THE DUKE'S KISS

Her mouth dropped open. "Are you *blackmailing* me into letting you court me, Your Grace?"

"Why, what an ugly way to put it. I'm merely asking for one more day in hopes that you'll change your mind. If you insist upon my returning to London after tomorrow, I'll do as you say without argument, and I won't trouble you again."

She let out a defeated sigh. He was a perfect villain, but alas, he was a villain who knew a great deal more about what had transpired in London than she ever wanted her mother to know. "One day only. I make no promises beyond tomorrow."

"Very well. We have an agreement then, Lady Francesca."

He caught her hands again, raised one to his lips, and before she could tug free, he pressed a kiss to her knuckles.

They both froze.

It was a chaste kiss, the merest brush of his lips, so soft she hardly felt it, aside from the warm drift of his breath, but instantly every inch of her was clamoring for him, goosebumps rising to the surface of her skin. She caught her breath, the slight hitch of it carrying over the ceaseless pattering of the rain.

He heard it. His eyes darkened, and he brought her hand to his mouth once again . . .

Books by Anna Bradley

LADY ELEANOR'S SEVENTH SUITOR

LADY CHARLOTTE'S FIRST LOVE

TWELFTH NIGHT WITH THE EARL

MORE OR LESS A MARCHIONESS

MORE OR LESS A COUNTESS

MORE OR LESS A TEMPTRESS

THE WAYWARD BRIDE

TO WED A WILD SCOT

FOR THE SAKE OF A SCOTTISH RAKE

THE VIRGIN WHO RUINED
LORD GRAY

THE VIRGIN WHO VINDICATED
LORD DARLINGTON

THE VIRGIN WHO HUMBLED
LORD HASLEMERE

THE VIRGIN WHO BEWITCHED
LORD LYMINGTON

THE VIRGIN WHO CAPTURED
A VISCOUNT

GIVE THE DEVIL HIS DUKE

Published by Kensington Publishing Corp.

Give the Devil His Duke

~ DROP DEAD DUKES ~

ANNA BRADLEY

ZEBRA BOOKS

Kensington Publishing Corp.

www.kensingtonbooks.com

ZEBRA BOOKS are published by

Kensington Publishing Corp.
119 West 40th Street
New York, NY 10018

All Kensington titles, imprints, and distributed lines are available at special quantity discounts for bulk purchases for sales promotion, premiums, fund-raising, and educational or institutional use.

Special book excerpts or customized printings can also be created to fit specific needs. For details, write or phone the office of the Kensington Sales Manager: Kensington Publishing Corp., 119 West 40th Street, New York, NY 10018. Attn. Sales Department. Phone: 1-800-221-2647.

Zebra and the Z logo Reg. U.S. Pat. & TM Off.

First Printing: August 2023
ISBN-13: 978-1-4201-5539-6
ISBN-13: 978-1-4201-5542-6 (eBook)

10 9 8 7 6 5 4 3 2 1

Printed in the United States of America

Grafton Public Library
Grafton, MA

CHAPTER 1

Once, when Franny was a child, her father had shown her a drawing in one of his history tomes of the gruesome fate that befell traitors to the English Crown. The rebels' severed heads had been boiled in water, doused with pitch, and displayed on wooden pikes along the south bank of London Bridge.

As a lesson in obedience, it had fallen short of the mark.

As a lesson in self-preservation, it had failed spectacularly, otherwise she wouldn't be crouched behind a shrub on a dark, deserted street, spying on her uncle Edward's townhouse.

She wasn't a rebel by nature, so much as by opportunity.

It was unfortunate, then, that all the stars had aligned to tempt her into tonight's bit of recklessness. It was a dark evening, for one, the pale starlight muted by a heavy layer of clouds. Then, the streets of Berkeley Square were deserted, the two short blocks between her and her uncle's house on Bruton Street beckoning like waggling fingers, luring her forward.

Or was it backward? Yes, backward, into the past.

If all that hadn't been temptation enough, Lady Crump had

retired early to her bed, leaving Franny alone with a kiss on her cheek, and a suggestion that she *amuse herself* for the rest of the evening.

Fate herself may as well have shoved Franny out the door.

The townhouse looked much as it had when she'd left it behind a decade ago, aside from the fence—a tall, iron affair, with a row of spikes running along the top edge. There were no severed heads, thank goodness, but it was still a bit forbidding for Mayfair. It might have been deterrent enough, if it hadn't been for the lamplight flickering in the dining room window.

That ruinous glow drew her from her hiding place to the edge of the street, and once she was there, well . . . it wasn't as if she'd get another chance like this one, was it?

Only a coward would forgo such an opportunity.

She darted across the street, the hem of her cloak flapping around her ankles, and ducked underneath a neatly pruned plane tree in a back corner of her uncle's garden. She rested her hand against the cool, rough bark of the trunk, and looked up through the spreading branches above.

It *looked* sturdy enough.

The leaves rustled as she grasped one of the lower branches and swung her foot up. It was just a bit of a shimmy to grab the next branch, an easy enough reach for a lady who'd climbed as many trees as she had after she'd been banished from London and found herself in the wilds of Herefordshire.

Hand over hand over foot, higher and higher she climbed, until she drew level with the window, her heart thudding with anticipation against her ribs, only to sink with disappointment when she peeked inside.

Susannah wasn't there.

A man was seated alone at the dining room table, an empty bottle of port in front of him, his heavy chin resting on his chest. His back was to the window, and there was rather less hair on his head than there had been ten years ago, but she'd know her uncle Edward anywhere.

He was asleep at his port, the drone of his snores so familiar she could picture the vibration of his thick lips in her mind's eye, the spittle clinging to the corners of his mouth.

She didn't linger, but left her uncle to his slumber, shimmying back down the same way she'd gone up, but in reverse—foot under foot under hand—her legs dangling as she searched out the thickest branches, testing her weight against each one.

Of all the things she'd longed for in the years after they'd left London—all the dreams she'd had during the long nights spent shivering in her bed in their drafty cottage in Herefordshire, her eleven-year-old heart breaking—of all the people she'd missed with the deep, aching misery of a wounded child . . .

Her uncle Edward hadn't been one of them.

Giles had had a perfectly respectable reason for calling on Lord Stanhope this evening. A proper, honorable, gentlemanly reason, as befit a proper, honorable, gentlemanly, er . . . gentleman.

He'd come here to . . . to . . .

Damn it, why *had* he come here tonight? It had something to do with a woman. Or a lady. One or the other. He couldn't recall now, because somehow the evening had taken a disastrous turn.

A disastrous, *drunken* turn. That wasn't supposed to happen, though perhaps he should have anticipated it, as Stanhope *did* serve an excellent port.

That was the best that could be said of Stanhope. The worst that could be said of him was that he'd blathered on about one thing and another at such tiresome length Giles had been obliged to keep drinking, his brain growing murkier with every word out of his host's mouth.

She's a great beauty, Basingstoke. Looks just like her mother, but with the Stanhope blue eyes.

Blue eyes, blue eyes . . . yes, that sounded familiar. He'd come to see Stanhope because of . . . something to do with blue eyes. But no sooner had he seized on the blue eyes than Stanhope began going on about *horses*, of all things.

It's rather like that pretty pair of matched bays of yours, eh, Basingstoke? Stanhope had leaned closer, his hot, sour breath wafting over Giles's face. *Nothing but the finest breeding stock will do for a duke.*

Wait. Giles paused on the sidewalk at the bottom of the steps.

Blue eyes, breeding stock, and . . .

Damn it, he almost had it, but it was hovering just out of reach—

. . . *My Susannah is the finest filly in London.*

Susannah! By God, that was it!

He'd come here tonight to ask permission to court Lady Susannah Stanhope. Not quite the thing, really, dipping so deeply into his cups while courting.

He was meant to be *be*sotted, not just sotted.

Still, he'd gotten the thing done. He'd professed his admiration and undying devotion and all that nonsense, then declared his intentions toward Lady Susannah, and Stanhope had said . . . *something*.

He couldn't recall what, exactly, his head being all muddled with port, but Stanhope was hardly going to refuse him, was he? Every nobleman in London was angling after Lady Susannah Stanhope, but *he* was the only duke, and Stanhope wanted to see his daughter made a duchess.

Why, he could have cast up his accounts all over the dining room table, and Stanhope still would have handed his daughter over with a smile.

So, he'd won his bride, and was the happiest of men in London tonight!

Wasn't he?

Yes, yes, of course, he was. He'd made up his mind to wed this year, and Lady Susannah was certain to be declared this season's belle. It went without saying that nothing less than society's most perfect diamond would do for the Duke of Basingstoke.

He was the happiest—and drunkest—of men, and utterly besotted with his future bride.

Or he would be, once they'd met.

As it was, he'd only ever laid eyes on the chit one time before, and that from a distance. He hadn't been able to see much of her, just that she was petite, with dark hair. According to every addlepated fool in London she had remarkably beautiful blue eyes, but he'd withhold judgment on that until he'd seen them for himself—

Thud.

He paused, squinting into the darkness. Were those footsteps, coming from Stanhope's garden, at this time of night? How curious. All manner of strange things tended to happen the week before the London season began, but he'd never heard of a Peeping Thomas skulking about Mayfair before.

Alas, he was far too deep in his cups to do anything about it—

"Dash it, you blasted thing."

What the devil? He stilled, listening. There was another thump, a ripping sound like cloth tearing, then, "Let *go*, damn you."

God in heaven. It wasn't a Peeping Thomas at all, but a Peeping *Thomasina*!

Well, that was another matter entirely, wasn't it?

He crept closer, peering into the darkness. Yes, just there, on the other side of the fence, a shadowy figure was skulking about near the fence, but she was hidden by the thick branches of the tree. "Come out of his lordship's garden this instant, madam, and present yourself."

Yes, that was *very* good—he'd hardly slurred at all—but the culprit didn't appear, and aside from a rustling of the branches, there was no reply.

Well, that wouldn't do. "There can't be any innocent reason for you to be prowling about his lordship's garden. Either you're a thief, or worse. Come out on your own, or I'll come in and fetch you myself."

There was a long pause, then a voice said, "I'm afraid you'll have to come in and fetch me, then, because I can't come out. I'm stuck."

He blinked. She didn't *sound* like a thief, with that soft, clear voice. Aside from that curse she'd uttered, she sounded like a lady. "Stuck? How can you be stuck?"

"Quite easily, I assure you, sir. The back of my cloak is caught on one of the spikes at the top of the fence."

How had she managed that? "Well, take off your cloak, then."

"Yes, I *did* think of that, but it's rather tight around my arms, and there's not much room to move, as the fence is directly at my back."

Well, she had made a mess of it, hadn't she? "Forgive me, madam, but you don't sound like a particularly skilled thief."

An indignant sniff floated out from under the tree. "I'm not a thief at all."

She had a rather pleasant voice, for a thief. "Of course, you are. Why else would you be prowling about a dark garden?"

It seemed an entirely reasonable question to him, but she let out a derisive snort. "As much as I'm enjoying our delightful chat, sir, I'm rather preoccupied at the moment, so if you don't intend to help me, perhaps it would be just as well for you to go on about your business."

Did she just *shoo him away*? You couldn't shoo away a

duke, for God's sake. It wasn't done. "The devil I will. I'm coming in to fetch you, then I'm turning you over to the watchman."

Alas, it was easier said than accomplished, given the height of the fence, the spikes, and his inebriated state. Why the devil did Stanhope need such a forbidding fence, for God's sake? He was an earl, not King George IV.

Finally, after a good deal of flailing about and a near castration with the sharp tip of a particularly aggressive spike, he managed to make it over the fence without maiming any vital body parts. He scanned the garden, lingering on every shadow, but she'd hidden herself well, like a proper thief would. "Some assistance, madam, if you would?"

There was a faint huff, then, "Just here."

She didn't sound as if she wanted to be rescued, but she'd pricked his curiosity now, and the ducal whims must be satisfied. He scanned the garden again, and this time he spied a dark, vaguely female shape flattened against the fence, her arms akimbo, the hood of the cloak pulled low over her head. "That doesn't look at all comfortable."

"It *isn't*. Would you be so good as to stop gaping, and help me down?"

Gaping? Impertinent. "You're a bit high in the instep for a thief, madam."

"I told you, I'm not a thief. I . . . ouch!" She let out a hiss and began wriggling against the fence like a worm on a hook. "Dash it, I've got a spasm in my neck."

"Well, twisting about like that isn't going to help it. Stop squirming." He strode across the garden, wrapped his hands around a pair of slender shoulders to still her, then reached behind her to inspect the state of her cloak. "Good Lord, a little to the left and this would have been a beheading."

The spike had her right at the tender place where the back of her head gave way to her neck, and it had caught a large fold of the fabric of her cloak. She might have squirmed and kicked all night, but she never would have gotten free. "Cease wriggling, if you please, madam."

"I'm wriggling because you're strangling me, sir!"

"So I am. I beg your pardon." He leaned closer, squinting in the darkness. He couldn't see a cursed thing, but after a bit of prodding with his fingers, he drew back. "Right, I'm going to have to lift you off the spike."

"*Lift* me? Surely, there must be another way?"

"There isn't. You're hopelessly tangled, and the knot is as tight as my fist."

"But—"

"I can either lift you off the spike, madam, or I can leave you here. The choice is entirely yours." He stepped back, crossed his arms over his chest, and waited.

She huffed and tsked and sighed, then finally gave herself up to the inevitable. "Yes, all right. Lift me off, please."

"Wise choice, madam." He wrapped his hands around her waist, then paused as an unexpected sensation crept over him, and an exceedingly improper one. She had a trim little waist, and it gave way to a most tempting swell of hips, and the most intoxicating scent wafted from her hair, something flowery, and not at all like he'd imagined a thief would smell—

"Please, sir, won't you hurry?"

"Er, yes. Of course. I beg your pardon. Put your hands on my shoulders. Yes, like that. Very good. Now hold on." He bent his knees, braced his thighs, and with one graceful heave, lifted her into the air—high, then higher still, until the curves of the luscious bosom she was hiding under that shapeless cloak was a breath away from his mouth, and her hood slid off the end of the spike.

Well, perhaps "graceful" wasn't quite the right word.

It might have been graceful if he hadn't been so sotted, but as it was, he toppled backward, and landed on his arse with an "Oof," his hands still wrapped around her waist.

"Oh, dear." She lay sprawled on top of him for a moment, panting, then struggled onto her knees and leaned over him, her brow creased. "Are you hurt?"

Giles didn't answer, but gazed up at her, speechless. Dark hair tumbled around a heart-shaped face with full pink lips, a pointed chin, and the most beautiful dark blue eyes he'd ever seen.

Stanhope blue.

Her presence behind the fence, her ladylike accent, those blue eyes . . . of course.

By God, she'd been telling the truth. She really *wasn't* a thief. There was only one explanation for her presence in the garden, only one person she could be.

He'd just peeled his future duchess off the tip of a spike.

He struggled up onto his elbows. "Lady Susannah?"

She stilled, her blue eyes going wide, then wider still, then quickly, before he could think to grab her, she scrambled to her feet and, in a whirl of torn muslin, fled to the edge of the garden, was over the fence in a trice, and gone without a backward glance.

CHAPTER 2

Charles Street, Berekley Square
A few days later.

Lady Francesca Stanhope had reached the dubious age of twenty-one years without ever dancing a quadrille in a London ballroom, and she wouldn't dance one tonight.

Wearisome things, quadrilles. Country dances were tolerable, but she hadn't come to London for the season to dance, or flirt her fan, flutter her eyelashes, or bask in the admiring glances of the dozens of eligible gentlemen prowling about the ballroom, eying the young ladies as if they were sweetmeats on a serving tray.

She hadn't come to giggle or gossip, or to sip ratafia from small silver cups.

Her one hope for the evening—her lone requirement, her single, fixed ambition for her first and only London season—was to remain entirely invisible.

Alas, that hope was fading with every turn she took in front of the looking glass. There *were* shades of pink that were acceptable for young ladies. The sweet, new pink of a peony about to burst into bloom, for instance, or the wholesome pale pink of a maiden's blush. The tender pink of a newborn baby's lips, and the translucent, silver pink of seashells.

And then . . . then there were the *other* shades of pink.

She turned this way and that in front of the looking glass, studying her reflection, but it was no use. No matter how much she squinted, it was the same from every angle.

It was, God help her, one of the *other* shades of pink.

Magenta. Raspberry. Persimmon. Azalea.

"It is a bit bright." Jenny, who was to act as Franny's lady's maid during her stay with Lady Crump, did her best to subdue the puffed lace sleeves of the gown. "But with your dark hair and fair skin, every color flatters you, my lady."

"It's not really the thing for a young lady in her first season to appear in such a bright color, is it? Perhaps another one of Lady Dorothea's gowns might be more flattering? Something a bit less vivid?"

Jenny shook her head. "They're all the same color as this one, my lady."

"What, *all* of them?" There were at least two dozen ball gowns in that wardrobe, and *all* of them were this shade of pink? Why, whatever modiste had willed so many infamous pink gowns into existence deserved to be driven out of London on the end of a pitchfork.

"I'm afraid so. Lady Dorothea is fond of pink."

This gown and all the others crowded into the wardrobe had been made for Lady Crump's niece, Lady Dorothea, but there'd been some sort of scandal, and poor Lady Dorothea had been hastily married off to the son of a country squire several weeks before the season began.

Lady Crump, kind soul that she was, had invited Franny to come to London for a season in Dorothea's place, but it had all been rather rushed. Even if Franny's mother had had the money for new gowns—which she didn't—there hadn't been enough time to have any made up.

So, it was to be pink, then, and not an acceptable shade of

pink, but a violent, shocking, blinding pink. It might not have
been *quite* such a disaster if it had been only the color, but the
gown was smothered in layers of ribbon and heavy blond
lace, as well.

Indeed, it was difficult to say whether the color, the fit, or
the extravagant trimmings were the worst of it. She blinked at
her reflection in the looking glass, then jerked her gaze away
again, appalled, but the offensive pink glare persisted even
after she'd averted her eyes, as if it had seared her retinas.

The color was the worst of it. Definitely, the color.

She braved another peek into the looking glass, but no, all
she could see was her neighbor's garden back in Herefordshire.

Mrs. Cornelius was fond of fuchsias.

Well, there was no sense making a fuss over it. What did
it matter if she *did* look like Mrs. Cornelius's fuchsias? It
wasn't as if she'd come to London to impress the *ton*, or catch
a husband—

"Francesca?" There was a brief knock on the door, and a
moment later Lady Crump sailed over the threshold. "Are
you ready, my dear? I've just sent Thomas to fetch the carriage, and . . ." Lady Crump gasped when she caught sight of
Franny and clapped her hand over her mouth.

Franny turned away from the glass with a smile and held
out her skirts for Lady Crump's inspection. "Will this do?"

"My dearest girl, you look positively ravishing!" Lady
Crump pressed a hand to her breast. "Why, you look like a
fairy princess!"

Franny bit her lip to hide her grin. She'd never admired
princesses, fairy or otherwise, but she wouldn't dream of
hurting Lady Crump's feelings by saying so. "You approve of
it, then?"

"Approve of it? That shade of pink is perfection on you!
Why, I said to Dorothea when we chose her color for the

season that not one in two dozen ladies could wear such a shade of pink, but you do it credit, my dear."

"Yes, but I do wonder, my lady, if the gown quite fits me? It's a trifle too loose in this part of the bodice, isn't it?" She pinched a fold of fabric at her waist between her fingers. "And perhaps it's a bit short for me, and too tight in the bust?"

"The tighter the bust, the better!" Lady Crump cackled. "Especially when a young lady has no money to entice a suitor. You may trust me, Francesca, when I say curves have worked miracles guineas could only dream of!"

That might be, but bright colors in nature were a warning of extreme toxicity, weren't they? A pink such as this was more likely to frighten the gentlemen off than to entice them. But then, she hadn't any use for London's fine gentlemen, so perhaps it was just as well.

"Come along, Francesca. The carriage is waiting. We're off for the first night of what is sure to be a most triumphant debut!" Lady Crump took her arm and marched her to the bedchamber door. "Leave it to me, and we'll have you wed well before the end of the season."

Triumph was, of course, a relative term, one young lady's failure being another's resounding success.

Another young lady, for instance, might court the attention of the *ton*, but as soon as they entered Lord Hasting's ballroom, Franny tucked herself into as inconspicuous a corner as she could find, as far removed from the dancing as she could get.

A wallflower among wallflowers.

It was a strategy that should have guaranteed invisibility, but the bright pink gown drew every eye toward her, until she felt like one of those poor caged animals in the Tower of London's menagerie.

If she could have made herself disappear with a snap of her fingers, she would have done so in an instant, but as she wasn't a magician, there was nothing for it but to keep her head high and ignore the pointed stares and snickers, even as she was ready to sink beneath the weight of all the unfriendly eyes upon her.

Lady Crump remained close, of course, and often reached over to pat Franny's hand in a consoling manner, but after an hour passed without a single gentleman approaching them for either an introduction or a dance, her ladyship fell into conversation with one of the other disappointed matrons nearby, the two of them chattering about the tediousness of balls, and wondering at the lack of discernment among London's gentlemen.

Still, there was one bright spot. Aside from her gown, that is.

No introductions meant no one in the ballroom knew her name.

That was *something*, anyway. It was a mere shred of the anonymity she'd hoped for, and it would be ripped away soon enough, but until then she might observe the company in peace.

Quite a spectacle it was, too.

So many elegant people gathered in one place! The silks and jewels alone were enough to make her gasp. Most of the young ladies present were a few years younger than she was, and they seemed different creatures from her altogether, in their pastel gowns, with dainty pearls or diamonds at their ears and throats, and fashionable clusters of curls framing their faces.

Yet the one face she was searching for, the one face she longed to see, eluded her. It was a face very like her own, with the same pointed chin and clear blue eyes.

Stanhope blue.

Or dragonfly blue, as her mother had always called it,

because to her fond maternal eyes it was the same crystalline blue of a dragonfly's wings.

Would she even recognize her cousin, when she did appear in the ballroom? A decade seemed a lifetime ago, and Susannah had been just a girl then. She was a young lady now, embarking on her first season, but surely, she wouldn't have changed so much Franny would no longer know her?

She'd written to Susannah countless times since the . . . well, since they'd been torn apart. She'd never received a letter in return, but there could be any number of reasons for her cousin's lack of response. Susannah had only been eight years old when it happened, and firmly under her father's thumb, even then. Either he'd forbidden her to answer the letters, or Susannah, poisoned against Franny by her father's lies, had made that decision herself.

She'd chosen to believe it was the former, but after ten long years of wondering, she'd find out for certain, soon enough.

They *would* come to Lord Hasting's ball, wouldn't they? It was the first ball of the season, and a very grand one. She perched on the edge of her gilt chair, her gaze lingering on every young lady with dark hair, but another half hour passed without a sign of them.

Was it possible they'd come and gone already, and she'd missed them? She'd hardly taken her eyes off the entrance, but more people crowded inside with every passing moment, until the ballroom had become a sea of indistinguishable shoulders and heads.

Perhaps she'd just move over a seat or two. Yes, that was better. From here she had an unobstructed view of . . . "Oh! Well, my goodness."

There were dozens of beautiful young ladies crowding the ballroom tonight, but none so striking as the one who'd just crossed the threshold.

"She looks like an angel, doesn't she?" A young lady with

glossy, golden-brown hair seated a few chairs away from Franny's had followed her gaze to the opposite side of the ballroom. "It's rather startling, really."

"It is, indeed." Franny rose halfway from her seat to get a better look at the young lady who'd caught her eye. She was standing in a shallow alcove to one side of the entrance, her golden hair gleaming under the candlelight from the chandeliers above. "Is she this season's belle?"

"By all rights she should be, but she's not one to put herself forward. Forgive me. I do beg your pardon." The young lady offered her a friendly smile. "It's dreadfully rude of me to speak to you without an introduction, but we've been sitting two chairs apart for nearly three hours now, and it seems silly not to speak to each other."

"Unforgivably so, yes, particularly since it appears no one else intends to speak to either one of us." Franny returned the young lady's smile. "Wallflowers must rely on each other for entertainment."

It was too blunt a comment to be strictly polite, but the young lady only laughed. "Indeed. Now, Lady Diana, our fair-haired goddess there, is said to be rather shy, and perhaps just a touch awkward. If you're looking for the season's belle, she's just arrived."

Franny followed her gaze, and her heart gave a frantic thump.

There, standing just behind the fair-haired goddess was a man who, for a single instant, a brief, suspended moment in time, so resembled her own beloved father that her heart gave a frantic, foolish leap in her chest. But then he turned his head, and just like that, he was her uncle Edward again, as unlike her kind, loving father as a man could be, for all that they were—had been—brothers.

But the young lady beside him, dressed in pale blue silk, her dark hair gathered into a shining mass of curls at the back of her neck . . . a raw, familiar ache bloomed in Franny's chest as she stared at Susannah.

She didn't know her cousin anymore, but oh, how she'd loved her once! She loved her still, but it was love based on a memory of who Susannah had once been, faded now, and worn thin at the edges.

"*That* young lady is Lady Susannah Stanhope. She's lovely, isn't she?"

"So lovely, yes." Susannah had grown from an adorable little girl with tangled dark curls into a stunning beauty. She was more petite than Franny was, and boasted a trim, tidy figure far more fashionable than Franny's generous curves, but otherwise they were as alike as sisters.

"Lady Susannah's father, Lord Edward Stanhope is just there," the young lady beside her added. "He's the tall man, with dark hair, and her mother, Lady Edith Stanhope, is on his arm."

Yes, there was no missing Aunt Edith, who was draped in a Pompeian red silk gown so luxurious, the cost of a single fold of it likely would have kept Franny and her mother in coal for three winters running.

But then nothing but the best would do for Aunt Edith.

"Lady Susannah favors her mother, aside from the color of her eyes. You can't tell from this distance, of course, but her blue eyes are the toast of London."

"Dragonfly blue," Franny murmured.

"Lady Edith was a renowned beauty in her day. She's handsome still, don't you think?" The young lady leaned closer, and lowered her voice. "Or she would be, if she didn't have such a disagreeable, pinched look about her."

Franny stifled a snort. "Oh, dear. Er, perhaps I'd better introduce myself. I'm Lady Francesca Stanhope. Lady Edith Stanhope is my aunt."

"Lady Francesca Stanhope!" The young lady flushed to the roots of her hair. "My goodness, I have put my foot in it, haven't I? I do beg your pardon. Lady Susannah is your cousin, then?"

"Yes." There was no point in hiding the truth, as everyone in London would discover who she was soon enough. "My father is . . . was Lady Susannah's father's elder brother."

"How do you do, Lady Francesca? I'm Miss Prudence Thorne. Or Prue, if you can bear it."

Franny scooted across the two empty chairs between them and took the seat beside her new friend. "It's a pleasure to make your acquaintance, Miss Thorne."

Miss Thone's gaze drifted from Franny to Susannah, and then back again. "I don't know how I didn't notice the resemblance between you and your cousin at once. You look very much alike. Perhaps, Lady Francesca, *you'll* become the season's Incomparable, instead of your cousin."

"In this gown? I think not." The Unbearable, perhaps, if there were such a thing. "You were saying you think Susannah will be this season's belle?" Her gaze wandered back to the golden-haired Lady Diana. It seemed impossible any other lady could be declared the belle while such a young lady as *that* existed.

"Well, one can never tell, of course, the *ton* being as capricious as a herd of wild cats, but yes, I think it's likely. There isn't another young lady in London who can equal Lady Diana for beauty, but she's quite reserved, and not one to court attention. Her family has kept her out of society for the most part."

It was true Lady Diana didn't have the air of someone conscious of her own beauty. She clung to the arm of the lady beside her, her gaze lowered. "Who is her family?"

"The lady beside her is her mother, Judith Drew, Her Grace, the Duchess of—"

"Basingstoke." A chill swept over Franny at the familiar name, the fine hairs on her arms rising. She could hardly get that name off her lips fast enough.

Judith Drew was the widow of the Seventh Duke of Basingstoke, a man so wicked, so blackhearted the best that could be said of him was he'd finally descended into hell before he had a chance to destroy another family.

By then, it had been too late for *her* family.

"Yes, and of course that means Lady Diana's brother is—"

"The current duke."

"Yes, indeed. Giles Drew, the Eighth Duke of Basingstoke. Have you seen him? He's even more beautiful than his sister, if you can imagine it. I'd be dreadfully annoyed with him, if he were my own brother."

Beautiful, was he? The gods *had* been generous to the Drew family, hadn't they? "Surely, no gentleman could be as beautiful as that young lady is."

"You may judge for yourself, soon enough." Miss Thorne glanced toward the entrance of the ballroom. "The duke is expected to join his mother in chaperoning Lady Diana this season."

"It's quite late, is it not?" If the duke did intend to chaperone his sister, he was taking his time about it.

"Nearly ten o'clock, I should think."

Goodness, was that all? It felt as if she'd been here for ages.

"He'll appear before too long, and I daresay you'll recognize him the moment he enters the ballroom." Miss Thorne gave her a mischievous grin. "If ever there was a gentleman who looks every inch the duke he is, it's the Duke of Basingstoke."

CHAPTER 3

The sun had been shining with unusual splendor on the morning Giles was born. He'd burst from his mother's womb red-faced and squalling, indistinguishable from every other infant, but for one thing.

His tiny baby's skull was graced with a crown of downy, golden curls.

His father had been so fond of the story of his only son's miraculous birth, he'd told it time and time again over the ensuing years, boasting of how the small army of doctors who'd attended the duchess had professed themselves amazed, and claimed those gilded ringlets could be nothing less than a blessing from the heavens themselves, a mark of celestial favor, a tangible promise of the Eighth Duke of Basingstoke's future greatness.

Tricky things, blessings. One could never be certain what shape they'd take.

"*Harder*, Your Grace." Lady Caroline's silken thighs clamped around Giles's thrusting hips, her heels thumping against his damp back. "Oh, oh *yes*, Your Grace!"

It was a great pity, really, that the heavens hadn't been more specific.

"Oh, oh, oh." Lady Caroline's grip on his hair tightened with every jerk of his hips. Good God. If he could still boast the headful of golden curls after she'd finished with him, he'd count himself fortunate.

Perhaps he should have gone to White's, after all. They did a lovely roasted grouse on Wednesday afternoons—

"Please, please . . . ah, *please.*"

If it hadn't been such a damnably dreary afternoon, he might have had a ride in Hyde Park, but he didn't fancy a dousing.

If it wasn't to be a ride in the park or a visit to White's, that left only—

"Faster, Your Grace!"

A discreet romp with a sultry beauty. Or even better, a discreet romp with—

"My lady is eager for you, Your Grace." Lady Caroline's lady's maid, a voracious young beauty named Clarissa—or perhaps it was Christina—teased the tip of her tongue into the hollow at the base of his spine.

Two sultry beauties.

Or, if the gentleman in question was blessed by the heavens themselves, marked with celestial favor and destined for greatness, then—

"More, Your Grace. Please, more!"

Three sultry beauties.

He'd be damned if he could remember the third lady's name—ah, yes, there she was, crawling out from beneath the covers—but she had red hair, and the prettiest pair of thighs he'd ever seen. He paused to nibble that smooth, pale skin before he collapsed face first into his rumpled silk sheets with a grunt.

With a quick, graceful move, the redhead threw a leg over his hip and hauled herself on top of him so her pert little bottom was perched atop his bare arse. "Having a nap, Your Grace? Don't say we've worn you out already."

"His Grace, worn out?" Lady Caroline lay sprawled on her back beside him. "I think not."

"Onto your back, Your Grace," Clarissa-Christina urged in a throaty whisper, catching his earlobe in her teeth. "My lady isn't finished with you."

He stifled a sigh and flopped over onto his back, feeling rather put upon, like a stallion cornered by a trio of demanding mares. There'd been a time, hadn't there, when he'd thought this a pleasant enough way to pass an afternoon?

"Up on your knees, my lady." The redhead caught Lady Caroline under her arms and maneuvered her until she was astride him. "Now lean back on me, and let me . . . ah, yes, that's it."

She grasped Lady Caroline's hips and rocked her into Giles's thrusts, the two of them swaying together, the bed letting out a protesting groan with every snap of his hips.

If it had been anything less than the mahogany monstrosity it was, such an energetic flurry of limbs—to say nothing of all the other bouncing appendages—might have reduced it to a pile of kindling, but the thing was as sturdy as a prison hulk floating on the Thames. The ladies might have climbed the posts and swung from the canopy, if they'd pleased.

They didn't, not this time, Lady Caroline contenting herself with gripping the silken bed hangings and wailing as her release swept over her. The hot pulses of her body drove him closer to the edge, the tight curl of his release gathering at the base of his spine . . . just a few more thrusts, and . . . *yes*.

Pleasure rushed over him, drawing his spine as tight as a bowstring and holding him suspended for an instant before hurtling him back down onto the bed, panting. Lady Caroline collapsed beside him, struggling to catch her breath while Clarissa-Christina and the redhead rolled about together, a writhing mass of arms and legs, grasping hands, and arching backs, the silk sheets clinging to sticky, sweaty flesh.

That arousing sight might have been enough to spur him into a renewed charge, but the two ladies appeared perfectly

willing to entertain each other, and while he wouldn't dream
of permitting any of his lovers to leave his bed unsatisfied—
he was a gentleman, above all—nor did he object if the ladies
chose to honor each other with their attentions.

At last, all four of them were sated and sprawled across
the bed in a tangle of limbs.

A *crowded* tangle—

"Your Grace?" There was a discreet tap at his bedchamber
door.

Ah, there was Digby. Really, the man's timing was impeccable. "Yes? What is it?"

"I beg your pardon, Your Grace." Digby opened the bedchamber door a crack, taking care to avert his gaze from the
pile of naked bodies lounging atop the bed. "It's nearly nine
o'clock. You have an engagement this evening, and Lady
Scott's carriage is waiting in the mews."

"Yes, very well." Giles waved a hand, and Digby withdrew, pulling the door closed behind him.

He rose from the bed, tugged his breeches over his hips,
and held out his hand to Lady Caroline. "Alas, my lady, time
is fleeting when one is engaged in the most pleasurable activ-
ities, is it not?"

Or was it the pleasure that was fleeting? It was one or the
other.

"Indeed, Your Grace." Lady Caroline accepted his hand
and allowed him to assist her from his bed. "Will I see you at
the ball this evening? Lord Hasting's entertainments are
always so amusing."

Lord Hasting's balls were about as amusing as a funeral,
but he'd be there nonetheless, along with the rest of the *ton*.
He forced his most charming smile onto his lips. "Of course.
I trust you'll honor me with a dance?"

"Naturally." Lady Caroline gave him a flirtatious flutter of
her eyelashes as he lifted her hand to his lips.

"Until tonight then, my lady."

Digby returned once the ladies had gone and began to scurry about, retrieving bits of discarded clothing from the floor and clucking like a mother hen.

"Never mind that, Digby." Giles threw himself onto his back on his bed, fumbled for his snuff box on the table, and helped himself to a generous pinch.

"Yes, Your Grace. You will take your dinner in your bed-chamber, followed by your bath, I presume?"

"As always, Digby, you presume correctly. You're a model of efficiency. Tell me, how is it that you always arrive to escort the ladies out at the precise moment I wish to be rid of them?" Really, the man's timing was nothing short of astonishing. It was as if he could read Giles's mind.

"I wait for the creaking to cease, Your Grace," Digby called from the depths of the wardrobe, his voice muffled.

"Creaking? What creaking?"

Digby emerged with a freshly pressed black evening coat and a spotless pair of breeches over his arm, and nodded at the rumpled bed. "The bed, Your Grace."

Giles raised an eyebrow. "I'll have you know, Digby, that this bed has survived generations of Basingstoke dukes, every one of us a licentious scoundrel. It's perfectly safe."

"Yes, Your Grace, but it does creak rather menacingly. You must be careful, Your Grace, not to break it. The wood will shatter, and you'll do yourself an injury."

"Don't be ridiculous, Digby. A splinter wouldn't dare lodge itself in a duke's arse."

"Yes, Your Grace. May I suggest the dark blue silk waist-coat for Lord Hasting's ball tonight?"

"Yes, whatever you like."

"May I also suggest, Your Grace, that you begin your preparations earlier than usual, so you won't be late?"

"Why, because Lord Hasting's balls are so endlessly entertaining?"

"For Lady Diana's sake, Your Grace."

Diana, the eldest of his three sisters, would make her first appearance at the ball this evening. She deserved better than one of Hasting's dull affairs, but it was the first ball of the season, so the Drew family would turn out for it, along with the rest of the *ton*.

"I haven't forgotten Diana, Digby, I promise you."

"Of course not, Your Grace. Will you have the sapphire and diamond cravat pin this evening?"

"I don't see why not." There was no need to question Digby's choices. The man's sartorial instincts would put Beau Brummel to shame. Digby was the consummate gentleman's gentleman, a genius with bootblacking, a magician with a cravat, and above all, he was the heart and soul of discretion. Nothing less than a fireplace poker could pry a single secret loose from Digby's lips.

Giles couldn't imagine how he'd get along without the man.

He helped himself to another pinch of snuff. "Go on, then, and pretty me up, Digby. I surrender myself entirely into your hands. You may do your worst, and I promise you I'll be as docile as a lamb."

"If memory serves, Basingstoke, you demanded Montford and I appear in Lord Hasting's ballroom no later than ten o'clock this evening." Maxwell Burke, the Duke of Grantham, made a great show of retrieving his gold pocket watch and opening it with a sharp flick of his thumb.

"Don't be absurd, Grantham. I never make demands." He didn't have to. People generally gave him what he wanted with little effort on his part.

He'd talked Montford and Grantham into attending tonight, just in case Diana's natural reserve led her to a lack of partners. The first ball of her first season mustn't be anything less than a stunning success, and he wouldn't have her standing about watching the other young ladies dance, or worse, banished to wallflower row.

Fortunately, Diana had been in the middle of a quadrille with the Marquess of Ormsby when he arrived, and his mother assured him every dance on her card had a gentleman's name penciled in beside it. Despite her shyness, she didn't need his help tonight. She was well on her way to conquering London society.

Which was just as it should be. There wasn't a single young lady in the ballroom who could compare to Diana.

So, he'd left his mother beaming as she watched Diana twirl about the floor on Ormsby's arm, and made his way over to his friends who, for all their grumbling, were loyal enough, and had rallied around Diana tonight.

"Ah. You did request it, then? Because it's now . . ." Grantham glanced down at his watch. "Half ten. You're *late*, Basingstoke."

Yes, well, they could blame Lady Caroline for *that*. Her ladyship was a delightful bed partner, but she did tend to drag the business out.

"For God's sake, Basingstoke, if you'd dallied any longer, one of us would have a foot stuck in the parson's mousetrap by now." Jasper St. Vincent, the Duke of Montford, shot a nervous glance around the ballroom. "Every marriage-minded mamma is staring at us and scheming. Even the card room isn't safe!"

"A rake like you, Montford? I'd wager your feet, to say nothing of the rest of you, are safe enough."

Montford snorted. "I'm a *duke*, Basingstoke. No duke is safe in a ballroom during the season. It's a bloody miracle poor Grantham here hasn't been kidnapped and dragged off to Gretna Green by now, with his fortune."

"What young lady would want an unpleasant fellow like Grantham?" Though it was true enough that as far as the marriage-minded mammas of the *ton* were concerned, the more dukes trapped in a ballroom, the better. No doubt dozens of them were even now plotting to make their daughters the next Duchess of Montford or Grantham.

Or Basingstoke, at least until his betrothal to Lady Susannah was announced.

Tempting, blue-eyed Lady Susannah. Lady Susannah, with her tumbled locks of dark hair, that tiny waist, and that tart tongue hidden behind those perfect, plump pink lips, like the most delicious secret. He may have been sotted the night of their fateful meeting in the garden, but a man didn't forget a lady like *that*.

"Has there been any sign of Stanhope yet tonight?" He glanced around, searching for a dark-haired lady in blue. Yes, she'd be wearing blue tonight, with those eyes.

For all that Lord Hasting was a dullard, his ballroom was such a crush Giles couldn't distinguish one person from the next, but somehow, as if Fate herself had decreed it, he found Lady Susannah at once. She was chatting with the lady sitting beside her, her face turned away from him, but there was no mistaking that cloud of dark hair, the delicate curve of that cheek.

He started toward her, but before he could take two steps, Grantham caught him by the shoulder. "Where are you going, Basingstoke?"

"Why, to dance with my lovely betrothed, of course." He shook Grantham off, but then paused, confused. The lady in question wasn't wearing blue, but pink—a rather violent shade of pink—and she was seated in one of the gilt chairs pushed against the wall on one side of the ballroom.

Wallflower row. Lady Susannah, relegated to wallflower row? No, certainly not.

"She's over there, Basingstoke."

Grantham nodded toward the opposite end of the ballroom, where Lord Stanhope was parading about like a peacock on the strut, his chest thrust out and his chin so high

Lord Hasting's guests were being treated to an intimate view of his lordship's nostrils.

Montford snorted. "Good Lord. He looks as if he's rehearsing being the father of a duchess, doesn't he?"

"He behaves like a court jester," Grantham muttered. "His daughter isn't as witless as he is, I trust."

"I don't know. I've hardly exchanged six words with the lady." Not with the dark-haired lady in the blue gown standing next to Stanhope, the lady who was, presumably, Lady Susannah Stanhope. He *had* exchanged more than six words with the dark-haired lady in the pink gown, who presumably was *not*.

"What's the matter with you, Basingstoke?" Grantham frowned at him. "You look as if you've seen a ghost."

He *had* seen a ghost, or an amazingly realistic figment of his drunken imagination. He glanced back at the young lady in pink, but then forced himself to turn away, dismissing her with a mental shrug. She wasn't his betrothed, but just one of many young ladies banished to wallflower row for the evening.

"Anyone can see poor Basingstoke is regretting this ill-advised courtship of his." Montford's lip curled as Stanhope pranced and swanned about. "I don't blame you, Basingstoke. I wouldn't want such a bloody fool as Stanhope for a father-in-law."

"I'm not marrying her father, Montford. Lady Susannah is a great deal more palatable than Stanhope is." At least, he hoped she was. It was difficult to tell with the length of a ballroom between them, but perhaps she was every bit as alluring as his garden goddess.

It was time to find out. "If you'll pardon me, gentlemen, my blushing bride awaits."

CHAPTER 4

"The Duke of Basingstoke has arrived, Lady Francesca." Miss Thorne tapped Franny on the shoulder with her fan. "I did promise he'd turn up, didn't I?"

Franny followed Miss Thorne's gaze, and a soft gasp left her lips. The Duke of Basingstoke had joined her uncle Edward's party near the entrance to the ballroom, but even from such a distance she could see he was . . .

Oh no, no, no. She couldn't be that unlucky.

Except, of course, she was *precisely* that unlucky, because the Duke of Basingstoke was none other than the drunken gentleman who'd rescued her from Uncle Edward's fence the night she'd arrived in London!

She dropped her head into her hands with a groan. Was it too much to ask that her savior turn out to be a coachman, or Uncle Edward's man of business, or some other man she'd never again be obliged to lay eyes upon?

"The young ladies call him Helios." Miss Thorne's voice was thick with suppressed laughter. *"Helios,* if you can credit it."

"*Helios*!" The Greek sun god? "Why, what utter nonsense."

Still, he was a bit . . . well, there was only one word for it. *Golden.*

Looking at him was rather like looking directly into the

sun. Reckless, foolish, a thing she always regretted as soon as she'd done it, yet even as painful white starbursts exploded behind her eyelids, she knew she'd do it again if given the chance, because, alas, there were few things more compelling than beauty and risk in equal parts.

What color eyes would a man such as the Duke of Basingstoke have? Brown, perhaps? A tawny brown, though, like a lion's, rather than a velvety brown. It had been too dark to tell in the garden that night, but she'd devoted quite a lot of time to speculating about the color of his eyes since their fateful encounter.

"I quite agree with you, Lady Francesca, though you must admit there is a certain *godliness* to him, though I feel perfectly ridiculous saying so, I assure you."

With those luxurious curls and that golden tint to his skin, there was no denying he was the sort who'd make the most stalwart young lady's heart quicken in her chest. Not *her* heart, of course. She didn't have any use for golden curls, and even less use for dukes.

"I suppose so, yes, but only because he's so tall." Broad shouldered as well, and imposing, with that long, lean frame. "My goodness, look at how everyone scurries out of his way as he passes through the ballroom!"

It would have taken a mere mortal an hour to get through that crush, but the Duke of Basingstoke passed through it as if he were Moses crossing the Red Sea.

Very well then, perhaps he *did* look a touch godly, but his father had been just as striking, and there'd been nothing in the least godlike about *him*. "What sort of a man can he be, if all of London fawns upon him as shamelessly as that?"

"The *ton* insists he's charming, honorable, a man without vice, and a paragon of the highest principles." Miss Thorne's eyes were twinkling.

"A man without vice!" Franny snorted. "Such a man doesn't exist."

"No, I daresay he doesn't, but even the highest sticklers claim the duke is a man of character and refinement."

The opposite of his father, then. "But can their account be credited?"

Miss Thorne shrugged. "I couldn't say, really, as I've never been introduced to him, but the *ton* has nothing but praise for him, and God knows they're sparing enough in their praise of everyone else."

Or else he was a duke, so they all acted as if he was everything he should be.

"Look, Lady Francesca, he's just invited your cousin to dance."

So he had. Susannah accepted him, of course—even if propriety didn't allow her to refuse him, Uncle Edward certainly would have—but wasn't there just the tiniest moment of hesitation on Susannah's part, the merest hint of reluctance? After all, Susannah knew as well as Franny did the destruction the previous Duke of Basingstoke had wreaked on their family.

Or more properly, the destruction he'd wreaked on Franny, her father, and her mother. God knew Uncle Edward had made out well enough.

But perhaps she wasn't being fair. Perhaps the current duke was nothing like his father had been. Perhaps he was everything the *ton* claimed he was—a virtuous, godlike creature born to make amends for the seven villains that illustrious line had heretofore produced.

He *had* freed her from that spike, after all.

Whatever the truth was, she had no wish to tangle with him. Her family had made that mistake once before with his father, and it had cost them everything they had.

No, the wisest course was to stay as far away as possible from the Duke of Basingstoke. It went without saying he wouldn't deign to trouble himself with anyone so insignificant as she. Indeed, she was relying on it. The last thing she wanted was to be thrust upon the notice of the *ton*.

All would be well, as long as he didn't recognize her as the same lady who'd been prowling around the garden. He'd been well into his cups. With any luck, her face was nothing more than an indistinct blur in his mind.

God knew she was due for a bit of luck.

The duke kept Susannah on the floor for two dances before escorting her back to Uncle Edward and Aunt Edith. The two tall, handsome gentlemen the duke had greeted when he'd arrived joined their party, and the six of them stood chatting; such a flawless sextet of *bon ton*, they looked as if they were posing for a painting.

"Oh, dear. Is it so late? Forgive me, but I must go and find my father." Miss Thorne jumped to her feet and held out her hand. "It was a great pleasure meeting you, Lady Francesca. Shall I save you a seat at the next ball?"

"Please do, yes. Something unobtrusive, if you would, as I foresee another pink gown in my future."

Miss Thorne laughed and pressed her hand. "Of course. Until then, my new friend."

"Until then." Franny turned to bid Miss Thorne goodnight and noticed Lady Crump beckoning to her from the corridor that led toward the ladies' retiring room.

She would have been pleased to spy for a bit longer, but even wallflowers required chaperones, so she rose to her feet to join Lady Crump. Really, aside from the whispers and appalled glances aimed her way when they'd arrived, it hadn't been *too* dreadful an evening, all things considered—

"Who the devil is that poor, unfortunate creature in the dreadful pink gown?"

She froze, her heart heaving into her throat. It was *him*— she'd heard that lazy drawl in her head a dozen times since the incident in the garden.

He'd moved a little away from Uncle Edward's party,

toward a shallow alcove to one side of the dance floor, and was speaking to one of the gentlemen, his back to her.

"Whoever slapped that awful gown onto her back should be horsewhipped."

She caught the back of a chair to steady herself, knuckles white. He was talking about *her*—he must be—his words as ugly as his face was beautiful.

One of his companions spoke, too low for her to hear, but the duke's reply reached her clearly. "She looks like a radish unearthed from some tragic patch of country mud."

Incredibly, a laugh bubbled up in her throat, though it was more hysterical than amused. She slapped her hand over her lips to smother it and glanced frantically around her, desperate not to hear whatever insult would emerge from his perfect lips next.

There was nowhere to hide, nowhere to go but right past him, but if she did, he was certain to see her.

A sudden, choking shame rushed over her. Somehow, *realizing* she'd overheard him insult her was far worse than simply having overheard him. It was the duke who should be ashamed, not *her*, and yet . . .

She remained where she was, frozen, her feet rooted to the spot.

"Bloody ridiculous, the entire thing. I despise the . . ."

She was saved from having to hear what else the duke despised aside from radishes, country mud, and pink gowns by the appearance of a fair-haired beauty, who emerged from around a corner and laid her gloved fingers on the duke's arm. "You promised me a dance this evening, Your Grace, and you know I adore a quadrille."

Franny waited, breath held, frozen stiff like a terrified rabbit until the duke led the lady to the floor, then she fled around the corner and into the corridor.

"Francesca, my dear, are you ill?" Lady Crump caught her arm and turned Franny to face her. "Oh, dear, you look a bit peaked. A lady's first ball can be overwhelming, can it not? Shall we go to the ladies' retiring room for a bit? I'll come with you—"

"No! I mean, no, I'm quite well, Lady Crump. I'll be out in a moment."

"Very well, dear. I'll request our carriage be brought round, then I'll come back to fetch you."

"Thank you, my lady."

Franny hurried down the corridor, darted into the ladies' retiring room and pressed her back to the wall, her too-tight bodice pressing against her ribs, squeezing the breath from her lungs.

Charming, kind, honorable . . . the ton has nothing but praise for him . . .

Pure, unadulterated hogwash. Lies, from beginning to end.

She met her own gaze in the glass, let out a little laugh, and shook her head.

Well, what if she *did* look like a radish? What of it? That is, no young lady wished to look like something that belonged on a dinner plate, particularly not something so uninspired as a radish, but in the end, what did it matter what some haughty duke thought of her?

Particularly *that* haughty duke.

His Grace, the Eighth Duke of Basingstoke, might be better at hiding his flaws from the *ton*, but he was as wicked a man as his father had been.

Tonight, she'd gotten a peek under that pretty golden mask he wore, and she wouldn't soon forget the ugliness she'd found there.

Helios, indeed.

CHAPTER 5

There wasn't a single soul to be seen on the streets of Mayfair at eleven o'clock the following morning. Only the most desirable or the most desperate of callers would choose to present themselves at the door of a lady of fashion the morning after the first ball of the season.

Franny wasn't the former—the odds were against her getting farther than her uncle's entryway—but neither did she like to think of herself as the latter.

At least, not *yet*.

She was resolute. Yes, that would do. Resolute, and unwavering in her determination to breach the wall of her uncle Edward's icy silence before the season ended, because if she didn't, she'd be forced to return to her mother as empty-handed as when she'd left.

And that, well, it didn't bear thinking about.

Her knock was brisk, firm. Her uncle's butler must have been stationed just on the other side of the door because it flew open at once, revealing a bewigged man in smart, navy-blue livery. He peered over her shoulder into the empty street behind her, his jowls quivering.

Proper young ladies didn't venture out alone. Not onto the streets, and not anywhere else. It had been more than a decade since she'd been in London, but there were certain things about Town one never forgot, like the taste of Gunter's violet ices, and the Cascade at Vauxhall Gardens.

And, of course, the hundreds of improprieties lurking around every corner, lying in wait for any lady who dared stir a step without a chaperone nipping at her heels. She'd been herded from one location to the next since she'd arrived in London. She'd borne it all with the docility of a sheep for the most part, but not this time, as it wouldn't do for Lady Crump to know she was calling on the Stanhopes.

So, impropriety it was. "Lady Francesca Stanhope, for Lady Stanhope."

The butler, who was called Coote—a name so perfectly suited to him she had to smother a snort every time she laid eyes on him—gave her a disapproving frown, but he waved her inside, and presented his silver tray for her card. "Wait here, if you would, my lady."

She'd spent enough hours yesterday on the straight-backed bench set into the alcove near the entryway to know it was a punishment to sit upon, but she settled down with a muttered apology to her backside and prepared for another excruciating wait.

Nor was she disappointed. Time dragged along as the grandfather clock on the first-floor landing ticked away one torturous minute after the next, until at last it chimed the hour.

Still, Coote didn't return.

She remained where she was, every limb still, her jaw tight and her backside numb, and waited. If her aunt Edith ever *did* intend to admit her, she intended to punish her first, because evidently a decade of silence wasn't punishment enough.

But she was at their mercy, and they all knew it.

There was nothing for her to do but to sit, wait, and watch the servants bustling about, hurrying through the corridors and up and down the stairs, which was a dull enough enter-tainment, until a footman carrying an enormous spray of pink roses in a crystal vase appeared, and set the elegant arrangement in the center of a round marble table at the base of the stairwell.

"My, how pretty." Now *here* was a pink she could approve of, such a pale blush of a pink it was nearly translucent, and the blooms themselves perfect layers of velvety petals.

"Aren't they lovely, miss?" A housemaid had paused in the entryway and was fussing with the arrangement, her dimpled cheeks flushed with pleasure. "The duke's got his own hothouses, and his flowers are always the nicest."

The Dukes of Basingstoke, Montford, and Grantham were all in London at the moment. It was quite an unnecessary surplus of dukes, really—but the maid could only be referring to the duke who'd danced the first two dances of the opening ball of the season with Susannah. "The Duke of Basingstoke?"

"Yes, indeed, miss. Lady Susannah is a lucky young lady."

Or an unlucky one, depending on how much the eighth duke resembled the seventh. Given that casual bit of cruelty she'd overheard last night, she'd wager the father's wickedness had implanted itself in the son.

Or the *sun*, as the *ton* would have it.

An unladylike snort slipped out at that, but she sobered again as the grandfather clock began to chime the quarter hour. The gentlemen who'd partnered Susannah at Lord Hasting's ball last night would be crowding the entryway soon enough, including the blasted Duke of Basingstoke.

Dash it. She didn't like to leave without some acknowledgment of her call from Lady Stanhope, but—

"Franny?"

It was a low hiss, soft enough she thought she'd imagined it, but a quick, light step on the staircase made her turn. She looked up, and her breath left her lungs in a rush.

Susannah.

Her cousin was standing on the second-floor landing,

wearing a pale, yellow carriage dress, the gleaming locks of her dark hair gathered into a smooth knot at the back of her neck and tied with a matching yellow ribbon.

Susannah gave her a hesitant smile, then lifted her hand in a shy wave.

A tangled ball of emotions rushed into Franny's throat, but she managed a smile in return, and lifted her own hand in greeting. "Su—"

"I beg your pardon, Lady Francesca."

Franny whirled around. After making her wait more than an hour, Coote had chosen this moment to return. She hardly spared him a glance, but when she turned back toward the staircase, it was deserted. Susannah had vanished as quickly as she'd appeared.

"Lady Stanhope is not at home," Coote informed her coolly, his face expressionless.

Not at home, indeed. Why, Aunt Edith was no doubt in the drawing room even now, her ear pressed to the door so she might hear Coote dismiss her after an interminable wait, because Lady Edith Stanhope was the sort who'd find it amusing to see her own niece humbled.

And humbled she would be, because she'd be back during calling hours tomorrow, and the next day, and the day after that, only to receive the same shabby treatment, until they finally relented and admitted her, because she didn't have any other choice.

"I see. How unfortunate. I'm sorry to have missed her." She reached into her pocket, pulled out her case, and dropped yet another of her cards onto the silver tray. Soon enough her aunt would have so many she could build another grand London townhouse with them. "I'll return tomorrow, then."

"Very good, my lady."

Coote opened the door, giving her just enough time to step out into the chilly afternoon before he slammed it behind her with such force, she nearly tumbled off the top step. She caught herself, and turned to glare at the closed door, just managing to restrain herself from giving it a hearty kick. "Why, you utter *devil*—"

"You have excellent balance, madam."

"Indeed, and a lucky thing I do, or else I might have . . ." She turned toward the voice, and her tirade ended with a humiliating gulp.

There on the pavement before her sat a dashing curricle with scarlet and gold wheels, pulled by the prettiest pair of sleek matched bays she'd ever seen, and beside it . . .

Beside it stood the prettiest duke who'd ever graced a London season.

Who else, but the Duke of Basingstoke?

Helios himself, complete with his winged chariot.

She stifled a groan. Why, of all the gentlemen Susannah had danced with last night, did it have to be *him* she stumbled across? Fate seemed determined to thwart her at every turn.

"Might have what?" He arched an eyebrow, a slight smile on his handsome lips.

He was directly out of a fashion plate—a perfect pink of the ton, from the tips of his gleaming Hessians with their silver tassels to the glossy black top hat artfully arranged over his golden curls.

His eyes *weren't* brown, after all, tawny or otherwise, but blue, and set into his angel's face like two flashing sapphires in a bed of pearls.

Goodness. His valet must be in raptures over him.

But then fine clothing could hide a multitude of sins, couldn't it?

"I do hope you aren't injured. You nearly fell down the stairs."

Oh, he was the perfect gentleman, wasn't he? Just as everyone in London claimed he was, except just last night, he'd called her a muddy radish in the same smooth, polite tone he was using right now.

The pink gown had been a catastrophe—there was no denying that—but even if it *did* make her look like a radish, how was it any business of his? Surely a duke must have a great many more important things to concern himself with. As for radishes, they were perfectly serviceable vegetables, and did not deserve to have scorn heaped upon them, any more than she did.

"I'm *fine*, thank you." She lifted her chin, marched down the stairs and with a final, dignified sniff began to sidle down the sidewalk, taking care to keep an eye on him.

"I'm relieved to hear it, madam." He took a step toward her. "As I said, you have impressive balance, but you aren't quite skilled enough to keep from impaling yourself on an iron spike, are you?"

Oh, *no*. She swallowed. "I beg your pardon?"

"Three nights ago, madam. I caught you sneaking about inside that very garden." He waved his walking stick toward the plane tree. "Don't say you've forgotten already?"

No, but she'd hoped *he* had. The man had been so deep in his cups he may as well have been at the bottom of the Thames, but not deep enough to have forgotten her face, damn him.

"I'll have your name, if you please, madam."

Ah, here was a stroke of good luck, at last. He didn't know who she was, and she wasn't going to help him along. The longer it took for him to realize it, the better it was for her. "But you already know my name. We've been introduced."

And so they had been, loosely speaking.

He was the peerless, the unmatched, the flawless Duke of Basingstoke, a man of reputedly impeccable character, a man rumored to be free of vice, and *she* was the lady he'd had the infamously bad manners to call a country radish.

There. Introductions complete.

"If I'd been introduced to you at Lord Hasting's ball last night, madam, I feel certain I would remember it."

"Oh, it wasn't at the ball. It was three nights ago, in the garden. I told you my name then. Indeed, I believe I repeated it several times, as you were a bit befuddled. Don't you recall it?"

For the first time since he'd emerged from his winged chariot, the Duke of Basingstoke looked puzzled, his handsome brow creased. "I do not."

She smothered a snort. "What a pity. Now, if you'll pardon me—"

"Are you acquainted with the Stanhopes?"

Not so well acquainted their butler had hesitated to toss her out the door—an event the duke had most certainly witnessed, along with the unladylike curse she'd uttered—but she said only, "In a manner of speaking, yes."

He advanced another step. "I'm not persuaded you ever did introduce yourself to me, madam. Regardless, I don't have the honor of knowing your name."

Not yet, no, but he'd find it out soon enough. The Drews were the only family in London aside from the Stanhopes who had any reason to be interested in her sudden appearance in town. There was bound to be all manner of unpleasantness when he discovered it.

"Well, there's nothing I can do about that, I'm afraid." She would have left it at that, but when she tried to scurry past him, the man had the nerve to step in her way.

"Certainly, there is. You can *tell it to me*."

Oh dear, he *did* look put out. Yet at the same time his handsome lips were quirked at the corners, as if he found her amusing despite himself, as one might a naughty puppy, or a spoiled child.

Amusing, indeed. He'd soon find out how amusing she could be.

All at once, she had had quite enough of the Duke of Basingstoke. "Perhaps it would nudge your memory if I were wearing a pink gown."

"I beg your pardon?"

She pasted a brilliant smile on her lips. "The poor, unfortunate creature in the dreadful pink gown? At Lord Hasting's ball last night? The radish, unearthed from some tragic patch of country mud?"

"You!" He jerked his head back in surprise, his gaze moving over her, taking in every detail of her appearance from her scuffed shoes to her shabby gray cloak. He lingered on her face, her lips, her hastily arranged hair, his perusal so slow and deliberate: every inch of her went hot with embarrassment.

Well, he recalled her *now*, certainly. Nothing but a consciousness of having behaved like a perfect cad could color the tips of a high and mighty duke's ears such a bright pink.

Ha! Now who was the radish?

Still, at least he had the decency to flush. That was something, at any rate.

But he didn't, as it turned out, have the decency to beg her pardon, because the next words out of his mouth weren't a groveling apology. "You can hardly blame me for not recognizing you as the lady in the pink gown last night, madam."

"Can't I?" Because she *did* blame him, and she had every intention of doing so until the end of eternity.

"Why, no, certainly not. The glare from the gown made it impossible for me to properly make out your features."

No sooner were these shocking words out of his mouth than the corner of his lip twitched in the beginnings of a smile that *might* have been charming, if she'd encouraged it to escape.

She didn't, no matter if she did feel just a twinge of curiosity to see how it would transform his face, but the Duke of Basingstoke was no friend of hers, and he might keep his almost-charming smiles to himself. "Is that your attempt at an apology?"

His lips were still twitching as he swept into an exaggerated bow. "I beg your pardon for my rudeness last night, madam. It was badly done of me. I'm Basingstoke," he announced, as if his belated apology and grand title were more than enough to excuse his shocking conduct last night.

In most cases, it probably was, as dukes were permitted to do as they pleased, for the most part.

But he might have been Prinny himself, and she still would not excuse his conduct. Not because he'd called her a country radish, but because a man who'd speak so unkindly about any lady was no gentleman.

"I know who you are, Your Grace." Everyone in England knew who *he* was, but after last night, perhaps she knew better than most, and thus better than most to stay away from him.

"Ah, but I still don't know who *you* are, madam."

She didn't answer, but cocked her head to the side, studying him. Really, he'd done her a favor last night. If he hadn't shown her who he was, she might have succumbed to the allure of those blue eyes, that charming smile.

Now, however, she was immune to him. He might bow, and smile, and flutter his eyelashes without it having the least effect on her. "Not to worry, Your Grace. I assure you, I'm far beneath your notice. Obscurity can, on occasion, be a delightful thing, can it not?"

She didn't offer him another word, but ducked around him and continued on her way toward Charles Street, humming under her breath, the natural good humor her aunt Edith had squashed now restored.

It wasn't every day, after all, that a poor, unfortunate creature like herself, a lady only just liberated from her tragic patch of country mud, had the satisfaction of leaving a duke speechless.

CHAPTER 6

"Giles!" Louisa, Giles's youngest sister, flew into the drawing room, her golden-brown curls bouncing and her chubby little legs a blur of ruffled white pantalettes.

"Hello, imp." He caught her up in his arms and pressed a loud, smacking kiss to the top of her silky head. "What are you doing, scampering about like a wild animal? Does Nurse know where you are?"

"No. I ran away from her," Louisa replied, with the bald honesty and utter unconcern of a six-year-old. "What's a bugle?"

"A bugle? It's a wind instrument, rather like a horn, used by the militia to signal battle positions. Why? Are you thinking of joining the cavalry?"

"No, silly." She plucked at his cravat, watching with interest as the flawless folds of Digby's Mathematical fell into disarray. "I heard Mamma tell Diana you made a bugle at Diana's ball last night. Did you, really?"

"Not that I recall, no." Though perhaps he should have, as a few deafening bugle calls might have lent a touch of liveliness to the proceedings.

"Mamma said you made a bugle, and then she said you were . . ." Louisa's brow wrinkled. "In . . . in . . ."

"Ingenious? Inspiring? Incandescent?" There was no harm in guessing, after all.

"Incorrigible." Amy, who'd reached the wise age of thirteen just the week before, and thus knew everything there was to know, appeared in the drawing room doorway. "And it wasn't *bugle*, Louisa, you peahen, but *bungle*."

Louisa's lower lip wobbled. "I'm *not* a peahen!"

"You *are*. Mamma said Giles made a dreadful bungle at the ball last night, and then Diana said she was sure you didn't mean it, and then Mamma said you never do, but thoughtlessness doesn't excuse you, and that's when she said you were incorrigible."

Well, this had all the makings of a delightful visit. "Have you got a proper greeting for your brother, Amy, or are you too grown up for that now?"

Amy ran across the room to him. He leaned down to catch her, Louisa still balanced on his hip, and she threw herself into his arms. "Have you come to take us for a drive in the park?"

"I have, indeed." He hadn't, but a drive was certain to be a good deal more amusing than a scold from his mother. "Of course, I have. Why else would I have come? Go and fetch your cloaks, and be quick about it, before—"

"Well, Giles, here you are at last. We've been expecting you for the better part of an hour." His mother swept into the room, the shamefaced nursemaid trailing after her. "Amy and Louisa, you're to go with Miss Peck at once."

"No!" Louisa stamped her foot. "I don't want to!"

"You will do as I say, Louisa."

"But we're to go for a ride with Giles!" Amy clung to his neck like a limpet.

"Not today. Go on, off to the schoolroom with you both. Miss Peck, if you would?"

"Tomorrow, imps!" Giles called as Miss Peck corralled his

sisters and whisked them away. "Good morning, Mother. You're in a temper today."

She gave him a tight smile. "Perhaps I've reached the end of my patience with incorrigible children, Giles."

Incorrigible. There was that word again.

"Whatever it is I've done, I'm sorry for it." Likely to be even sorrier before he escaped the drawing room by the looks of things, despite having been an utter paragon of exemplary behavior last night.

He'd attended Hasting's cursed ball, had made certain Diana was properly partnered, and had danced attendance on Lady Susannah and taken her into supper, just as a proper bridegroom should. He'd even persuaded Montford and Grantham to attend, which had been no small feat, especially in Montford's case, as he had a pathological abhorrence to anything related to the season, or marriage.

His mother turned an incredulous look on him. "You mean to say you don't know what's happened?"

"No. I haven't the vaguest idea." Nor did he care much. His mother was forever in a fit over something.

"For pity's sake, Giles, what have you been doing all morning?"

"Enduring a scold from a wily female." Prim, pinched lips flashed in his mind's eye, dark hair bundled into an untidy knot at the back of a long, graceful neck, cheeks flushed red with temper—

"You *what*? No, never mind." His mother held her hand up. "I don't want to know."

"No, likely not."

His ears were still burning from the set-down he'd endured at the hands of that tart-tongued vixen. It wasn't often a young lady unleashed the full force of her temper upon him.

Or ever, come to think of it.

He'd rather enjoyed it, but he *hadn't* cared for the way she'd looked at him—pure scorn, hidden behind the thinnest, most brittle of veneers. No young lady had *ever* looked at him like that in his entire life.

None had ever dared.

After glaring at him as if she'd happily strangle him with his own cravat, she'd had the nerve to run off without telling him her name. But as soon as he'd caught sight of her face, it was as if he'd been struck by a bolt of lightning. Fine, pale skin, a heart-shaped face with a pointed, stubborn chin, and those blue eyes . . .

It was *her*, the impertinent garden nymph and last night's country radish, all rolled up into one delectable, impudent—

"Oh, Giles! There you are." Diana hurried into the drawing room, a newspaper under her arm. "I'm so glad you're here."

"Well, I'm pleased someone is." He gave his mother a reproachful look, then pressed a kiss to his sister's cheek. "Your first ball was a brilliant success, Diana. Every eye in Lord Hasting's ballroom was on you and Ormsby when you danced together last night."

"They do complement each other, don't they?" His mother's frown softened into a beaming smile as her gaze fell on her eldest daughter. "Lord Ormsby would do very well for you, dearest."

Giles sniffed. "A trifle dull, isn't he?" Surely, at least *one* of them should have an animated spouse.

Just like that, his mother's frown was back. "On the contrary, Giles, the Marquess of Ormsby is just the sort of decent, honorable gentleman I could hope for, for Diana. I can't think of a single objection you could have to him."

"None whatsoever, as long as Diana likes him. *Do* you like him?" He raised an eyebrow at Diana, and her cheeks went pink. "Ah, ha. That blush says you do."

"I hardly know him, but he does appear to be—"

"Of course, she likes him," his mother interrupted. "What's

not to like about Lord Ormsby? He's a perfect gentleman. Never mind that now. We have another matter to deal with."

"Yes, something about a bugle, or so Louisa tells me."

"It's a great deal worse than a bungle." His mother settled on the edge of a chair near the fireplace. "Indeed, I haven't the faintest idea how we're to address it."

Giles just managed not to roll his eyes. "What have I done *this* time? Was my cravat pin crooked, or my linen wrinkled? Did I call some young lady by the wrong name?"

Diana and his mother glanced at each other. "Er, perhaps you'd better just read it yourself." Diana slid the paper out from under her arm and handed it to him.

He took it with a huff and threw himself onto a settee. The paper had been folded so the account of Lord Hasting's ball was on top. He skimmed over the article, but it appeared dull enough, just the names of the people who'd attended, with the usual long-winded account of who'd danced with whom, some gushing over the jewels and clothing, and—

> . . . grievous lapse in the gentlemanly manners for which he is so universally admired, the Duke of B— was overheard to compare the unsuspecting young lady to "a radish that's been unearthed from some tragic patch of country mud."

He jerked upright. What the *devil*? How in the world had the *Morning Post* gotten ahold of the ill-tempered remark he'd made about the country radish—

That is, the garden nymph—

No, damn it.

That is, the young lady in the pink gown?

"You look surprised, Giles. Dare I hope you did *not*, in fact, refer to a young lady as a 'country radish' at Lord Hasting's ball last night?"

"No! That is, I *did* say it, but . . ."

But he hadn't imagined anyone could *hear* him, least of all the lady herself. There'd been six rows of chairs between them, and a ballroom of chattering, laughing *ton* surrounding them.

"For pity's sake, Giles!" His mother leapt up from her chair. "Wasn't it bad enough that everyone in the ballroom was laughing at that poor girl without *you* having to make it worse?"

"If you'd be so good as to let me finish, Mother. I did say it, yes, but to Montford and Grantham *only*. I've no idea how the *Post* got ahold of it."

"Someone overheard you, of course!" His mother paced to one end of the room, turned on her heel and marched back. "There's always someone listening, Giles. You, of all people, should know that."

"We were in an alcove, engaged in a private conversation! I never intended for my comment to reach anyone's else's ears."

Diana shook her head. "There are no private conversations at a ball, Giles, especially not for *you*."

"I regret saying it, I assure you, but I fail to see why the newspapers should bother with it. My opinion on some young lady's gown is hardly newsworthy."

"That depends on the young lady." His mother snatched up the paper and handed it back to him. "Keep reading."

He skimmed down the page again, searching for his own name. He found it a few paragraphs down, and read the passage aloud. "'Could it be that the D— of B—would prefer the scandals of the past remain in the past? Might the lady's sudden appearance in London have sparked a churlish rancor in that manly breast?' For God's sake!" He tossed the newspaper aside. "Rancor! Over *what*? A pink gown?"

"Keep reading." His mother snatched up the paper and handed it back to him.

He hardly dared. But he sat up and gave it his whole attention this time. Near the end of the column, he found what his mother wanted him to see. "'Mightn't the duke's vicious attack on Lady Francesca Stanhope bring the hurt feelings of the past to life once again? Could it be a hint of another scandal to come?'"

Oh, good Lord. No. It couldn't be.

But it was, right there in black and white, for all of London to see.

His country radish, his deliciously cheeky garden nymph, was none other than Lady Francesca Stanhope.

Lady Francesca Stanhope.

Good God, what he had *done*?

"She's Lady Susannah's first cousin," his mother said, when he didn't speak. "Lord Stanhope's elder brother's only child."

Of course. How had he not realized it at once? That night in the garden, he'd mistaken her for Lady Susanna because they so closely resembled each other! They had the same thick, dark hair, the same clear, crystalline blue eyes.

Her eyes alone should have given it away. Only the Stanhopes had eyes that color.

That pert mouth, though. That was Lady Francesca's alone.

"You do realize who she—"

"I know who she is, Mother. What in God's name is she doing in London?"

That unfortunate branch of the Stanhope family had buried themselves in some obscure village in Herefordshire, the last he'd heard. They hadn't set foot in society since the scandal nearly ten years ago.

"Lady Crump is sponsoring Lady Francesca for a season. Her ladyship has remained loyal to Lady Maria Stanhope, despite all the ugliness that attached to Lady Maria after the scandal." His mother sighed. "Lady Maria and I were great friends once, you know. Of course, that ended after your father . . . well, I was excessively fond of her."

"Yes, so you've said before." The trouble was, his father had *also* been excessively fond of Lady Maria Stanhope.

For a time, that is, before he'd broken her. Before he'd broken them all.

Lady Maria had had the damnable bad luck to catch his father's eye when she'd accompanied her husband to London to visit her dear friend, the Duchess of Basingstoke. His father had seduced Lady Maria, ruining her, then he'd killed Lord Charles Stanhope, Lady Maria's husband, when the man challenged him to a duel over his wife's honor.

A true gentleman, a gentleman with even a shred of proper feeling would have refused such a challenge, but his father hadn't been a gentleman.

He'd been a villain.

Society tended to look the other way when it came to villainous dukes, but Lord Charles and Lady Maria had been great favorites among the *ton*, and his father had already had one toe over the line that separated an aristocratic rake from an utter scoundrel, even before he'd trifled with Lady Maria.

That scandal had sent him careening over the edge. Even now, there were still those who shook their heads over that wretched, ugly business. The *ton* had never forgiven his father for it, and God knew they hadn't forgotten it. Even now, ten years later, his family still hadn't been washed entirely clean of the stain.

Lady Maria and her daughter had vanished from society after Lord Charles's death, but now here was Lady Francesca Stanhope, an innocent victim of his father's perfidy, landed smack in the middle of London for her first season, right alongside her cousin, and in a shockingly vivid pink gown, no less!

And *he*, the son of the man who'd destroyed her family, had insulted her.

Lady Francesca Stanhope. Good *Lord*, what a bloody mess.

If there was one thing guaranteed to turn the *ton*'s scrutiny back on his family, it was the sudden and inexplicable presence of Lady Francesca Stanhope in London, and the gossip in the *Post* was certain to make it worse.

A hint of another scandal to come . . .

They were a single day into the season. Lady Francesca had attended *one* ball, and already the newspapers had taken notice of her, and were breathlessly reporting on a meaningless skirmish over the color of a gown as if it were the next Trojan War.

"Do you have any idea what you've done, Giles? If the *ton* digs up your father's scandals, it could impact Diana's prospects this season."

His mother was right. If they got their teeth into that bit of gristle again, there was no telling what it would take to pry it loose. He needed to see this business set to rights at once, for Diana's sake, before the spark caught and they had a raging conflagration on their hands.

"Honestly, Giles, I never would have believed my son could speak so disparagingly to a young lady. I was under the impression I'd raised a gentleman."

"I *wasn't* speaking to Lady Francesca." He couldn't even say now why he'd remarked on Lady Francesca's gown to begin with. The pink gown had caught his eye as he'd made his way back across the ballroom after two nearly silent dances with Lady Susannah. Montford had asked him his opinion about the young ladies present, and the next he knew, he'd started raving about radishes.

To be fair, it was difficult to overlook that shade of pink, but he certainly wasn't in the habit of critiquing ladies' gowns, especially to Montford and Grantham, who didn't give a damn whether a gown was purple or pink, satin or silk. "I never meant to offend her. I'll make amends for my blunder, Mother. I promise it."

"My dear boy, I'm not certain it will be that simple." His mother dropped back into her chair with a sigh. "Her husband's death wasn't the end of Lady Maria's misfortunes, you know. Lord Edward Stanhope laid the blame for his brother's death squarely at her feet and forced her and her daughter to leave London. Lady Francesca has every reason in the world to resent our family."

"I promised you I'd take care of it, Mother, and I will."

"But what can you do, Giles?" Diana bit her lip. "Everyone at the ball was already laughing at her, and now her name's been dragged into the newspapers. Really, it's quite dreadful of you."

It wasn't his finest hour, certainly. "I'll invite Lady Francesca to dance at Lord Wilmot's ball tomorrow night." It would sooth her ruffled feelings and go a long way toward silencing the *ton*'s wagging tongues. "I'll beg her pardon and do what I can to make amends."

His mother studied him for a long moment. "Has it occurred to you, Giles, that Lady Francesca may not *want* to dance with you?"

He blinked at her. Not want to dance with him? Of course, she'd dance with him. He was the Duke of Basingstoke, for God's sake. If Lady Francesca had come to London to find a husband, she really couldn't afford *not* to dance with him. "Every young lady in London wants to dance with me."

His mother huffed. "Really, Giles, one of these days you're going to come upon a young lady you can't charm."

"Perhaps, but it won't be Lady Francesca Stanhope." There wasn't a young lady in London who'd refuse a dance with the Duke of Basingstoke. "I flatter myself she'd prefer a dance with a duke to an evening spent languishing on wallflower row."

"Is that so?" His mother raised an eyebrow. "You're my

son, Giles, and I love you, but I confess I'm rather looking forward to seeing you humbled."

Humbled? Nonsense. "Yes, well, I'm confident my humiliation won't happen at Lord Wilmot's ball tomorrow night."

"Lady Maria must not have accompanied Lady Francesca to London. I know Lady Maria Stanhope, and she never would have permitted her daughter to set foot outside the door in such a gown. It's a pity she isn't here. I'd dearly love to see her again, if she'd agree to see me, that is."

"You may see her yet, if Lady Francesca makes a match this season." That was unlikely, however, either with or without the pink gown. The *ton* might sympathize with Lady Maria and her daughter, but that didn't mean they'd be forgiven for being penniless.

"Try not to worry, Mother." He tossed the paper aside, rose to his feet, and pressed a quick kiss to her cheek. "I'll see you at Lord Wilmot's ball tomorrow evening."

CHAPTER 7

"Well, my dear, another night, another ball." Lady Crump dropped into a chair with a sigh. "It's another crush, for all the good it will do us."

There'd been no mention of a triumphant success when they'd left Charles Street for Lord Wilmot's ball tonight, nor had her ladyship reiterated her promise to deliver a bridegroom before the end of the season. Once the Duke of Basingstoke's radish comment had appeared in the *Morning Post*, the wind had rather died under poor Lady Crump's sails.

Her ladyship looked out over the sea of gilt chairs and let out another disconsolate sigh. "Dear me, these balls do start to blend into one another when one is forced to observe from here, don't they?"

"They do, rather." If she didn't know it to be impossible, Franny would have sworn she'd attended this very same ball two nights ago.

Lord Wilmot's ballroom was nearly identical to Lord Hasting's ballroom, with the same soaring crystal chandeliers, the same gilt-pier glasses upon every wall, and the same tiny chairs with the same glum young ladies sitting upon them. All but Miss Thorne, alas. It was a cruel blow, indeed, as Prudence Thorne was the only young lady in London who could have made such an evening bearable.

Plenty of speculative glances had followed Franny as she made her way from the entrance to wallflower row, and there'd been no shortage of whispers trailing in her wake, but there was rather less snickering than there had been at Lord Hasting's ball, and some of the gazes were curious rather than disdainful.

They all knew who she was, now. The Duke of Basingstoke had seen to that.

The duke, and the *Morning Post*.

"Do endeavor to smile, won't you, Francesca?" Lady Crump tapped Franny's arm with her fan. "I grant you things appear a touch grim just now, but no gentleman wishes to dance with a young lady wearing such a fierce frown upon her face."

Dance with her? Such an optimistic, indomitable spirit Lady Crump had! Why, there wasn't a single gentleman here who'd venture a dance with *her*, whether she smiled or not. Not after they'd read the *Post* yesterday.

The Duke of Basingstoke had seen to *that*, as well.

Radish, indeed.

If it hadn't been humiliating enough before, now all of London knew he'd compared her to a root vegetable. Whatever had become of comparing a lady to a summer's day, or to the sun, or her eyes to the stars in the heavens? There was a reason not a single line of poetry comparing a lady to a radish existed.

But she'd already made up her mind that it didn't matter what the Duke of Basingstoke thought of her. The more distance she kept between them, the better, and as for the other gentlemen roaming about, they wouldn't pay her any mind no matter what she wore.

Which was just as well, really.

She hadn't come to London for *them*. She'd come to make

her peace with her uncle Edward, no matter if she did have to tiptoe upon eggshells to do it.

"Look, Francesca, the Duke of Basingstoke has arrived with his mother, and his sister Lady Diana. My goodness. I'm quite displeased with the duke at the moment, as you know, dear, but one can't deny that he quite eclipses every other gentleman in the room."

"Indeed." There was no mistaking *him* for another, lesser gentleman, was there? Not a single one of the gentlemen in attendance tonight cut quite as regal a figure as *he* did, with his impeccable dress, everything in the height of fashion, from the black evening coat stretched smoothly over his broad shoulders to those absurdly fetching golden curls.

But his clothing wasn't any more a reflection of him than the pink gown she wore tonight was a reflection of *her*, for all that the *ton* would never admit it.

Though one did wonder whether they were all still singing the duke's praises after they'd read about his ill-natured comment in the *Post*. Did they all still think him a proper, honorable gentleman? It was rather a foolish question, really. They'd sing as loudly as they ever had, whether they thought him proper or not, because he was a wealthy duke with an angelic face.

"He and your cousin look well together, don't they?" Lady Crump watched from behind her fan as the duke approached Susannah and offered her an elegant bow. "It looks as if he'll open the dance with her, just as he did at Lord Hasting's ball. He's quite singled her out this season, has he not? I daresay he's taken with her."

Was he, though? Oh, he was behaving just as a besotted gentleman should, with that dazzling smile and those lingering glances, but there was something artificial about it, as if he were putting on a performance. There was no sincere warmth in his expression, no—

"Oh, dear. That's not . . . oh, dear. I'm afraid something's gone awry."

At Lady Crump's anxious clucking, Franny turned her attention back to her companion. "What is it, my lady?"

"Whatever is he doing? He's going off without taking your cousin to the floor!" Lady Crump grasped Franny's arm. "My goodness, I don't believe I've ever seen your aunt so red in the face before! Goodness, she looks to be on the verge of an apoplexy."

Aunt Edith had gone as red as . . . well, a radish, in fact.

Susannah didn't lack a partner for long—Lord Ormsby appeared instantly and swept her into a country dance, but that did little to sooth Aunt Edith's ruffled feathers. She was glaring at the duke's back as if she hoped he'd burst into flames on the spot.

"It almost looks as if he's—why, what in the world?" Lady Crump's grip tightened around Franny's arm. "He's coming this way, and he's looking right at you, Francesca!"

No, surely not. "I'm certain you must be mistaken, my lady. He can't be."

But Lady Crump *wasn't* mistaken. The duke was striding across the ballroom toward the gilt chairs, looking very much like a man who had a specific destination in mind.

And those blue eyes were fixed on *her*.

Meanwhile, the entire ballroom was looking at *him*.

What in the world was he *doing*? Was she once again to be made a sacrifice to another of the Duke of Basingstoke's dramas?

Franny half rose from her chair, intending to flee to the ladies' retiring room before he could reach her, but Lady Crump jerked her back down with a hiss. "Sit down this instant, Francesca! The entire ballroom can see he's coming to you. You *will not* publicly insult the Duke of Basingstoke! It is *not done*."

Why not? He'd publicly insulted *her*—so publicly there

likely wasn't a single person in London who hadn't read about it—and now he was going to make matters worse by calling her to the attention of every smirking aristocrat in Lord Wilmot's ballroom!

To her *uncle's* attention, and in the very worst way possible.

She could *not* be seen to be rivaling her cousin for the duke's favor. If even a breath of gossip to that effect reached her aunt and uncle, she'd never get so much as a toe through the door of their townhouse ever again.

Dear God, what was she to do?

"I cannot fathom what has possessed the man," Lady Crump hissed into her ear. "But His Grace has chosen to single *you* out for his attention, and there is naught for you to do, Francesca, but receive it."

"But I don't want His Grace's attention!" Franny tugged at her arm, but Lady Crump held on with a strength truly astonishing in such an elderly lady. "Indeed, Lady Crump, you must let me go!"

"My dear girl, I'm very sorry for it, but there isn't a thing to be done about it now. The duke is nearly upon us, and a young lady does not scamper across a ballroom like a wild animal to avoid a dance with the Duke of Basingstoke!"

All at once, Franny could see with a sort of dazed, horrifying clarity how the next few moments would unfold, and the echoing ramifications they'd have over the next few days, weeks, months, and years, like a line of dominoes falling.

The duke would stop in front of her, sketch a bow, and say . . .

What? Would he murmur a heartfelt apology for his abominable behavior at Lord Hasting's ball? Insist that he'd always been fond of radishes? That he adored country mud, and had meant the remark as a compliment, or—

But what did it matter what he said? He'd already ruined her. His solemn promenade across the ballroom was more than enough to set every tongue wagging, and Aunt Edith was glaring at her as if her fingers itched to snatch every hair from Franny's head, and—

Oh, dear *God*, this entire drama was certain to be reported in the *Post* tomorrow, wasn't it? Her uncle was going to be furious! He'd see to it that she was sent back to Herefordshire empty-handed, and she and her mother would be right back where they'd started, their mounting debts unpaid, and not enough money for coal to keep their cottage warm this winter.

The duke kept coming, another step, another, closer and closer still, until at last he stopped in front of them, and it was too late to do anything but sit there and wait for everything she'd hoped for to crumble to dust around her.

"Lady Crump. How do you do? I trust you're having a pleasant evening?"

"Oh, Your Grace! How kind of you to enquire. I'm very well, indeed. I was just saying that Lord Wilmot's balls are always among the most enjoyable of the London season."

"Perfectly delightful, yes. I wonder, my lady, if I may trouble you for an introduction to this young lady with you?"

"Why, of course, Your Grace! This is Lady Francesca Stanhope, niece to Lord and Lady Stanhope, and cousin to Lady Susannah."

"How do you do, Lady Francesca? It's a great pleasure to make your acquaintance at last." He bowed over her hand with flawless graciousness, but there was no mistaking the emphasis he put on those last two words.

Was this a punishment for her rudeness to him yesterday, then? Oh, *why* could she never learn to hold her sharp tongue? For an instant, Franny squeezed her eyes closed, but there was nothing for it, no way out of it. She looked up, met his blue eyes, and froze.

The young ladies call him Helios . . .

The Greek sun god, in all his startling radiance.

It was absurd, yet at the same time, she couldn't tear her gaze away from him.

She'd been in too much of a pique yesterday to take in how tall he was, how broad his shoulders, but it wasn't his size, his piercing blue eyes, or that perfect face that tied a lady's tongue in knots.

It was something else, something that slid out from under her fingertip the moment she tried to pin it down, but she could feel it as palpably as a touch on her hand, or a whisper in her ear. He had a presence about him, a power in that lean body, barely suppressed, as if he were an instant away from bursting into motion. It was there in his wide stance, his straight shoulders and back, and the way he was looking at her, directly into her eyes.

But his mouth . . .

How had she not noticed his mouth when they'd spoken yesterday?

She'd never seen a man with a mouth like his in her life. The startling color, a splash of crimson in that flawless face, as if he'd spent the afternoon eating sweet cherries and licking the sticky juice from his lips.

Pure sin, as if the devil himself had drawn it there.

It was the one feature in his face that gave his wickedness away.

"Are you unwell, Lady Francesca? You've gone rather pale all of a sudden."

Another lady might not have heard it, that hint of amusement in his tone, a touch of arrogance, as if he believed he could mock a lady he'd only just been introduced to and never be held to account for it, but *she* heard it, and it was as if he'd tossed a basin of icy water in her face.

Did he find it amusing to single her out?

Of course, he did. It must entertain him to toy with her, as a cat did with a mouse, because when one was the Duke of Basingstoke, then everything was a game, wasn't it? But it wasn't a game to *her*. Her mother wouldn't survive another winter in their cold, damp cottage in Herefordshire. Her presence in London was literally a matter of life and death.

Her spine snapped straight. "I'm not in the least unwell, Your Grace."

And she *wasn't*, not anymore, but she was a bit of a coward still, because even as he leaned closer, she became aware she was pressing back against her chair, away from him, because underneath those fashionable clothes, behind that charming smile, the Eighth Duke of Basingstoke was every inch the devil his father had been.

"Will you join me for a quadrille, Lady Francesca?" He bowed again, and held out his hand with the air of a man who hadn't any doubt she'd accept it. Indeed, of the hundred or more ladies in attendance tonight, she was likely the only one in the entire ballroom who wouldn't trade her soul for a chance to dance with the Duke of Basingstoke.

But none of those ladies were at the mercy of a man like her uncle Edward. None of them were facing a growing mountain of debt, or the declining health of a beloved mother. None of those ladies had experienced a heartbreaking loss at the hands of this man's father.

And none of them could imagine what it was like to be as desperate as she was. "Thank you, Your Grace, but I don't intend to dance this evening."

Lady Crump gasped. "Francesca! My goodness, I can't have heard you right. You can't have just refused to dance with the duke."

But she could. She *had*. "I beg your pardon, Your Grace. If you'll excuse me, Your Grace, Lady Crump."

Lady Crump stared at her, stunned, and her hand fell away from Franny's arm.

Franny didn't give the duke a chance to say anything more, but leapt to her feet and raced out of the ballroom to the ladies' retiring room without looking back, as if the devil himself were chasing her.

The devil, or the Duke of Basingstoke.

CHAPTER 8

The dozens of eyes boring into the back of Giles's skull were putting him off his pheasant pie.

"Well, Basingstoke?" Grantham took up his wineglass and settled back against his chair. "Let's have it out, shall we? What do you have to say about that business at Wilmot's ball last night?"

Giles abandoned his fork with a huff. A perfectly good pheasant pie, wasted, but they may as well get this over with now, as neither of his friends had ever been able to hold their tongues worth a damn. "Not a blessed thing."

And he didn't—not a single, bloody word.

Though if he *did* have something to say, he might ask Lady Francesca Stanhope what in God's name she thought she was *doing*, fleeing the ballroom as she'd done last night, leaving him gawking after her like a great fool, with every eye upon him? He might hint that such mulishness was unattractive in a young lady, or perhaps he'd point out that she'd nearly brought poor Lady Crump to tears with her antics.

He might tell her that such a violent shade of pink didn't flatter her.

No, perhaps not that last thing, as that sort of remark was what had gotten him into this mess to begin with, and it wasn't even *true*, damn the chit. Not one lady in a thousand could wear such a blinding pink, but Lady Francesca some-how contrived to look like a flower in it.

The *Morning Post* had printed an account of the entire humiliating episode, of course, and had had the gall to refer to him as humbled by her rejection. *Humbled*, just as his mother had warned. They'd even had the nerve to imply he deserved it, after the radish debacle.

And it wasn't just the *Post*. *The Times*, the *Morning Herald*, and the *Morning Chronicle* that had also reported it, and they'd gleefully taken up Lady Francesca's cause. Somehow, refusing to dance with him had made her the darling of London's scandal sheets.

"I wagered Grantham you wouldn't come to White's at all today." Montford stretched his legs out in front of him in a careless sprawl. "I'm out fifty bloody pounds because of you, Basingstoke."

"You made a fool's wager, Montford. Why should you think I wouldn't come today? We always dine at White's on Wednesday afternoons." Every damnable gentleman in the dining room with them had likely made the same wager, and it gave Giles a grim sort of satisfaction that they'd all lost their money.

"Yes, that's so, but it isn't every day a nonpareil like the Duke of Basingstoke is brought low with a few words from a lady in a lurid pink gown." Montford exchanged an amused look with Grantham, his dark eyes dancing with merriment. "We thought perhaps you'd stay abed for a bit, licking your wounds."

And there it was.

Giles managed a shrug, but the gnashing of teeth inside his head was deafening. "Wounds? I'm surprised at you, Mont-ford. You can't believe either I or anyone else will take any notice of what Lady Francesca Stanhope does."

Except, of course, that all of London had taken notice of it. At least two dozen amused stares had followed him across

White's dining room, and he could have sworn he'd heard Lord Allen titter, the scoundrel.

"I don't know if that's true, Basingstoke." Grantham took a judicious sip of his wine. "Lady Francesca's name is on the lips of everyone in London. That's quite a trick, for a lady who lacks fashion, family, and fortune."

"Pretty face, though." Montford nudged Giles. "And that's to say nothing of her other eye-catching assets. She looks just like her mother did at that age, according to my grandfather."

Giles grunted. "Your grandfather is a decrepit old bounder, Montford."

Still, there was no denying the girl was pretty. She resembled her cousin, with the same dark hair and heart-shaped face, but Lady Francesca's blue eyes had a spirit Lady Susannah's lacked, and Lady Francesca's figure was . . . well, poor Lady Susannah looked rather like a plucked chicken next to all of Lady Francesca's delicious curves.

Montford laughed. "True enough, but whether she meant to or not, Basingstoke, Lady Francesca has stumbled upon an ingenious way to transform herself from a wallflower into the most interesting young lady in London. You can be sure every chit at Wilmot's last night is now lamenting the fact they didn't think to cut you first."

"She didn't *cut* me. She simply declined to dance with me." Still, it was as close to a cut as *he'd* ever received. Ladies didn't refuse to dance with him, particularly not ladies of so little consequence as Lady Francesca.

She wasn't in a position to refuse anyone, yet she'd done just that, while all the *ton* gawked at the spectacle, their jaws hanging open.

And not a single jaw wider than *his*.

He'd crossed an entire ballroom to solicit her hand. Such a magnanimous gesture on his part would have set the chit up for the rest of the season.

And she'd *refused* him.

Still, even as he'd stood there, gaping at her back as she'd rushed off to the ladies' retiring room, there'd been a flicker of something in his chest that had felt suspiciously like . . .

Admiration.

It had been a tiny, unwilling, resentful flicker, yes, but a flicker, nonetheless.

No one ever refused him anything.

She was brave, he'd give her that. Irrational, naïve, and careless of her own interests, but brave, too. Perhaps it shouldn't have surprised him, though. She'd kept her head up when the *ton* had been snickering over that disastrous pink gown.

"It's rather remarkable, really, that she *did* refuse you," Montford said, as if he'd read Giles's mind. "I can't make any sense of it. If anything, the girl was more conspicuous at Wilmot's ball than she was at Hasting's, after that radish business."

Heat crawled up the back of Giles's neck at the reminder. He hadn't intended the remark for anyone but Grantham and Montford, but that didn't excuse his behavior. A gentleman didn't make a derogatory comment about a lady's appearance, *ever*, and God knew comparing a lady to "a radish unearthed from some tragic patch of country mud" *wasn't* complimentary.

"Montford's right about the dance. Why would Lady Francesca give up a chance to dance with a duke?" Grantham fixed his cool gray gaze on Giles. "One dance with Basingstoke here would have liberated her from wallflower row for the rest of the evening, if not the season. Why would she refuse such an advantageous opportunity?"

But she hadn't simply refused, had she? It had been more than that. She'd appeared utterly horrified by even the suggestion of a dance with him, then she'd fled the ballroom as if the plague were chasing her.

"Lady Francesca's dance card would have been filled with the names of London's most fashionable gentlemen after a single quadrille with you," Grantham went on. "Isn't the girl here to catch a husband? If so, she made a rather drastic mistake, refusing you."

Drastic, and *foolish*, and despite what else he might think of Lady Francesca, the girl was no fool. She was as close to being a laughingstock as anyone he'd ever known, but rather than acting in her own best interests, she'd stuck her dainty little nose in the air, and ran away from him.

It didn't make *sense*. *She* didn't make sense. "I haven't the faintest idea, but I can't let it stand."

Grantham speared a sliver of pheasant on the end of his fork and raised it to his lips. "Can't let what stand?"

"Lady Francesca's refusal. This absurd dispute between us is stirring up all that old, ugly business between my father and her family. You'd think she'd want to see an end to *that* scandal as much as I do." He'd offered for Lady Susannah in part to put to rest any lingering gossip about a feud between the Stanhopes and the Drews, and now here was Lady Francesca, poking at the bees' nest, setting all the angry bees loose again.

"Why should she want that?" Montford sliced off a bite of meat and popped it into his mouth. "Excellent pheasant, eh?"

Giles looked at Grantham, then they both looked at Montford. "What do you mean, why should she want it? No young lady wants to be the subject of gossip."

Montford snorted. "What you mean, Basingstoke, is *you* don't want to be the subject of gossip. You and Lord Edward Stanhope have every reason to want to see that old scandal buried, but it doesn't do Lady Francesca any good to silence the wagging tongues. She and her mother are already ruined. If you want her cooperation, you'll have to give her something more than that."

Giles glanced at Grantham, then back to Montford. "What do you suppose she wants?"

Montford glanced up from his plate, surprised. "Damned if I know. You might ask her, Basingstoke. I daresay Lady

Francesca would be more amenable to your schemes if there was something in it for her."

"Odds are she merely wants to make an advantageous marriage. Isn't that what every young lady in London for the season wants?" Grantham drained his wine and signaled the waiter for another glass.

It was, but Lady Francesca didn't strike him as being much like every other young lady. Or *any* other young lady, come to that.

"If she is after a match, you've made it difficult for her with that radish business," Grantham pointed out, "She's likely holding a grudge against you for it."

"Who's to say she's holding a grudge?" Montford demanded. "I can think of dozens of reasons she might not want to dance. Her feet might have been tired."

"Tired from what, Montford? Sitting in a gilt chair all evening?"

"How should I bloody know? Perhaps her slippers pinched her toes. Or perhaps she simply didn't want to dance with *you*, Basingstoke. Did that ever occur to you?"

It had, yes, but only *after* he'd handed the impertinent chit an opportunity to make an utter fool of him. His mother had tried to warn him this might happen. He should have listened to her.

Grantham laid his fork aside. "I don't pretend to know Lady Francesca's mind, but it wouldn't be surprising if she did hold a grudge against you, Basingstoke. She and her mother fared a great deal worse over that business with your father than Lord Edward and his family did."

"Too right," Montford said. "If you really wanted to silence the wagging tongues, Basingstoke, you'd marry Lady Francesca, not Lady Susannah."

Marry Lady Francesca! Good Lord, what a thought. She'd drive him to Bedlam within a fortnight. "I'd prefer to marry Lady Susannah, if it's all the same to you, Montford."

It was true, however, that Lady Francesca might be pleased to cause his family trouble. "I don't deny she has reason to despise me, but her feelings are utterly irrelevant to the matter at hand. She's here now, and she's thrust herself upon the *ton*'s notice with that foolishness over a simple dance."

"Ballocks, Basingstoke. It didn't start with the dance, it started with the pink gown, the blame for which lies with Lady Crump, not Lady Francesca." Montford pointed his knife at Giles. "God knows you didn't help matters, calling the girl a muddy radish."

"I didn't call her a—"

"You may as well have done."

It was lowering, to be lectured on his behavior by a rake like Montford. "Yes, very well, but the point, Montford, is she has the *ton*'s attention now, and the more she kicks and screams, the more likely she is to hold onto it."

If Lady Francesca chose to be stubborn, it would only be a matter of time before every gossip in London was shrieking about another dispute between their families, and the *ton* once again gnawing on the bones of his father's old scandals. They weren't likely to take his family's side in the fracas, either. They'd waited years for his father to be punished for what he'd done to Lord Charles and Lady Maria, only to be cheated of justice by his father's death.

Except it wouldn't be his father who'd be punished. It would be Diana, and Amy, and Louisa, and his mother, and God knew they'd been punished enough, as his father had done a rather grand job of mucking up the entire family before his death two years ago.

Even now, despite all he'd done to woo the *ton* and make them forget his father's sins, a hint of the stench still lingered about his family, faint but unmistakable.

But it ended here.

The misfortune of being born to Frederick Drew was punishment enough.

Lady Francesca would *not* make a mess of Diana's season. Her first introduction to society had been a triumph, and triumphant it would remain until she was safely wed to a gentleman who was nothing like their father had been.

Nothing like *him*, either.

"Well, what do you intend to do, Basingstoke?" Grantham toyed with the wineglass between his fingers. "You can't force Lady Francesca to dance with you."

"*Force* her? What do you take me for, Grantham? I wouldn't dream of forcing her to do anything at all. There won't be any need for that. Lady Francesca is a woman, and as susceptible as any other woman to a gentleman's charms."

"Another gentleman's, perhaps." Montford smirked. "I beg your pardon, Basingstoke, but she didn't seem all that charmed by *you* last night."

"I didn't endeavor to charm her." He'd yet to come across a lady who didn't thaw when he exerted himself. "I'm certain I can persuade Lady Francesca to see reason, one way or another."

"Oh?" Montford raised an eyebrow. "How certain are you, Basingstoke? Certain enough to wager on it?"

"Only a scoundrel wagers on a lady, Montford, and you've already lost fifty pounds to Grantham."

"Let me worry about my pocketbook, eh, Basingstoke? Now, do we have a wager, or don't we?"

The mention of a wager had caught the attention of several of the gentlemen nearby. Giles drew out the moment, swirling his wine in his glass before tossing the last of it back, and setting it on the table. "I don't wager on ladies, Montford. I will say this, though. I intend to make peace with Lady Francesca, and will certainly dance with her at Lady Sandham's ball next week. You may do what you will with that information, gentlemen, as long as you keep my sister's name out of it."

"It doesn't count if you have to drag her to the floor, Basingstoke," Lord Allen called out.

"On the contrary, Allen, I can promise you the lady will be all smiles when I lead her out. Now, if you'll pardon me, Grantham, Montford, I'm off to pay a call on Lady Crump."

He rose from his chair, ignoring the gentlemen who rushed to the betting book to wager over whether the Duke of Basingstoke could persuade Lady Francesca Stanhope to dance with him at Lady Sandham's ball.

If he should happen to run across Lady Francesca in Lady Crump's drawing room, then all the better. He'd engage her for two dances before he took his leave, this matter would be settled, and Lady Francesca would quickly find herself, if not the belle of the season, certainly no longer a wallflower.

CHAPTER 9

"Ouch! Dash it!" Franny yelped, yanking out the embroidery needle lodged under her thumbnail. She stuck her thumb in her mouth to catch the welling drop of blood, but it was already too late. Instead of a white carnation, the delicate bluebird she'd been embroidering now had gore dripping from its beak.

Why did she continue to bother with such an odious, tiresome pursuit? Embroidery never distracted her from her whirling thoughts as she hoped it would, and her finished pieces were forever being spoiled by smudged, bloody thumbprints.

She tossed the piece aside and turned to gaze out the window, her chin in her hand, but there wasn't much to see aside from the tops of a handful of dripping trees in Berkeley Square, their leaves reduced to a brown smear by the rain streaking the glass.

It was fitting, really, that it should be such a damp, dreary day. Fitting that she should have stabbed herself with her embroidery needle, and bloodied that poor, innocent bluebird. It was her punishment for having committed the most heinous, unspeakable act any young lady in the history of the London season had ever dared commit.

Refusing to dance with a duke.

Such a grievous sin! It was a wonder her head hadn't been liberated from her neck, impaled on a pike, and mounted on London Bridge.

Lady Crump had been so horrified by Franny's behavior she'd chased her across Lord Wilmot's ballroom last night, cornered her in the ladies' retiring room, and insisted they leave at once. But alas, the drama hadn't ended there. Her ladyship was still so beside herself this morning, she'd lectured over breakfast until Franny's ears were ringing.

Once she'd worn out her tongue at last, Lady Crump had gone off to Bond Street to pick up a few bits and pieces for Lady Sandham's ball next week, leaving Franny alone to think about her shameful lapse in manners.

No one seemed in the least concerned with the Duke of Basingstoke's lapses. They appeared to have forgotten them entirely, and she was evidently meant to forget them as well, and to blush and stammer and curtsey gratefully when the scoundrel who'd called her a country radish asked her to dance.

Proper young ladies didn't seethe with resentment against poor, innocent dukes. They didn't seethe at all, over anything, but particularly not against a duke who'd deigned to show his favor with such a noble gesture as the Duke of Basingstoke had made last night.

Except it hadn't been noble at all, had it? He'd been smirking the entire time! "Noble, indeed—"

Clop, clop, clop . . .

Dear God, now what? She peered through the window down to the street below. A carriage had stopped outside Lady Crump's townhouse. She couldn't make out the crest, but the wheels were painted scarlet and gold, much like—

Oh, *no*. It simply couldn't be!

But it was. There was no mistaking the gleam of those golden curls under the brim of his top hat as he leapt down from his curricle, tossed the reins to his tiger, and bounded up the front steps.

She scrambled to her feet and rushed to the door, intending to flee to her bedchamber, but Percival, Lady Crump's butler, was already coming up the stairs. "Lady Francesca? The duke of—"

"No need to announce me, Percival." The Duke of Basingstoke was striding down the corridor on Percival's heels. "Lady Francesca knows who I am. How do you do, my lady?"

"The Duke of Basingstoke," Percival finished.

"Yes, thank you, Percival. I can see him." She couldn't fail to see *him*. His tall frame and wide shoulders filled the doorway, his sheer presence swelling into every corner of the small parlor before he'd even crossed the threshold, taking up all the space in the room.

He seemed to take up all the space in *every* room.

All the air, too. She'd been enjoying perfectly normal respirations all morning, but now that *he'd* appeared, she'd gone suddenly breathless.

What was he *doing* here?

He was the last person in the world she wished to see, but she didn't dare send him away after the almighty uproar simply refusing to dance with him had caused. "Good afternoon, Your Grace."

"Lady Francesca." He swept into an elegant bow. "Where is Lady Crump? Don't say she left you here to receive callers alone."

"It's past calling hours, Your Grace." It was as broad a hint as she dared, but the duke chose not to recognize it, because one could do as one pleased, when one was a duke. "Do feel at liberty to leave your card for Lady Crump—"

"On the contrary, Lady Francesca, I've come to speak to you, and it's just as well if we keep this business between ourselves. There's no need to involve Lady Crump."

Business with the Duke of Basingstoke? How ominous.

"Forgive me, Your Grace, but I wasn't aware there *was* any business between us."

He regarded her in silence, his sharp blue eyes taking in every shift in her expression until a hot blush rose to her cheeks. What did the man mean, staring at her as if she were a butterfly pinned to a board?

"Last night you refused to dance with me," he said at last. "Why is that, Lady Francesca?"

For pity's sake! All this fuss, because she didn't want to dance with him? One would think she'd set Lord Wilmot's ballroom aflame. "Are you in the habit of calling on ladies the day after a ball, demanding an explanation for their refusal to dance with you, Your Grace?"

"Not at all, Lady Francesca."

"Well, then—"

"You're the only lady in England who's ever dared to refuse to dance with me."

Dear God, had there ever been a more arrogant man than he?

She dropped down onto a settee with a huff. She'd hoped for so little from her one season. Her only goal had been to see her uncle Edward, and negotiate some sort of agreement with him, preferably while avoiding the notice of the *ton*.

How had it come to *this*?

It should have been simple enough, keeping away from the Duke of Basingstoke. He should regard her as well beneath his notice, and she regarded him as well beneath *hers*, though not for any reason he'd understand.

Instead, it felt as if he'd been hounding her since she set foot in London. Everywhere she turned, he was *there*, upsetting all her plans to remain invisible. It wasn't bad enough he'd seen to it her name was dragged into the *Morning Post*. Now nothing would satisfy him but dragging her onto the dance floor, under the prying eyes of the *ton*.

Now he was *here*, in the smallest parlor tucked into the

darkest corner of Lady Crump's grand London townhouse, making himself comfortable on an adjacent settee and demanding answers to all manner of intrusive questions.

He crossed one long leg over the other. "You don't much like me, do you, Lady Francesca?"

It wasn't an accusation, or even a question. It was a statement, without so much as a flicker of emotion behind it. "Am I also the only young lady in England who has ever dared to dislike you, Your Grace?"

He didn't answer, merely raised one golden eyebrow, and she let out another huff. "I have no opinion regarding you whatsoever, Your Grace. I hardly know you." Nor did she want to. If she never heard another word about the Duke of Basingstoke again, it would be too soon.

Well, perhaps she *did* have an opinion about him after all, then.

"There's no need to be coy, Lady Francesca. You do have an opinion, and it's a most implacable dislike."

Whether she liked him or not appeared to be of little consequence to him, so there wasn't any reason not to tell him the truth, was there? "Very well, since you insist upon hearing me say it aloud, then no, Your Grace. I *don't* like you."

He'd called her a radish, for pity's sake. That was more than reason enough to excuse her from having to dance with him, if not the *real* reason.

"Ah, I thought not, but you see, my lady, it doesn't matter whether you like me or not."

At last, a point upon which they could agree! "You're quite right, Your Grace. It doesn't matter at all, which is why I fail to understand what you're doing here now."

"Permit me to enlighten you. While your feelings toward me are irrelevant, your *behavior* toward me matters a great deal, indeed."

"I don't see why it—"

"It's quite simple, really. I am betrothed to your cousin."

For an instant, her mind went blank, and she could only gape at him, numb with shock.

Betrothed to Susannah?

"We haven't yet announced it, but Lord Stanhope and I have agreed upon it. It's quite a settled matter. Lady Susannah will become the Duchess of Basingstoke before the end of the season."

Betrothed. Susannah was *betrothed* to the Duke of Basingstoke.

"The ugliness between our families does neither of us any credit, Lady Francesca, and you refusing to dance with me has stirred the scandal up again—"

"That *isn't* what stirred up the scandal!" Why, how dare he attempt to blame this mess on *her*! "A country radish, Your Grace? I give you credit for being inventive, at least. The rest of the *ton* was satisfied with merely laughing at me."

"Nonetheless, it's past time we put it behind us. The marriage between myself and Lady Susannah is, in part, intended to mend the rift."

He'd spoken of himself, Susannah, and Uncle Edward.

But there was no mention of *her*, and no mention of her mother. No mention of her father, who'd lost his life over the "ugliness," as the duke called it. All was now forgiven, it seemed, because the duke and her uncle Edward had decreed it to be so.

Her uncle Edward, who'd yet to reach out to either herself or her mother, despite ten long years having passed. Her uncle, who hadn't deigned to admit her to his presence since she'd arrived in London. His forgiveness didn't appear to extend to *them*, but then that was hardly surprising, was it?

Neither she nor her mother could make Susannah a duchess.

And the duke, with that mass of golden curls . . .

Helios. It was a proper nickname, because everything about him was golden. Not just his appearance, but his title, his wealth, his influence, and his power. It had been *his* father who'd ruined her family, caused all of their troubles, yet he'd never suffered a single moment for any of it, any more than Frederick Drew had suffered. Any more than her uncle Edward or her aunt Edith had suffered.

No, punishment was reserved for people like her and her mother.

She stared at him, into those lovely blue eyes, and a chill rushed over her, goosebumps puckering her flesh. Why had she even bothered coming to London at all? She should have seen from the first how this would end—

"Allow me to be perfectly frank, Lady Francesca. I'm afraid I can't permit you to upset my plans for the season."

"*Me*, upset your plans?" He and her uncle had made their plans without the least consideration for her or her mother. How, then, could he suppose anything *she* did would make any difference to anyone? "I couldn't, even if I wished—"

"On the contrary. Every gossiping tongue in town is wagging over your presence in London. A truce between us will help to silence them, but it could become very unpleasant, indeed, if you continue to hold a grudge against me."

A *grudge*? Her mother had been ruined, her father murdered, and she'd been left with an emptiness so deep inside her heart nothing could ever fill it, and he called it a *grudge*?

"You have the eye of society upon you, Lady Francesca," he went on. "It's up to you to wield it wisely, as it would be a great pity if another rift between our families damaged your cousin's marriage prospects."

"Damage Susannah's prospects?" She stared at him. "Do you mean to say you'll jilt my cousin unless I agree to a public truce with you?"

"What I mean to say, Lady Francesca, is that there can be no hint of discord between us. My sister Diana is in her first season, and a scandal will damage her reputation. I will not permit her name to be on the lips of every telltale in London, I assure you."

"I see. It is, however, perfectly acceptable to you if *my* name is on the lips of every telltale in London? Or in all the papers, for that matter?" If only gossip had been the worst of what she and her mother had suffered. They could have borne that.

"I beg your pardon for that remark." He caught her gaze, and held it. "It was unforgivable, and I regret it."

An apology from the Duke of Basingstoke? She hadn't expected *that*.

He leaned back in his chair, his sharp blue gaze on her. "What is it you *want*, Lady Francesca? Why did you come to London? If you choose to be accommodating in this business, I'd be pleased to return the favor."

It was a generous offer, but rather late to be of much use. Or was it?

Was it truly the case that she could upset her uncle Edward's plans by a public refusal to make peace with the Duke of Basingstoke? Could a quadrille or a country reel at Lady Sandham's ball influence whether or not her cousin became a duchess?

The duke seemed to think so. If he was right, then he'd just handed her a precious gift, a way past her uncle's wall of deafening silence.

No, not a gift, a *weapon*.

"The next time I offer to take you out to the floor, Lady Francesca—and there *will* be a next time, at Lady Sandham's ball next week—I sincerely hope you will think twice before you refuse me."

And if she *did* refuse him? What then? "If I didn't know it to be impossible, Your Grace, I might think you were *ordering* me to dance with you."

"That would hardly be gentlemanly of me, would it? As I said, I'd be pleased to offer you something in return for your cooperation, but you didn't answer my question." He leaned closer. "What do you *want*?"

You just gave it to me.

But the less he knew about her business with her uncle, the better. "I'll be happy to share a dance with you at Lady Sandham's ball, Your Grace, or engage in any other public displays to convince the *ton* I bear no lingering resentment against your family." More than happy, provided she got what *she* wanted from her uncle first. "Indeed, might I suggest you confer with my uncle if you have any further requirements of me?"

His eyes narrowed suspiciously. "Just like that? All is forgiven?"

"I wish to see my cousin happy, Your Grace. If Susannah wishes to become the Duchess of Basingstoke, then I wish it for her." Whether Susanna truly did wish it or not remained a mystery. All she could be certain of was that her *uncle* wished it, and for her purposes, that was all that mattered.

The duke didn't look quite convinced, but he rose to his feet, towering over her, a smile playing about his lips as he gazed down at her with those blue, blue eyes.

He took her hand and raised it to his lips. "A truce then, my lady."

CHAPTER 10

Franny rushed to the window as soon as the duke left the small parlor and watched as he mounted the box of his curricle, accepted the reins from his tiger, and drove off in the direction of her uncle's townhouse on Bruton Street.

He wasn't wasting any time. Good.

She tiptoed from the small parlor into the corridor and peered down into the entryway below. There was no sign of either Percival, or Lady Crump.

At last, some good fortune! She seized her chance and raced down the stairs.

Oh, Lady Francesca, you startled me!" Betsy, one of the downstairs housemaids was in the entryway, cleaning cloth in hand, polishing the gilt wall sconces to a blinding shine. "Is something amiss, my lady? You look a bit wild."

Only a bit? Well then, she appeared more composed than she felt. "Oh, no, I'm perfectly fine, Betsy, thank you. Do you happen to know if Lady Crump has returned from Bond Street yet?"

"Not yet, no. Is there something I can do for you, my lady?"

"No—er, that is, yes, now that I think about it. Would you be so kind as to choose one of Lady Dorothea's ball gowns for me for Lady Sandham's ball? It's not until next week, so we've time to make, er, a few adjustments to whichever one you choose."

She didn't like to send the servants scurrying about, but she needed Betsy away from the entryway, so she didn't see her rush out the door unaccompanied. It would get back to Lady Crump, who'd already quite reached the end of her patience.

"Of course, my lady."

"Thank you, Betsy." As soon as Betsy disappeared up the stairs, Franny dashed out the front door, and hurried the few blocks to Bruton Street. There, parked right outside her uncle's townhouse was the fine, scarlet-and-gold-wheeled curricle, just as she'd hoped it would be.

She ducked out of sight, bursting with impatience until at last the duke emerged. She waited until he'd climbed aboard his curricle and driven off toward Hyde Park before she dashed from her hiding place and ran up the steps to the front door.

Her knuckles hardly had a chance to meet the wood before Coote appeared, his jowls aquiver, as usual. "Lady Stanhope is not at home—"

"I'm not here to see Lady Stanhope." No, she was well past that now. "Please tell *Lord* Stanhope I require a word with him." She pulled out her card and thrust it at Coote. "Give him this."

Coote might scowl all he liked, but her uncle wouldn't turn her away—not this time. At last, after dozens of calling cards and hours of fruitless waiting in the entryway with Coote's suspicious eye upon her, she would finally have her interview with the almighty Lord Edward Stanhope.

Coote plucked the card from her fingers and waved her over the threshold into the elegant marble entryway, then turned on his heel and disappeared down a corridor to the left of the staircase.

There was another enormous bouquet displayed on the

round marble table today—orchids this time, the delicate blooms so large and fine they could only have come from the Duke of Basingstoke's hothouses.

My, he was a devoted suitor, wasn't he? There wasn't a single gentleman in London who sent prettier flowers than the duke. Such a pale, delicate purple. It would be a grand thing, to have one's own hothouses—

"I beg your pardon, my lady. His lordship will see you now." Coote appeared at her elbow, a sour expression on his face. "If you'd be so good as to follow me."

Yes, no doubt Uncle Edward *would* see her. He hadn't much choice.

He was seated behind the same massive mahogany writing desk her own father had used when he'd been the earl, and they'd stayed in the London townhouse. She'd sat upon his lap countless times, playing with the brass pulls while her father wrote letters, or read to her from one of his many books.

But her uncle had never been the sort of man to dangle his child on his knee, and the desk looked rather different with his forbidding presence behind it. The entire room looked different, or, no—it looked the same, but it *felt* different, oppressive.

"Well, Francesca. How do you do, my dear? It's been far too long since we've had the pleasure of your company in Town."

"Indeed, it has, Uncle, though you might have had the pleasure sooner, if my aunt had admitted me any of the other half dozen times I've called since I arrived in London." No sense mincing words, was there?

Another man might have had the grace to flush at that, but not her uncle Edward. He only waved a negligent hand. "I don't concern myself with my wife's callers, niece, any more than I do with her hat trimmings or her silk gowns. She may do as she likes, as long as she doesn't trouble me with any of it."

He plucked her calling card from his desk, worrying one corner with his thick thumb. "To what do I owe the pleasure of your visit, Francesca?"

"Oh, I think you know, Uncle." If he didn't, she wouldn't be here right now. "I understand you wish to marry my cousin to the Duke of Basingstoke. How fortunate, that I happened to come to London just in time to learn of Susannah's impending nuptials. Otherwise, I doubt I would ever have known about it until after she became the duchess."

He shrugged, his pudgy shoulders straining against the seams of his coat. "I don't see how Susannah's betrothal is any business of yours, Francesca."

"No, neither did I, at first." She cocked her head to the side, as if considering it, then shrugged. "But you see, Uncle, the *ton* has taken quite an interest in my presence here in London, and as the gossip grows more intense, it occurs to me I may have a role to play after all."

"A role? My dear girl, you think yourself a great deal more important than you are. The *ton* isn't likely to trouble themselves with some upstart of a chit with no money, and a mother who's a—"

"The newspapers say otherwise, Uncle. It's unfortunate, isn't it, that all the ugly gossip regarding the Drews and Stanhopes has resurfaced as it has?"

"I haven't any idea what you—"

"I believe the Duke of Basingstoke is rather concerned by it, or so he indicated when he called on me this afternoon. I can't help but think, Uncle, that it would be a great deal better for your purposes if talk of that dreadful scandal remained buried."

Uncle Edward was no longer smiling. "Now you see here, you interfering little—"

"But the *ton* does like their gossip, don't they? Did you read this morning's *Post*?"

"I don't give a bloody damn what the bloody *Post*—"

"No? I'm surprised to hear that, given how concerned you were when it was my *mother's* name on every tongue. It's a trifle awkward for it all to come back up now, when the duke and Susannah are so soon to announce their betrothal. I daresay all the rumors could be put to rest without much trouble if these silly disagreements between myself and the Duke of Basingstoke reached a peaceful conclusion."

"You can't mean to—"

"On the other hand, the rumors could become a great deal worse, depending on how I choose to approach them." She met his gaze without flinching, because surprisingly enough, it was a great deal easier than she'd imagined it would be to threaten someone.

Or perhaps it was just easy to threaten *him*.

But then veiled threats did seem to command her uncle's attention far more effectively than family loyalty ever had.

Uncle Edward slammed his fist down on the desk. "Are you *threatening* me, girl?"

"Why yes, Uncle. I am. You see, my mother and I—"

"Lady Maria made her choices." He glared at her, patchy spots of red color staining his cheeks. "She may live with the consequences of them."

The callous indifference in his tone was even more chilling than resentment or anger would have been, and her heart curled in on itself, hardening to protect itself from that icy blast. "She never made a choice."

Her uncle might like to call what had happened between Franny's mother and Frederick Drew a seduction, but that didn't make it the truth. The truth was, it had been nothing less than an assault. Her mother had had the tragic misfortune of being in the wrong place at the wrong time, and that single, isolated moment of chance had ended in their utter destruction.

And her mother had been blaming herself for it ever since.

"I beg your pardon, Uncle, but you don't seem to have any qualms about marrying my cousin into the family that ruined us. I commend you on your generous heart, though I suppose it's easier to forgive a duke, particularly one still in need of a duchess."

His dark eyes—eyes she'd once thought very like her father's—narrowed to cold, hard slits. "What is it you *want*, Francesca?"

"Odd, but that's the second time today someone's asked me that." Or, to be perfectly accurate, it was the second time in the past ten years. "It's quite nice to be asked. I want money, of course. What else?" Threats and money were her uncle's stock in trade. He understood them in a way he never would compassion, generosity, or kindness.

"My dear girl, such a vulgar discussion of money is hardly appropriate for a young lady of your—"

"Forgive me, Uncle Edward, but I've discovered it's only those people who have money who find discussions of it vulgar. In any case, I'm afraid you've left me with no other alternative."

"So cynical, for such a young lady! I shudder to think what my poor, dear brother would think if he—"

"I will *not* speak to you about my father, Uncle. We both know how disgusted he'd be that you've treated myself and my mother as you've done. Let's not pretend otherwise."

"How dare you speak to me in that manner!"

But she *did* dare. After ten long years, and by the strangest twist of fate imaginable, at last she had a way to force her uncle's hand.

The time for silence was over.

"No, how dare *you*!" She shot to her feet and leaned over

the desk, her nose mere inches from her uncle Edward's. "How *dare* you make your own brother's child *beg* you for something you should have given with an open heart."

Fury burned through her, her heart shuddering within her, her chest aching with the force of it, unleashed after a decade of silence. He'd let them sink into the most abject poverty out of nothing more than pure greed. That he could look her in the eye and act as if he'd ever cared for her father made bile sting her throat.

It ended here. Right this minute.

"Next week, at Lady Sandham's ball, the Duke of Basingstoke will ask me to dance, and I will graciously accept his hand."

"Then what?" Uncle Edward shot her a resentful look. "I suppose you'll want your money."

"Indeed, I will." She snatched up the card still sitting in the middle of his desk, took up his pen, and scrawled a number on the back. "I'll come the morning after the ball, and *you*, Uncle, will see me, and you'll hand over a bank draft for that amount without a single word of argument. If you don't, I'll remain in London, and I'll make certain to keep the *ton* entertained for the rest of the season."

She'd be gritting her teeth the entire time, but she'd do it for her mother's sake. It was astonishing what one could endure when lives literally depended on it.

Uncle Edward took up the card, a vein in his forehead pulsing when he saw the number. He raised his gaze to her face, eyes narrowed. "You'll accompany us on a promenade tomorrow afternoon, as well. The duke insists on it."

"Very well, Uncle." A dance, a promenade, it made no difference to her. She'd run a footrace through Covent Garden, as long as it got her what she wanted.

"Once I hand over the draft, you will leave London at once, and return to Herefordshire."

"With pleasure." Susannah may have her duke, Basingstoke his duchess, and Uncle Edward the fawning approval of the *ton* he so delighted in, and she . . .

She would have the means to take care of her mother. It was all she'd ever wanted to begin with, and with any luck, once she had it she'd never be obliged to set foot in London again.

CHAPTER 11

If the London season was nothing less than deadly *ton* warfare—and there was little question of that—then the afternoon promenade was the bloodiest of its skirmishes.

Under the thin veneer of politeness and elegance, it was bloody down to its roots.

Anyone who dared venture into Hyde Park during the fashionable hour with anything less than the precision of a military campaign was a damned fool. Giles was no fool, so when he sailed out the door of his townhouse the following afternoon, his gold-tipped walking stick in hand, he was dressed for battle.

Digby, who'd been briefed on the significance of this afternoon's promenade had, after much agonizing and wringing of hands, at last outfitted him in a bottle-green tailcoat with spotless, cream-colored trousers, and a crisp white neckcloth tied in a flawless Gordian Knot. His Hessians had been shined to a high gloss, not a single thread of his silver tassels out of place.

He marched from his Park Lane townhouse into a fine afternoon of blue skies and an invigorating breeze, and made his way to the Marble Arch, where he was to meet the

Stanhopes, Lady Crump, and Lady Francesca, so they might all play at being the best of friends for the benefit of the *ton*.

After several days of chasing after Lady Francesca Stanhope like a dog running in circles after its tail, he'd at last put everything she'd knocked askew back into its proper place. There would be no further mention of her name in the *Morning Post* or any other scandal sheet, those scoundrels at White's were no longer snickering behind his back, and the words "radish" and "country mud" had been forever banished from his lips.

He was once again the golden Duke of Basingstoke, the opposite of his wastrel of a father in every way, and very soon to become betrothed to Lady Susannah Stanhope, the belle of the London season. They would announce their engagement at Lady Sandham's ball next week.

Until then, with Lady Francesca's destructive tendencies neutralized, there would be no more chaos and no more bloody surprises, no matter what she tried to—

Wait. Was that . . .

What the devil?

He stopped in the middle of Park Lane, half a block away from the Marble Arch, gaping at the taunting flutter of the skirts of a bright pink gown. "Hell, and damnation."

It was *her*. Of course, it was her. Who, other than Lady Francesca Stanhope could contrive to make a scene by doing nothing more than standing beside a column, her dark hair tucked neatly under a ladylike straw bonnet?

She was waiting in front of one of the columns at the Marble Arch, her pink walking dress like a daub of bright paint against the white marble canvas of the arch. There was no missing her in that gown, no fading into the background for Lady Francesca. It was such a blinding pink it looked like the sun was rising in that corner of the park. Worse, over the top of the gown she wore a pelisse with a great quantity of heavy . . . was it netting, or lace?

She looked like a boiled salmon caught in a fisherman's net, but the mortifying thing was, even in that offensive costume, he couldn't tear his gaze away from her.

Either he was afflicted with a sudden and powerful desire for boiled salmon, or Lady Francesca Stanhope had caught his attention in a way every other lady this season had failed to do.

Including his betrothed.

She was precisely where she'd promised she'd be, and at the agreed-upon time, but if ever there was a lady who could follow every command to the letter and *still* manage to create a scandal, it was her, and damned if she hadn't found a way to turn every eye on her, simply by doing exactly as she'd been told to do.

To be fair, it was unlikely anyone had *told* her a proper young lady didn't appear in Hyde Park during the fashionable hour without a chaperone. Not a single one of London's inhabitants would have thought such a warning necessary.

Consequently, she was alone.

Alone under the Marble Arch, one of the busiest places in Hyde Park, perfectly situated to make herself, once again, the talk of the *ton*.

He strode toward her, teeth clenched. "Lady Francesca."

She turned, and an angelic smile curved those perfect pink lips. "Oh, good afternoon, Your Grace. How do—"

"There's nothing good about it." He caught her by the arm and tugged her into the shadows of one of the trees beside the Arch. "What in the world do you think you're doing? For God's sake, don't you have any sense at all?"

"I beg your pardon?" She blinked up at him, surprised. "Weren't we meant to promenade today?"

Surprised. She'd be the talk of every drawing room in London by tomorrow, and the woman had the gall to look *surprised*. "Where is Lady Crump?"

"Lady Crump?"

"Yes, Lady Francesca, Lady Crump. You *do* remember her, don't you? She's that sweet-tempered, white-haired lady who agreed to sponsor you for the season? The lady who's meant to accompany you when you venture into public places? Hyde Park, for instance?"

She raised an eyebrow at his tone. "My, you're in a temper, and on such a lovely day, too. Pity."

Good Lord, the woman would drive a saint to commit mortal sin. He sucked in a long, slow breath through his nose, counted to ten, and released it. "Lady Crump, Lady Francesca. Where is she?"

"She didn't fancy a promenade this afternoon and bid me to go without her." She gave a careless little shrug, as if this were an end to the matter.

She was lying. With perfect ease, and not as much as a blush on that cheek. "Do you take me for a fool, Lady Francesca?"

She frowned. "Of course not, Your Grace. Why would you—"

"Quiet, if you please." He held up his hand to silence her. "You'd have me believe that *Lady Crump*—the same Lady Crump who dissolved into tears when you refused to dance with me at Lord Wilmot's ball—"

"For pity's sake, we're not back to that again? I thought we'd agreed to—"

"The same Lady Crump who dissolved into tears when you refused to dance with me at Lord Wilmot's ball," he repeated, his back teeth grinding together. "That Lady Crump told you to come to Hyde Park by yourself during the fashionable hour, and undertake the promenade, alone?"

"I'm hardly *alone*, Your Grace. My uncle Edward will arrive at any—"

"Is your uncle here right now, Lady Francesca?"

"Well, no, but he's—"

"No, he isn't, and as I'm a single gentleman, your reputation is at even greater risk being seen alone with me than if you were by yourself. I find it difficult to believe you aren't aware of that." There was no reason he should care about the reputation of a lady who clearly had so little use for it herself, but his hands were curling into fists, hot anger twisting through him.

"Of course, I'm aware of it, but I'm not a fragile, naïve young lady in her first season. The *ton* have long since washed their hands of me, and now I may do as I wish. Freedom, Your Grace, is one of the few benefits afforded a lady without family, fortune, or reputation, and I've grown accustomed to roaming about as I please in Herefordshire."

"You roam as you please because there's no one to see you in Herefordshire aside from a dozen or so herds of sheep! The *ton* is a great deal more exacting about a young lady's behavior, I assure you."

"How strange, when they're so very like sheep in every other way." She peeked up at him, a small smile on her lips, her eyelashes fluttering against the shafts of sunlight filtering through the leaves of the tree above, catching the blue and making it twinkle.

It *wasn't* charming, that twinkle. "What does Lord Stanhope say about you wandering the streets of London alone?"

"My *uncle*?" She laughed, but there was a bitter edge to it. "Not a blessed thing. I doubt he's even aware of it."

Not aware of it? Lady Francesca was his niece, for God's sake. Surely, he must take some interest in her welfare? "Then perhaps I'll have a word with Lady Crump, Lady Francesca, and make *her* aware of it."

Ah, now that got a reaction. Her eyes narrowed, and she laid a hand on his forearm. "That wasn't part of our arrangement, Your Grace. I've agreed to help you, but that does *not* give you the power to dictate what I may and may not do, nor will I have you worrying Lady Crump."

He might have paid more attention to her warning if she hadn't been touching him, but she *was* touching him, a fold of his coat caught between her slender fingers. It was a light touch, but her hand seemed to burn through the layers of wool between them, heating his skin, the muscles of his forearm twitching under her palm, her white glove stark against the dark green superfine. "I don't mean to dictate to you, Lady Francesca, only to keep you from ruining yourself with your reckless antics."

Someone had to, and no one else seemed to give a damn what she did.

"Do you suppose I care a whit about ruin, Your Grace? It's rather a luxury to care about such a thing, isn't it?"

A luxury? What the *devil* did that mean? "I don't under—"

"Good day, Basingstoke."

Giles glanced over Lady Francesca's shoulder. Stanhope was approaching the Marble Arch, Lady Edith clinging to his arm, with her daughter on her other side. "Stanhope."

"Shall we get this charade over with? I have rather a busy . . ." Stanhope trailed off, his cold blue eyes settling on Lady Francesca's hand, which was still resting on his arm.

She snatched it away. "Uncle Edward, Aunt Edith, and Susannah. How do you do?"

Lady Susannah glanced between him and Lady Francesca, and for an instant she seemed to still, an odd expression crossing her face, but in the next moment it was gone, swallowed in the shy smile she offered her cousin. "Good afternoon, Franny."

"Francesca." Lord Edward gave her a cool nod.

Lady Edith, however, didn't spare her niece a single word.

The cut direct, from her own aunt? It was well known there was no longer any love between Lord Stanhope and his deceased elder brother's daughter and widow, but he hadn't expected such deep enmity, or such pettiness.

"Good afternoon, Your Grace." Lady Edith, who was all smiles for *him*, sank into a deep curtsey.

"My lady." Giles bowed to Lady Edith, then turned to offer his arm to Lady Susannah, who accepted it with a polite smile. He returned it, and laid his hand briefly over hers, but there was no tug in his belly, no twitch of his muscles, no tingling sensation at Lady Susannah's touch.

"Franny?" She turned and offered her cousin her other arm, and they set off toward Rotten Row, with Stanhope and Lady Edith following behind them, a companionable group of five out for an afternoon stroll.

Or so they must appear, to any of the *ton* who chose to look, but even as he devoted all of his attention to Lady Susannah, his nerve endings were still burning with the imprint of Lady Francesca's fingers against his arm.

"I can't recall a sunnier day yet this season!" Lady Edith gushed. "Such a pleasant afternoon for the promenade. Don't you agree, Your Grace?"

Giles blinked up at the sky. The sun was indeed shining with unusual fervor, and they were indeed on the strut during the fashionable hour, prancing down Rotten Row in their finest fashions, so all might see and admire them.

That much, he could agree with. As for it being pleasant . . .

It might have been *that*, too, if Lady Edith could manage to hold her tongue, but she'd kept up an unceasing stream of inane chatter since they'd entered Hyde Park.

"How pleasant it is, to see so many fashionable people outside enjoying the weather, is it not, Your Grace? Why, it looks as if the entire upper ten thousand is on the promenade this afternoon!"

"It does, indeed." Their party had attracted a good deal of attention, too, Lady Francesca in particular, who was the

object of more than one curious glance, but if she was aware
of their stares, she gave no sign of it.

Or perhaps she simply didn't care. She strolled quietly
along the pathway, her arm linked with Lady Susannah's, a
serene smile on her lips. She hadn't said more than a half
dozen words since they'd entered Rotten Row, and all of those
had been whispered in a soft undertone to Lady Susannah, for
her ears only.

"Oh, look, there's Lady Eustace! How do you do, my
lady? We're just on the promenade with the *Duke of Basingstoke*, Lady Eustace!" A half dozen heads turned at Lady
Edith's piercing shriek, and one man clapped his hands
over his ears. "Are you acquainted with Lady Eustace, Your
Grace?"

This time, Giles didn't bother to reply. Even when Lady
Edith paused long enough to allow it, she didn't listen to his
answers, and so he let his mind drift where it would.

That turned out to be a mistake, because it drifted in one
distinct direction, and once it landed there it refused to be torn
loose, and clung stubbornly, like a limpet to a sea-tossed rock.

He *should* have been focused on his betrothed, but instead
his thoughts were wild, wayward things, each one more inap-
propriate than the last.

Lady Francesca's dark lashes fluttering against the sun
filtering through the trees above them, the press of her fingertips against his coat sleeve, the rush of color in her cheeks
when she'd delivered him a set-down . . .

It was fortunate that Lady Edith couldn't read his mind, or
she'd be appalled to discover her daughter was being slighted
in favor of Susannah's cousin. Even *he* was appalled. Any
other gentleman would have been delighted to have Lady
Susannah on his arm, but as agreeable as she was, and as
pretty as she looked this afternoon, his attention insisted on
drifting to her maddening cousin—

"My dear Susannah looks lovely in blue, does she not, Your Grace?"

"I beg your . . . oh, yes. She does, indeed." He wrenched his attention from Lady Francesca to his betrothed, who was as lovely as he'd ever seen her in a peacock-blue walking dress with a matching pelisse and hat. The color brought out the remarkable blue of her eyes.

At least, if he recalled correctly, it did. Lady Susannah hadn't looked directly at him since they'd embarked on their stroll. She kept her gaze bashfully averted, as befitted a proper young maiden.

He'd expect nothing less, yet at the same time, Lady Francesca's refusal to meet his gaze was driving him to distraction, and with every step they took, that vacant smile on her lips was becoming more infuriating. Meanwhile, Lady Edith was whittering on and on about *blue*, of all bloody things, her grating voice a punishment to his ears.

"That shade of blue is the height of fashion this season. I think it's a perfect match for Susannah's eyes. Don't you think it's perfect for her, Your Grace?"

"Perfect, indeed." Lady Francesca had the same blue eyes as her cousin. What would *she* look like, wrapped head to toe in peacock blue?

"Cost a pretty penny, that rig, with all the ribbons and furbelows and whatnot, but nothing less than the best for a future duchess, eh, Basingstoke?" Stanhope nudged Giles with a wink.

"Indeed." Giles's smile stretched thin against his clenched teeth. It was his fifth "indeed" since they'd embarked on their walk, and it had been less than a quarter of an hour.

"Lady Alethea wore a similar blue to Lord Wilmot's ball the other night, Your Grace, but I feel it necessary to just hint that her gown was not *quite* the same shade of blue.

Lady Alethea's was not a true peacock blue, you understand, Your Grace, but more of a—"

"Dragonfly blue?"

Giles nearly stumbled over his own feet. The pleasure that flooded him at the sound of Lady Francesca's voice was far greater than it should have been, rather like the strike of a particularly plaintive note in a favorite piece of music.

"Dragonfly blue!" Lady Edith scoffed. "Why, how absurd. There is no such shade as dragonfly blue."

"Indeed, there is. It's the blue of a dragonfly's wings, of course. Surely, you've seen that blue before, Aunt Edith?"

Lady Edith huffed. "On a dragonfly, yes, but not anywhere—"

"Our eyes, Aunt Edith. Mine, and Susannah's." Lady Francesca's chin hitched up, and she held Lady Edith's gaze. "My mother always described them as dragonfly blue."

Lady Edith's cheeks flushed red. "Your *mother*! How dare—"

"Yes, Aunt Edith, my mother. She was one of your dearest friends once. Surely, you remember her?"

There was a moment of stunned silence, then Lord Edward said, in a voice that would have frozen water, "Now you see here, girl—"

"She hasn't forgotten *you*, Uncle Edward, nor you, Aunt Edith. Not at all, though it's been so many years." Lady Francesca stared at them each in turn, her face like stone, but it softened when she turned to her cousin. "And you, Susannah. She remembers you with the greatest affection, indeed."

Lady Susannah glanced at her father, then swallowed, and whispered timidly, "Lady Maria was always kind to me."

It was the longest speech Giles had ever heard her utter, and brave, in its own way, judging by the way Stanhope was glaring at her. He felt the first faint stirrings of approval for his betrothed, but his attention was once again drawn back to Lady Francesca, as if he were a fish with a hook embedded in its flesh, and she was holding the rod.

"Shall we finish our walk?" She reclaimed her cousin's arm, and as calmly as if she hadn't just brought the entire party to a dead stop, continued her amble down Rotten Row.

CHAPTER 12

"Francesca, my dear girl, I was beginning to think you were going to sleep the day away. I nearly sent Jenny in to wake you." Lady Crump was seated in the breakfast room, tea in hand, a plate of pastries at her elbow, and the table before her covered in . . . newspapers?

Franny paused in the doorway, blinking. It wasn't just *The Times* or the *Morning Post*, but a veritable pile of newspapers, and at least half a dozen of them were scandal sheets. "What are you—"

"Only look, Francesca!" Lady Crump waved one of the papers in the air. "All of London is talking about you!"

"Oh, no. What is it *this* time?" Franny dropped into a chair with a groan. "No, never mind. Let them talk, if they must, but I don't want to hear a word of it." It was certain to be a pack of lies, whatever else it was. "Thank you, Williams," she added, seizing the steaming cup of tea the footman placed in front of her.

By the looks of things, she was going to need it.

"Oh, but you must! It's the most remarkable thing, Francesca. Just listen!" Lady Crump snatched up the *Post* and spread it out in front of her. "Lady Francesca Stanhope, looking as lovely as an autumn rose in a fetching pink frock—"

"An autumn rose!" Franny snorted. "I'm a rose now, instead of a radish?"

"Yes, fickle, are they not? I feel quite vindicated, as I did say from the start that shade of pink is perfection on you. But just listen! 'Lady Francesca Stanhope, looking as lovely as an autumn rose in a fetching pink frock, was seen in the elegant company of the Duke of Basingstoke at the Marble Arch yesterday.' Weren't you meant to promenade with your aunt and uncle, and Lady Susannah? How did Basingstoke happen to be there?"

"He, ah, that is, we . . . he met us there. But how does the *Morning Post* know any of this?" More to the point, why should they care?

"Why, someone saw you, of course. There are no secrets in London, my dear. Now, where was I? Oh, yes. 'Elegant company of the Duke of Basingstoke at the Marble Arch yesterday. Lady Francesca and His Grace appeared to be engaged in a passionate argument—'"

"Passionate argument? What passionate argument?" He'd attempted to lecture her about propriety, and she'd given him the set-down he deserved. There'd been nothing passionate about it, although he did have a curious knack for rousing her temper.

Lady Crump frowned at her over the top of the paper. "My dear Francesca, if you'd only let me finish, all will be revealed."

"I beg your pardon, my lady. Do go on."

"Thank you. Now, where was I? Oh, yes. 'Appeared to be engaged in a passionate argument over the lady's reluctance to permit His Grace to escort her to the promenade. In the end, the lady was compelled to accept His Grace's arm, a flattering blush coloring her cheeks.' My goodness, Francesca! The *Post* says the duke *compelled* you to take his arm, despite your maidenly resistance!"

Maidenly resistance? That was a *fanciful* interpretation,

but less preposterous than what the *Post* had actually written. "How in the world does someone *compel* another person to take their arm? Surely, not even the Duke of Basingstoke could manage such a thing. It's utter nonsense. He didn't compel me to do anything at all."

"Well, of course not, dearest. But it's all rather curious, isn't it? The duke has ever been a darling of the scandal sheets, but they've quite turned on him of late. It's not just the *Post*." Lady Crump nodded at the newspapers scattered over the table. "All of these say the same thing."

"For pity's sake! There must be hundreds of words of print here, and all of it lies. What's to be done?"

"Why, not a thing, child, other than to ignore it." Lady Crump folded the *Post* and dropped it atop the pile with a sigh. "It's not particularly complimentary to the duke, is it? Between this and that radish business, it's almost as if someone is determined to paint him in an unflattering light."

Franny pushed her cup of tea aside, her stomach twisting. "Who do you suppose would do such a thing?" The *ton* was enamored of their golden duke, weren't they? Miss Thorne had told her they believed he could do no wrong. Whatever could have happened to Miss Thorne, come to that? She seemed to have simply vanished.

"I haven't the vaguest idea, but the duke would do well to be careful of the company he keeps." Lady Crump scowled down at the papers, but an instant later her brow cleared, and she gave Franny a bright smile. "There is one piece of pleasant news."

Franny braced herself. "What is it?"

"Now, what have I done with it? Ah, here it is." Lady Crump plucked up a thick, ivory-colored card with a half dozen lines in an elegant scrawl written on one side. "The Duchess of Basingstoke is hosting a musical evening tonight, and she's invited us to attend. Isn't that delightful, Francesca?"

"Yes, indeed." Delightful, and *sudden*.

The duke was not, it seemed, satisfied with yesterday's promenade, and now required another performance for the benefit of the *ton*. She'd do well to remember it was nothing more than that when he was gazing down at her with those sparkling blue eyes.

"Her Grace will have Madame DuPlessis on the harp tonight. I'm *mad* for Madame DuPlessis. It's quite an honor to be invited, as Her Grace is selective about her guest lists— only the absolute pinnacle of fashion, you know, Francesca."

"Ah, so we're the pinnacle of fashion now, are we?"

"It appears so. Oh, and I have *just* the gown for you to wear, dearest!"

"Is it pink?" It was, of course—they all were—but strangely, she'd grown fonder of the color as the days passed. It was nothing at all like what other young ladies wore, but then she wasn't like the other young ladies, and there was no sense in pretending otherwise. "I do hope it's pink."

"It is, indeed." Lady Crump beamed at her. "And you're certain to look smashing in it."

The Duchess of Basingstoke's music room was utterly still, every breath held as Madame DuPlessis's fingers stilled on the strings, and the last notes of the final trio of Pleyel's harp sonatas faded into silence.

Her mother had always adored Pleyel. When she was growing up, the house had often echoed with the notes of his harp and pianoforte pieces. The townhouse on Bruton Street had a fine music room, and she'd spent many hours there as a child, plucking at various keys and strings and listening to her mother play.

The music had fallen silent when they left London. Her mother rarely sang anymore—not since Franny's father died, and as they didn't have the luxury of an instrument in Herefordshire, her own music lessons had come to an abrupt end.

Her poor, youthful heart had broken in two at the loss. In those darkest of days, she'd believed the music was gone forever, but the strains of the sonatas she'd warbled as a child were there still, winding and twisting inside her chest as if they'd been there all along, sleeping, awaiting the chance to burst into life again.

She closed her eyes and let herself float on the memory of the bright, glittering cascade of notes Madame DuPlessis had coaxed from the harp, but they popped open again when she felt a small, gloved hand slide into hers.

Susannah.

Franny hadn't dared to look at her cousin since she'd sat down beside her, but now she risked a sidelong glance to her left and caught Susannah's smile, as familiar to her as the music rippling through her, goosebumps rising on her skin.

Sleeping, but there still. There, all along.

Uncle Edward hadn't been pleased when the Duke of Basingstoke had seated her next to Susannah, of course, but not even Uncle Edward dared naysay the duke.

Soon after she'd arrived tonight, His Grace had taken her arm and led her to the first row of chairs, where her uncle Edward and aunt Edith were seated, with Susannah between them. Her uncle had cast such a livid glare at her approach she'd actually backed up a step, but the duke had laid his hand over hers, his palm warm against her knuckles, and offered Susannah an elegant bow. "Will you sit next to your cousin this evening, my lady?"

For an instant, Susannah had appeared terrified, but then she'd cast an uncharacteristically defiant glance at her father, and lifted her chin. "Indeed, I will, Your Grace."

So, Uncle Edward had been faced with a choice between arguing with the Duke of Basingstoke in the middle of the duchess's drawing room, with all the *ton* looking on, or giving up his chair to his niece, and taking the empty one beside his wife.

He'd done the latter, with a false good grace that had turned Franny's stomach, but since then he'd been seething with a dark fury as palpable as the vibrations of Madame DuPlessis's harp strings. If a glare could have incinerated her, she'd have been reduced to a pile of ash before the first dozen notes.

Such pointed resentment should have ruined her evening, but her uncle's animosity was wasted on her. Between the music and Susannah's affection, it was by far the most pleasant evening she'd spent since she'd arrived in London.

The duchess's townhouse on Curzon Street was everything a duchess's residence should be, or at least everything Franny had ever imagined one to be, as she'd never been inside a duchess's house before. The music room was the size of a ballroom, and the finest she'd ever seen, with the light from dozens of candles casting a soft glow on the gleaming lines of the pianoforte, which had been placed in the center of the room, with the harp beside it.

"Will you play tonight, Lady Francesca?"

A tall, lean, broad-shouldered shadow passed over her, and Franny looked up into the handsome face of the Duke of Basingstoke. "Play?"

"For the company." He nodded toward the pianoforte. "May I escort you to the bench?"

"The bench?" Dear God, she wasn't meant to exhibit her musical skills tonight, was she? "I, ah, no thank you, Your Grace. I—I don't . . ."

Don't play. Her fingers hadn't touched the keys since she'd left London a decade ago.

There was no reason she should be ashamed of that—there was no shame in having suffered hardship—yet with the glittering *ton* surrounding her, the other young ladies like gauzy butterflies, resplendent in their silks and flashing jewels, she couldn't make the words leave her mouth. "I don't—"

"I'll play, shall I, Your Grace?" Susannah gave Franny's hand a surreptitious squeeze, then hurried to her feet.

The duke frowned down at Franny for a moment, his forehead creased, before turning a distracted smile on Susannah, and offering her his arm. "Yes, of course, my lady."

A heaviness settled in Franny's chest as she watched him escort her cousin to that beautiful pianoforte, the dark blue superfine of his evening coat tight across his broad shoulders, with Susannah beside him, her celestial-blue silk gown shimmering in the candlelight like a pool of water touched by the sun.

She played the Allegro assai from Mozart's Sonata in F, and it was beautiful, both to hear the music flowing from her fingertips in a tumbling cascade, and to watch her play, her body swaying with the movement of her slender arms, which were wrapped fingertip to elbow in pristine white silk gloves.

But along with the beauty there was heartbreak, too: memories of the past hidden between each rippling note, and the future there, too, the line between them so much more tenuous than she'd ever realized before—a decade of losses and injustices, sorrows and regrets, dusty with cobwebs, but there still, no matter how deeply she'd tried to bury them. Somehow, they gathered together in the moment, the music swelling inside her head, her heart beating in six-eighths time, a knot in her chest pulling, *pulling . . .*

It was too much. All at once, it was too much, and she was on her feet—*how?* The folds of her silk skirts slippery in her damp hands, her feet catching on her hems as she stumbled from the music room—*where?* Down the first corridor she came to, bursting through a pair of French doors at the end and onto a stone terrace.

Yes. Here, she could breathe. She could close her eyes, and just *breathe*.

How long had she been there, the black sky infinite above her, the cool night air caressing the bare skin of her arms, when he found her?

"You're ill, my lady." His voice was low, a deep, dark velvet, as if it were a part of the night itself.

"No." She wasn't ill, she was . . . she didn't know what she was. "I just . . . I couldn't breathe."

It wasn't what she'd meant to say. She'd meant to say something meaningless—it was too warm inside, she was dizzy, she'd feared a swoon—an acknowledgement of her odd behavior that revealed nothing. Yet somehow, this man—a man she didn't know, or trust—*this* man, of all men, had somehow compelled her to tell the truth, without having asked a thing from her.

Perhaps that was why. Words came easier, when no one demanded them of you.

There was a brief silence, then the click of his pumps across the stone terrace. He appeared in her periphery, leaning a hip against the balustrade. "It's not easy for a young lady to display her musical skills for company, or so my sister Diana tells me."

"It wasn't that." Though it was comforting to know a young lady as perfect as Lady Diana experienced the same fears and misgivings as a regular mortal like herself.

"Ah."

"Ah? That's all?" He wasn't going to ask what had made her flee the music room, likely sending poor Lady Crump into a panic, and making herself the laughingstock of London?

"Well, I—"

"I don't play the pianoforte," she blurted, then caught her lower lip between her teeth. Dash it, that was the trouble with telling one truth. Other truths insisted upon following it, until they were gushing from one's lips.

Exclamations of shock, a derisive laugh, an uncomprehending frown—none of these reactions would have surprised her—but he merely shrugged. "No?"

"I did, when I was younger, but . . ."

But her Uncle Edward tossed her and her mother out of their home, and they'd spent the past ten years living in a cold, damp cottage in Herefordshire without a pianoforte, never mind a music room.

Er, no. That was about a dozen truths too many. "But I don't anymore."

"Do you not enjoy playing?"

"I did enjoy it once, very much. Perhaps I'll have the chance to learn again, someday." Though it wasn't likely. The money she'd managed to pry from her Uncle Edward's tight fist wouldn't stretch to luxuries.

"You have other impressive, if rather unusual talents, Lady Francesca."

She did? "Like what?"

"Climbing trees, spying through windows, and flaying the skin from a gentleman's bones with your extraordinarily sharp tongue. That last thing especially."

He grinned then, suddenly, a wicked, boyish grin, so unlike any expression she'd ever seen on his face before—so unlike any expression she'd ever imagined she *could* see on any duke's face—for a moment she could only stare dumbly at him.

But then a laugh bubbled up in her throat—a hearty, full-throated laugh that chased the ugliness from her mind and set her back to rights again at once. "Do you refer to your own skin, and your own bones, Your Grace?"

"Indeed. You'd be heartily ashamed of yourself if you saw the scars you've inflicted, but not to worry, Lady Francesca. I'll keep your wicked secrets."

"Nonsense. I don't *have* any secrets." Or she hadn't, before she'd come to London. "Did you follow me out here to keep me from climbing your mother's trees, and peeking into your windows, and scolding your footmen?"

"No. I came on Lady Crump's account." His smile faded. "She's . . . distraught."

"Oh." She bit her lip, guilt washing over her. "Yes, I imagine she must be."

He held out his hand to her. "May I take you to her?"

She stared at his gloved hand, hesitating. It appeared an exceptionally large, strong, capable thing, that hand. It was the sort of appendage that coaxed a lady into letting down her guard. Touching it didn't seem like a wise idea—

"You may take my hand without fear of mischief, Lady Francesca. I promise you I haven't hidden a poisonous snake inside my coat sleeve."

"Well, no. Not with a coat as handsome as *that*." No gentleman of any sense permitted a serpent to squirm about inside the sleeve of a coat that turned his eyes the blue of sapphires.

She laid the tips of her fingers in the center of his palm, he wrapped his hand around them, and yes, even with their gloves between them, the warm reassurance of his grip was profound, dizzying.

"Are you a connoisseur of gentlemen's coats, Lady Francesca?"

"Not at all." Neither of gentlemen's coats, nor of gentlemen themselves. "May I ask you a question, Your Grace?"

"You may, my lady."

He was ushering her through the French doors that led back into the corridor, but she held back for a moment, and he paused. "Why did you take the trouble to seat me next to my cousin tonight? You must have seen that my uncle Edward didn't like it."

He looked surprised. "No, but you *did* like it, didn't you?"

"I did," she said softly. "Very much."

"That's why I did it, Lady Francesca—for no other reason than I thought you'd like it."

It wasn't until after he'd returned her to Lady Crump and they were tucked into the carriage and on their way back to Charles Street that the full meaning of his words struck her.

He said he'd done it for *her*.

Not for Susannah, his betrothed.

For her.

CHAPTER 13

"Attention! All admirers of circus pageantry, military spectacles, and amazing feats of equestrian skill, report to the drawing room at once!"

A stampede of footsteps came thundering down the stairway, and an instant later Amy and Louisa charged into the drawing room and threw themselves at Giles, knocking the wind from his lungs.

"Ready, sprites?" He was to take his younger sisters on a much-anticipated visit to Astley's Amphitheater today. He didn't have any interest in attending himself, of course. It was all a very great bother to *him*, the circus being far beneath the notice of a duke, but children were simple-minded creatures, and apt to be diverted by things like astonishingly realistic battle reenactments, with crashing cymbals cleverly timed to accompany the explosions.

Or so he'd heard. He hadn't paid much attention, really.

"I want to see the dancing ponies!" Louisa thrust out her chubby little arms to him, and he swept her up, balancing her on his hip. "We *can* see the dancing ponies, can't we, Giles?"

"Of course, we—"

"You can see a pony any old time, Louisa." Amy caught his hand in hers and began tugging him toward the drawing room door. "I want to see the rope walkers! Jane Turner says they wear sparkly skirts, and dance about on the thinnest bit of silver wire imaginable!"

He set Louisa back on her feet and caught her little hand in his. "Well, if Jane Turner says so, who am I to—"

"Might I have a word with you, Giles, before you go?"

They'd nearly reached the entryway door, but at the sound of his mother's voice he froze, and Louisa and Amy went instantly still beside him. "Hush now, girls. If we don't move or speak, she may not see us."

An exasperated huff came from behind him. "I've no desire to ruin your fun. It will only take a moment, and then you may be on your way."

A moment, indeed. Nothing *ever* only took a moment. "Very well, what's so important it can't wait for—" He broke off with a groan when she handed him a copy of *The Times*, folded open to the gossip section. "Good Lord, what *now*?"

"It's *The Times*' account of our musical evening last night."

He took the paper and skimmed the first few lines of print. "Whatever it is, the best course of action is to pay no mind to . . . for God's sake! I never tried to *force* Lady Francesca Stanhope to play the pianoforte last night, nor did I . . ." He squinted down at the paper. "Chase her out of the music room when she declined!"

"You *did* chase her, but they make it sound a great deal more improper than it was. Who do you suppose carried such an exaggerated tale to the scandal sheets?"

He hardly heard her. "This is unconscionable! This reads as if I trampled over a dozen elderly countesses in my haste to get to Lady Francesca, then threw her over my shoulder, carried her kicking and screaming to the pianoforte, and dropped her onto the bench!"

Louisa let out a high-pitched giggle, and Amy slapped a hand over her sister's mouth. "Hush, Louisa."

"I could hardly have forced her, given she didn't play!

Indeed, there isn't a gentleman in London who could force Lady Francesca Stanhope to do a single, cursed thing! She's the most stubborn, willful chit I've ever encountered."

"This little morsel could only have come from one of our guests, and I'd dearly like to know who it was, because they seem determined to give the impression that you're preoccupied with Lady Francesca."

"*Preoccupied* with Lady Francesca?"

"I didn't even realize she'd declined to play before I read about it in *The Times* this morning. Someone must have been paying close attention to the two of you to have noticed it at all."

"Why should I care whether or not Lady Francesca plays the pianoforte? I daresay it would shock the London gossips to know I don't give a *damn* who—"

"Giles! Mind your tongue." His mother nodded toward Amy and Louisa, who were watching this exchange with wide eyes. "Still, I can't blame you for being annoyed. It's rather like that radish business all over again, is it not?"

He'd been reading through the blasphemous article a second time, his blood boiling, but at the mention of radishes, his gaze shot to his mother. "It is, isn't it?"

He would have sworn no one but Montford and Grantham were anywhere near him when he'd made that remark, but Lady Francesca *must* have overheard it rather than just read of it in the *Post* the next morning, because when he met her in front of Stanhope's townhouse, she mentioned he'd also called her a "poor, unfortunate creature."

That part hadn't been printed in the *Post*.

Then last night, once again, she'd been uniquely situated to report the details of an incident that very few people could have overheard. And hadn't there been some other bit of nonsense in the scandal sheets about their argument at the Marble Arch?

But why should Lady Francesca want her name dragged

into the papers? It didn't make sense, although she did have reason to resent his family, didn't she? And God knew her uncle hadn't done a single thing to earn her love, or her loyalty. A scandal would be an excellent way to take revenge on them all, wouldn't it? She had told him herself she didn't care a whit about her own ruin. "It's Lady Francesca."

His mother frowned. "What is?"

"It's Lady Francesca who's tattling to the scandal sheets. Indeed, I can't think how we didn't realize it before this."

His mother was staring at him as if he'd gone mad. "You mean to say, Giles, you think Lady Francesca Stanhope—that lovely young lady who was all generosity, all graciousness last night, despite the ugliness between our two families—"

He snorted. "Of course, she was gracious to you. You're the Duchess of Basingstoke."

"I see. And the brightness in her eyes when I mentioned her mother, Giles? Was that also because I'm the Duchess of Basingstoke?"

"Brightness in her eyes?" Had Lady Francesca been *crying* last night? That was . . . none of his business, damn it, and certainly *not* a piece of information he felt any particular way about.

Not distressed, nor worried. Especially not either of those two things.

"I don't know how you can imagine a lady of Lady Francesca's sensibilities would do something so low as tattle to the scandal sheets, but perhaps *The Times* has the right of it, and you are preoccupied with her, Giles."

"Don't be absurd, Mother." His thoughts might drift to Lady Francesca now and again, but he was hardly *preoccupied* with her.

"Very well, then." His mother raised a skeptical eyebrow, but whatever nonsense she'd gotten into her head about Lady Francesca, she chose to keep it to herself, thankfully.

"Amy, Louisa, forgive me." He turned to his sisters. "I'm afraid Astley's is going to have to wait for another day."

Amy's face fell. "But—"

"I want to see the dancing ponies!" Louisa squeezed her eyes shut and screwed up her lips in a way that warned a storm of anguished tears was approaching. "You said I might see them, Giles!"

"I know, sprite, and see them you shall. We'll go tomorrow, and afterwards I'll take you to Gunter's, and you may have your favorite violet ice, and Amy, her favorite orange flower."

"It's only a day, Louisa." Amy turned a shrewd eye on Giles. "Do you *promise* you'll take us tomorrow, to both Astley's and Gunter's?"

"I swear it on my pair of matched bays." He dropped a kiss on Amy's head, then lifted Louisa's chin and dabbed at her tears with his pocket handkerchief. "All right?"

It took a bit of cajoling before the promise of the violet ice soothed Louisa's ruffled feelings, but at last her tears were dried, and he was on his way to Lady Crump's, the blasphemous copy of *The Times* clutched in his fist.

But when he arrived, Lady Crump's butler, Percival, informed him that Lady Crump and Lady Francesca were not at home.

"Where are they?" He ground out through gritted teeth.

Percival blanched. "Madame Laurent's shop, Your Grace, on Bond Street."

Well then, it seemed he was going shopping.

Every single female in the city of London was crowded inside Madame Laurent's fashionable Bond Street shop, all of them chattering, laughing, shrieking, and gasping at once. Buttons, ribbons, and bits of lace and tangled thread were strewn about the glass countertops, a pair of young ladies was about to come to blows over a length of pale pink silk, and a third sat in a chair in the corner, weeping.

It was utter mayhem, and the *noise*! He'd never heard such an unholy ruckus in his life. They put the monkeys in the Royal Menagerie to shame.

He stood on the threshold for an instant, frozen with horror, then turned at once to flee, but Madame Laurent, who was far too wily a businesswoman to let a duke escape her clutches, stopped him before he could get away. "Your Grace! It's such a pleasure to see you! Have you come to fetch Lady Diana's gown for Lady Sandham's ball?"

"No, er, I mean, yes!" He wasn't in the habit of collecting Diana's gowns at the modiste's, but he could hardly say he'd come in search of Lady Francesca so he might shout at her, could he? "Yes, indeed, I have, Madame Laurent."

"Very good, Your Grace. I have it right—"

"I beg your pardon, Madame Laurent, but did you happen to see Lady Crump in your shop today? I require a word with her, and I thought perhaps if she *was* here . . ."

"She is, indeed, Your Grace. I've put her in a private room with Lady Francesca, and Lady Susannah and her mother. Lady Stanhope wasn't pleased at it, but I've only one private dressing room, you see, and Lady Crump arrived first, and then the younger ladies insisted on sharing. Shall I fetch Lady Crump for you?"

It was tempting, but Madame Laurent's patrons were already casting curious glances at him. No, it wouldn't do. It was entirely too public. "You're very kind, Madame Laurent, but that's not necessary."

"Very well, Your Grace. Would you prefer to wait in my sitting room while I see to Lady Diana's gown?"

"Perhaps that would be best." Before the ladies descended on him in a swarm.

"Of course. If you'll just come with me, Your Grace."

"Thank you." He followed her to a comfortable chamber tucked into the back corner of the shop, breathing a sigh of relief as he sank down on a plush velvet settee to wait. There was a reason gentlemen avoided the modiste like the plague—

"I don't know what Madame Laurent is thinking, banishing us to this miserable little room!"

What the devil? He jerked upright. The sharp exclamation came from his right, mere inches from his ear.

"It's too crowded for the four of us, and this settee a punishment to sit upon."

He stilled, listening. That voice, it sounded like—

"I'm perfectly comfortable, Mamma."

"Yes, well, I'm glad of it, but we're not all as pleasantly situated as you are, Susannah."

By God, it *was*. Lady Stanhope in an ill temper, and Lady Susannah, attempting to sooth her.

"Perhaps you'd be more comfortable in the main part of the shop, Lady Stanhope. Pray don't let us keep you here, if you're so dreadfully uncomfortable."

That was Lady Crump, her tone waspish, but then Lady Stanhope had a talent for driving even the most mild-mannered people into a temper. Good Lord, how would he ever countenance her as a mother-in-law? Perhaps Montford was right, and he hadn't thought this betrothal through properly.

Not that it mattered, now. He and Stanhope had already agreed they'd announce the betrothal tomorrow.

The thing was as good as done.

And it wasn't as if he had any objection to Lady Susannah. No reasonable gentleman could object to her. There wasn't anything *wrong* with her, and he'd have to choose a duchess sooner or later. It may as well be her, and it may as well be now.

That he hadn't managed to conjure as much as a flicker of interest in her mattered not at all. She wasn't to blame for it.

Lady Susannah was a lovely, sweet-tempered young lady, and she'd make an admirable duchess. It wasn't her fault he preferred ladies with a bit of spirit, ladies more like—

"Will you try on the evening-primrose silk, Susannah?" It was Lady Francesca's voice. "It's such a pretty color, and it will look lovely with your dark hair."

More like Lady Francesca, damn her, and damn his mother as well, for planting the idea in his head.

He was *preoccupied* with her. Preoccupied, with a sharp-tongued, blue-eyed, maddening chit who'd nearly decapitated herself sneaking into her uncle's garden, for God only knew what nefarious reason. Preoccupied, with a lady who wandered about the London streets *alone*, without a single care for her reputation. Preoccupied, with a lady who may well be carrying unflattering tales about him to every bloody scandal sheet in—

"The evening primrose is out of the question. The color is far too bright. One would think you, of all people, would know that, Francesca," Lady Stanhope snapped. "I do hope you're not attempting to manipulate your cousin to appear in public in an unflattering gown."

"Mamma! Franny would *never*—" Lady Susannah cried.

At the same time Lady Crump hissed, "How *dare* you suggest—"

"Now that we're on the subject of unflattering gowns," Lady Stanhope interrupted in smug tones. "Wherever are you getting all those dreadful pink garments, Francesca?"

"They belong to my niece, Lady Dorothea." Lady Crump's voice was shaking with fury. "And Francesca looks perfectly *lovely* in all of them!"

"Indeed, she does," Lady Susannah agreed.

"*Borrowed* gowns? Oh, dear." Lady Stanhope tsked. "But it's not the thing at all, for a young lady to wear such a bright color in her first season. The blue, if you please, Susannah. The duke prefers you in blue."

"I don't need another blue gown, Mamma, and this one is just like the blue silk Madame Laurent made for me at the start of the season."

"It isn't at all alike, you silly child. That gown is sky blue, while this one is French blue, and that silver Brussels lace is exquisite, and in the height of fashion."

"If you prefer this one, Mamma, then let's give the other one to Franny. The cut doesn't suit me, but it would look wonderful on—"

"Certainly not, Susannah! I have that gown in mind for you for Lady Fortin's rout. No, the pink gowns will do very well for Francesca. Now, you will do as I say this instant, and put on the blue gown."

There was a sigh, then a shuffle of footsteps as Lady Susannah presumably did what her mother ordered, and tried on a blue gown that was, no doubt, just like every other blue gown she'd worn this season.

For all Lady Stanhope's protestations, he didn't give a damn about Lady Susannah's blue gowns.

The pink gowns, however . . .

Lady Crump had loaned them to Lady Francesca for the season, because . . . well, what other reason could there be, except that she didn't have any gowns of her own?

And the pianoforte—what had she said about the pianoforte last night?

I did enjoy playing. Perhaps I'll have the chance to learn again, someday.

Every young lady in England with the means to do so played the pianoforte. It was odd, indeed, that Lady Francesca, the daughter of an earl, didn't play.

Unless *she didn't have the means*.

He curled his fingers around the head of his walking stick.

Just how tight was Lord Edward pulling Lady Francesca's and her mother's purse strings? So tight she couldn't afford a new gown? So tight, they couldn't afford to keep an instrument? What sort of circumstances were Lady Francesca and her mother living in, out in the Herefordshire countryside?

"Yes, that gown will do nicely. Stay as you are, Susannah, and we'll have the girl pin—Susannah! What are you doing?"

"I don't want it. I told you, Mamma, I don't need another gown."

"Hush, child. I'll be the judge of what you—"

"Indeed, Mamma, I won't wear it." Lady Susannah's hard, flat tone said she wouldn't be bullied into changing her mind.

Well, then, she had a touch of her cousin's willfulness, after all.

"Why, you wicked, ungrateful girl! You'll wear it if I say you'll—"

"No, I won't. Franny, will you help me with these buttons in the back?"

"Susannah!" Lady Stanhope gasped, outraged. There was a stunned silence, then the door to the private dressing room flew open and slammed again with an echoing thud.

"I beg your pardon, Franny, for my mother's dreadful . . . Franny? Are you unwell?"

He slid to the edge of the settee with every muscle tensed as he waited for her reply.

"Yes, I'm perfectly well. It's just your cameo, Susannah. Where, ah, where did you get it?"

"My father gave it to me just before the season started. It's lovely, isn't it?"

"It is. I've never seen a lovelier one."

Was there a slight hitch in her voice? He stilled, waiting for her to speak again.

"Shall we go, then?" Lady Francesca asked a moment later, voice bright.

Perhaps he'd imagined it.

The dressing room door opened again, there was a rustle of skirts as they passed by the sitting room, and then they were gone.

"Your Grace?" Madame Laurent appeared a few moments later, looking harried. "I do beg your pardon for making you wait, Your Grace! Lady Fishburne had a bit of a mishap with one of the satin turbans, but at last I have Lady Diana's gown ready."

"Thank you, Madame Laurent. If I might just trouble you about another matter?"

"Why, of course, Your Grace."

"I believe you have a French-blue silk gown trimmed in silver Brussels lace on the premises?"

"Indeed, I do, Your Grace."

"I'd like to have it, if I may. If you'll provide me with a pen and paper, I'll write down the direction of the recipient, but first I must ask, Madame, that you keep this business strictly between the two of us. It's a surprise, you see."

"Oh, yes, of course, Your Grace!"

"I have your promise, Madame?"

"It will remain between the two of us only, Your Grace. You have my word on it."

CHAPTER 14

"I wonder, Jenny, if we might forgo the ringlets tonight, and leave my hair as it is."

Jenny hesitated, a lock of Franny's hair in one hand and a pair of heated tongs in the other. "Ringlets at your temples are the height of fashion, my lady."

"Yes, I know, but I think we've quite left those dizzying heights behind us this season." Franny glanced at the pink gown spread out on her bed, then met Jenny's eyes in the glass, her lips quirked. "Wouldn't you agree?"

"I suppose I would, at that." Jenny set the tongs aside with a sigh. "I'll brush it so it gleams, then smooth it back from your face and tie it with a pink ribbon. Will that do, my lady?"

"Perfectly, yes." Franny let her eyes fall closed as Jenny ran the brush through her hair in long, soothing strokes. Tonight, Susannah and the Duke of Basingstoke would announce their betrothal to the *ton* at Lady Sandham's ball, and tomorrow . . .

Tomorrow, she'd present herself on her uncle's doorstep, collect the agreed-upon sum, and return to Herefordshire, leaving London behind, likely never to return again.

She was relieved at it—of course, she was. No more promenades with her uncle Edward's cold eyes upon her, no more taunts and slights from her aunt Edith's sharp tongue, no more pink gowns or staring *ton*, or long evenings confined to wallflower row.

But at the same time, no more Susannah, or Lady Crump. No more Jenny, who'd faithfully curled and smoothed and squeezed and fretted until she'd fashioned her into as elegant a young lady as the pink garments would allow.

No more Duke of Basingstoke.

Not that she'd miss *him*, of course, with his scolding and arrogant demands, and those sapphire-blue eyes always upon her, watching her. Still, he'd been kind to her the night of the duchess's musical evening, when she'd been so overset. Somehow, he'd known just the right thing to say to—

"Francesca, dearest?" There was a soft knock, and Lady Crump's muffled voice came from the other side of the door. "May I come in?"

"Yes, of course, my lady. Please do."

The bedchamber door opened, and Franny turned away from the looking glass to see Lady Crump enter, followed by a footman burdened with a large, cream-colored box.

A dressmaker's box.

"Just lay it on the bed there, George, if you would. Thank you. You may go."

"What's this, my lady? Did you change your mind, and order the green silk from Madame Laurent, after all?"

"No, this isn't mine, my dear. It's for you, and there's this one, as well." Lady Crump reached into her pocket, pulled out a long, narrow box, and set it on the dressing table in front of Franny.

"For *me*?" She stared down at the pale gray, velvet box. "But this looks like a jeweler's box."

"It does, yes."

"But who would send *me* anything in a jeweler's box?"

"Percival told me one of the Stanhopes' footmen brought it a little while ago."

"One of the Stanhopes' footmen? Oh, dear, you don't

suppose Aunt Edith tucked a poisonous viper inside a jeweler's box and sent it to me, do you?"

"I can't abide your aunt Edith, and would put nothing past her, but I believe your cousin sent this."

"Susannah? What do you suppose is in it?"

Except she already knew what was in the box, didn't she? There was only one thing it *could* be. She hadn't said a word to her cousin this afternoon at Madame Laurent's, but Susannah must have noticed her reaction when she saw the cameo. She'd been too shocked to hide it.

Lady Crump smiled. "There's one way to find out, isn't there?"

Jenny pressed closer. "Open it, my lady!"

Franny swallowed, then drew in a steadying breath, but her hand was still shaking a little as she reached for the box, and opened the lid. "Oh, my goodness."

There it was, her mother's cameo, nestled carefully in a protective layer of pale gray silk. It was a simple piece, nothing at all like the extravagant jewels her aunt Edith wore, just an onyx oval set into a plain gold frame, with a silhouette of a gentleman's face in ivory.

Her father's silhouette.

He'd given the cameo to her mother, less than a month before he'd been killed in the duel with Frederick Drew. Franny gazed down at it, her eyes filling with tears. How her mother had treasured it! How she'd wept over the inscription, after her husband's death.

For Maria, my dearest love. Ever yours, Charles.

And how she'd wept again, when it had been taken from her and given to Uncle Edward as part of the Stanhope estate.

"How did she know?" Franny traced her fingertip over the gentleman's face. "How could Susannah have known?"

"She's sent a note with it." Lady Crump reached into the jeweler's box, plucked up a piece of paper from the silk wrappings, and handed it to Franny. "Perhaps she's explained."

Franny fumbled the bit of paper open and read aloud. "My dear cousin. I've never seen anyone look at a necklace as you did this cameo this afternoon, with such sadness and longing at once. I realized there must be more to it than I knew, so I teased my mother's lady's maid until she confessed the truth. This could never be mine as much as it is yours, and so, it belongs to you, now. No arguments please, Franny, for all the refusals in the world won't make me take it back again. Your loving cousin, Susannah."

"Oh!" Lady Crump pressed a hand to her chest. "What a lovely thing for her to do! Lady Susannah truly is an angel."

"She always has been." Franny met Lady Crump's misty gaze in the glass, her own eyes stinging as she fought to hold back the tears that would not be denied. "Oh dear, I'm all soggy now."

"What do you suppose is in the other box?" Jenny was hopping up and down in excitement. "That's one of Madame Laurent's boxes!"

Franny glanced at Lady Crump. "You don't suppose . . ."

"The French-blue ball gown?" Lady Crump crossed to the bed, Franny following after her, and the two of them stood there, staring down at the cream-colored box. "It must be the gown, mustn't it? What else could it be?"

"One of Madame Laurent's ball gowns!" Jenny clapped her hands. "Won't you open it, my lady?"

Lady Crump nudged her closer to the bed. "Go on, Francesca."

The twine surrounding the box had already been loosened, so she pulled it off the end, then lifted the top off the box. The gown was buried under a dozen layers of paper to protect it, but a fold of French-blue silk could be seen peeking through.

Jenny gasped. "Oh, my goodness, such a pretty blue!"

Lady Crump brushed the layers of paper aside and fingered the hem of the gown. "The silk is very fine, the petticoat white satin, and that lace! Brussels, of course, and a prodigious quantity of it."

Franny stared down at the gown, a strange pang at her heart. She'd never had a gown like this one, had never owned a ball gown at all, let alone one so exquisite, and there was a secret part of her—a silly, girlish part that wanted nothing more than to wear something so fine, to feel the brush of white satin against her legs, and watch the candlelight play over the sparkling silver lace.

What would it be like, just once, to dance in such a gown?

This was the last ball of her only season. She'd never have another chance to wear a gown like this, but she'd started with the pink, and it only seemed right to end with it. "It's stunning, but I . . . I think I'll wear the pink."

"The pink!" Jenny wailed, but then snapped her mouth closed, her cheeks coloring. "I beg your pardon, my lady."

"It's all right, Jenny." Lady Crump gazed down at the blue gown for a moment, then picked it up and held it in front of Franny. "You do know, Francesca, that I won't be offended if you'd rather wear the blue. I did wonder, after the radish ordeal, if I'd done you a disservice, thrusting Dorothea's pink gowns upon you as I did. I thought—"

"You didn't, my lady. You did no such thing." Franny slipped her hand into Lady Crump's. "I'll never forget all the kindness you've shown me."

"You're a good girl, Francesca." Lady Crump let out a watery little laugh. "But I think you should wear the blue."

"You do? Truly?"

"I truly do, dear."

Franny traced her finger over a length of the silver lace. It was so soft and fine, like a cloud. "If you're sure, my lady."

Jenny let out a little squeal, then turned to Franny. "And the necklace, from Lady Susannah? You'll wear it, too, won't you?"

"I will, indeed." She returned to the dressing table, and

carefully lifted the necklace from the box. The cameo had been strung onto a length of white silk ribbon. "Do you suppose we can find a blue ribbon for it, in place of the white, Jenny?"

"Blue ribbon? Why yes, my lady, I do believe we can."

"My goodness, Francesca, do sit still, won't you? Your beautiful gown will be all wrinkled within the hour if you keep squirming in that manner."

"I beg your pardon, my lady." Franny straightened her back against her chair and folded her hands in her lap, but not more than five minutes passed before she was struggling to see over the sea of heads blocking the entrance to the ballroom.

She touched the pendant at her neck, the ivory silhouette of her father's face cool under her fingers. Where was Susannah? She must see her, thank her—

"Look, my dear!" Lady Crump gripped Franny's wrist. "The Duke of Basingstoke has arrived. Smile, and perhaps he'll ask you to dance again!"

Franny followed Lady Crump's gaze. A smiling Duchess of Basingstoke had paused under the archway, then moved forward again, revealing . . . yes, there he was, with his pretty, fair-haired sister on his arm.

An involuntary, and unwelcome sigh broke from her lips. Whatever else one might say about the Duke of Basingstoke, he did justice to his exquisite, fashionable clothing. As lovely as Lady Diana was, there were more eyes following his progress across the ballroom than hers.

How would she ever manage to stand up with him in a dance?

"There's Lady Susannah, at last, and looking so pretty in her pink gown. I do love a young lady in pink. Go on, then, Francesca, I know you're anxious to see her. Go and wish her a good evening." Lady Crump gave her an indulgent smile. "Perhaps then you'll calm down a bit."

Susannah wasn't in one of her usual blue gowns tonight, but in pale pink, and for all that she looked beautiful in it, she was as pale as the silk, her shoulders tense, and she was looking frantically around the ballroom, as if searching for someone. When her eyes met Franny's, she jerked her chin toward the corridor, her meaning unmistakable.

Franny nodded and leapt up from her chair. "I believe I will go and bid Susannah a good evening, my lady."

She'd just left wallflower row behind her when she noticed the duke was also making his way toward the Stanhopes from the other side of the ballroom. Anyone looking at the eagerness with which he hurried across the floor would think him utterly besotted with Susannah, so much so he was unable to be away from her for another moment.

But it was just another performance, a charade for the benefit of the *ton*.

It wasn't that he wasn't kind to Susannah. He *was* kind, and solicitous—perfectly so, but though he admired Susannah— she was lovely, and everyone admired her for her kindness as well as her beauty—there was no passion between them, or even any sincere affection, really. He wasn't in love with her, nor was she in love with him.

In truth, they were one small step removed from being strangers.

But mustn't Susannah know that, already? It wasn't as if she looked upon the duke with a fonder eye than he did her. Wasn't it more than likely she'd long since reconciled herself to a *ton* marriage, where a lady traded her chance at real love to make a spectacular match? Wouldn't every other young lady in this ballroom have done the same?

It didn't sound much like the sort of bargain Susannah would make, but it *did*, alas, sound like one her father would make for her, and Susannah had always been a dutiful daughter.

She skirted around the edges of the dance floor, her gaze jumping from Susannah to the duke, who was winding his way toward her from the other side. They were each about halfway to their goal when he noticed her.

They both paused mid-step, their eyes locking. His blue eyes widened as he took her in from head to toe, a tiny smile lifting one corner of his lip. He gave her a mocking bow, and then he was off again, his long legs eating up the distance between himself and Susannah.

Dear God, how ridiculous it was, both of them rushing toward her as if they were on a hunt, and poor Susannah was the doomed fox, but that didn't keep Franny from quickening her steps.

It wouldn't have been enough—he almost certainly would have reached Susannah first, but if there were any drawbacks to being an elegant, fashionable duke, it was that it was impossible for him to cross a ballroom without being stopped by acquaintances every step of the way.

Whereas she, well, the *ton* might be watching her every move with bated breath, and some might even wish her well, but no one wanted to actually *talk* to her. As it happened, the duke became trapped in a conversation with elderly Lady Fishburne and was still caught when Franny reached her cousin's side.

Susannah grasped her arm. "Come with me to the ladies' retiring room."

She didn't wait for a reply—indeed, there was no time, as the duke slipped quickly through Lady Fishburne's clutches—but tugged Francesca from the ballroom and down a hallway toward the ladies' retiring room.

"For pity's sake, Susannah. You nearly tugged my arm from its socket. Whatever is the matter?"

"Shh. Not here. Follow me." They bypassed the ladies'

retiring room, ducked through a closed door and into a dim room that turned out to be the library. Susannah pulled the door closed behind them and leaned her back against it. "There's something I need to tell you."

Franny gripped her cousin's hand, uneasiness stabbing her chest. "You look strange, Susannah. Something's gone awry, hasn't it? I can see it by the expression on your face. Tell me at once."

"It's about the duke. I don't . . . I can't . . . I don't love him, Franny." Susannah buried her face in her hands. "I've left it too late, haven't I? Oh, dear God, it's too late, and I—I don't know what to do."

"It's alright. You're alright, dearest." Franny wrapped her fingers around Susannah's wrists and gently lowered her hands from her face. "What brought all this on, Susannah? Did something happen with the duke?"

"No! He's done nothing wrong, but he doesn't love me anymore than I do him, and I'm afraid we're about to make a terrible mistake." Susannah gripped Franny's hand between both of hers, her fingers as cold as ice. "What should I do? Tell me what to do, Franny!"

"I can't do that, Susannah. I wish I could." She *wanted* to, so much. She would have given anything to be able to promise Susannah she wouldn't be made to do anything she didn't wish to do, and for it to be the truth.

But she knew her uncle too well for that. Susannah was being sacrificed to Uncle Edward's ambitions.

Susannah pressed her fingers to her temples. "I-I can't think. I can't . . . be here. Will you help me, Franny? Please? Surely, you must see I can't face Basingstoke tonight?" Susannah's big, blue eyes—eyes so like Franny's own, were bright with unshed tears. "You're the only one I can turn to. I need your help."

Franny had been too young to stop what had happened to her own mother, but she wasn't too young to help her cousin.

"You must leave the ball, at once, Susannah. Right now. There can't be a betrothal announcement without you here, and it will give you a chance to think about it tonight. By to-morrow morning, you'll know what you should do."

"But my parents, and Basingstoke! My father will be furious if I leave, Franny!"

He would, indeed—so furious Franny shuddered to think of it, but it couldn't be helped. "The betrothal announcement can be made just as easily at the next ball as it can be tonight. One thing I've learned about London, cousin, is that there's *always* another ball."

Susannah gave a half-hearted laugh. "Yes, that's true."

"I'll have a servant fetch you a hack, and you'll be home before anyone realizes you've gone. Once you're on your way, I'll tell your father you were taken ill, and went home. Stay here. I'll come back to fetch you in a bit."

"Franny!" Susannah caught her hand before she could dash out the door. "Before you go, I have to tell you . . ."

"Yes? Quickly, Susannah. Your father is likely already looking for you."

Susannah bit her lip, her throat working, then she caught Franny to her in a fierce hug. "I just wanted to tell you that you look beautiful tonight. That gown was made for you, and the cameo looks lovely with it, cousin."

"My dear Susannah! You're so very good to me. How shall I ever thank you?"

There wasn't time to say more. She hurried through the door, but something made her pause for one last glance at her cousin before closing it behind her.

Susannah was standing near a window, her slender form silhouetted against the darkness, a pale shaft of moonlight turning the pink silk of her gown a pearly white.

CHAPTER 15

"Do stop gaping in that absurd manner, Giles, and try and pay attention, won't you? Lord and Lady Stanhope have just arrived with Lady Susannah."

Giles followed his mother's gaze, and yes, there was Stanhope, posing under the archway that led into the ballroom, so the *ton* would have adequate time to admire his daughter.

His mother let out a soft gasp. "My goodness. Lady Susannah looks lovely tonight, does she not?"

"She always looks lovely." Lovely and pastel.

She was wearing a ball gown in such a pale shade of pink it was nearly white, with strings of pearls woven among the inky locks of her hair. More than one male gaze lingered appreciatively on her, but his attention kept drifting back to another dark-haired lady sitting in one of the chairs arranged on one side of the dance floor.

There was nothing pale about *her*.

She hadn't helped herself to Lady Dorothea's dressing closet tonight. No, tonight, she was an angel in French-blue silk, so lovely she made his throat ache. Did she suppose she could hide from him on wallflower row? Fade into the background, in her pale blue gown? She couldn't fade into the background in any gown. There was no *not* seeing her, no matter what she wore.

Not for him.

Once a lady had scolded a gentleman as fiercely as she'd scolded him, he could never fail to be aware of her again, but would sense her presence whenever she was near, in the same way he did a gathering storm. And then she *did* glare rather charmingly, those clear blue eyes narrowing, then darkening with pique.

She was turned away from him as she chatted with Lady Crump, but suddenly her back straightened, as if she could feel the heat of his stare burning through the delicate silk of her gown. She turned, her gaze caught his, and then . . .

The audacious chit looked him right in the eyes, thrust her pert little chin in the air, and looked away.

This, mere days after she'd agreed to behave nicely for the *ton*.

Or had she agreed? He'd thought so at the time, but looking back on it, all he could remember was how delightfully cross she'd looked on the afternoon he'd called on her at Lady Crump's, the tight, yet somehow inexplicably fetching press of her lips.

No doubt it was the novelty of the thing that intrigued him, and nothing to do with *her*—

"Giles? For pity's sake, what are you doing?" His mother had been watching Diana move through the first figures of a minuet on Lord Ormsby's arm, but now she turned back to him with a frown. "Lady Susannah is waiting."

That he was dwelling on the shape of Lady Francesca's lips instead of rushing across the ballroom to bid his betrothed a good evening was perhaps a matter for some concern, but contrary creature that he was, Lady Francesca's glowers and pinched expressions were somehow far more enticing than Lady Susanna's smiles.

"Giles?" His mother's frown deepened. "Aren't you meant to dance the first two dances tonight with Lady Susannah?"

"Indeed." The first two dances and a betrothal announcement tonight, to be followed soon afterwards by the rest of his life: only why did the rest of his life suddenly seem so much longer than it had last week? "I suppose it's too late to unseal my fate now, isn't it?"

His mother's eyebrow rose. "Is that a sincere question, or are these dramatics? If it's the former, then no, it's not too late until we're seated at your wedding breakfast."

"I reconciled myself to this marriage weeks ago, Mother, and I'm reconciled to it still." For better or worse, until the sweet relief of death, or, no, that wasn't quite how the vows went, but it was something of that sort.

"Oh my, yes, you're the very picture of the delighted bridegroom. But if you're going, you'd best hurry, because Lord Stanhope already looks like a thundercloud."

"He always looks like that." Stanhope was forever on the verge of falling into a temper over one thing or another. "He's certain to be a delightful father-in-law, is he not?"

"Giles—"

"It's all right, Mother. I'm going." There'd be no marriage without an announcement, so he may as well get on with it, and present himself to the Stanhopes like a fatted pig dropped on a butcher's doorstep.

He made his way through the crowd, one eye on Lady Francesca, who was hurrying toward Lady Susannah from the other side of the ballroom, dodging acquaintances as he went, until Lady Fishburne—who was a good deal quicker than such an elderly lady should be—caught him and regaled him with an excruciatingly detailed account of her recent trip to Brighton.

"I'm delighted your gout was so dramatically improved by taking the waters, my lady," he interrupted at last, pasting on his most charming smile. "Indeed, I don't know how I could have enjoyed myself tonight if you hadn't informed me of your renewed health."

"Thank you, Your Grace. How kind you are."

He sketched a polite bow and made his escape, winding his way through the crowd until he reached his future in-laws on the other side of the ballroom. "Good evening, Stanhope, and Lady Stanhope."

"How d'ye do, Basingstoke? Shall we get this thing done, then?"

By "this thing," Giles could only assume Stanhope was referring to the betrothal announcement. "Hadn't we better wait for Lady Susannah to return first?" He'd never been betrothed before, but wasn't the lady usually present for such things?

"What?" Stanhope looked around, as if he were searching for a misplaced walking stick. "For God's sake, where's the girl got to, Edith? She's meant to dance the first two dances with Basingstoke!"

"I believe I saw her leave the ballroom just now with her cousin. Their gowns must have required some mysterious alterations." Giles spoke lightly—it didn't make a damn bit of difference to him when they made their grand announcement.

Lord Stanhope's heavy brow lowered. "Gone off with *Francesca*? Where?"

"Now, my lord, she's merely gone to the ladies' retiring room, and will be back at any moment." Lady Stanhope laid a hand on her husband's arm. "You can hardly blame the dear, sweet child for wishing to look her best on such an important night."

"I can, and do blame her, devil take the girl—"

"Perhaps you might fetch your mother and Lady Diana, Your Grace, and invite them to join us?" Lady Stanhope gave him a bright smile. "I'm certain Susannah will be back by the time you return."

"Of course." Giles bowed, and made his way back across the ballroom, where he found his mother chatting with Lord Ormsby, who'd just returned Diana to her side.

"Good evening, Your Grace." Ormsby offered him a polite greeting, then bowed over Diana's hand. "Thank you for the dance, Lady Diana."

"My lord." Diana curtsied, a shy smile on her lips.

Ah, so that's how it was, then. Giles waited until Ormsby vanished back into the crowd, then nudged his sister. "So, it's to be Ormsby, is it, Diana?"

Diana's cheeks turned a deep, rosy red. "I never said—"

"You didn't need to. A young lady doesn't blush like that unless she's smitten."

"Don't tease, Giles!"

"Hush, Giles, and let your sister have her secrets." His mother gave Diana a fond smile, and smoothed a stray lock of hair back from her forehead. "Though I can't help but hint, dear, that if it is to be Lord Ormsby, I approve of your choice."

"As does your wicked, teasing brother, though I can't help but notice no one asked *my* opinion. One marriage at a time, however, if you please, Diana." Giles held out his arm to his sister. "Let's get this business settled with the Stanhopes first, shall we?"

Diana took his arm, and the three of them sallied forth, every eye in the ballroom watching their progress as they made their way over to the Stanhopes.

But Lady Susannah hadn't returned, and if Stanhope had looked like a thundercloud before, he was now a hurricane.

"Oh, dear." His mother's step faltered. "What do you suppose has happened?"

"Alas, my blushing bride vanished to the ladies' retiring room before I could even bid her a good evening, and as there's no sign of her, it appears she's yet to return."

"Oh, Your Graces, and Lady Diana." Lady Stanhope cast an uneasy glance at her husband, then rushed forward to meet them. "I do beg your pardon, but our niece has informed us our daughter was taken suddenly ill and has had to return home."

"Ill? How unfortunate, but I shouldn't worry, my lady. She's likely just fatigued," his mother said, and gave Lady Stanhope a reassuring smile. "As far as our announcement is concerned, it's a brief delay only. I daresay next week's ball will do as well as this one."

"Ill? How curious. Lady Susannah appeared in perfect health when she arrived." Giles eyed Lady Francesca, who was standing beside her aunt, her lower lip caught between her teeth, her blue silk gown turning her eyes a haunting blue. "What ails her, Lady Francesca?"

She eyed him the way a prisoner standing upon the gibbet eyes the hangman, which was appropriate, really, given she had as much chance of escaping him.

"I, ah, I couldn't say, exactly, Your Grace, but I believe the duchess is correct, and my cousin is merely fatigued."

"I see. How unfortunate."

There went that poor, swollen lip, caught once again between her teeth. "My cousin was sorry to disappoint you, Your Grace."

"It's rather bad timing, isn't it? It's a pity, as I was very much looking forward to dancing a cotillion. Indeed, I'm *expiring* for want of a cotillion."

Out of the corner of his eye he saw his mother and sister turn to stare at him, both frowning, but it was already too late. Absurd, contrary, feeble-minded fool that he was, he couldn't make himself look away from Lady Francesca.

Lady Crump was speaking to her, but Lady Francesca didn't appear to hear her. She remained still, her gaze trapped by his, her eyes so blue, so impossibly wide, if he closed the space between them, he'd fall into them entirely.

Fall in, and drown in that endless blue.

He handed his sister off to his mother, and with a deep bow, held out his hand to her. "Will you dance, Lady Francesca?"

She hesitated, and for an instant, he was certain she'd refuse, but then she held out her hand. His much larger one swallowed the tips of her gloved fingers, and he led her out to the floor.

Moments later, she was in his arms, the long, slender line of her back warm and alive under his palm, so close her scent teased his senses, dizzying him.

She smelled like the country.

Not like radishes or mud, thankfully, but the pleasant scents one associated with the country, like fresh breezes and flowers, green, growing things, soft, cool rain, and—

Dear God, he'd slipped into poetry.

He shook his head, as it needed clearing, and gazed down at the top of her dark head. "Well, Lady Francesca, is it as terrible as you imagined?"

She met his gaze, a fetching little wrinkle appearing between her eyebrows. "Is what terrible?"

"Dancing with me." Dancing with *her* wasn't anything like dancing with another young lady, nor was it as he'd imagined it would be.

That is, if he'd imagined it at all, which he *hadn't*.

Not much, anyway.

If she'd been any other lady he'd expect a pretty blush, a dozen stumbling denials, and a few sentences of awkward flattery, but Lady Francesca had yet to attempt to flatter him, and she wasn't a lady who stumbled.

Not over anything.

So, he waited with considerable curiosity for her reply.

"Not at all, Your Grace." Her lips quirked in a smile that was both angelic and wicked at once. "But then it couldn't possibly be as terrible as I imagined it would be."

It was strange, what happened next. His lips gave a decided twitch, his most charming smile began to feel a bit slippery, then slipperier still until it slid from his mouth altogether, pushed aside by . . .

A real smile?

"Well, my lady, I'm . . . flattered? Insulted? I'm not quite sure which." One thing he wasn't, however, was *bored*.

Stranger still, her lips gave a reluctant twitch of their own, as if goaded into it by his. "You *did* ask, Your Grace."

"Yes, but I didn't expect you to tell me the truth."

One dark, dainty eyebrow rose. "Are people in the habit of lying to you, Your Grace?"

"I'm a duke, Lady Francesca. People are in the habit of telling me what I wish to hear."

"Oh, dear. How dreadful it must be, to be a duke. I quite pity you, Your Grace."

"I don't believe you do, as I can say without the slightest hesitation that *you*, Lady Francesca, have hardly said two words I wished to hear since we spoke that morning on Bruton Street."

She shrugged, but the reluctant smile lingered at the corners of her lips. "Perhaps that's only because I don't know what you wish to hear."

"A hint then, Lady Francesca." He bent his head so his lips were closer to her ear. "I'm not fond of hearing the word 'no.'"

Good Lord, was he *teasing* Lady Francesca Stanhope? Worse, was he flirting with her?

"Ah. It's fortunate, then, that you're so seldom obliged to hear it, Your Grace."

It was indeed, but as it happened, a denial from some lips stung a trifle more than it did from others, just as a kiss from some lips tantalized in a way another kiss never could. A kiss from her deep pink lips, for instance, would be sweet and tart at once, the pale skin of her neck so soft under his palms, and . . .

His gaze locked on the blue ribbon she wore around her neck, the oval pendant nestled at the base of her throat. "Your necklace." He slid his fingertip under the pendant, his knuckle brushing against the warm hollow of her neck, the skin there unspeakably soft. "Haven't I seen your cousin wear this very same cameo?"

She swallowed, the slight, delicate movement of her throat against the backs of his fingers sending a hot rush of blood to his groin.

"You have, yes. She made a present of it to me."

"It suits you." He studied the pendant for another moment before letting it drop from the edge of his finger back into the notch of her throat. "The gentleman. Who is he?"

But he knew—he already knew, because he could see it in her expression, a curious mix of defiance and anguish. "My father. He had the necklace made for my mother, as a gift."

The cameo belonged to Lady Maria? Then how had Lady Susannah happened to have it? He darted a glance toward Stanhope, who was watching them with an expression of pure venom on his face, then back to Lady Francesca, who seemed to be taking great care not to look in her uncle's direction.

The lady had secrets. He could see it in her face, the way her thick, dark lashes suddenly hid her eyes, the press of her teeth against the deep pink of her lip. "That afternoon a few days ago, Lady Francesca, when I called on you at Lady Crump's, I asked you then why you'd come to London, what it was you hoped to achieve while you were here. It's occurred to me since then that you never answered my question."

"You're mistaken, Your Grace."

"No, you said only that I'd already given it to you." He hadn't noticed it at the time, but it had been a strange thing for her to say. "You never said what it was, but instead sent me off to see your uncle."

As if against her will, her gaze shot to Stanhope, and a soft sound escaped her throat, as if she were . . . frightened of him? No, it wasn't that, precisely. Any lady who dared scold a duke wasn't likely to be frightened of much, but she was wary, certainly.

"It's best, Your Grace, if I don't comment on my uncle's affairs."

She thought it best, or Stanhope did? "If Lord Stanhope has intimidated you in any way, Lady Francesca—"

"No! No, it's nothing like that. The dance has finished, Your Grace."

To his surprise, the last few notes of music were fading, and gentlemen were escorting their partners from the dance floor. "So it has. Will you favor me with another?"

He wasn't ready to let her go. Not yet.

"Thank you, Your Grace, but I'd better not."

There was little he could do but offer her his arm and return her to Lady Crump, the light touch of her hand searing through his coat sleeve, warming the skin underneath.

She and Lady Crump departed the ball soon afterwards, leaving him with a memory of thick eyelashes falling over blue eyes dark with secrets, and the ballroom somehow dimmer in her wake.

Chapter 16

The sun was just peeking over the horizon when Franny jolted awake, her heart thrumming in her chest, her breath short, and a warm, tingling sensation between her thighs.

She'd had a dream, a most, er, disquieting dream. She was dancing with a gentleman. He *wasn't* a gentleman she recognized—indeed, he was a perfectly anonymous gentleman, not specific in any way, but he—well, he did have golden hair and blue eyes, but then so did dozens of other gentlemen in London, so that was neither here nor there.

They were dancing, in the dream, but the ballroom around them was deserted. They were alone, just the two of them on an empty dance floor, and he was whirling her around and around until she was dizzy and laughing, her arms around his neck, and his hands on her waist.

It was rather an improper dance, if the truth were told.

But what followed, as the music slowed, then faded into silence, was far more improper. The strong hands around her waist tightened—tighter, then tighter still, the heat of his palms bleeding through the silk of her gown—and he was urging her closer, against a shockingly warm, muscular body, his blue eyes darkening as he leaned over her, and then his lips were pressed against her ear, whispering . . .

I'm not fond of hearing the word "no."

Then those hard, hot lips settled on hers, teasing them apart, his hands drifting lower, stroking her hips, and then . . .

Nothing. She woke up before she found out where his hands might wander next, the dream still clinging to her and urging all manner of wicked things, but she shook off the remnants, leapt from the bed and washed quickly, then hurried into her clothes and tiptoed down the hallway, taking special care not to make a sound as she passed Lady Crump's bedchamber door.

It was becoming quite a habit, stealing from Lady Crump's townhouse in the early hours of the morning. She despised sneaking about like a thief, but it wouldn't do for Lady Crump to know of her illicit dealings with her uncle Edward, particularly since she might take it into her head to report her findings back to Franny's mother.

That *certainly* wouldn't do, and so Lady Crump was left to slumber on in blissful ignorance, while Franny crept along the dim streets, and prayed that all would go well, so she'd never be obliged to sneak anywhere, ever again.

Once she'd concluded her transaction with her uncle—and it would be quick, as there was no sense lingering over *that* unpleasant business—she'd return to Charles Street, wait for Lady Crump to wake, and explain that her mother's health necessitated an immediate return to Herefordshire.

By this time tonight, she'd be back home at their little cottage in Ashwell, back within reach of her mother's comforting arms, only now her pocketbook would be full. There might even be enough money to send her mother to Brighton for a short spell. The sea waters were meant to do wonders for a consumptive chest.

After more than a decade of scrimping and scraping and calculating the necessity of every penny they spent, she and her mother would at last manage to snatch a little bit of comfort and security from the ruin to which her uncle had condemned them.

It wasn't a happy ending—it never could be, without her father—but it was something.

Perhaps she should be ashamed of herself for what she'd done—the sneaking about, the half-truths and outright lies, the blackmail, and the disloyalty to her father's memory—but she wasn't ashamed. She'd done what she needed to do.

And shame was rather a luxury, wasn't it?

It tended to get pushed aside in favor of survival.

As she'd expected, Charles Street was deserted, all of the fashionable people still tucked into their warm beds while their servants labored over fires and kneaded bread and sponged the stains from last night's ball gowns.

Her uncle's townhouse on Bruton Street was still and silent, but she knew he was awake, waiting for her. If there'd been any way for him to cheat her, he certainly would have, but she'd been rather specific in her threats of what would happen if he went back on his word.

Pride had ever been Uncle Edward's fatal flaw.

The one thing her uncle could be trusted to do was act in his own best interests, if not anyone else's. Not even his own daughter's.

She hesitated, squinting up at the house, and a flurry of movement at one of the third-floor windows caught her eye. For some reason, the draperies hadn't been drawn, and she could make out a figure on the other side. It looked as if they were rushing back and forth across the room.

How strange. Susannah hadn't truly fallen ill, had she?

Franny ran up the front steps and rapped on the door, expecting to come face-to-face with Coote and his quivering jowls, but to her surprise, the door flew open with such force it crashed against the inside wall with a crack, but whoever had opened it had already disappeared in a flurry of footsteps.

She crossed over the threshold into the entryway, and on the other side . . .

"What in the world?" It was utter pandemonium, with

servants scurrying this way and that, up and down the stairs and from one hallway to the next, nearly crashing into each other in their haste. A silver tray lay upturned on the floor, surrounded by a haphazard collection of glass bottles of smelling salts, one of which had smashed, leaving a sharp, medicinal order hanging in the air.

Uncle Edward could be heard above the mayhem, his bellows echoing throughout the hallways from two floors above. "I don't give a bloody damn if King George himself appears on our doorstep! We are *not* at home to visitors. *Coote*! Do you hear me, man?"

His voice was hoarse as if he'd been shouting for hours, the walls of the townhouse rattling with each thunderous scream. Franny stood at the bottom of the stairs listening, her mouth open in shock as he raved on and on, but none of what he said made any sense at all. No sooner would he issue an edict, than he'd contradict himself in the next moment.

"Have the carriage made ready this instant, Coote! I must have the carriage! Have it brought round to the mews at once!" But as soon as the servants scurried to do his bidding, he'd change his mind. "Get away from that door this instant, Coote! Not a single person in this house, whether they be family or servant, is to venture a single *toe* over that threshold unless they wish to feel my wrath come down upon them with a force that will crush them where they stand!"

Franny's heart was shuddering inside her ribs, her uncle's fury and violence beyond anything she'd ever witnessed before in her life, but it wasn't his crazed gibbering that made the sweat break out on her temples, and the hair on the back of her neck stand upright.

It was the wailing. A continuous, shrill, ear-piercing shriek.

It was her aunt Edith, and she was in screaming, breathless hysterics.

Dear God, what had happened? Something terrible, dreadful

beyond imagining, and there was only one voice she couldn't distinguish among the cacophony.

Her cousin Susannah. Where was Susannah?

One of the housemaids ran by just then, and she reached out and grabbed her by the arm, tugging her to a halt. "What's happened? Tell me at once!"

The maid gaped at Franny with wide, tear-filled eyes. "It's the young lady, Miss, she's . . . she's—"

"She's *what*? For pity's sake, say it, will you?"

The maid's mouth opened and closed, a frantic gulping, so Franny grasped her shoulders and gave her a firm shake. "What's the matter with Lady Susannah? Where is she? Is she sick, or hurt, or—"

God forbid, was she *dead*?

"Gone!" The maid choked on a screech loud enough to rival Aunt Edith's. "She's *gone*!"

"Gone?" Gone where? With whom? And *why*? For pity's sake, why? "I don't understand. Where has she—"

"*You!*"

Uncle Edward's deafening shout bounced off each of the four corners of the townhouse before hitting her squarely in the chest. She staggered backwards from the force of it, and stumbled against the table, sending a blue and white porcelain vase crashing to the floor.

Slowly, she looked up, up, up until her gaze met Uncle Edward's.

Immediately, she wished she hadn't. He was standing on the top step of the second landing, towering over her, one long, pudgy arm extended, his thick finger pointed directly at her. "This is *your* doing!"

"*Me*? I don't—"

"*You* persuaded her to leave the ball last night before her betrothal to the duke could be announced. *You've* been filling her head with silly, romantic notions since the day you arrived in London, inserting yourself into our family and poisoning our daughter against us!"

She gaped up at him, too stunned to say a word.

"Now you've come to collect your money, have you? Well, you may turn right back around again, my fine lady, for you won't see a penny from me. Susannah is no longer betrothed to the Duke of Basingstoke!"

No longer betrothed? "What—"

"That's right, girl, you heard me! Your cousin is *ruined*, but I daresay you're happy about that, aren't you? The best we can hope for now is she'll be made a marchioness, and that's if he doesn't decide to toss her aside before they even make it to the church! I would, in his place. Foolish, wicked, ungrateful chit!"

A *marchioness*? How? Had her uncle lost his wits?

"She would have become a duchess! Do you hear me, girl? A *duchess*! Instead, the Stanhope family has once again been disgraced. First your cursed mother, and now Susannah! What if Ormsby refuses to marry her, eh, girl? What then? A young lady who would have been a *duchess*, reduced to nothing more than a common whore!"

Oh, dear God. Dear *God*. Had Susannah run off with the Marquess of Ormsby? But how? When? Had he followed her home from Lady Sandham's ball last night? Caught up to her before she entered the house? Or had the two of them been planning this for some time? Had she inadvertently made it that much easier for her cousin to escape a marriage to the duke when she'd arranged to send her home last night?

And if she had, if she *had* . . . oh, her thoughts were all muddled!

But if she had, wasn't it for the best? Nothing less than the sincerest affection could have induced Susannah to flee the protection of her family and run off with Lord Ormsby.

Well, sincere affection or profound stupidity, but no, Susannah was naïve, certainly, but she'd never been a fool.

No, she must be most desperately in love with Lord Ormsby to do such a thing.

And if she was desperately in love with him, shouldn't she *be* with him? It was shocking it should happen in such a scandalous manner, of course, but then nothing short of an elopement could have freed Susannah from a marriage with the duke.

As for Lord Ormsby, there was no question he *would* marry Susannah. A gentleman didn't risk running off with an earl's daughter—to say nothing of a *duke's betrothed*—unless he was madly in love with her.

There would be a scandal, yes, but Susannah would be the Marchioness of Ormsby. She wouldn't be a duchess, but she'd be married to the man she loved. The scandal would pass, and once it did, wouldn't everyone get what they wished for most, in the end?

That is, everyone but her uncle Edward—

"You will leave my house this *instant*, Francesca, and you may be certain you'll never set foot in it again. As for you and your mother, neither of you will receive so much as a shilling from me!"

With that, reality came crashing down around her.

When Susannah had fled with Lord Ormsby, she'd taken all of Franny's leverage with her. Uncle Edward and Aunt Edith weren't the only ones who wouldn't get what they'd wished for.

She and her mother wouldn't, either.

There would be no comfort, no security, no trip to Brighton. Nothing but the cold, damp cottage that was stealing her mother's health one labored breath at a time.

No hope.

There would be no happy ending for *them*.

"I told you to *get out*, and a curse upon you!" Uncle Edward thundered, his words crashing down upon her head like a dark pronouncement from above.

For one long, agonizing moment, everything went still. Footsteps ceased to echo, doors ceased to slam, and the servants froze in their places. Even Aunt Edith's wailing abruptly ceased. The entire house went silent as they all stared at her, waiting to see what she'd do.

But there was only one thing *to* do, wasn't there?

She backed toward the front door, stumbling a little as her heel met the edge of the threshold, and then onto the top step that led down the stairs.

Behind her, the door to the townhouse slammed closed, and a shudder gripped her, like cold, skeletal fingers squeezing her neck. It was the sound of a thousand doors, all slamming closed at once.

The sun had only just risen an hour ago, but for her, it had already set, leaving nothing but night on the other side.

CHAPTER 17

If Giles's stomach hadn't been howling with hunger, he might have slept the entire day away, but there were still a few hours of daylight left when he pried one eye open, blinking as a watery glow filtering through the gap in the draperies fell over his face.

"Devil take you." He rolled over, buried his face in his pillow, and pulled another over his head. There wasn't much reason to leave his bed today. He was still in London, still betrothed, and the season was still dragging onward, but all those things would be as true tomorrow as they were today.

He'd left Lady Sandham's ball early last night, soon after Lady Francesca had, since he was no longer required to play the doting bridegroom. He'd find himself back in that role soon enough—Lord Tyne's ball was next week—but he'd taken advantage of his unexpected freedom by going on a proper tear with Montford and Grantham.

Now, predictably, his head felt as if it had met the wrong end of a fireplace poker, his eyes were gritty, and his mouth was as dry as sawdust.

To make matters worse, there was a distinctly unpleasant nip in the air. He couldn't feel it, swathed in his cocoon of silken sheets as he was, but he knew what that cold white light coming through the window meant, the rattle of the pane, the relentless pattering against the glass.

It was the first day of November. Soon enough, he wouldn't be able to set foot outside his door without being tossed about by bone-chilling wind and pummeled by icy drops of rain.

He'd spent the night alone, tormented with thoughts about his dance with Lady Francesca. Somehow, when he hadn't been paying attention, his preoccupation with her had turned into . . . something else. He couldn't say *what*, precisely, but it was damned unsettling, rather like a serpent twisting about in the pit of his stomach.

One thing was certain, though. It *wasn't* desire.

She did have lovely blue eyes, yes, and he was a bit preoccupied with her mouth, but only because it was a conundrum, what with those plump, sweet lips hiding a tongue like a rapier, and then she could wear a scandalously pink gown like no other lady he'd ever seen.

But none of that meant he *wanted* her.

A proper gentleman's mouth didn't water over the cousin of his future betrothed, for God's sake, and the reflection of himself he saw in Lady Francesca's eyes was hardly flattering. Yet at the same time, as much as he might wish otherwise, one glance and he was drowning in them.

He rolled over onto his back with an irritable groan and threw his arm over his eyes. His head was fit to burst, and hunger was gnawing at him. Despite the late hour, not a single servant had yet appeared with a tray.

Where the devil was Digby? The man was always unfailingly prompt, but there hadn't been any sign of him yet today. What good was being a duke if his servants left him to starve in his own bed?

He shoved his pillows aside, fumbled for the bell, and yanked on it with the sort of violence that usually brought a half dozen servants running. But instead of the scurry of footsteps, his command was met with oppressive silence.

So, he yanked it again, and then again.

Nothing.

Damn it. He tossed the coverlet back, his stomach letting out an angry whine, and padded to the door of his bed-chamber, intending to jerk it open and let out a ducal howl terrifying enough to make the dead shudder in their graves.

That was when he heard it. Whispering, in the hallway outside his bedchamber.

He paused with his hand on the doorknob. The door was a thick, sturdy one, but not so thick he couldn't hear Digby engaged in a heated discussion with his butler, Trevor.

They were *chatting*, while he expired in his bed from lack of sustenance?

". . . duchess has already sent a half dozen notes, demanding that His Grace present himself in Harley Street at once. I assure you, Mr. Digby, we ignore Her Grace at our own peril."

God in heaven, what was his mother in a strop about *this* time? Whatever it was, she would have to wait, because he wasn't presenting himself anywhere until he'd broken his fast.

". . . whole business is dreadful enough without further upsetting His Grace by waking him before he's had the proper rest, Mr. Trevor."

"You do us no favors by delaying the inevitable, Mr. Dig—"

Giles wrenched the bedchamber door open. "Is something amiss, Trevor?"

Nothing ever rattled Trevor. He was an impeccable servant, the epitome of the impassive butler. Several years ago, there'd been a rather large fire in the kitchens. It had spread to the stillroom, setting off a series of small explosions, but Trevor hadn't so much as twitched.

Now, however, Trevor blanched when he saw Giles

standing in his bedchamber doorway, while Digby, who was considerably less stalwart, let out a faint shriek, the dishes on the silver tray in his hands wobbling enough to upset the teacup in its saucer.

"I . . . er, no, Your Grace, nothing's amiss. Mr. Digby here was just about to bring you your tray."

"Well, Digby?" Giles nodded at the tray. "I assume that's my meal?"

"Yes, Your Grace."

Trevor nudged Digby forward. "Serve His Grace his meal at once, Mr. Digby. Go on."

"Before I collapse, if you'd be so kind, Digby." Giles moved away from the doorway and waved his valet in with an impatient flick of his fingers.

Digby shot an inscrutable look at Trevor, who gave him a helpless shrug.

"What the devil is the matter with the two of you?" For God's sake, he should have remained in his bed with the coverlet over his head. "You're acting like two naughty schoolboys sent to the headmaster for a thrashing."

"Er, I beg your pardon, Your Grace." Digby passed into the bedchamber and Giles followed after him, slamming the door behind him.

"Will you take your breakfast in bed, Your Grace, or at the table?"

"The bed." He dropped back into it with a huff and tugged the coverlet over his legs.

Digby fussed with the dishes, the scrape of porcelain setting Giles's teeth on edge, but at last he set a tray with coffee, scones, and the newspapers in Giles's lap.

Then he darted to the other end of the room, well out of reach. "Will that be all, Your Grace?"

Giles raised an eyebrow at him. "It looks as if it will have to be, since you're halfway out the door already."

Digby looked as if he were an instant away from bursting into tears. "I beg your pardon, Your Grace, I—"

"Never mind. Just *go*."

Digby managed a quick bow, then he shot through the door as if the hounds of hell were after him. Trevor was waiting in the hallway still, but instead of both of them going away, as proper servants would do, they set to whispering again like a pair of clucking hens.

Whatever the trouble was, Giles was already bored of it.

He unrolled the paper and spread it across his lap, but instead of the *Morning Post*, as usual, Digby had brought the *Cock and Bull* instead, a scandal sheet so notorious the *ton* all professed themselves unable to stomach it, though of course they all devoured it as voraciously as they did their morning chocolate.

He lifted his coffee to his lips as he skimmed over the page. The scoundrels at the *Cock and Bull* had uncovered another delicious tidbit, it seemed, about some rakehell or other who'd compromised an innocent young lady—

"Damnation!" Coffee spurted from his lips and sprayed across the lines of newsprint in front of him, the rest of it catching in his windpipe and sending him into a coughing fit that had him gasping for breath, and tears pouring from the corners of his eyes.

It wasn't just any rakehell this time. This time, it was *him*. His name was splashed across the front pages of the *Cock and Bull* as surely as his first sip of coffee was.

The Duke of B— and Lady F—a S—e, Caught Out!

He and Lady Francesca, caught out? Caught out at what? As far as he was aware, they hadn't done a thing to be caught out at.

He brought the dripping paper closer to his face, his heart pounding.

> Sinful lust . . . dangerous preoccupation with
> the lady since she arrived in London . . .
> preference for blue-eyed ladies, much like his
> father . . . pursued the innocent with single-
> minded intent . . . dark-haired siren . . .
> unbridled lust . . . a private dressing room . . .

Unbridled lust! What unbridled lust, and what did a dressing room have to do with—

Oh, no. His gaze shot down the page, nausea rolling though
his empty stomach. Why, those scoundrels! They were too
cowardly to say it outright, but one would have to read it with
one eye closed not to see they were implying that *he*, the Duke
of Basingstoke, had dallied with Lady Francesca Stanhope in
the private dressing room in Madame Laurent's shop!

Hell and damnation, this was an utter disaster.

No wonder Digby had been terrified to bring him his tray
today. No servant wanted to deliver his master's ruination
with his morning coffee.

And ruination it was, a total annihilation. He didn't need
to read past the first few lines to see that, but a strange, numb
horror dragged his eye to the next line, then the next, and it
only got worse from there.

> . . . firsthand account from a source close to . . .
> blue silk gown worth a king's ransom . . .
> dance with Lady F—a at Lady S—m's ball
> last night . . . besotted with . . . one wonders
> what the Duchess of B— makes of her son's
> depravity . . . a scandal worthy of his wicked
> father . . .

He lowered the paper to his lap in a daze. A rake, a
seducer, a despoiler of innocence, a scoundrel the likes of

which London hadn't seen since his father's death—one outrageous lie after the next, right there in black and white, every delectable morsel of it for the gossips to swallow along with their morning chocolate.

But *how*? How had they managed to stitch together a few bits of truth to create a full cloth of such outrageous lies? God knew the scandal sheets had left more than one nobleman's reputation in tatters without troubling themselves much with the truth, but he'd never before seen such blatant fictions presented as if they were facts.

Or perhaps he had, every time he'd read the newspaper, and simply hadn't realized it. Well, he'd now been paid back a thousandfold for his ignorance.

He snatched it up and read through the story again, line by line this time. It read like some sort of twisted fairy tale, with just the right balance of romantic and titillating detail calculated to catch the *ton*'s fancy.

An innocent young lady comes to sinful old London, is preyed upon by a nobleman with more coin than morals, and, in an astonishing case of history repeating itself, he ruins her without a twinge of regret, just as his father ruined her mother a decade earlier.

What could be more spectacularly lurid than that?

And that last line, *a scandal worthy of his wicked father.*

The *ton* hadn't expected proper behavior from the Seventh Duke of Basingstoke. They'd known who he was and had lost patience with him long before he'd ruined Lady Maria and Lord Charles Stanhope.

The same wasn't true of the Eighth Duke of Basingstoke.

He'd spent the two years since his father's death doing all he could to recover his family's good name, to wrench his family's shattered reputation back from the edge of the cesspool his father had nearly plunged them into, and give London the Duke of Basingstoke they felt they deserved.

But in the privacy of his own bedchamber, he was much

like every other jaded aristocratic gentleman in London. He'd had a torrid affair with Lady Caroline Scott, had debauched her and multiple other ladies besides, all at once, and in this very bed.

That was bad enough, but it wouldn't have ruined him, if only because there was little that could ruin a man of his rank and fortune in the eyes of the *ton*. If a single gentleman of means paid his debts of honor, treated his mistresses generously, and didn't cheat at cards, he might for the most part do as he pleased.

As long as he *wasn't* the Duke of Basingstoke, and the lady whose innocence he'd reportedly stolen *wasn't* Lady Francesca Stanhope.

That he hadn't actually ruined her meant precisely nothing. *A scandal worthy of his wicked father.*

For a few fleeting years, he'd been a respectable gentleman, a man of honor and integrity, the first in a long line of Dukes of Basingstoke who hadn't been an utter villain.

But not any longer. What would become of his mother and his sisters now? What of Diana's season, her prospects, her chance of a marriage to Lord Ormsby, or any other decent gentleman? Then there was Lady Susannah to consider. A scandal of such monstrous proportions was more than reason enough for her to jilt him.

Finished. All of it, finished. In one day, all his efforts had been destroyed.

His name would already be on the lips of every gossip in London, and the scandal would be as bad as his father's ruination of Lady Maria Stanhope had been, the stain every bit as dark as Charles Stanhope's blood on his father's hands.

No, worse even, because Lady Francesca was an innocent, and because the *ton* had done him the favor of believing him to be an honorable man, or at least pretending to believe it, and he'd repaid their generosity by trifling with the innocent daughter of the lady his father had ruined.

They wouldn't forgive that.

"Trevor!" He shoved the tray off his lap, uncaring when the cup overturned and coffee splattered everywhere. "Trevor, Digby, I need you both at once!"

His servants had certainly been waiting for the summons. Trevor was at his bedside at once, Digby hovering over his shoulder. "Your Grace."

"Trevor, send a note to my mother letting her know I will call on her as soon as I'm able, then remain in the entryway. I am not at home to callers today."

"Yes, Your Grace." Trevor left the bedchamber at a run.

"Digby, I need your services, and be quick about it, man. I should have called on Lady Susannah hours ago." It was a bloody miracle Stanhope hadn't appeared in his bedchamber by now, shrieking for an explanation.

"Yes, at once, Your Grace." Digby scurried to the dressing closet and returned a moment later with pantaloons, shirt, waistcoat, and a coat clutched in his arms. Despite his trembling hands, his tied tongue, and bouts of dizziness, he managed to pull Giles into some semblance of order.

He had his carriage sent to the mews and was halfway to Bruton Street before he allowed himself to think once again about Lady Francesca.

He'd never intended for her to find out he'd been the one who'd sent her the blue ball gown. She knew now, of course, and no doubt she regretted wearing it to Lady Sandham's ball last night.

Regretted dancing with him, as well.

Of course, she knew the story for the lie it was, but she wasn't any less ruined for it being a lie than she would have been had it been the truth.

He could hardly blame her, if she regretted ever knowing him at all.

His stomach gave a sharp lurch that definitely *wasn't*

hunger, but there was no sense dwelling on it, as he couldn't do a thing about it just now.

Lady Susannah was his first concern, and his mother and sisters his second.

As for Lady Francesca, something would have to be done about her.

This wasn't the time to consider what, but that time would come, and soon.

CHAPTER 18

"You know what's wrong with London, Digby? Do you know, my good man, what makes this bloody city such an unholy torment to live in?" Giles tried to point his finger at his valet, but the damn thing kept wobbling about. "Go on, have a guess."

Digby's Adam's apple bobbed. "Er, is it all the h-horse dung dirtying the streets, Your Grace?"

"Dung? You can't say dung to a duke, can you?" Giles tossed back half the brandy in his glass, wincing as it burned its way down his throat. That was the trouble with brandy—the more you drank, the hotter it burned. Or was it the other way around? "Do you know, Digby, I don't think anyone's ever said the word dung to me before."

"I-I beg your p-pardon, Your Grace, I shouldn't have—"

"Never mind, Digby. You didn't know." Giles waved the dung away with a flick of his wrist and the rest of the brandy in his glass splashed over his hand. "Damn it."

Digby leapt to his feet. "I'll fetch a cloth, your—"

"No, never mind it. Sit down, my good fellow." He had something important to say about dung, and—no, wait, not dung, but London. He had something important to say about *London,* and Digby needed to hear it, because it was very wise, and he may not be able to recall it later.

He may not be able to recall it *now*, come to that.

It was something to do with treachery and filth, and . . . oh, yes, he had it now. "The trouble with London, Digby, is the vile, treacherous gossip in every corner of this filthy city! The gossip, and the despicable, smirking *ton* who . . . who smirk over it."

"Yes, Your Grace."

"A man can't even admire a lady's blue eyes without every fool in Mayfair having an opinion about it! It's a bloody travesty, Digby!"

"A travesty indeed, Your Grace."

"Dragonflies," Giles announced, abandoning his glass and raising the bottle to his lips.

"I beg your pardon, Your Grace?"

"Dragonflies, Digby! The color of her eyes. Really, do try and keep up, will you?" He took another healthy swig from the bottle and dragged his arm over his lips.

"Er, yes, Your Grace."

"Her gowns were pink. I'm fond of pink, Digby. Not pale pink, mind you, but a vivid, robust pink. When it comes to pink, I always say, the brighter, the better."

"Yes, Your Grace."

"But the pink doesn't matter, man! No, it's the . . . the . . ." What was it that mattered again? "The gossip!" Yes, that was it. "The gossip, and the scandal sheets, and the dung." He took a long pull from the bottle. "I tell you, Digby, if Dante had ever lived in London, there'd be ten circles of hell rather than just the—"

"Basingstoke!" A sharp knock on his study door interrupted him. "Are you in there?"

"Damn it, it's Gransham, and probably Montford with him." Giles held his finger up to his lips. "Not a peep, Digby. If we're quiet, they might give up and go away."

He and Digby both kept very still, but it didn't do a damn

bit of good. Grantham burst through the closed door without so much as a word of apology.

"What the devil d'you want, Gransham?"

"He's whittering on about Dante again. I heard him from the other side of the door." Montford was right behind Grantham. "We got here just in time."

"I didn't invite you in, Gransham. You either, Montford. Go away. Digby, throw them out on their arses, would you? There's a good fellow."

"I beg your pardon, Your Grace." Trevor rushed in, breathless. "I did tell their Graces you weren't at home to visitors, but they insisted upon coming—"

"S'all right, Trevor, you poor bastard." He waved his brandy bottle at Trevor. "Every bloody gossip in London's been on my doorstep today, Gransham, none of 'em invited or welcome, and all of them having a run at poor Trevor, but he didn't let a single one of 'em past the entryway. Trevor, you're a for . . . a for . . . a fortress! Yes, that's it. Do you fanshy a drink, my good man?"

"Give me that bottle, Basingstoke, before you hit someone with it." Grantham made a grab for the brandy bottle, but Giles snatched it away and curled a protective arm around it.

"No. It's mine."

"You're slurring, Basingstoke. That means you've had enough."

Giles held up the bottle he was cradling in the crook of his arm to have a look. Half-empty, already? When did that happen? "Who's shlurring? Not me."

"Yes, *you*. You sound like a drunken doxy on the floor of a gin palace." Montford leaned over him and sniffed. "Smell like one, too."

Grantham plucked the bottle out of Giles's hand and passed it to Trevor. "Here. Take this."

Trevor, ever loyal, turned to Giles. "Your Grace?"

He waved him away. "S'all right, Trevor. You can have it."

"Very good, Your Grace. Shall I remove Mr. Digby?"

Giles squinted at Digby. "Eh, I suppose you'd better, before he casts up his accounts." He waited until Trevor had closed the door behind them, then faced his friends, let out a belch, and announced, "Gennelmen, I'm ruined."

Grantham rolled his eyes. "You're a duke, Basingstoke. Dukes can't be ruined."

Montford snorted. "Can't they? God, that's a relief."

It didn't seem right for Montford to be laughing, considering how bloody awful things were, but on the other hand, there was something rather funny about a ruined duke—a duke so wicked he'd lust after the blue-eyed cousin of his betrothed, a duke filthier even than the dung on the streets.

The Duke of Dung.

"Ha." God, that was funny. Except, wait. Wasn't *he* the duke in question?

No, not so funny, after all.

Montford dropped into a chair near the fire and crossed one booted foot over the other knee. "Have you spoken to your mother?"

"I've been interrogated, and released." Giles attempted a salute and poked himself in the eye. "Ouch."

Grantham took the seat next to Montford. "Dare I ask what the duchess had to say?"

"Say? Something about dung, I think."

"Dung!" Montford glanced at Grantham. "Are you certain it was dung, Basingstoke?"

Huh. It didn't sound right, really. "Now you mention it, I think it was Digby who was talking about dung."

"Think hard, Basingstoke." Grantham leaned toward him. "Your *mother*, the *duchess*. What did she say?"

"Oh, I remember now. She said Diana's season is over. Finished. Done. She's ruined, because of me. Terrible thing,

ruination. Terrible to see Diana cry, you know. Her eyes got
all red, and her cheeks all wet, and then my mother started
weeping, and then Amy joined in. Everybody bloody wept."

A brief silence fell, then Montford asked, "Even Louisa?"

"No. Not until my mother took her violet ices away."

"Violet ices?" Grantham frowned. "Why should your
mother take away Louisa's violet ices because you got caught
in a scandal?"

"No, no, no. Pay attention, Gransham. The trouble is, there
are no violet ices in Kent."

"You mean to say your mother is taking your sisters back
to Kent?"

"That's what I said, isn't it? There's no Gunter's in Kent,
you know." There wasn't much of anything in Kent, really.

Grantham and Montford glanced at each other. "Anything else?"

"Some other things, yes. Sad things. Don't bear repeating." Except that wouldn't make it go away, would it? "She
said it's best if I don't see Diana, or Amy, or Louisa until the
scandal dies down."

Well, maybe they *did* bear repeating, then.

"Christ, Basingstoke," Montford muttered. "That's a devil
of a thing."

"It is. Stings, you know." He didn't blame his mother,
though. It wasn't *her* fault he'd turned out to be the Duke of
Dung. Wicked, just like his father.

"Well then, we'll simply have to do as your mother demands, and find a way past this scandal, won't we?"

"Good thinking, Gransham." Grantham had always been
a clever one. That was probably how he'd made all those
piles of money. "I say we wait for the *ton* to forget about it. It
shouldn't take more than a decade or so. Now, what did I do
with that bottle of brandy?" He leaned over to search under

his chair, and a flood of bile rushed into his throat. "Oops. Some of it may be on the way back up."

Montford rose, jerked his chair back a few feet, then plopped back down on it again. "No offense, Basingstoke, but these are new boots."

"We're not waiting for the *ton* to forget it, Basingstoke," Grantham said. "We'll find another way out of it."

"Damn right we will. What way?" He hadn't had any good ideas himself, although that might be because he'd crawled to the bottom of a bottle of brandy as soon as he'd returned home from his mother's.

It was the weeping that did it. Four pairs of big blue eyes filled with tears. No man could withstand that without brandy. If ever a situation called for drunkenness, it was this one. "I want my brandy back. Where's Trevor? Need to ring for Trevor." Where the devil had the bell gone?

"Wait." Montford jerked his head up. "You haven't said a word about Lady Susannah! Your betrothal, Basingstoke. What of your betrothal?"

"Done. I am no longer betrothed to Lady Susannah Stanhope, but not because I ruined her cousin."

Grantham's mouth dropped open. "You didn't *actually* ruin her cousin, did you?"

"No, of course not. Do you take me for a defiler of virgins, Gransham? Never laid a finger on her, although . . ." He beckoned them both closer with a wriggle of his fingers and lowered his voice. "I did *think* about laying a finger on her. Maybe even two." He wriggled two of his fingers. Or four. It was hard to tell. "Never did it, though."

That was important, wasn't it? That he'd never actually done it?

"If it wasn't your lustful urges that put an end to your betrothal with Lady Susannah, Basingstoke, then what did?"

Ah, now *there* was a question. "*Her* lustful urges!"

"*What*?" Grantham gaped at him. "You can't mean to tell me shy, sweet, blushing Lady Susannah Stanhope was involved in some sort of clandestine affair!"

"Yes, I bloody can, because that's precisely what I *am* telling you. She's run off with Ormsby." And here he'd thought this would be a dull season. "Plenty of scandals to choose from, Gransham. That'll make the gossips happy, eh?"

Shouldn't *someone* be happy?

"*Ormsby!*" Grantham's mouth dropped open. "The Marquess of Ormsby? Impossible! I don't believe it!"

"Believe it, Gransham. They're gone, likely halfway to Gretna Green by now, or wherever it is marquesses . . . marquesses? Is that how you say it?"

"Yes, yes." Montford waved at him impatiently. "Go on, Basingstoke."

"Wherever it is marquesses take their ill-gotten brides." He beckoned them close again. "I found an almighty tumult at the Stanhopes when I called this afternoon, too. Servants running about like . . . like . . . things that run. Lady Edith in fits, and Stanhope raving incoherently about King George, of all things."

"Well, I'll be damned." Grantham shook his head. "I wouldn't have thought the girl had it in her."

"Me neither, but she's wilier than she pretended to be. It takes spirit to flee a duke, eh, Gransham? I like her more now than I did before. I'd wish her well, if it weren't for . . . something."

There was *some* reason he couldn't wish her well— something she and Ormsby had done he didn't like, but he couldn't quite remember . . . "Oh, right. She made Diana cry. She took Ormsby away from Diana and broke her heart. It's not fair. One lady's happiness shouldn't come at the expense of another's."

Yes, that was very good. Perhaps he should write that down—

"That's unfortunate." Grantham sighed. "I'm sorry for Diana, but I shouldn't worry, Basingstoke. Young ladies' hearts are resilient things. She's certain to—"

"You're no longer betrothed, Basingstoke," Montford interrupted. "You won't be marrying Lady Susannah."

"I *know*, Montford. Isn't that what I just said?" Was anyone even listening to him?

"No, you don't understand, Basingstoke. Don't you recall what the three of us discussed that day at White's?"

"I recall you wagered Gransham fifty pounds I wouldn't appear for luncheon, and lost your money, just as you deserved."

"Not the wager, for God's sake. I mean in regard to Lady Francesca. Grantham here reminded you that Lady Francesca and her mother fared a great deal worse over that business with your father than Stanhope and his family did."

"I know that, *too*, Montford. What of it? I don't see—"

"My God, Montford!" Grantham leapt to his feet. "You're a genius!"

Montford, a genius? How much brandy had he had?

"That day at White's, Basingstoke. Montford told you if you really wanted to silence the wagging tongues, you'd marry Lady Francesca, not Lady Susannah. Of course, that was out of the question then, as you'd already offered for Lady Susannah, but you're no longer betrothed, so—"

"Oh, you mean I should marry Lady Francesca in Lady Susannah's place? No, I can't. It won't do."

Grantham held out his hands, as if he were attempting to calm a cornered animal. "Just listen for a moment, Basingstoke. The *ton* thinks you've ruined Lady Francesca. The only way to save your reputation as well as hers is to—"

"Marry her. Yes, I know that, Grantham, but—"

"A marriage to Lady Francesca is the perfect way to put you back in the *ton*'s good graces. The only way, really. I don't see that you have much choice, Basingstoke."

"I don't deny it, Montford, but you see—"

"The *ton* is on Lady Francesca's side, Basingstoke. They have been since she appeared at Lord Hasting's ball, and you called her a muddy radish."

"Will you stop saying that, Montford? I never called her—"

"They want a romance between you two. You recall that bit in the *Post* about your 'passionate argument' with Lady Francesca at the Marble Arch? Then there was that other thing about you chasing her all over the drawing room at your mother's musical evening—"

"Lies! I never *chased* her any—"

"A marriage between the two of you makes perfect sense," Grantham interrupted. "The *ton* was never satisfied with the conclusion of that ugly business between your father and Lady Maria. They all wanted to see her vindicated. If you were to marry Lady Francesca now, make her the Duchess of Basingstoke—"

"They'd forgive you anything, then. You must see it, Basingstoke—"

"For God's sake, will you two be quiet and listen to me? I've already offered for Lady Francesca." Or he'd tried to, anyway. It would have worked, too, if she hadn't run off.

Montford glanced at Grantham. "Are you sure of that, Basingstoke?"

Was he *sure*? He was drunk, not delusional. "Of course, I'm sure."

"I see. Then you're betrothed to Lady Francesca?"

"Don't be ridiculous, Grantham." If he were betrothed to Lady Francesca, he'd have said so at once. "Of course, I'm not betrothed to her."

Grantham threw his hands up in the air. "Your turn, Montford."

"Think hard, Basingstoke. Did you see Lady Francesca *before* you drank half a bottle of brandy, or afterwards?"

Why was Montford speaking so slowly? It was annoying. "I never spoke to her at all. She ran off back to Herefordshire before I got the chance, didn't she?"

"Ah, now we're getting somewhere." Montford rubbed his hands together. "You mean you called on Lady Francesca at Lady Crump's, intending to make her an offer, but she'd already left for Herefordshire by then?"

"That's it, Montford! Good man!" Maybe Montford was a genius, after all.

"Christ." Grantham collapsed against his chair. "That was bloody exhausting."

"I don't know what you're complaining about, Grantham. I'm the one who has to go to the country. There's *mud* there. My boots will get muddy, and Lady Francesca's going to refuse me, and then I'm going to be standing about like a fool in ruined boots, without a betrothed."

"*Refuse* you?" Grantham gaped at him. "Don't be ridiculous, Basingstoke. She isn't going to refuse you. She hasn't any choice but to marry you. She's ruined."

Yes, but she didn't *know* she was ruined. Lady Crump had told him Lady Francesca left early this morning, and the *Cock and Bull* was an afternoon paper.

"Grantham's right, Basingstoke," Montford soothed. "Besides, every young lady wants to become a duchess."

Not Lady Francesca. She didn't care about being ruined. She'd told him so herself, and worse, she'd never been impressed with his dukery. Ducalness? "Perhaps I'd better have another drink."

"Good idea, Basingstoke. Ring for Trevor, Montford. Quickly, man. We need more brandy."

Montford tugged on the bell, and Trevor appeared instantly. "More brandy, Trevor!"

"Yes, right away, Your Graces!" Trevor hurried off, then returned a short time later bearing a tray with a fresh bottle of brandy and three tumblers.

Montford poured a generous measure into each of the tumblers, handed them around, then raised his glass. "To Basingstoke and his bride, Lady Francesca Stanhope!"

CHAPTER 19

The trouble with Herefordshire was that it was in the *country*.

Not the country in the way the leafier parts of London were the country, with a few extra trees in orderly rows or an unnecessary patch of grass here and there—but the proper English countryside, with all the accompanying distressing details.

Tedium. Insects. Sheep.

Giles shuddered. Horrible, wooly, unpredictable creatures. And the mud!

He gripped the strap and held on for dear life as Fenwick, his driver, careened over one rutted, muddy cow path after another. At this rate, he'd have to have his carriage resprung, and that was to say nothing of the damage being inflicted on his horses.

Of course, Lady Francesca couldn't have simply remained at Lady Crump's townhouse in Berkeley Square. No, she had to send him scurrying about the countryside, chasing her into every godforsaken corner of England. He should have known she'd find some way to make courting her as difficult as possible.

Courtships were a devil of a business, even under the best of circumstances.

Courting the reluctant daughter of the lady whose husband

his father had murdered in a duel—the lady whose happiness his father had destroyed forever—all while navigating the wilds of Herefordshire *weren't* the best of circumstances. Then there was that radish business. What were the odds Lady Francesca had forgiven him for that?

"Where in God's name *are* we, Fenwick?" He had to shout through the vent to be heard above the rattling and squeaking of the carriage wheels. He didn't like to open his mouth, as the dirt was already thick upon his tongue, but they'd been bouncing along for ages. They must be nearing the border of Scotland by now. "You're quite certain we haven't missed it?"

"Yes, Your Grace. Ashwell is south of Bedford, and we haven't reached Bedford yet."

"Ashwell?" He would have sworn it was Ashfield, and God knew there were a great many fields rolling by outside the carriage window. "Aren't we going to Ashfield?"

"I don't believe so, Your Grace. I've never heard of an Ashfield in Herefordshire, but there's an Ashwell, right enough. We can't be more than a few miles away now."

A few miles. He could manage a few miles, and once he'd bundled Lady Francesca into his carriage and carted her back to civilization, he needn't ever give either Ashfield—or Ashwell, for that matter—another thought.

He settled back against the squabs, his fingers still clutching the strap, and gritted his teeth against the abuse the deplorable state of the roads was inflicting upon his backside.

It was another lifetime before the carriage began to slow. They'd passed a pretty little village a few miles back, with a church rather more handsome than one might expect in a country hamlet like this, but they'd left behind any pretensions to grandeur once they'd left High Street.

"Stop, Fenwick."

Fenwick pulled the horses to a stop in the middle of the

deserted lane and leapt down from the box. He appeared at the window a moment later. "Is something amiss, Your Grace?"

"This can't be right." He waved a hand at the series of dwellings separated from the narrow, rutted lane by nothing more than a scraggly hedge. "These are cottages."

"Yes, Your Grace. This is Woodforde Close."

That was the direction Lady Crump had given him, but surely Lady Maria and her daughter didn't live *here*? This was little more than a pitiful speck in the middle of a great swathe of mud, with a half dozen grimy white cottages floating atop it.

The scandal with his father had landed Lady Maria and her daughter in reduced circumstances, certainly. Everyone in London knew that. The *ton* had proclaimed to anyone who'd listen that they'd been ruined, but they tossed the word *ruined* about so indiscriminately, it had ceased to have much meaning.

But *this*, this was true ruination, in the bitterest sense of the word.

This, then, was what came of running afoul of his father. All of London had breathed a sigh of relief when the wicked bones of the Seventh Duke of Basingstoke had been consigned to the Drew family tomb, but Giles had only to look around him now to see that the damage his father had done had outlived him.

Everyone who'd ever crossed his father's path, anyone who'd ever been unfortunate enough to catch his attention, had suffered at his hands. It was staggering, really, to think of how many lives he'd ruined.

Was *still* ruining, even now, two years after he was dead and buried.

His father had done this to Lady Maria and her daughter, had reduced them to this, and then Stanhope had put the final nails in their coffin by allowing his own niece and his brother's widow to sink into the most abject poverty without lifting a single finger to help them.

"Shall I turn back, Your Grace?"

Giles let his gaze rove over the roofs of the cottages, the thatch sparse in places, and dripping from a recent downpour, before resting once again on his coachman's puzzled face. "No, Fenwick." There was no turning back now. It was a decade too late for that. "Go on. It's the last cottage at the end of the lane."

"Drat." Franny sat back on her heels, frowning down at the streak of mud she'd just transferred from her forehead to the sleeve of her gray dress. It was her last clean one. "We'll have to launder again."

"Aye, Ashwell's a dirty place this time of year." Hannah, their maid of all work, cast Franny a sidelong glance. "You haven't been in London so long you've forgotten that, have you?"

"No, but our little patch of it is rather dirtier than I remembered."

Hannah worked her way down the row, her big, raw hands firm around her trowel, turning over one neat patch of dirt after another. "No dirtier than London. Mrs. Cornelius says you can't walk down a street without wading through piles of horse dung as high as your hip."

Franny plunged her own trowel into the dirt, came up empty and gave another vicious stab, her arm aching, until at last the ground yielded up one of the bulbous vegetables she'd been digging for. "This is an absurd amount of work for a scant basket of pitiful turnips. I don't even *like* turnips." Did anyone? They tasted like soap.

Hannah grunted, and plunged her trowel into the dirt. "Ye'll be happy enough for 'em when winter arrives."

Franny let out her own grunt in reply. Happy, over turnips, boiled, roasted, and mashed? Turnip stew? Braised turnip and rutabaga? On the contrary, it was enough to put a lady off eating altogether.

She stared down at the gaping holes she'd left in the dirt, the shreds of dull purple turnip skins that remained buried blurring in front of her eyes. "She's getting worse."

There was no need to say anything more than that. Hannah knew what she meant, and who she meant, without her having to explain a thing. Her mother always grew weaker when the weather turned cold, her lungs struggling to take in even the shallowest breaths, but it was happening earlier this year, and the decline was sharper.

"She always does, when the weather turns," Hannah said evenly. "She's no worse off than she was this time last year."

Not long ago, there'd been a time when Hannah's reassurances would have comforted her, but she'd been in London long enough for the blinders to be torn from her eyes.

During the weeks she'd been gone, she'd thought about home every day. She'd longed to be here, tucked into her tiny bedchamber with the sloped roof, but in her mind's eye, the cottage had been cozy, comfortable—a trifle dim in the late afternoons, yes, as the drawing room windows faced east, but somehow, she'd managed to convince herself the light was restful, soothing.

But instead of the snug little nook she thought she'd left behind, when she returned home she found a shabby cottage with a cramped drawing room, narrow hallways with peeling wallpaper, the fireplace bricks blackened with soot, and spreading patches of damp staining the ceiling.

The cottage was dark and chilly, the furnishings threadbare. There was no coziness to be found here, no warmth. She might have borne that well enough, but as it turned out, one could be deceived when it came to their memories of *people*, too.

Especially the people they loved the most.

"She *is* worse than she was at this time last year, Hannah.

She's worse than she was just last *month*, before I left for London, and there's not a thing that can be done about it!" Fury and panic curled into a tight, hot ball in the center of her chest. Her fingers tightened around the trowel, and the next thing she knew, she'd hurled it halfway across the garden. "What's the use, Hannah? What's the use of anything?"

There was no help forthcoming from her uncle Edward—not now, and not ever. Even now, days later, she shuddered to recall his face, scarlet with fury, and the high-pitched wails of her aunt Edith. She might not have done the horrible things her uncle had accused her of doing, but given how drastically wrong things had gone, it was difficult not to feel she was guilty of something quite dreadful, indeed.

Hannah said nothing, but rose calmly to her feet, stepped over the furrowed rows of the vegetable garden, and picked up the trowel. She studied it for a moment, then held it up. "Look at that. You got one."

There, caught on the tip of the trowel was a single, muddy, pathetic little radish. Franny stared at it, tears clogging her throat, but she sucked in a breath and choked them back. Weeping had never done her much good before, and it wouldn't now, either. "I did, didn't I? Perhaps I should spend less time digging, and more time throwing things."

"No harm in tossing a few things about." Hannah marched back across the garden, dumped the sad little radish into the basket, plucked the basket up from the ground, then settled her large, warm hand on Franny's shoulder. "You're worn out, is all it is. Wicked old London took it out of you, you poor thing. I'm going in to fetch your mother's tea. You come in when you're ready."

Franny nodded, then reached up to squeeze Hannah's hand, but once Hannah had gone, her shoulders sagged, and the foolish, useless tears she'd been fighting since she returned to Ashwell began to leak from the corners of her eyes.

They had enough money to get through the winter. Barely. If nothing went wrong, and something *always* went wrong.

The one bit of good news was that their situation wasn't *quite* as dire as it had been before she'd gone to London. After that dreadful scene at her uncle Edward's, she'd bid Lady Crump a tearful good-bye, but before she left London behind, she'd had her ladyship's coachman stop at a jeweler in Piccadilly, and she'd sold them the cameo Susannah had given her.

It had hurt terribly to let it go a second time instead of giving it back to her mother, as she'd longed to do, but the cameo, as precious as it was, would do little to soothe them when there was no tea or bread in the house.

It had fetched a nice sum. Enough to pay off their debts with the tradespeople in Ashwell, with a few coins left. Soon enough, however, they'd be right back where they'd started, and short of leaving her mother and Hannah here alone and going out to work, she hadn't any idea what could be done about it. If it did come to that, Lady Crump would help her find a proper place, but until such a time came, she didn't intend to breathe a word to her mother about it.

Not about *any* of it, in fact.

Not Uncle Edward, or Susannah, or Lord Ormsby, or the Duke of Basingstoke.

Certainly, not about the Duke of Basingstoke.

It was best if her mother remained ignorant about what had transpired in London. It wasn't good for her to become agitated, and she couldn't fret over what she didn't know. It wasn't as if Franny was telling a lie, keeping it from her. It was a little harmless omission, nothing more. They were useful, practical things, on occasion.

No, she'd simply have to work this mess out for herself. She'd find a way to make it work. She always did.

She just had to *think*. So, she plopped down onto her backside in the middle of the dirt, heedless of the damp, drew her knees up and dropped her chin onto her folded arms.

The steady drizzle falling from the sky was turning her vegetable bed to mud, but she remained where she was, considering ways to get them out of their predicament, then discarding them just as quickly, her head spinning, until at last she became aware of a familiar clopping sound coming up the rutted pathway that led to the cottage.

Horses? It sounded like it, and the rattle of carriage wheels. Theirs was the farthest dwelling down this road, but they rarely received visitors, and certainly not those who could afford to keep a carriage.

She leapt to her feet, her heart thumping as the sound of the hooves splashing through the muck drew closer, until at last a pair of equine heads emerged from the tunnel of overgrown trees overhanging the lane, and behind it, a carriage, a very fine one done in a handsome black lacquer, the wheels painted in dazzling shades of scarlet and gold.

Scarlet and gold. Scarlet and gold . . .

She froze, everything but her mouth, which dropped open in shock.

Helios, and his winged chariot!

But *no*. It couldn't be. It simply couldn't be. It was impossible.

There was no reason in the world to suppose it was *him*. There must be dozens of carriages with scarlet and gold wheels in London.

Hundreds of them.

There was a crest emblazoned on the door, but she was too great a distance away to make it out, and soon enough the carriage vanished behind the tall hedge that lined the road.

She hiked her skirts in her hands and dashed across the garden, heedless of the thick mud splattering her hems and clinging to the soles of her half boots. The vegetable gardens were quite a distance from the cottage, and by the time she reached the drive she was gasping for breath, and both the passenger and the driver had disappeared inside.

She flew toward the door, her heart thumping anxiously, rattling inside her chest with every beat. It took very little for her mother to become overwhelmed, and the sudden appearance of a duke in her tiny drawing room was overwhelming, indeed.

Especially *that* duke.

"Mother!" The front door hit the wall with a crash as she rushed through it, then bounced back to slam shut behind her. "Hannah?" She rushed down the short hallway leading to the drawing room, the soles of her half boots so slippery with mud her feet skidded out from underneath her with every step, until at last she came to a stop.

Dear God, what was she seeing?

A broad-shouldered, fair-haired gentleman in fawn-colored pantaloons, an impeccably cut dark brown coat, and tall black boots polished to a high gloss was standing in their cramped drawing room. His back was to her, but she didn't need to see his face to know who he was.

There was only one gentleman in all of England who could make it through the mud and muck of the Hertfordshire countryside without getting a speck of dirt on his boots, and he was bowing over her mother's hand.

"Francesca, my dear." Her mother's gaze met hers over the golden head, her eyes as wide as saucers in her pale face. "We, ah . . . we have a visitor."

Upon hearing her name, he turned, a handsome, charming

smile upon his handsome, charming lips, his long, lean body bent in a handsome, charming bow. "Lady Francesca. How perfectly lovely to see you again."

Of course, it was *him*. Only *he* could have so intimidated the Herefordshire mud that it was too frightened to besmirch his boots.

None other than His Grace himself, the Duke of Basingstoke.

CHAPTER 20

"May I help you to tea, Your Grace? I daresay you're fatigued after coming all this way from London."

Tea. Her mother had just offered tea to the Duke of Basingstoke.

"Thank you, Lady Stanhope. Tea would be delight—"

"No!" There would be no tea, and no delight. Not while she was here to put a stop to it.

"Francesca!" Her mother stared at her, appalled.

Franny's cheeks heated. "I mean, er, what I meant to say, Mother, is I'm certain whatever brings the duke to Ashwell won't permit him to make a long visit. Isn't that right, Your Grace?"

"Not at all, Lady Francesca. Indeed, I have important business in Ashwell, and I intend to remain here for as long as it takes to bring it to a successful conclusion. Weeks, if necessary." The duke gave her his most maddening smile. "I am a trifle parched, after the drive. I'd be delighted to join you for tea, Lady Stanhope. You're very kind."

"Wonderful." Her mother smiled. "Do sit down, Your Grace."

Incredibly, he had the gall to accept her mother's invitation. He took the place on the settee closest to the fire—her *mother*'s place, the villain—crossed his long legs, and sat there chatting politely about the journey from London and the weather in Herefordshire, as if it were perfectly normal for a duke to happen down a remote cow path deep in the country, and pop inside for a bit of refreshment.

"You became acquainted with Francesca while she was in London, I presume, Your Grace?" her mother asked, passing him a cup of tea.

Franny jumped in before he could utter a word. "His Grace is a passing acquaintance. Nothing more." A passing acquaintance she'd dreamed about kissing, yes, but that was neither here nor there.

"Would you call it merely a passing acquaintance, Lady Francesca? It was more than that, I think."

Had he just fluttered his eyelashes at her? Why, what did the man *mean*, fluttering at her like a coquette at a country fair? She gritted her teeth. "I would call it a passing acquaintance, Your Grace, if even that."

He took a small sip of his tea. With every brush of his beautiful, ducal lips against the edge of her mother's faded rose-patterned teacup, Franny's temper was rising. At least, her temperature was. It was wretchedly warm in here.

His full, firm lips pursed in a pout that made heat flood her cheeks. "I rather hoped you looked upon me as a gentleman, er . . . friend, my lady."

A gentleman *friend*? Young ladies didn't have gentlemen friends, they had gentleman *callers*. Dear God, did he mean to imply he was—

"As it happens, Lady Stanhope, my mother is well acquainted with Lady Crump, so your daughter and I were quite thrown together these past weeks. Calls, promenades, a musical evening, dancing together at balls—"

No, her feelings for him weren't at all *friendly*. "We danced once, Your Grace. *Once*."

"Ah, but it was a memorable dance, was it not, my lady?"

He gazed at her, and let out a long, deep sigh—a lovelorn sigh, as if he was . . .

Pining. *Pining*, for her!

She gulped down some tea, her eyes watering when it scalded her throat. "Indeed, I hardly remember it."

Her mother looked between them with a baffled expression. It made no sense at all that a gentleman—a duke, no less—should come all the way from London to tiny, insignificant Ashwell to call on a young lady he hardly knew.

"It was a cotillion. You told me I'd given you the very thing you wanted most when you came to London. Do you not recall it, my lady? I do. Quite clearly, indeed." He smoldered at her over the edge of his teacup, his gaze holding her captive, but underneath the flirtation, his blue eyes burned with resolve.

She caught her breath.

Whatever it was the duke had come for, he didn't intend to leave without it.

Lady Maria Stanhope *should* have despised him on sight. Given how closely he resembled his villain of a father, she should have shoved him off her front steps and onto his arse in the mud, then slammed the door in his face.

As it happened, Lady Maria Stanhope was a tiny, fragile lady, and so frail she couldn't have menaced a butterfly, much less have tackled a large duke, but the servant who'd gone to fetch the tea—a solid lady with the hands of a bare-knuckle boxer—might have made quick work of him.

But he wasn't assaulted, insulted, or even frowned upon. Not by Lady Maria, that is.

Lady Francesca, on the other hand, was hostile enough for all three of them.

Passing acquaintances, indeed. Lady Fishburne was one of

his passing acquaintances, and he wasn't tormented with erotic dreams about *her*.

"May I offer you more tea, Your Grace? Francesca, would you see if Hannah has any fresh scones? I'm sure the duke would enjoy—"

"There are no scones, I'm afraid." Lady Francesca crossed her arms over her chest, her frigid gaze on him. "Alas, not a single scone."

"Some bread and cheese instead of the scones, then."

Lady Francesca opened her mouth, no doubt to unleash her tart tongue upon him—perhaps to hint that if he wished for tea, he might return to his grand townhouse in London for it—but Lady Maria raised an eyebrow at her, and her mouth closed with a snap.

"If you'd be so good as to go and see, Francesca?"

Lady Francesca rose with a huff and left the room.

Silencing Lady Francesca, with a mere quirk of an eyebrow? That *was* a neat trick. He'd pay a king's ransom to have Lady Maria teach it to him. He and Lady Francesca would have to come to terms somehow or other, as it wouldn't do for them to be at each other's throats once they were married. Such a skill as that would contribute greatly to their chances of wedded bliss.

"My lady." The large woman with the stooped shoulders and the enormous, raw-knuckled hands marched into the drawing room, with Lady Francesca trailing after her. The servant—Hannah—plonked a tray down onto a wobbly table, paused only long enough to cast a suspicious look at him, then marched back out again without a word.

"Here we are, Your Grace." Lady Maria poured another measure of weak tea into his cup and passed it to him. "Are you comfortable? I daresay you're chilled to the bone, traveling on such a blustery day!"

"Quite comfortable, my lady, thank you." He *wasn't* comfortable in the least, of course, because there was no comfort to be had in this room.

The chair Lady Maria had offered him looked like it was one duke's arse away from collapsing entirely, but a discreet glance told him it was the sturdiest of the furnishings in the room, and the room itself was . . . well, there was no other word for it but *grim*.

The cottage was tiny and dark, and so damp and cold it must be pure misery in the winter months. If he could judge by the pallor of Lady Maria's cheeks, her skeletal hands, it had taken a drastic toll on her health.

All this time, he'd persisted in thinking himself and his family the primary victims of his father's perfidy—

"How does your mother do, Your Grace? Did she accompany you to Herefordshire?"

"No, I'm afraid business kept her from it." The business of spiriting his sisters off to Kent, that is, in what would doubtless prove a vain attempt to outrun his scandal.

"What a pity. We were . . ." Lady Maria trailed off, her pale cheeks flushing. "We were dear friends, at one time."

"Yes, she speaks of you fondly, my lady, and sends her best." Or she would have done, if she'd known he was coming here at all, but there was no reason for his mother to know a damned thing about any of this until he'd secured Lady Francesca's hand.

And secure it he would, despite the frosty glances she was casting his way. No matter, he'd thaw her out soon enough.

A perfectly innocent thawing, of course. For the most part.

"And your sisters, Your Grace? Francesca mentioned to me Lady Diana is in the midst of her first season. I daresay she's taking great pleasure in it."

Oh yes, as much pleasure as any young lady whose every girlish dream has been shattered. Those tear tracks on her cheeks, her repeated assurances that his scandal wasn't to blame for her heartbreak. Just thinking about it was enough to make him long for his brandy bottle. "She, ah . . . yes, of course, it's been very . . . the season can be overwhelming for a young lady, as you know, Lady Maria, but Diana has taken nicely."

Or she had taken, before he'd destroyed all her hopes.

"It's difficult for the young ladies, isn't it? I was terrified to embark upon my first season, but Francesca never hesitated when Lady Crump was kind enough to offer her a chance at her own." Lady Maria beamed at her daughter, glowing with pride. "But then Francesca's never been afraid of anything, not even when she was a girl."

That he could believe. Lady Francesca had the nerve of a cavalry commander. She'd make an admirable duchess, if she ever learned to hold her tongue. "It's a pity Lady Francesca's season came to such an abrupt end. I trust your health has improved, my lady?"

"My health?" Lady Maria darted a glance at her daughter, her brow creased. "Forgive me, Your Grace, but I don't under—"

"Shall I fetch more tea, Mother?" Lady Francesca leapt to her feet and snatched up the plate on the tea tray. "More scones?"

"I thought you said there were no scones, Francesca." Lady Maria gave her daughter a narrow look.

"Er, well, we do have a duke in the house, Mother. I'm sure Hannah's made some up by now. If you'll excuse me, I'll be right back." Lady Francesca fled the drawing room as if her heels were ablaze, leaving him and Lady Maria staring after her.

A few stunned moments passed, then Lady Maria cleared her throat. "I beg your pardon for my daughter's behavior, Your Grace. I can't imagine what's come over her."

"Forgive me, Lady Maria, but I was under the impression Lady Francesca was obliged to return to Herefordshire on account of your health." Or so Lady Crump had told him, and he had no reason to think she hadn't believed it to be the real reason.

Had Lady Francesca been telling lies, then?

"My health is indifferent, Your Grace, but it hasn't taken any significant turn recently." Lady Maria glanced at the door through which her daughter had just fled, her expression troubled. "I didn't send for Francesca to return home."

Lying to Lady Crump, and to her own mother, and keeping secrets from them both? My, Lady Francesca *was* wicked, wasn't she? It made one wonder what other secrets she was keeping, and from whom.

It couldn't be a coincidence she'd left town so quickly after Lady Susannah had run away with Lord Ormsby. Had she had a hand in it, then? She'd been the one to offer Lady Susannah's excuses the night she'd disappeared from Lady Sandham's ball, and they'd gone off on some mysterious errand to the ladies' retiring room just before that.

Had Lady Susannah confessed to her cousin she was leaving with Lord Ormsby that night? Had Lady Francesca encouraged her to flee? If so, then she'd played a part in breaking Diana's heart.

Not to mention making an utter fool of *him*. She owed him a bride, damn it.

A step sounded in the corridor outside the drawing room, and both he and Lady Maria turned to see Lady Francesca in the entryway, a plate of scones in her hand.

She hesitated for an instant, her eyes meeting his before skittering away again, then she hurried across the room and plunked the plate down on the table. "I, ah, I beg your pardon. I must have overlooked these before."

"Er, thank you, Francesca."

Lady Francesca returned to her seat, folded her hands together tightly, and rested them on her lap, every line of her body tense.

Lady Maria did her best to keep the conversation going as

they each choked down a scone and another cup of tea, chatting determinedly about the weather and a variety of other innocuous topics, but Lady Francesca remained stubbornly silent.

By the time they'd finished the tea, poor Lady Maria had given up trying to prod them into the niceties, and had fallen into a baffled silence. Meanwhile, Lady Francesca was gaping at him as if she thought she could guess what he was doing here if she only stared at him hard enough.

It was most disconcerting.

"Tell us, Your Grace, what brings you to Herefordshire on such a rainy afternoon?"

Lady Francesca's voice was like a pistol shot, and he startled, choking on the bite of scone he'd just taken.

"Oh, dear. Are you quite alright, Your Grace?" Lady Maria retrieved his teacup, filled it with lukewarm tea, and passed it to him. "Please have some more tea."

"Thank you, my lady." He gulped down some tea and cleared his throat, while Lady Francesca watched him with narrowed blue eyes, no doubt hoping he'd choke.

Such an unusual blue, her eyes, so clear, and somehow bright and dark at once. How had she referred to that color, again?

Dragonfly blue.

The same blue as her cousin's eyes. It was strange, really, that the two ladies could so closely resemble each other, and yet the experience of looking into Lady Francesca's eyes could be so different than looking into Lady Susannah's.

Had he ever looked into Lady Susannah's eyes? If he had, he couldn't recall it.

Perhaps that's why she'd run off with Ormsby.

Lady Francesca, on the other hand . . . he could recall with perfect clarity the first time he'd looked into her eyes, that night he'd caught her prowling about like a thief in Stanhope's garden. It had been too dark to get more than a glimpse into them, but even then, before he knew her name or had even properly seen her face, that brief flicker of blue had put an ache in the center of his chest, and another in his groin.

Of course, the second time he'd looked into her eyes she'd refused to tell him her name, and then she'd treated him to a scold that made his ears ring.

"Your Grace? What brings you to Herefordshire?" Lady Maria, who was clearly trying to puzzle out what had passed between him and her daughter, repeated Lady Francesca's earlier question. "You said you have some business here in Ashwell?"

Ah. Now they were coming down to it. Lady Maria was too polite to ask outright, but she wanted to know what he was doing here, in their cottage, drinking up all their tea and eating their scones, all while engaging in an excruciatingly polite argument with her daughter.

Now it had come down to it, there was no sense in dancing around it, was there? "I do, yes, my lady. My business . . ." He hesitated, glancing at Lady Francesca. "My business, Lady Maria, concerns your daughter. I've come to Ashwell for *her*."

There could be no mistaking his meaning.

No one moved. No one even appeared to breathe for what felt like an eternity.

But then Lady Francesca leapt to her feet, this time with such force she knocked the tea tray off the wobbly little table and sent the plate with the remaining scones on it crashing to the floor. "Would you care to take a stroll in the gardens, Your Grace? I daresay you'd appreciate the chance to stretch your legs before you *return to London*."

Well, that was plain enough.

He glanced out the window. The slice of sky visible through a gap in the worn draperies was a sulky gray, drops of rain splattering the glass. There'd be mud in the garden to contend with, and quite possibly sheep.

There was still time to leave, to return to London and forget his designs on Lady Francesca. It had been pure madness, coming here, a moment of utter foolishness born at the bottom of an empty bottle of brandy.

Yet when he rose to his feet and opened his mouth, he didn't take his leave. Instead, he stepped over the broken plate of scones and offered his arm to Lady Francesca. "I'd be delighted to walk with you, my lady."

He wasn't going anywhere. Not without her.

Lady Francesca Stanhope *would* become the next Duchess of Basingstoke.

She simply didn't know it yet.

CHAPTER 21

The Duke of Basingstoke was too handsome for Hereford-shire.

Franny paused outside the front door, the cold rain dripping down the back of her neck, resentment swelling in her chest as she took him in from the top of his shining head to the tips of what were no doubt his maddeningly magnificent toes.

He was too tall, too golden haired, too fashionable, too everything.

It was *offensive* that all that perfection should be concentrated in a single man.

It was one thing for him to appear to such advantage in a ballroom. He *was* a duke, after all. He was meant to be tall, elegant and handsome. His flawlessly tailored coats were meant to stretch seamlessly over his broad shoulders, his breeches to display the long, lean muscles of his calves and cling like a second skin to his bulging thighs—

No, dash it. There would be no ogling his thighs. No notice taken of his thighs in any way. Certainly, no notice taken of any bulging.

But this was the *country*. By every rule of fair play, he should look absurd standing about the yard in his fine coat and blindingly white cravat.

But dukes were immune to such things, evidently. *She* might look tragically out of place amongst the *ton*, like a kitchen maid who'd stumbled into a glittering ballroom, but *he* somehow contrived to look like a blooming rose atop a pile of. . . well, muddy radishes.

Even the rain couldn't dampen his appeal. The skies had unleashed a cold, miserable drizzle upon them, but instead of plastering his fair hair to his head in an unflattering mash, the droplets clung to his thick eyelashes, making them sparkle like stars.

Then there was the mud. The cottage yard was overflowing with it. The stone fence, the rough boards of the ramshackle shed, the pails and hoes and shovels were all splattered with it. One step into that quagmire should have been the end of those shiny boots of his, but of course, the humble country muck wouldn't dare sully Helios's spotless Hessians.

Not so, her own boots, or any other part of her. The cuffs of her sleeves and the hems of her skirt were all caked with mud, and there was a suspiciously itchy patch on her forehead. It could only be more mud, which meant she'd missed a spot when she'd washed up.

She must look a fright, like she'd been rolling around in the garden beds.

It wasn't *fair*—

"Why are you looking at me like that, Lady Francesca?"

His deep voice startled her from her seething. "Looking at you? Don't be absurd. I'm not looking at you." She certainly hadn't been gaping at his thighs, no matter what he—

He squinted at her. "Yes, you are, and with the strangest expression, as if you're calculating my measurements in order to determine which part of your garden will best accommodate my lifeless body."

"Nonsense." She didn't want a thing to do with his body.

"I was merely trying to decide where we should walk. You did say you wished to walk, did you not, Your Grace?"

He glanced at the ocean of mud spread out before them and shuddered. "Er, well—"

"Come, Your Grace. I'll take you through our garden." Their vegetable garden, that is. There wasn't a single flower to be had there, only rows upon rows of mounded dirt, the furrows between them inches deep with rainwater.

Even *his* boots couldn't withstand such a dousing as that.

"Very well." He drew her arm through his, wincing at the wet squelch of their footsteps as she led him deeper into the garden. "It's a great pleasure to meet your mother, Lady Francesca. I can understand why my mother speaks so highly of Lady Maria. She's gracious and kind."

"She is, indeed." Far *too* kind, really. If her mother had been any less so, he would never have made it into the drawing room, but she wouldn't dream of turning a visitor away, even the son of the man who'd ruined her. She simply wasn't the sort of lady who'd blame the son for his father's crimes, even when she'd been the victim of them.

"These are the potatoes. This row, and that one, there." She pointed at a long furrow of upturned earth. "They were harvested already, in the latter part of the summer."

"Potatoes? Yes, ah, an admirable vegetable, indeed."

The Duke of Basingstoke didn't, of course, give a single thought to potatoes beyond their appearing at his dinner table properly seasoned and buttered, but he was going to get a lesson on root vegetables regardless, if only to prevent him from broaching the real reason he'd come to Ashwell.

Her.

Short of dropping to one knee in the middle of their drawing room, he couldn't have made his intentions any clearer. Her mother's eyes had nearly popped from her head, which was hardly surprising, given Franny hadn't breathed a single word about the Duke of Basingstoke since she'd returned home.

As far as her mother knew, she'd never even laid eyes on the duke. She must have been shocked indeed to find him suddenly in their shabby drawing room, drinking all their tea and quibbling over scones.

My business concerns your daughter. I've come to Ashwell for her.

Dear God, she'd nearly sprayed her mouthful of tea everywhere when he'd said that.

As for her heart, well, it may as well give up its foolish fluttering at once. Handsome dukes didn't chase penniless young ladies into the country to beg for their hands in marriage because they were in love with them.

This wasn't a romantic novel, for pity's sake. Young ladies with mud smeared across their foreheads *didn't* become duchesses. No, this was all merely another of the duke's charades, much like the one they'd enacted for the *ton* over the past few weeks, except this particular charade wasn't simply a promenade in Hyde Park, or a dance at a ball.

Marriage, to the Duke of Basingstoke? That charade would require nothing less than the rest of her life.

It was, of course, out of the question. The sooner he understood that, the sooner he'd ascend his chariot and be on his merry way back to London, where he belonged.

Still, there was no harm in helping him along, was there?

She began to search for furrows with puddles so deep the silver tassels on his boots would never recover. "Here, Your Grace, are the radishes."

"The, ah, the radishes?"

"Yes. Have you something you wish to say about the radishes, Your Grace? Some clever observation you wish to make upon their color, perhaps, or some ingenious comparison you wish to draw between radishes and something else?"

"God, no. I learned my lesson, I assure you."

He gave her a lopsided smile that set her silly, naïve heart aflutter once again, but she ignored the pattering against her ribs and continued to make her way through the garden. "This is garlic, right here, and onions just beside them, here."

"You can't imagine my disappointment, Lady Francesca, when I discovered from Lady Crump that you'd left London so suddenly, weeks before the end of the season."

"You were disappointed to find *I'd* gone? What of Susannah, Your Grace? I would think the sudden departure of *your betrothed* would have been a great deal more disappointing to you."

He shrugged. "Less so than you might think."

She paused beside the onions, biting back a curse as icy water seeped through the thin soles of her half boots. "My, you *are* cheerful, for a gentleman who's just been jilted. One might think you never really cared for Susannah at all."

But she'd suspected that from the start, hadn't she? He was a proper suitor, and would undoubtedly have been a proper enough husband, but the duke's heart was far from broken at Susannah's defection.

Really, Susannah had done them both a favor, leaving London as she had.

"I wish Lady Susannah and Lord Ormsby joy, but you see, my lady, I find myself rather unexpectedly without a bride, just as I'm most in need of one, and—"

"Carrots, Your Grace, just here—"

"—fortunately for me, I knew at once where I might find a blue-eyed, sharp-tongued lady who—"

"We have beets, as well, right next to the carrots!" She tugged her arm free of his and hurried down the row. Yes, it was better to put some distance between them, before that low, coaxing voice of his muddled her thoughts and made her want things she shouldn't.

But he followed her and caught her wrist, stilling her.

"Stop it, Francesca. I didn't come all the way to Ashwell to hear about—"

"Rutabagas!" she cried, rather desperately. "Do you care for rutabagas, Your Grace?"

"No. I don't care to eat them, and I care even less to talk about them. I don't give a damn about rutabagas. I came to Ashwell for one reason. I came for *you*, to ask you to marry me."

"Marry you?" She'd known it was coming, of course, and the only proper response was a robust refusal, but instead what came out of her mouth was, "Did you really just offer your hand to me in the same breath as you cursed rutabagas?"

His lips twitched. "That depends. If I did, does it make it more or less likely you'll accept me?"

She sighed. "Come now, Your Grace. You must see how absurd this is. You can't simply fit me into my cousin's place, now that Susannah's run off with Lord Ormsby."

"Is that what you think this is?" He threw his head back in a laugh. "Are you under the illusion, Lady Francesca, that you and your cousin are anything alike? The similarities between you begin and end with your dark hair and blue eyes."

"Well, why are you pestering me to marry you, then? Has it slipped your mind, Your Grace, that you're the Duke of Basingstoke, and may have your choice of the most beautiful young ladies in London?"

"I don't want a beautiful young lady. I want *you*."

She choked out a laugh. "Why, how charming you are, Your Grace! What lady could possibly say no to such a flattering offer?"

"I didn't mean . . . for God's sake, you know very well I didn't mean that the way it sounded. Now, don't make a fuss, and let's get on with it, there's a good girl."

A *fuss*? God above. "I think, Your Grace, that your wits have quite deserted you."

Perhaps he really *did* want to marry her, or he thought he

did, but even if that was the case, it wasn't for the right reasons. He didn't truly want *her*, but only to achieve the same ends he'd set out to achieve by marrying Susannah. "Is the recent gossip in the scandal sheets behind this sudden proposal of yours?"

His blue eyes narrowed, his gaze sharpening on her face. "What gossip?"

"The gossip my arrival in London occasioned, of course." What other gossip was there? "The day you called on me at Lady Crump's, you told me you offered for Susannah in part to mend the rift between our families. Now that she's gone off with Lord Ormsby, in order to silence the *ton* for good on the subject of your father's crimes, you need to marry *me*."

"Francesca—may I call you Francesca, now we're to be wed?"

"Wed! You forget, Your Grace, that I haven't accepted you."

"Not yet."

Not ever. Perhaps it made sense for the Duke of Basingstoke to marry according to the whims of the *ton*, but aside from Lady Crump, she didn't owe society a blasted thing, and she wouldn't marry to please them.

She wouldn't marry to please anyone but herself.

"I don't deny I wish to see the past put to rest, Francesca. Is it truly so terrible if that *is* one reason I wish to marry you? Surely, you must see a marriage between us would benefit us both?"

She looked around her, at the sodden, muddy field that served as their garden, the endless rows of vegetables that would make up the majority of their winter table. She glanced behind her at their dilapidated little cottage. The roof was sagging, the thatching wearing thin in places, and the chill in the drawing room grew more pronounced with every successive winter, and today, they'd been obliged to serve him tea without sugar or cream, the tea leaves weak from being used twice already.

Shamed heat scalded her cheeks. How pitiful they must seem to him. How amazed he must be, that a lady with so little to hope for would even think to refuse him. "Do you mean to say, Your Grace, that you offer for me out of pity?"

"No!" He seized her hands. "I could never pity you, Francesca, but you must see what a great difference our marriage would make in your circumstances. Your mother's health alone—"

"My mother told you not an hour ago that while her health is indifferent, she hasn't taken any recent significant turn for the worse—"

"But that's not the truth, is it?" His fingers tightened around hers. "She needs better care than she can get in Ashwell. The advice of a London doctor could do wonders for her, and perhaps a few months in Bath, or Brighton."

"It's time you returned to London, Your Grace." She withdrew her hands from his. "I'm sorry you made such an uncomfortable journey for nothing."

"It's too late for me to return to London. I intend to spend the night in Ashwell, at the Three Tuns. May I have your permission to call on you and your mother again tomorrow?"

She shook her head. "I don't see any point—"

"I wonder what Lady Maria would think, Lady Francesca, if she knew what you got up to while you were in London? I must say I'm shocked—*shocked*—to discover how little she seems to know of your antics. Running about Hyde Park without a chaperone, and climbing your uncle Edward's trees in the middle of the night? Lying to Lady Crump about your reasons for leaving?"

Her mouth dropped open. "Are you *blackmailing* me into letting you court me, Your Grace?"

"Why, what an ugly way to put it. I'm merely asking for one more day in hopes that you'll change your mind. If you insist upon my returning to London after tomorrow, I'll do as you say without argument, and I won't trouble you again."

She let out a defeated sigh. He was a perfect villain, but alas, he was a villain who knew a great deal more about what had transpired in London than she ever wanted her mother to know. "One day only. I make no promises beyond tomorrow."

"Very well. We have an agreement then, Lady Francesca."

He caught her hands again, raised one to his lips, and before she could tug free, he pressed a kiss to her knuckles.

They both froze.

It was a chaste kiss, the merest brush of his lips, so soft she hardly felt it, aside from the warm drift of his breath, but instantly every inch of her was clamoring for him, goosebumps rising to the surface of her skin. She caught her breath, the slight hitch of it carrying over the ceaseless pattering of the rain.

He heard it. His eyes darkened, and he brought her hand to his mouth once again.

She watched, mesmerized as the full, sensuous lips she'd dreamt of kissing parted over the back of her hand. This kiss was soft, as soft as a dragonfly's wing tickling her skin, but he lingered this time, a hint of damp heat as he stroked the tip of his tongue over her sensitive flesh.

By the time he withdrew, a delicious ache had bloomed deep in her belly, and her head was swimming with dizziness.

"Until tomorrow, my lady."

She nodded, breathless, and watched as he made his way across the soggy yard and climbed into his carriage. His driver set the horses' heads toward the village, and off they went, the carriage rattling over the rutted road.

She stood for a long time after he'd gone, the hand he'd kissed pressed to her chest, her heart shuddering against her palm before she ran back to the cottage, slipped inside and fell back against the door.

It was just a kiss, just a kiss . . .

"Francesca? Is that you?"

"Yes, Mother." She brought her hands to her cheeks, felt

the heat of her skin against her fingertips, and took in a long, slow breath before making her way to the drawing room, the hems of her skirt leaving a trail of damp across the stone floor.

Her mother had just woken from her afternoon doze. "Has the duke gone?"

"Yes, he . . . yes." *But before he left, he asked me to marry him, and I . . . refused?*

Dear God, had she really just refused the Duke of Basingstoke's hand?

Her mother waited, but when Franny said no more, she asked, "Back to London?"

"No. He's, ah, he's decided to spend the night at the Three Tuns tonight. He'll come back tomorrow morning to say . . . er, good-bye."

Among other things.

"Well, then. I'll look forward to seeing him tomorrow. He's terribly handsome, isn't he?"

"He's, ah . . . well, he's very, er . . ." For pity's sake, she sounded like a besotted schoolgirl. "I'm going upstairs to change out of my wet clothes, Mother."

"Yes, all right, dearest. Take your time."

Franny did take her time. The rest of the night, in fact, and her mother, bless her, didn't disturb her, but let her have her privacy.

But for all that she spent the rest of that afternoon, the evening, and most of the night thinking about him, she came to only one definitive conclusion about the Duke of Basingstoke.

She shouldn't have let him kiss her hand. That kiss was where the trouble had started. Before that kiss, she'd been quite resolved against him, but now . . .

Now, nothing. She was *still* resolved. Of course, she was.

Still, she should never have let his handsome lips anywhere near her. It was all shockingly improper, and if she hadn't let him kiss her hand, she wouldn't be lying in her bed right now, cursed with sleeplessness, reliving over and over again the moment when his warm lips brushed against her bare skin.

How could his lips have been so warm? It was *raining*, the November air raw and blustery. His lips should have been cold and wet, his kiss clammy, like a fish flopping against her hand, not a flutter of a dragonfly's wings, for pity's sake.

Instead, his kiss had seared her, his hot mouth like a brand against her flesh, and now she'd have to live with the memory of that kiss.

What would it have felt like, if he'd kissed her mouth?

She threw her arm over her eyes, groaning as sleep slipped further away.

CHAPTER 22

"What is the proper attire for a gentleman embarking on a country courtship, Digby?"

Hessians, or top boots? A wool coat, or linen? Navy blue, or black?

Digby, who'd arrived at the Three Tuns quite early this morning in response to Giles's summons, plucked up a pair of pantaloons from one of the two overflowing trunks he'd brought with him from London. "Er, beige kerseymere, Your Grace?"

Giles eyed the pantaloons. "Is that what a country gentleman wears to a wooing? Kerseymere?"

"I, ah, I can't say for certain, Your Grace, but it seems a logical choice."

"Logical? My dear Digby, what's courtship got to do with logic?" Nothing whatsoever, particularly when one was courting Lady Francesca Stanhope, as none of the usual things seemed to work with her. "You do understand, Digby, how essential it is that I get this right?"

"Yes, Your Grace, of course." Digby rummaged through the trunk again and held up another pair of pantaloons. "Nankin?"

"God, no." Giles waved the nankin pantaloons away. "I suppose the kerseymere will have to do."

"Very good, Your Grace."

"I trust you to put the rest of the costume together, Digby, but nothing too ducal, if you please." He hadn't missed the dark look his prospective betrothed had cast at him when they'd ventured into her garden yesterday. His pantaloons had seemed to earn her particular ire.

It was disconcerting, as dukes tended to receive warm welcomes wherever they went, but mightn't Lady Francesca have felt that same sort of discomfiture when she'd come to London—as if she'd landed somewhere she didn't belong, and wasn't welcome?

Had that only been a few weeks ago?

The pink gowns couldn't have made it any easier for her, to say nothing of his radish comment. A comment for which she didn't appear to have forgiven him.

He could only hope she approved of kerseymere. Otherwise, he'd be on his way back to London before teatime. He'd never before devoted so much thought as to how to best please a lady, but then he'd never had to. People tended to be pleased with him no matter what he did.

People other than Lady Francesca Stanhope, that is. She was the exception to every rule, it seemed.

But of course, it wasn't really his clothing that mattered. It hadn't been his Hessians she'd rejected yesterday, but *him*. A bloody unpleasant shock it had been, too. Until she'd ordered him to return to London, he'd never given a thought to the possibility that she'd actually *refuse* him.

Young ladies didn't *refuse* to marry dukes, for God's sake, particularly not young ladies who were facing a long, comfortless winter in a chilly cottage and a steady diet of root vegetables to dine upon.

Those damnable potatoes, and that cheerless drawing room, with nary a decent chair to sit upon, and Lady Maria's drawn, pale face behind that cracked teapot full of weak tea . . .

He was a selfish man, perhaps, and he'd come to Ashwell for selfish reasons. When he and his coachman had set out for Herefordshire, he'd thought only of his family's honor, his reputation, the ruin of Diana's season, and her future prospects.

But when he'd arrived in Woodforde Close and witnessed for himself how Francesca and her mother lived, it had changed everything.

He wasn't a monster, nor was he a fool. If it hadn't been for Frederick Drew, Lady Maria and her daughter would be living a very different life than the one they were obliged to live now. What had happened to them had been an undoing, a ruination, while his blackguard of a father had gone on his merry way, never thinking twice about the damage he'd wrought, or all he'd taken from them.

Nothing short of everything.

But he wouldn't do the same. He *couldn't*. He simply could not leave them here in such dire circumstances, no matter how determined Francesca was to force him to go. She was as prickly as a porcupine, and it wouldn't be an easy matter to win her over, but he'd do whatever he must to see to it that when he returned to London, Francesca and her mother would be with him.

Including lying.

The lady didn't yet know she was ruined, as she'd left London to return to Herefordshire before she'd seen the *Cock and Bull*. The proper thing—the *honest* thing—would be for him to tell her all of it, leaving nothing out, including the conversation he'd overheard at Madame Laurent's that day, and the fact that he'd been the one who'd sent her the blue silk ball gown.

But if he did, if he did . . .

She'd never agree to marry him. She'd think he was using her to restore his own reputation, and that would be the end of any chance he had of making her his duchess.

And to be fair, wasn't that precisely what he was doing? Using her?

It had begun that way, yes, but that was before he'd—

"I have it, Your Grace!" Digby, who'd been rummaging around in the trunks, was holding up a selection of clothing for Giles's inspection. "Will this do, Your Grace?"

Ah yes, his courting costume.

"The kerseymere pantaloons, a plain linen shirt—no ducal ruffles, Your Grace—your cravat tied *a la Oriental*—very plain, Your Grace—a dark brown linen coat—dark brown being a country color, Your Grace—with dark brown top boots." Digby beamed.

"No waistcoat?"

Digby sobered. "The waistcoat is a tricky garment, Your Grace. I've given it a good deal of thought, and I think you might forgo it, although I own it's a risk."

"Very well, Digby, we'll leave off the waistcoat. Now help me dress, and I'll be on my way."

For better or worse, he was going courting.

He'd been so anxious about looking the part of the proper suitor, he hadn't given much thought at all to what he'd *do* with Francesca once he arrived at the cottage. "Well, Lady Francesca, how shall we amuse ourselves today?"

"Isn't it up to the gentleman to manage the courtship, Your Grace?"

Cheeky chit. "I believe so, my lady, but as this is only my second day in Ashwell, perhaps you'll advise me." Country courtships seemed to be limited to walking, as there wasn't much else to do, aside from climb trees, and she'd already mastered that skill.

"Oh, but I wouldn't dare attempt to advise a duke, Your Grace, and our humble country amusements would likely only bore you. How do you amuse yourself in London?"

"I ride, or promenade, or go to White's, or the theater. The usual ways. I did take my younger sisters to Astley's

Amphitheater last week. That was rather more entertaining than I'd expected."

"Astley's Amphitheater! How wonderful! I *so* longed to go when I was a child. My father always meant to take me, but . . ." She trailed off, her face clouding.

"Shall we have another walk in the garden?" he asked quickly, to distract her from the dark turn her thoughts had taken.

"Are you certain you wish to venture into the garden again, Your Grace?" She glanced at him from the corner of her eye. "You didn't seem to care much for the beets and carrots yesterday, and if I recall, you went as far as to curse the rutabagas."

"Nonsense. I adore root vegetables. It's the mud I object to."

"Alas, we're sure to encounter mud wherever we venture. This is Herefordshire, you know. But the pathway that leads to High Street is dry enough, and my mother requires a few things from the shop. Would you care to walk to town?"

"I'd be delighted to accompany you, my lady, but fetch your servant first, if you please."

She raised an eyebrow. "You do remember, do you not, Your Grace, that I told you I'm accustomed to wandering about as I please in the country?"

"And *you* remember, do you not, Lady Francesca, that I reminded you that as I am a single gentleman, it's far worse for you to be seen in my company than it is for you to be seen alone?"

Despite his efforts to blend in, in his country garb, it wasn't every day a duke pranced down High Street in a small village like Ashwell. He was sure to be noticed, and he wouldn't have the fine citizens of Ashwell looking askance at his betrothed.

Prospective betrothed, that is. For now.

She huffed out a breath, but disappeared back into the cottage, and came out a moment later with Hannah, who was wiping flour from her hands and muttering crossly to herself, but after treating him to a suspicious glower, she fell into step behind them on the pathway that led to the village.

It was a fine day to embark on a courtship, a brisk wind overnight having chased the clouds away, and he had Francesca as much to himself as he ever would.

There was nothing for it now but to charm her into marrying him.

It should be easy enough. He was a duke, for one, and in the two years since he'd become His Grace, he'd successfully charmed most of London. A few pleasantries about the weather, a bit of delicate flattery, and she'd soften quickly enough. It shouldn't take more than a day or so for her to find him irresistible.

Right, then. The weather was as good a place to start as any. "It's such a pleasant day for a walk. It's unusually warm for November, is it not, Lady Francesca?"

"Do you call this warm, Your Grace? The ground was frosted over when I woke this morning, and it still feels rather chilly to me."

Chillier *now*, certainly, with that frosty reply. "Perhaps it only seems warmer because the sun is shining. Aren't sunny days a rarity in this part of Herefordshire in the autumn?"

"No rarer than in London, I think, Your Grace."

Well, then, she had rather decided opinions about the weather, didn't she? If he said the sky was blue, the contrary chit would likely disagree with him. Another topic, perhaps. "These trees along the pathway, Lady Francesca. They're wonderfully, er . . . tall, and sturdy. I don't believe I've ever seen this species before."

"They're oak trees, Your Grace."

"Oak?" Well, damn it, so they were.

"Yes, Your Grace. There are hundreds of them in Hyde Park."

This wasn't going well at all. If neither the weather nor

the trees could crack that icy exterior, that left only one thing. "You look very pretty today, Lady Francesca."

She snorted. Actually snorted!

"Do I, indeed, Your Grace? Do my eyes sparkle like diamonds, or stars? Are my lips like roses, or . . . no, perhaps they're more like cherries? Is my hair like velvet, or the deepest, darkest midnight?"

The infuriating woman was *laughing* at him.

This was pure torture. What the devil was the matter with her? He'd never before encountered a lady more determined *not* to be charmed.

But then she'd never seemed to care much for flattery, come to think of it, nor had she ever been impressed with the grand Duke of Basingstoke. Indeed, the only time he'd ever gotten a satisfactory response from her was the night of his mother's musical evening, when he'd followed her out onto the balcony.

I don't play the pianoforte.

It had cost her something, to tell him that one small truth, but she'd done it, and he'd responded in kind. Oh, he'd teased her about her sharp tongue as well, of course, but he hadn't *performed* for her, any more than she'd performed for the glittering *ton* gathered in his mother's drawing room that evening.

Good Lord, it wasn't going to be enough to be the witty, charming Duke of Basingstoke, was it? Not for her. He was actually going to have to be *himself*, and that was going to be difficult, given he hardly knew Giles Drew anymore.

He'd spent a great deal more time being the duke.

He cast a glance at her from the corner of his eye, but the sides of her bonnet were so deep, all he could see of her face was the very tip of her nose. It was quite the ugliest bonnet he'd ever seen, a drab brown affair adorned with a wide ribbon of the same dull brown.

Was she trying to put him off, with that bonnet? "It won't work."

She turned to him with a frown. "I beg your pardon?"

"If you're trying to frighten me off with that appalling bonnet, it won't work."

She stared at him, open-mouthed. "Do you mean to say, Your Grace, that you don't care for my bonnet?"

It was *not* a charming thing to say. The Duke of Basingstoke would never dream of saying such a thing, but Giles Drew . . . well, he was a rude devil, it seemed, and not one for delicate flattery.

But this was the first time she'd met his eyes all morning. He'd call her a muddy radish again, if it got her to look at him. "I don't care for it in the least. It's dreadful." He stepped closer, and gave the ribbon tied under her chin a gentle tug. "But you might wear one of your muddy gardening pails on your head, Francesca, and I still wouldn't be able to tear my gaze from you. So, as I said, it won't work."

Color flooded into her cheeks, but just as her lips parted to reply, a gruff voice rang out from behind them, chasing the birds from the branches. "I'll thank you to keep your hands to yourself, Your Grace."

It was Hannah, of course, just when things were getting interesting. How a woman of that size could manage to sneak up behind him was a mystery, but she'd picked up a large stick along the way that could just as easily be used to bludgeon an amorous duke as it could be a walking stick.

"You don't want to make an enemy of Hannah, Your Grace. She's a bit overprotective, and not fond of aristocrats as a general rule." Francesca smiled up at him, her blue eyes alight with laughter. "She says you're all scoundrels."

He couldn't argue with *that*, so, even as his fingertips ached to trace the long, graceful lines of Francesca's neck, to stroke that smooth, pale skin, he lowered his hands and stepped away from her. "I beg your pardon, Miss Hannah."

Hannah grunted. "If we're going into town, we better get on. I don't like Lady Stanhope's tea to be late." She trudged past them, evidently fed up with their dawdling.

They trailed along after her, and walked the remaining mile into town in silence, but he caught Francesca sneaking a glance or two at him, though whenever he tried to catch her eye, she flushed up to the roots of her hair and ducked back behind the safety of her bonnet.

It was . . . well, damn it, it was adorable. If Hannah and her stick hadn't been hanging about, he would have ducked under there with her, but he didn't fancy losing any appendages.

Ashwell wasn't a town so much as a village, but it was a pretty place, the stained-glass windows of St. Mary's Church glittering in the weak November sun, and a row of tidy shops made of handsome gray stone lining High Street.

Francesca paused in front of the largest of these, a general store with a small bay window. There was a bright blue sign hanging from an ornate iron pole proclaiming it to be WESTCOTT'S in neat white lettering. "Will you fetch the post, Hannah?"

Hannah's only reply was another grunt, but she made her way past Westcott's to the other end of High Street, while he followed Francesca up the stairs and into the shop.

"Lady Francesca, how do you do?"

"Good morning, Mr. Westcott."

"I'm pleased you came in today, my lady. I've just got a delivery of new teas that might do well for your mother. Now, where did I put that box?" Mr. Westcott, a small, balding man with a kind face had just bent to rummage in some boxes when he caught sight of Giles and blinked owlishly from behind the spectacles perched on his nose. "Oh, good day, sir . . . er, my lord . . . that is—"

"His Grace, the Duke of Basingstoke, Mr. Westcott." A

resigned little sigh accompanied this introduction, as if
Francesca were bracing herself for the fuss that would inevitably follow the sudden appearance of a duke in Ashwell.

"Oh, my. His, ah, His Grace, the . . . the, ah—"

"How do you do, Mr. Westcott?" Giles stepped up to the
counter, cutting off the man's stammering. "Shall we have a
look at the tea?"

"Yes, of course, Your Grace." Mr. Westcott fumbled ner-
vously with the box, but at last he managed to unearth some
of the parcels of tea and spread the selection on the counter.

"Which of these did you think a proper choice for Lady
Stanhope, Mr. Westcott?"

"The Bohea, if you please, Mr. Westcott," Francesca interrupted. "You know it's my mother's favorite."

Was it truly Lady Maria's favorite, or just the least expen-
sive? "The Bohea, certainly, but I wonder, Mr. Westcott, if
you have any medicinal teas?"

"Yes, Your Grace. I have Imperial Hyson, and this Assam.
Some of the green teas are meant to be quite restorative, but
the flavor is subtler. If Lady Stanhope prefers a bracing black
tea, Lady Francesca, this souchong will do very well for her."

"You're very kind, Mr. Westcott, but I think the Bohea
will—"

"A packet each of the Assan and Imperial Hyson, and two
each of the souchong and Bohea, if you'd be so good, Mr.
Westcott."

Mr. Westcott beamed. "Of course, Your Grace!"

"What do you think you're doing?" Francesca hissed, as
Mr. Westcott bustled off to measure the tea. "I can't accept
gifts from you—"

"It's not for you. It's for Lady Maria. In fact, Lady
Francesca, I forbid you to drink any of it."

She gave an impatient huff. "You know very well it
doesn't matter which one of us drinks the tea, Your Grace."

He took her arm and led her to a quieter part of the shop.

"It will give your mother comfort, and may well do her some good. My own mother would wish for me to do this. If you prefer it, the gift may be from the duchess."

Francesca scowled at him and muttered under her breath about "high-handed dukes," but at last she relented. "Very well, for my mother's sake only."

With that, she marched off to another part of the shop.

He waited until she was distracted by a display of soaps and candles, then returned to Mr. Westcott, who was wrapping the tea in brown paper. "A cone of sugar as well, and some drinking chocolate, Mr. Westcott, if you please."

"Certainly, Your Grace."

Giles glanced over his shoulder, but Francesca was still occupied at the other end of the shop. "One more thing, Mr. Westcott. My mother, the Duchess of Basingstoke, has charged me with settling any remaining balance on Lady Stanhope's account, but it's, er . . . a delicate matter, and I prefer it be kept private."

Mr. Westcott leaned over the counter, lowering his voice. "I understand perfectly, Your Grace, but there is no outstanding balance. Lady Francesca came in yesterday and settled the bill herself."

Francesca settled the bill? "This was yesterday, you said, Mr. Westcott?"

"Yes, Your Grace, immediately upon her return from London."

That was curious. It seemed unlikely Lord Edward had suddenly developed a conscience in regards to his niece and sister-in-law, and Francesca wouldn't have allowed Lady Crump to pay the debt. Where had the money come from, then?

He couldn't ask, of course, and there was no time to ponder it, because Francesca appeared, hands empty of either candles or soap. "If you're ready, Your Grace, Hannah is waiting outside for us."

"I'll have my boy deliver these to Lady Stanhope at once, Your Grace." Mr. Westcott gestured to the paper-wrapped packages.

Francesca cast a suspicious eye over them. "That looks like more than just tea, Your Grace."

"Thank you, Mr. Westcott." Giles took her arm and hurried her from the shop. She'd discover the sugar and chocolate for herself soon enough, but by then there'd be little she could do but unleash the edge of her tongue upon him.

A fate he'd happily endure, for the pleasure of sweetening that tongue with chocolate.

CHAPTER 23

Ashwell, like every country village in England, had its fair share of meddlesome old ladies, and the following day when Giles arrived at the cottage, he found all of them crowded into Lady Maria's tiny drawing room.

He paused in the hallway, taking in the sea of lace-capped gray heads with dawning horror. Was it too late to escape to the garden? Even a swim in the mud would be preferable to—

"They descended on us this morning like a swarm of locusts, determined to see the Duke of Basingstoke for themselves." Francesca appeared in the hallway behind him, a plate of freshly baked scones in her hand and a sly smile on her lips. "You'd best prepare yourself, Your Grace, because they're curious about you."

Curious? The elderly ladies of Ashwell put the Spanish inquisitors to shame. They prodded and poked and ogled and chattered at him until it felt as if a flock of magpies had nested between his ears.

"How long do you intend to remain in Ashwell, Your Grace?"

"I've not yet determined, Mrs. Terwilliger, but I hope to—"

"Have you and Lady Francesca been acquainted for long, Your Grace?"

"No, only since the start of the season, Mrs. Alderman, but we—"

"We don't get many dukes here in the country, Your Grace." A gray-haired old lady seated beside him looked him up and down, then dismissed him with a sniff. "We don't have much need of dukes in Ashwell."

Giles replaced his teacup in the saucer without taking a sip. It had long since gone cold, anyway. "No, I don't imagine you do, Mrs., er . . . Mrs. Dowd?"

That was her name, wasn't it? Or was it—

"It's Mrs. Dowden, Your Grace." Francesca gave him a sweet smile.

He scowled back. She was enjoying this far too much.

"We're all enormously fond of Lady Francesca, Your Grace. Such a good girl she is, and such a comfort to her poor mother! One doesn't like to think of such an innocent, tender-hearted young lady being taken advantage of by a wicked, conscienceless rake, does one?"

Wait, was *he* the wicked, conscienceless rake in this scenario?

He didn't know of many wicked, conscienceless rakes who sat for tea with the mother of the lady they intended to debauch, but he gave Mrs. Cornelius a solemn nod. "No, indeed, Mrs. Cornelius. The very thought appalls."

Beside him, Francesca smothered a laugh.

It was the third such warning Mrs. Cornelius had delivered since she'd arrived ten minutes earlier. No matter how politely he responded to her questions, the lady seemed convinced he had nefarious designs on Francesca's virtue, and was determined to frighten him off.

"This is *your* fault," he muttered to Francesca from one side of his mouth.

"My fault? I don't see how."

She pressed a hand to her chest, her eyes as wide and innocent as a kitten, but she was biting her lower lip to hide her grin. She looked so fetching with that tender, pink lip caught between her teeth, for a moment he forgot what he was saying.

Oh, yes. That this inquisition was all her fault. "You suggested we venture onto High Street yesterday. If they tear me limb from limb, it will be on your head, my lady."

"I think your limbs are safe enough, Your Grace, unless you attempt to evade their questions."

"I wouldn't dare." But he'd keep an eye on Mrs. Cornelius, whose comments about innocent young ladies suggested she might have heard the libelous story about his having ruined Francesca. The *Cock and Bull*'s circulation was limited to London, but town gossip reached into every corner of England. Someone in Ashwell would hear of it soon enough, and once they did, they'd take the tale straight to Lady Maria.

It was only a matter of time.

He should have predicted that this would happen and told Francesca the truth about the scandal at once, but he couldn't tell her *now*—not after delaying it for three days. She'd accuse him of the worst sort of deception, and he'd find himself on his way back to London alone.

No. It wouldn't do. He'd simply have to persuade her to marry him before the scandal had time to reach as far as Ashwell.

Another day, perhaps two.

Mrs. Dowd, er, Dowden, was still chattering away, and he nodded along, his most attentive expression fixed on his face, but his gaze kept wandering to Francesca, who was seated to Mrs. Dowden's left, nibbling on one of Hannah's fresh scones, her small, white teeth sinking into the soft flesh of the pastry, her dainty lips pursing slightly as she chewed.

Heat streaked through him, searing his lower belly and gathering in a hot pool of want between his legs. It was a *scone*, for God's sake, but with her, it didn't seem to matter what she was doing. He only had to glance at her to want her.

She could be engaged in the most mundane of tasks—brushing her hair, for instance, or pulling on a pair of stockings—

He smothered a groan and shifted in his chair.

Those were two exceedingly bad examples.

He wasn't leaving Ashwell without her. He *couldn't*—

"Won't you tell us all about the London fashions this season, Your Grace?" Mrs. Alderman swept a disapproving gaze over him. "Have all the aristocratic gentlemen given up wearing waistcoats?"

The ladies remained for some time, quizzing him about the London season, his mother, his sisters, his house in town, his country seat in Kent, and his business in Herefordshire until his throat grew scratchy from too much talking, and not enough tea.

By the time the last of them took their leave it was late in the afternoon, and Lady Maria looked pale and exhausted.

"You don't look well, Mother." Francesca was gathering up the scattered teacups and spoons and loading them onto the tea tray. "Won't you go upstairs, and have some rest?"

"Oh, but the house is in a shambles, and poor Hannah has been baking all day—"

"I'll help Hannah, Mother. You needn't worry about that."

"What, you're going to go off and tidy the kitchen, and leave the duke to amuse himself? No, Francesca. I can—"

"Please don't delay your rest on my account, Lady Maria. I'm perfectly able to—"

"His Grace can amuse himself for a short time, Mother. Indeed, I insist you go up at once."

Lady Maria sighed, but she rose unsteadily to her feet. "I suppose a brief rest wouldn't hurt."

"Good." Francesca gathered up the laden tea tray and turned toward the kitchen. "I'll come check on you in a little while."

"Yes, alright."

Lady Maria made her way up the stairs, but there was

something off about her gait, and the hand clutching the wobbly railing was shaky. "Wait, Lady Maria, let me help you." Giles started toward her, but he was still several steps behind when she faltered, her hand falling away from the railing.

An instant later, her legs buckled.

"Lady Maria!" He leapt toward her and caught her limp body in his arms just before she fell backward and tumbled down the stairs.

There was a crash from the kitchen, then a thunder of footsteps. Francesca rushed into the drawing room, with Hannah right behind her. "Mother!"

"Her bedchamber, Francesca. Where is it?"

"This way." Francesca ducked past him and darted up the stairs.

He followed after her with Lady Maria clutched against his chest, his throat tightening at how slight she was, how fragile, like a child in his arms.

Francesca led him into a small bedchamber and threw back the coverlet on the bed in the center of the room. "Here, Your Grace."

He strode to the bed and laid Lady Maria gently down on it, then stood back as Francesca tucked the coverlet around her and began chafing her wrists. "Mother? Can you hear me?"

"Here, my lady." Hannah passed a small bottle of smelling salts to Francesca.

"Mother?" Francesca waved the salts under her mother's nose, and Lady Maria's eyelids fluttered open. "She's waking up."

"Does this happen often?" Giles asked quietly. Their response was too perfectly coordinated for this to be the first time.

Francesca hesitated, then, "It's happened once before."

"There she is." Hannah leaned over the bed and took Lady Maria's hand. "You're just fine, my lady, just a bit of a swoon.

Too much exertion today, that's all. Take the duke downstairs, Lady Francesca."

"No, I won't leave her."

Hannah shook her head. "It's not proper, His Grace being up here in your mother's bedchamber."

"But—"

"It's alright, Francesca." Lady Maria's voice was weak. "Do as Hannah bids you."

"Go on, now, both of you." Hannah waved them off. "I'll sit with her."

Francesca looked as if she'd argue further, but after a glance at her mother's face, she nodded, pressed a kiss to Lady Maria's forehead, and left the bedchamber.

He followed her back downstairs to the drawing room, where she perched on the edge of a chair, her arms wrapped around herself and her face white. "It's never happened on the stairs before. I don't . . . I should have realized she couldn't—"

"You couldn't have known, Francesca."

"You did." She looked up at him. "You knew."

"No. I happened to be standing there, that's all."

"If she'd fallen down the stairs . . ." Her voice caught, and she hid her face in her hands.

He couldn't stand it, seeing her like this, so small and broken. He'd go anywhere, do anything so he never had to see her like this again. He crossed the room, knelt on the floor at her feet and urged her hands away from her face. "But she *didn't*, Francesca. She didn't fall. She's perfectly fine."

"This time." Her eyelashes were damp with tears.

He reached into his pocket, found a spotless and perfectly pressed handkerchief—thank God for Digby—and gently dried her tears. Then he rose to his feet and held out his hand to her. "Come. We're going for a walk."

She gazed up at him with big, watery blue eyes, but she

didn't argue—just fetched her cloak and bonnet, and let him take her outdoors.

The sun set early in Ashwell in November, but there were still a few weak rays to be had on one side of the garden. He took her there, the mud be damned, pausing beside the long rows of vegetables she'd described to him in such wearying detail two days earlier. "Tell me more about your rutabagas, my lady."

"Rutabagas?" She glanced around the garden in a daze, as if she'd never seen it before.

Her mind was still inside the cottage, in the bedchamber with her mother, so he cast about for a distraction, and his gaze landed on that dreadful brown bonnet. "This bonnet has to go, my lady. Yours isn't a face that should be hidden." He tweaked the brim. "It looks like you're wearing a beaver on your head."

She stared blankly at him for an instant, then let out a shaky laugh. "What an ungentlemanly remark, Your Grace. Why, only two days ago you told me you'd learned your lesson about insulting young ladies. You'll be calling me a country radish again, next."

"Nonsense. You're not even wearing pink."

Another of her soft laughs rippled around him. "A country potato, then."

Ah, yes, that was better. There was that impudent tongue. "It's your own fault I called you a radish at Lord Hasting's ball. You do realize that, do you not?"

"*My* fault? How could your shocking rudeness be my fault?"

He shrugged. "Because you put me out of temper that night."

She planted her hands on her hips. "*I* put you out of temper? I never spoke a word to you the entire evening!"

"No, but you see, I began searching for you the moment I entered the ballroom." He caught her shoulders and turned her toward him, so he could see her face. "As soon as I saw you, I thought you must be the same lady I'd caught sneaking around Stanhope's garden a few nights earlier."

"Well, I *was* the same lady."

"Yes, but I soon discovered you were *not* Lady Susannah Stanhope, and thus, not the lady I was betrothed to." God, how disappointed he'd been, how frustrated to discover the lady he'd been dreaming about for days *wasn't*, in fact, the lady he was going to marry.

At least, he'd thought so then. Now, well, it remained to be seen, but the way she was looking at him, with that softness in her eyes . . . she'd never looked at him in quite that way before, and his heartbeat quickened hopefully.

"You called me Lady Susannah, in the garden that night."

"Yes." He moved closer, until her back came up against the stone fence surrounding the garden. "And you ran away from me."

"I had to. I was afraid you'd take me to my uncle, and I couldn't let him find out I'd been there."

"I know that now, but at the time I couldn't make sense of it. I thought you must be Lady Susannah. It was the only explanation I could think of for you to be in that garden, and though I'd only seen your cousin once before, I knew she had dark hair, and astonishingly beautiful blue eyes." He touched his fingertips to her chin, raising it so he could look into her eyes. "Just like yours."

She swallowed. "Dragonfly blue."

"Yes." Dear God, those eyes. She might share that distinctive blue color with her cousin, but those eyes were hers alone.

They were the only eyes he'd ever drowned in.

"Y-you never said much about that night in the garden, afterwards."

"No. I couldn't. I was forbidden from saying a word, because I was courting your cousin." He stroked his fingers down her throat, biting back a groan. Had there ever been anything as soft as her skin?

Her eyes dropped closed at his touch, and he leaned closer and whispered, "How could I tell you, Francesca, that when I saw you in the garden that night, with those blue eyes and all that dark hair tumbling about your shoulders, I thought by some magical stroke of luck, I'd secured the hand of the most beautiful lady in London?"

"Your Grace, I—"

"I thought myself the most fortunate man in the world. You can imagine my disappointment, then, when I arrived at Lord Hasting's ball only to find I'd made a mistake. That I *wasn't* betrothed to my bewitching garden nymph, but to another lady who, as sweet and lovely as she is, was never going to satisfy me, because she wasn't *you*."

"And then you called me a country radish?"

"And then I called you a country radish." He let his forehead rest against hers.

"Your Grace." Her hands came up and caught his forearms, squeezed.

"Not *Your Grace*, Francesca. I've liberated your cloak from an iron spike, insulted you at a ball, offered you my hand, and now I'm about to kiss you. We're well past formalities."

"You, ah . . ." She glanced up at him from under her lashes. "You're about to kiss me?"

"God, yes." Nothing in the world could have stopped him from kissing her then, her cheek first, just the barest brush of his lips, then the stubborn curve of her chin, then the corner of her mouth, and her lips . . .

How often had he dreamed of kissing her lips? Since that first night in the garden? How many times had he imagined how her sweet, pink mouth would feel under his, how it would taste? He let his lips hover over hers, their breath mingling, then slowly, slowly, he covered her mouth with his own.

It was a soft kiss at first, hesitant, a delicate exploration, her breath catching as his tongue teased her lower lip, nipping and suckling until she parted for him on a gasped breath, and he slipped into the damp, pink heat of her mouth.

Everything spun away from him then but *her*, the long, slender line of her back against his palms, her rib cage shifting with each of her quickened breaths, the stroke of her fingertips against his sleeve, and her sounds—God, her sounds—soft gasps and whimpers, and the quick hitch in her throat as he deepened the kiss, his tongue growing more insistent as desire pooled in his belly.

"Francesca . . ." He urged her closer, his breath stuttering at the brush of her thighs against his, his hand on her lower back tightening into a fist around a fold of her cloak, urging her closer. "You're so lovely, Francesca, so beautiful."

A choked sigh left her lips, and then she was touching him, a light stroke of fingertips against his cheek before she sank her hands into his hair, tugging gently until he thought he must go mad from the delicious torment.

Perhaps he did go a little mad, because with each brush of her tongue reality spun further away until he lost his head entirely, and was kissing her with wild abandon, devouring every inch of soft skin he could reach—her neck, the pulse point in the hollow of her throat fluttering against his tongue, and she was matching him, gasp for gasp, and kiss for kiss—

Too much. It was too much, too *good*.

He pulled back, groaning, but he couldn't quite make himself let her go without one final kiss, a quick, hot press of his lips against hers. "Francesca, I—"

"Yes," she murmured. "Yes."

"Yes?" His head was spinning, his body so aflame with desire he could hardly think, but *yes* . . . did she mean . . . was she saying she would—

"Yes, I'll marry you."

A thousand thoughts flooded his head at once—triumph, that she would be his at last, but worry was right on its heels, because he hadn't told her the whole truth about why he'd come here for her.

Yet one thought silenced all the others, and it was the only thought that mattered.

He didn't care why she'd chosen to marry him, he cared only that she *did*.

"Are you sure, Francesca?" He caught her face in his hands and caressed her cheek, closing his eyes at the slide of her soft skin under the pad of his thumb. "Are you sure you . . . want me?" His throat caught on the last word.

Her hands came up to grip his wrists. "Yes, I'm sure."

He wanted her—had wanted her for what felt like a lifetime—and now, at last, she would be his. "I'll leave for London tomorrow to arrange for a special license, and will return by the evening of the following day. We'll marry the next morning."

She nodded, and he caught a lock of her hair between his fingers and brought it to his lips.

Three days, that was all. Three more days, and Lady Francesca Stanhope would become the Duchess of Basingstoke.

CHAPTER 24

"Come away from the window, Francesca. You'll catch your death with that draft."

"Yes, Mother." Franny turned away from the window, only to whirl back toward it again, her heart leaping when she caught a flurry of movement out of the corner of her eye, but an instant later, it sank in her chest.

It wasn't him, but only a few crows, squabbling over a bit of carrot they'd unearthed from the garden.

The duke—Giles, that is, she *must* remember to call him Giles—had left early in the morning the day before, and hadn't yet returned. He'd told her he'd be back before this evening, so he wasn't late, precisely, but the shadows were lengthening with each passing moment, and the lane outside the window remained stubbornly deserted.

There was no sign of Helios or his winged chariot, and she, fool that she was, had spent the better part of the afternoon with her nose pressed against the glass.

"Here, Francesca. Come and sit down with me, dearest." Her mother patted the empty space on the settee.

Franny dragged herself away from the window and plopped down beside her mother with a sigh. "What a dreadfully long day it's been."

A dreadfully long *two* days, in fact.

"Yes, the intervening days between a proposal and a wedding do tend to drag for a young lady. Be grateful you don't have to wait six weeks, as I did."

"Six weeks? That's an eternity! I wouldn't have survived it."

Her mother chuckled. "I'm pleased to hear you're so eager for the duke's return, Francesca."

Who was eager? Certainly not *her*. It was just that now the decision had been made, she'd just as soon get on with it, that was all.

"I confess it did occur to me that you . . ." Her mother's smile faded. "That you agreed to the match for my sake, rather than your own."

That had occurred to Franny, as well, dozens of times since that unexpected "yes" had slipped from her lips in the garden two nights ago. The duke—*Giles*—had seemed surprised she'd accepted his hand, but he couldn't have been more surprised than she was.

In that moment, if he'd asked, she almost certainly would have claimed she'd agreed for her mother's sake, but later, lying awake in her solitary bed in her dark bedchamber, the truths she denied to herself in the light of day always found her.

And the truth was, this wasn't about her mother.

It was about the way Giles had looked at her that first night they'd met in her uncle's garden. The way he'd scolded her at the Marble Arch, because he was concerned about her reputation, more concerned than she was, herself. It was about his kindness toward her on the terrace the night of his mother's musical evening. It was the grief in his face when she'd run into the drawing room and found him cradling her mother in his arms.

It was in his kiss, in the gentle way he touched her, even

as she could feel the tightly leashed passion vibrating inside him.

She didn't trust easily—not after the way her uncle Edward had treated them—but for better or worse, she *trusted* Giles Drew. She didn't know when it had happened, nor could she explain it in words. It was a feeling, deep inside her, the trust a part of her in the same way her love for her mother was.

Woven into her very bones.

So, she'd told him yes, and that one small word had changed everything. With a single syllable, she'd put the rest of her life in Giles's hands. All she could do now was hope she'd made the right choice.

"Francesca?" Her mother laid a hand over hers, her expression anxious. "You didn't agree to marry the duke for me, did you?"

"I don't claim I'm unaware of the advantages of the match, Mother. It's no small thing, becoming a duchess." She smiled and squeezed her mother's hand. "But no. I agreed to marry him for *myself*."

Her mother studied her face. "Is something else troubling you, then?"

"No, I'm perfectly well, it's just . . ." She glanced at the window, swallowing at the fading light. "What if he doesn't come back?"

Mightn't a return to London have brought him to his senses? Reminded him that he was a *duke*, for pity's sake, and might have any lady he wanted, and needn't settle for one of no name, wealth, position, or fashion—a lady whose only claim to distinction was a succession of blinding pink gowns?

"I don't think you need to worry about that, my dear. I've seen the way the duke looks at you, and he is most assuredly coming back." Her mother hesitated. "I thought perhaps you were worrying about your wedding night."

Her wedding night? Oh, dear God, her wedding night!

How in the world had *that* detail managed to slip her mind? Especially after that kiss they'd shared in the garden? His hands roaming over her, the hot press of his lips against hers, the warm drag of his tongue, demanding her response, and every inch of her quivering . . .

She snatched up a pillow, pressed it to her face and let out a groan.

Her mother pulled the pillow away. "Oh, dear. You *are* fretting, aren't you?"

"Well, I am *now*!"

Her mother laughed. "Perhaps we might just touch on what you can expect. Gentlemen's bodies are—"

Oh, no. They weren't truly going to discuss gentleman's bodies, were they?

". . . blood rushing to certain appendages . . ."

Clop, clop, clop . . .

Wait, was that—

". . . become engorged . . ."

Was she imagining the sound of hoofbeats? She stilled, listening, but no, the rattle of carriage wheels and the clop of horses' hooves were unmistakable.

She rushed to the window, her heart leaping into her throat, and yes! There was the chariot, with Helios himself emerging from it, the last rays of the sun snatching greedily at the glints of gold in his fair hair, like a pickpocket snatching a handful of coins.

My, he looked . . . well, much handsomer than any gentleman should.

"For pity's sake, Francesca, do come away from that window. Do you want the duke to see you with your nose pressed to the glass?"

No, no, she didn't want that. She flew back to her chair, her stomach twisting with anticipation, but he was taking an age to get to the door. She sat, her nerves stretching tighter and her heart thudding in her eardrums.

At last, there was a knock at the door, the echo of Hannah's footsteps trudging down the hallway, a low murmur of voices, and then he was there, his tall frame filling the doorway of the drawing room.

She rose to her feet, her knees trembling.

"Lady Francesca." His face lit up, and he strode toward her and caught her hands in his. "I—"

"I thought you'd never return," she blurted, then her cheeks promptly burst into flame. It was one thing to think it, but quite another to confess to it.

His smile widened. He squeezed her hands and turned to offer her mother a bow. "Lady Maria, how do you do? I've brought someone to meet you."

Only then did she notice another gentleman had accompanied Giles into the drawing room. He was small and slender, with fine, gray hair brushed back from an unlined face.

"This is Dr. Baillie, my personal physician. I've informed him of your delicate health, and he kindly offered to accompany me to Ashwell to examine you, with your permission, of course. Dr. Baillie, this is my betrothed, Lady Francesca Stanhope, and her mother, Lady Stanhope."

"How do you do, Lady Francesca, and Lady Stanhope." Dr. Baillie gave them each a polite bow, then turned to her mother with a kind smile. "I'm pleased to offer you my services, my lady."

"Why, how kind you are, Dr. Baillie. Indeed, I'd consider myself fortunate to have your opinion. Might my servant sit in for the examination? She's been a most excellent nurse to me, and will be better able to answer any questions you might have than I can."

"Of course, if you wish, my lady." Dr. Baillie stood back to allow Hannah to pass, then followed them up the stairs.

Franny watched them go, then turned to Giles, tears clogging her throat. Never, not once since her mother's health had begun to deteriorate had anyone offered them such a kindness.

"It was good of you to bring Dr. Baillie all this way to . . ." Her voice caught as she swallowed back a sob. "We're most grateful to you."

Giles said nothing.

"Your Grace? Giles?"

He advanced on her, slow but deliberate, his gaze intent on her face, and his eyes so very, very blue.

"Are you . . . is something amiss?" She braced her hand on the back of the settee to steady herself. The way he was looking at her, the hunger in those blue eyes, dear God, he looked as if he intended to devour her.

He caught her around her waist, then tugged her close and lowered his lips to her ear. "Did you miss me, Francesca?"

Every inch of her skin exploded in goosebumps at that low, husky growl. "I—I—"

He caught her earlobe between his teeth in a quick, gentle nip before soothing the tiny sting with a stroke of his tongue. "I missed you. You're all I can think about."

"I . . . oh, my goodness." She grabbed his shoulders as his tongue flicked out to taste the sensitive skin behind her ear before he worked his way down her neck, his lips leaving a trail of fire across her skin.

"Tell me you missed me, Francesca." His hands tightened around her waist, his mouth open against her neck, the brush of his tongue over her skin stealing her breath, her very reason.

"I—I missed you, Giles." She *had*, more than she'd thought it was possible to miss anyone.

He groaned, his breath hot against her neck, and then his mouth was on hers, his tongue licking delicately at the seam of her lips, coaxing her to open for him, then surging inside with another low, rumbling groan when she did as he demanded.

"Francesca, dear God, you taste so good." He buried his

hands in her hair and kissed her again and again, until they were both gasping. His hands dropped to her hips, urging her closer against him, something hard and hot pressing into her lower belly.

Was that the appendage her mother had referred to? Because it *was* engorged, intriguingly so. What would happen if she got closer still, just close enough to rub up against—

A choked sound fell from his lips. "I can't . . . you'll make me . . . we have to stop, sweetheart."

He set her carefully away from him, then shoved a hand through his hair, his cheeks flushed. "Thank God we're to be married tomorrow. Any longer, and I'll forget I'm a gentleman."

"Mrs. Cornelius will come after you with a garden hoe, and that's to say nothing of Hannah." She bit her lip to smother a laugh. "I'll be made a widow before I can become a bride."

"You'll be made a duchess. *My* duchess. I beg your pardon, madam, but that lip is mine." He extricated her lower lip from her teeth with gentle fingers. "If anyone's going to bite it, it'll be me."

"Is that so?" It was terribly high-handed of him, yet when he took her mouth again to nibble and tease her lower lip she wrapped her arms around his neck, gasping softly as her breasts were crushed against his chest, the tips tightening into hard points.

"You're driving me mad," he panted, sliding his hand down her spine.

What would that be like, to drive such a man mad with kisses? It would be terribly exciting to find out, but perhaps not *here*, in her mother's drawing room. She broke the kiss, but her fingers, acting entirely without her permission, curled against his waistcoat, wrinkling the fine silk.

"I brought you something from London." He kept her

close, his hands on her waist, but nodded to the box he'd set aside on the settee. "Lady Crump sent this, with her compliments."

It was the box from Madame Laurent's shop. "The blue ball gown Susannah sent me?"

"Susannah? What makes you think Susannah sent you the gown?"

"It arrived at Lady Crump's door along with the cameo." It had never occurred to her that someone else might have sent the gown, but now that she thought of it, Susannah's note hadn't mentioned the gown at all, only the cameo.

But who else would have sent her a ball gown? No, it must have come from Susannah.

He opened his mouth, closed it again, then shook his head. "I suppose she must have sent it, then. Lady Crump thought you'd like to wear it to our wedding."

That was like Lady Crump, to be thinking of her. "I would like it, very much."

He drew her toward the settee and lifted the top off the box.

Franny peeked inside, and there, cradled in the layers of paper, was the blue ball gown. She let out a little sigh at the sight of it. "It's as exquisite as I remember."

Giles stared down at the gown for a long moment, then turned his gaze to her, his eyes soft. "Not as exquisite as the lady who will be wearing it. Will you wear the cameo, as well?"

Oh, how she wished she could! The cameo was the closest she could get to having her father with her on her wedding day, but it was lost to her forever now. "No, I . . . I don't think so."

He frowned, but before he could ask any questions, they heard voices in the hallway above, and a moment later Dr. Baillie appeared, with Hannah following after him.

"How does my mother do?" Franny hurried toward the stairs, but Dr. Baillie stopped her.

"Not to worry, Lady Francesca." He offered her a calm smile that had no doubt soothed the worries of many a patient's families. "She's in her bed, sleeping peacefully. Your mother is a lovely lady, and an exceptionally strong one. Her lungs are weak, certainly, and she's far too thin, but proper rest and nutrition will do wonders for her. I recommend a month taking the waters, to start."

A month, taking the waters? Franny's heart sank. They couldn't possibly afford to send—

"Brighton, or Bath?" Giles asked.

"Either will do, I should think."

"I have a house in Bath that will do nicely for her. You'll accompany her, doctor?"

"Of course, Your Grace, if you wish it. We can leave from here after your wedding tomorrow, in my carriage. Miss Hannah, you'll accompany your mistress? Ah, good," he said, at Hannah's affirmative grunt. "Lady Stanhope will be more comfortable if you come along."

Franny looked from Dr. Baillie to Hannah, and from Hannah to Giles. Well, they'd settled that rather neatly, hadn't they? How wonderful it must be, to have the solution to every problem right at one's fingertips, and not a soul to consult aside from themselves—

"Lady Francesca? Does this meet with your approval?" Giles turned to her with eyebrows raised. "It means Lady Maria won't be with you for your first month in London."

She let out a long, slow breath, the tightness in her chest loosening. By this time tomorrow, Giles would be her husband, but not her lord and master, despite what the law might say. "She should go to Bath at once, of course."

Dr. Baillie nodded, satisfied. "It's settled, then. I look forward to returning her to you in much improved health in a month's time, Lady Francesca."

"Thank you, Dr. Baillie."

"If you could give me a moment, Dr. Baillie, we'll return to the Three Tuns for the night."

"Of course, Your Grace."

Giles took her arm and led her into the hallway outside the kitchen. "I brought Dr. Baillie from the inn in my carriage and must return with him now."

"Yes, very well. Thank you for your kindness to my mother. I can't say how much I—"

"Shh." He pressed his fingertips to her lips. "I'm fond of Lady Maria, and pleased to help her, both for your sake and her own." He stroked his thumb over her lower lip, his eyes darkening when they parted under his touch. "Will you be alright tonight?"

She smiled. "I should think so, yes." She had been every other night for the past ten years.

"Until tomorrow at St. Mary's then, my lady." He leaned down and dropped the sweetest, gentlest of kisses on her lips. "My duchess."

He and Dr. Baillie took their leave then. She ran to the window to watch him go, rolling her eyes at Hannah's snort. "Oh hush, you."

Once the carriage was out of sight, she gathered up the dressmaker's box and climbed the stairs to her bedchamber, closing the door behind her.

She laid the box on the bed, opened the lid, and drew the gown out. It would be a ludicrously grand addition to her humble little wardrobe closet, but such fine silk would wrinkle dreadfully if the gown wasn't hung properly.

She reached under the top layer of blue silk to smooth the white satin petticoat underneath, and her fingers caught on something tucked underneath it, stitched into the gathers at the waistline.

What in the world?

She spread the gown out on the bed, lifted the skirts, and found a small silk bag, like a reticule, sewn into the skirt at the back of the gown. A pocket? In a ball gown? How curious. She smoothed the skirts back down, carefully turned the gown over, and there, at the back of the skirt, hidden in the folds of blue silk was a slit, no more than four or five inches long.

She slid her hand inside it, and her fingers brushed a tiny, folded paper packet. She drew it out and opened it, and inside found a sewing needle, two bits of thread, one blue and one silver, and a neatly folded length of the silver Belgian lace.

Why, how ingenious! It wasn't at all the thing for a ball gown to have a pocket, but Madame Laurent had hidden it so cleverly, and tucked the little mending kit inside, so the hem of the gown might be easily repaired if it was torn at a ball.

But there was something else in the little pocket, aside from the mending kit, so she reached inside a second time and drew out another paper packet, this one folded over and over again so it might fit through the slit.

She lit a candle, unfolded the paper, and spread it out on the bed.

It was a letter.

My dearest cousin . . .

Of course! Who else could have put it there, but Susannah? No one else would have even realized the pocket was there, but Susannah had tried on the gown herself when they'd visited Madame Laurent's shop, and must have noticed it then.

She stared at the letter, the lines blurring as tears filled her eyes. All this time, she'd believed Susannah had run off without a word to her, but she *had* written, after all. She must have slipped the letter into the pocket when they'd embraced in Lady Sandham's library, right before Susannah left the ball.

The ball, her parents, Giles, and London, all in one desperate flight. How brave Susannah was! She dragged the back of her hand over her eyes and returned her attention to the letter.

> *My dearest cousin, you'll know by now that I've fled*
> *my father's house and protection. I know your*
> *generous heart, Franny, and trust you will forgive me*
> *for my recklessness, and for what I'm about to tell*
> *you. I have a confession to make. . . .*

A confession? What could Susannah have to confess?

She settled on the bed, her back against the headboard, drew her knees up, and began to read.

CHAPTER 25

The entire population of Ashwell attended Franny's wedding to the Duke of Basingstoke. She couldn't say with any certainty how they'd all discovered there was to be a wedding at all, but neither was she surprised when they filed into St. Mary's Church.

They had their ways, and it wasn't every day one of their own became a duchess.

For her, the ceremony passed in a blur of faces—smiling lips and teary eyes; voices—their marriage vows, his spoken decisively, confidently, hers whispered; and sensations—his long fingers wrapped around hers, the soft brush of his kiss against her cheek.

Later, when they were in the carriage on their way to London, other fleeting impressions came back to her—the scent of orange blossoms, the whisper of her satin petticoat against her thighs, the tears in her mother's eyes as she bid her good-bye.

One month apart seemed an eternity.

And now she was married—a wife, and a duchess—with her new husband seated across from her in the carriage, and he was staring at her.

Staring, a streak of hectic color high on his cheekbones, his eyes a turbulent dark blue, fierce and sleepy at once, his gaze roaming from her lips down the line of her neck, from the pulse beating wildly in the hollow of her throat to her hands, wrapped tightly in white kid and clenched in her lap.

She couldn't meet his gaze without a shiver slipping down her spine, tension and anticipation, eagerness and nerves all at once, a tight, pulsing ball of heat in her lower belly.

He didn't speak much during their drive, but left her in peace to untangle the complicated emotions that swept over her, relentless waves of them, the next following right on the heels of the one before, but never, not once, did she imagine he'd forgotten her.

He heard her every smothered sigh, noticed her every nervous twitch. Every inch of him was aware of her, attuned to her, straining toward her, but it wasn't until they'd reached the outskirts of London that he ventured to speak. "Are you weary, Your Grace?"

Your Grace. How strange that sounded.

His low, husky voice wrapped around her, coaxing another shiver to the surface of her skin, stealing her breath. "Perhaps a little. Are . . . are you?"

A smile drifted across those sensuous lips. "No, Francesca." His gaze met hers, blue eyes burning, and he didn't look away. "I've never been more awake in my life."

She'd never tried to imagine what a duke's bed might look like, but even if she had, she wouldn't have imagined *this*.

It was . . . well, massive was the first word that came to mind, but even that didn't capture the sheer enormity of it. It was a monstrous thing made of thick slabs of some dark, shiny wood, the columns on each of the four corners thicker than both her thighs squeezed together, so tall they nearly touched the ceiling, and the entire thing was draped in acres of bed hangings in dark blue silk.

"Oh, my." If ever there'd been a bed grand enough for a duke, it was this one.

"You needn't look so terrified." Giles came up behind her and curled his hands over her shoulders. "You'll find it's quite comfortable, for all that it looks like it will swallow you whole."

"Am I to sleep in here, with . . . with you, then?"

His fingers tightened on her shoulders. "Not if you don't wish to."

Did she wish to? She hardly knew. She hardly knew anything anymore.

He released her abruptly, then strode to the other side of the room, ripping off his jacket and dropping it onto a chair on his way. "You have your own apartments, of course, just here." He threw open a door. "There's a shared sitting room between us. Your bedchamber and dressing closet are on the other side of it."

"The other side," she repeated faintly. It seemed an awfully long way away. "I, ah, I'd prefer to—"

"Yes?" He seemed to be holding his breath.

"I'd prefer to stay here with you, for now." Her cheeks exploded with heat at the admission, but she made herself meet his gaze. He was her husband now. Surely, she could speak truthfully to him. "If that's acceptable to you?"

He stilled, his hands freezing on his cravat.

Oh, no. Had she said the wrong thing? Did he not want her to—

"Acceptable?" He jerked the cravat free from his neck, tossed it onto the chair and strode across the room to her. "It's more than acceptable. You're my wife, Francesca, and I want you in my bed. Tonight, and every night afterwards. Is that what you want?"

"Yes."

He released a long, slow breath. "Good. That's good, sweetheart."

Words gathered in her throat, but he reached for her then, his fingers moving down the buttons of her pelisse, releasing them one by one, and a rush of breath was all that emerged from her lips.

He slid the pelisse from her shoulders, then with one quick tug, he untied the ribbons under her chin, and the bonnet went onto the chair, along with the pelisse.

And then, one by one, he began to pull the pins from her hair. "I've wanted to do this since I first laid eyes on you." His eyes went darker with each lock that tumbled over her shoulders, until the last pin hit the floor. He gazed down at her, his throat moving in a rough swallow, and reached out to caress a lock of her hair. "So lovely."

Her belly leapt at the wondering smile on his beautiful lips. So lush and red, those lips, so strangely tempting.

His gaze darted to her throat, and he reached out and stroked his fingertips down her neck. She jerked at the touch, and his gaze snapped back to her face. "Do you like that, Your Grace?"

It wasn't a question, really, and the sound that tore loose from her throat wasn't an answer. It wasn't even a word, but he didn't seem to expect one. He continued to slide the warm pads of his fingers over her skin, his thumbs skimming her collarbones, then drifting higher, brushing over her lips, parting them. "Open."

Her breath rushed from her lungs in a gasp as he brushed his mouth over hers. The kiss was soft, tentative—a question, rather than a demand. He traced the tip of his tongue over her lips, then tugged her lower lip into his mouth to suck on it.

A low, needy whimper left her throat, and she wrapped her fingers around his forearms, holding on as his tongue darted between her lips. His mouth was so warm, his lips soft but firm, and somehow kissing him was different this time, familiar and strange at once.

Was that because he was *hers* now, and she was his?

Then Giles slipped his tongue inside her mouth, and she didn't think at all.

He kissed her and kissed her, and she took it all, every stroke, lick, and bite making her strain toward those lips, greedy for more.

He gave it to her. He gave her everything.

He teased and tormented, tracing his tongue over her lips again and again until at last he yielded to her broken pleas for more. Then he took her mouth harder, suckling on her swollen lower lip until she was panting for him.

By the time he tore his mouth free of hers, he was just as breathless as she was.

Giles held her gaze as he removed his waistcoat, then tugged his shirt over his head and let it fall to the floor. His boots followed, until he stood before her, bare but for his pantaloons, the massive plane of his chest rising and falling with each of his quickened breaths. "Do you want me, Francesca?"

Smooth, golden skin layered over tight muscles, a spattering of golden hair in the center of his chest, and lower, under his belly button, disappearing into his pantaloons . . .

Oh, *yes*. She wanted him. Her fingers ached to touch, to stroke. "I do. I want you, Giles."

"Then come to bed." He held out his hand.

She took it, her heart pounding, and he led her across the room. "Lie down," he whispered, easing her onto his bed with a gentle hand on her shoulder.

She did as he asked, but she was trembling, hectic breaths she couldn't control tearing from her throat. What was she meant to say to him, to do to him? How—

"Shh." He lay down beside her, gathered her into his arms and brushed a sweet kiss across her lips. He soothed her with gentle kisses until the tension drained from her body and she melted against the bed.

"May I take this off?" He was toying with the hem of her skirts, which had somehow crawled up her legs while he was kissing her, and were wrapped around her thighs.

"I, ah . . ." Oh, God. If he took off her gown, she'd be nearly bare before him, and he'd see everything, know everything—

"I would never hurt you, Francesca. I just want to touch you. Will you let me?"

She paused, then swallowed, nodded.

He made quick work of the buttons, drew the gown over her head, then settled her back down on the bed without removing her shift. "There, that's better."

Then, he began to touch.

Lightly at first, his fingertips sliding down her neck. He caressed her throat and swept his hands over the quivering skin of her shoulders. She twitched under his palms as he traced the contours of her waist, the soft curve of her lower belly. "Beautiful," he murmured as his lips followed the path his hands had taken, his tongue trailing over her abdomen.

He let his hands drift down to cup her hips, stroking his thumbs over the curves. She hardly noticed when he slipped a hand under the hem of her shift and let it rest on her thigh, his other hand skimming up her belly to cup one of her breasts.

That, she noticed.

He teased her, brushing the pad of his thumb lightly over one of her nipples, pausing to tease the stiff tip before moving to her other breast, pinching gently with his fingertips before he sucked the rigid peak into his mouth.

"Ah, God." She moaned, her back arching, her fingers twisting in his hair as he licked the sensitive tip. "Oh, oh, please."

"I want to take care of you, Francesca. Will you let me take care of you, sweetheart?"

The hot drift of his breath over her wet nipples tore another cry from her throat. In that moment, she would have done anything, promised him anything. Her fingers tightened in his hair, dragging his mouth closer to her breasts. "Please."

His hot mouth closed over the tip of one breast, his fingers trailing down her belly, teasing and caressing, and her hips rose and fell in rhythm with the slide of his fingers over her quivering skin, whimpers and half-broken pleas falling from her lips.

"Yes, Francesca. Just like that. That's so good, sweetheart." He grasped the hem of her shift and with a quick jerk drew it over her head, then he leaned over her, his lips against her ear, his hand slipping lower to caress the insides of her thighs. "I promised I'd take care of you, and I will, but you need to trust me. Can you do that?"

She could do anything, would do anything, as long as he didn't stop. "Yes."

He didn't make her wait. He pressed her thighs open wider, dragged his tongue down the center of her belly, then buried his face . . . oh. Oh, dear God, his face was . . . it was . . .

Between her legs. "That's . . . I—I can't . . . oh!" Her hips jerked when his tongue found her center, a desperate moan tearing from her throat.

"Yes, you can, Francesca." His fingers tightened on her trembling thighs as he licked and sucked at the tiny nub. It seemed to go on forever, his clever tongue teasing and circling until her body was as tight as a bowstring.

He drew back, his blue eyes wild. "Everything, Francesca. Give me everything."

"Ah, God, *please*. Giles, please." She was panting, her hands clenched in the coverlet beneath her, her entire body twitching and straining as Giles went back to devouring her, the tip of his wicked tongue fluttering over her needy core.

He growled against her damp flesh. "So sweet, Francesca, you taste so good."

"*Yes*. Harder, harder. Don't stop, don't . . ." She let out a keening cry, her hands sinking into his hair as sweet, sharp pleasure exploded between her thighs. Her back bowed as it unfurled inside her, ribbons of bliss fluttering through her, stealing her breath, her reason.

Giles groaned, licking her madly through her release, his mouth gentling as the tension seeped from her body and her hips sank back down onto the bed. She spread her arms wide, dazed. "I didn't know," she murmured, when she'd caught her breath. "I've never . . ."

He reached up and swept the damp hair off her brow. "Never found your pleasure before."

Heat rushed into her cheeks, but she nodded. "No. Never."

Her entire body felt liquid, her legs like jelly, but she struggled up onto her elbows to gaze at Giles, who was sitting back on his heels, breathless, and my goodness. This must be what people meant, when they said someone appeared debauched.

He looked half wild, his lips swollen, and his bare chest sheened with sweat. The appendage her mother had mentioned, the one apt to become engorged with blood, was pressed tightly against the straining fabric of his pantaloons, the tip of it trapped between his taut stomach and his waistband.

It looked . . . uncomfortable.

Even a lady who didn't know much about a gentleman's appendages must be able to see *that*. Hesitantly, she slid her hand over his thigh. "Are you . . . is that . . . should I . . ." She nodded at the engorged appendage, and it . . . dear God, was it getting bigger?

It was! It stirred and lengthened right before her eyes.

Giles let out a low moan and her eyes shot to his face. His cheeks had reddened, two bright spots of color spreading over his cheekbones. "I need you. Will you touch me, Francesca?"

She glanced back at the appendage, her tongue creeping out to touch her lower lip. It looked like a rather sensitive appendage, but she wanted to bring him pleasure, just as he'd done for her. "Yes. I want to touch you."

He stripped off his pantaloons, tossed them aside, then lay on his back on the bed. "Come here, sweetheart."

She edged closer, her cheeks burning with embarrassment, and . . . something else. His appendage was—not beautiful, exactly, but impressive. Long, hard, and pulsing against his belly, the tip damp and flushed a dusky red.

But what was she meant to *do* with it?

He answered that question by taking her hand and putting it directly on him, sucking in a sharp breath through his teeth when she closed her hand around him. "It's so hard, and *hot*."

She hadn't expected that.

He let out a shaky laugh, then caught her hand in his, closing her fingers more tightly around his length, and then he began to stroke up and down, showing her what he liked, his lips parting on a soft moan as she slid her hand eagerly over his pulsing length. "Ah, so good, Francesca. So good for me."

She stroked and teased, desire twisting in her belly as he writhed against the bed. She gave it a little squeeze, and he threw his head back with a guttural moan. "You're making me so hard. Going to make me come, sweetheart."

She watched, mouth open as he thrust into her fist, beads of sweat gathering at his temples and sliding down his neck. His breath was coming faster with each jerk of his hips until at last he pulled away with a tortured groan. "I need . . . I want to be inside you."

He rolled onto his side and slid one leg between hers, pausing to caress the sensitive skin there before gliding his thumb over her hungry nub, circling and rubbing until she was pushing back on his hand.

"Do you like this?" He slid the tip of his finger inside her, then paused. "Does this feel good?"

"Yes, yes." She pushed back again, desperate, and he responded, easing his finger carefully inside before sliding it back out again. She chased it with her hips, all embarrassment forgotten, whimpering until he slid it inside her again, pumping slowly in and out until her hips took up the rhythm.

"So needy, Francesca. It drives me mad, seeing you like this." He pressed a hot, open-mouthed kiss between her breasts. "Do you need more?"

"More." She writhed against the bed. "I want you inside."

"Not yet, sweetheart. I don't want to hurt you. Soon."

"Need you." She gripped his wrist, groaning and pleading, her hips working against every thrust of his fingers. "I want you. Please."

She keened when he eased his fingers out, then gasped when he nudged his hips between her thighs, the impossibly hard, hot length of him pressing against her entrance. Her eyes flew open. "Oh."

Giles pulled back and leaned down to press a tender kiss to her lips. "It's alright if you need me to stop—"

"No." She pressed her knees against his hips. "I don't want to stop."

He nudged against her entrance again. "I'll go slowly," he whispered, when she tensed. "I want to make you feel good, Francesca."

Slowly, the tension eased from her body and she opened her thighs to him.

He circled her weeping nub with his thumb, spreading the wetness there, then he slid halfway inside her in one long, smooth stroke. "That's it, sweetheart," he murmured, when her breathing quickened. "So good, Francesca, so wet for me."

He kept his hips still as he stroked and teased, coaxing her into another frenzy, waiting until she was squirming and gasping beneath him before he began to move. Slowly, he pushed inside. One inch, another, his jaw tight, and incredibly, she stretched around him, her heat pulling him deeper, deeper, until after what felt like a lifetime, her entire lifetime, he was buried inside her body.

He eased out, then back inside her again, a groan tearing from his lips. "Is that good? Do you need more?"

She stared up at him, mouth open. Her lips parted, but instead of words, only a low, hungry groan emerged. Giles gazed down at her, eyes slitted, his hips jerking desperately as she met his restrained thrusts, and goodness, he was so beautiful she couldn't resist capturing his face in her hands and bringing his mouth down to hers.

She whimpered a protest when he tore his mouth free, but it quickly became a hiss of pleasure when he wrapped his hot mouth around one of her nipples, suckling her as he drove himself into her.

The delicious knot inside her was tightening again, her release sliding closer, a pleading whine tearing from her throat. "Yes, yes."

Giles took her hips in his big hands and wrenched her closer. "Come for me, Francesca."

He thrust into her again, again, his eyes closing, his fingers prodding delicately between her damp folds and stroking her swollen nub until her thighs were shaking. "*Yes*," he urged, when she chased his hand with quick snaps of her hips, breathless cries falling from her lips.

She cried out, and a second later her release crashed over her, his blue eyes on her face as she thrashed against the bed.

"Yes, so good, Francesca. Come for me, come . . . ah!" He threw his head back and pumped helplessly into her, taking her mouth in a savage kiss as he shuddered over her trembling body.

He went limp once the spasms subsided, and let his head drop into the curve between her neck and shoulder. His lips moved lazily over her neck before he rolled onto his back on the bed. "Come here, sweetheart." He wrapped an arm around her waist and settled her against him, urging her head down onto his chest.

His skin was damp, his chest rising and falling with his

shuddering breaths, his heart thundering under her cheek. His strong arm was wrapped around her, his big hands stroking her back, but when long moments passed and she didn't speak, he struggled upright and gazed down at her face, his brow furrowed. "Francesca? Are you alright, sweetheart? I didn't hurt—"

"Mmm." She was sprawled out against the pillow, her limbs heavy, her heartbeat slowing. She wanted to gaze at him, talk to him, but his bed was so comfortable, like resting on a cloud, and she was so warm with the long length of his body tucked against her that her eyes insisted on drifting closed.

He let out a soft laugh. "You look content."

"Mmmm."

He leaned forward and dropped kisses onto her forehead, her eyelids, her cheeks, and her chin, then pulled the coverlet over them and wrapped her in his arms. "Sleep, sweetheart."

CHAPTER 26

His new wife had a tiny mole on her left arse cheek.

Giles abandoned the breakfast tray a servant had left on a side table and crept closer to the bed. He'd left her curled around a pillow with the coverlet drawn up to her neck, but she'd shifted since then, revealing the long, slender line of her spine and one curved cheek to his mesmerized gaze.

He'd kissed every inch of that creamy skin last night. How had he missed that delectable little mole? An oversight, indeed, and one that must be addressed at once. He sank down onto the bed, pausing to trail his fingertips down her spine, then leaned over her and—

She let out a little squeak and peered up at him with sleepy blue eyes. "Giles? Did you just *bite* my . . . my . . ."

"Your arse? Certainly not. It was hardly more than a nibble."

"A gentleman does not bite a lady, Your Grace!" She snatched at the coverlet and dove back underneath it, her face a picture of feminine outrage. "At least, not without her permission."

"I'm not a gentleman, I'm a duke. We do as we please." He dragged the coverlet back down again and dropped a kiss on the base of her spine, right above that delicious backside, then trailed his lips up to the graceful hollow between her shoulder blades. Good Lord, her skin was soft, as soft as a—

"Ouch! What the devil?" He spat out a mouthful of pillow.

"Serves you right, biting a lady while she's sleeping." Her stubborn little chin shot up, but she couldn't hide the smile lurking at the corners of her lips, or the flush of pleasure on her cheeks.

"You're a very naughty duchess, Francesca." He caught her ankle and tugged her toward him. "I should turn you over my knee for such insolence."

She kicked and squirmed, breathless laughter spilling from her lips. "Don't you *dare*!"

He didn't dare. Not *yet*, at any rate, as she was still a bit too innocent for such racy bed sport, but neither did he let her go. Instead, he caught her in his arms, rolled quickly onto his back and dragged her on top of him, arranging her thighs so they were on either side of his hips, and steadying her with a hand on her waist.

"Ah, that's much better." It was rather an impressive maneuver, really. "Now I have you where I want you."

"So you do. What do you intend to do with me, Your Grace?"

"I haven't decided yet. There are so many tempting options, you see." He drew tiny circles on her thigh with one fingertip, taking in the way her eyes darkened and her breath quickened, the way her lips parted on a quiet gasp as he teased his knuckles over the secret skin of her inner thighs.

He wanted her again . . . and again, and again, but she'd be tender this morning. There were other ways to give her pleasure, however, and he hadn't spent nearly enough time worshiping her breasts last night. He released her hip and slid his palms up her belly, but he stopped when his thumbs brushed the undersides of her breasts.

Stopped, and waited, swallowing at the sight of those dark

curls against her pale skin, her half-lidded blue eyes. "Do you want me to touch you, Francesca?"

"Yes," she whispered.

If he could have held off, made her plead and writhe for him, he would have, but he couldn't wait another moment. He slid his hands up and cupped her breasts, and she was—*dear God*, she was lovely, soft, and firm at once, a perfect handful of supple flesh. He rubbed back and forth in a light caress, his mouth going dry when her nipples beaded into tight points under his palms.

"You're so beautiful, sweetheart." His voice shook as he cradled her bare breasts in his palms, his skin dark against her pale flesh. Even in his most heated fantasies he hadn't anticipated anything as perfect as her, her creamy skin crested with the sweetest blush-pink nipples he'd ever seen. "Does that feel good?"

Her strangled whimper shot straight to Giles's cock. "So pretty. See how they peak for me, Francesca? How they beg for my touch?" He drew lazy circles around her nipples with his thumbs. "They flush a darker pink for me the more I tease them."

Her tongue darted out to wet her lips, and her eyes slid closed. "Yes."

"No, Francesca." He pinched her nipples between his thumb and finger. "Watch me touch you." He waited for her to open her eyes, then he squeezed and tugged on her nipples until she was shaking in his arms and they'd turned a deep, cherry red.

Slowly—oh, so slowly—he slid one hand down her belly until his fingers brushed the soft nest of dark curls between her legs. She jerked in his arms when he teased his fingertip into her cleft and stroked her. "Ah, that feels so . . . Giles—"

"Shh. Just let me make you feel good, sweetheart." He teased his fingers over her damp flesh, and a low groan tore from his lips. "You're so wet. So hot and wet for me. Open your legs, and let me touch you."

She spread her thighs wider for him, her breath catching on a moan as he stroked her. Yes, this was what he wanted, for her not to think, to be so mindless with desire she obeyed her body without question. "That's it, sweetheart. Yes, Francesca. Just like that."

"Don't stop. Please." She squirmed and gasped as he teased and petted her. "Ah. Don't stop."

"Never. Not until you come for me." He slid his fingertip into her opening, gathered the moisture there, and then dragged it back up to draw slow, slippery circles around her nub.

She cried out, and he couldn't stop himself from thrusting his cock against her. "Do you feel that, Francesca? I'm so hard for you, sweetheart. I want you so much. I want to watch you come for me."

She was panting now, her gasps trailing off into helpless moans.

Giles pressed one hand between her shoulder blades. "Come here, sweetheart. Closer. Put your nipple in my mouth. *Yes*," he hissed when she pressed her breast to his lips. "Now spread your legs wide and come for me."

He suckled her nipple and moved his fingers faster over her swollen flesh. God, she was so wet, her tender nub so hard under his circling fingers. She had to be close, so close . . .

"*Giles*." Her body tensed, his name on her lips part scream, part moan, and then she jerked against him, her back arching as her release thundered through her. He closed his eyes and gritted his teeth, ruthlessly holding back his own climax as he stroked her through hers.

His fingers slowed and gentled as her spasms faded, and after a moment she fell against him, her body limp. His cock was weeping, leaking with need, but he remained as he was, cradling Francesca and stroking her damp hair.

He'd never been more satisfied in his life. It was almost as if . . .

Francesca's pleasure was his own.

That had never happened before. Had it?

He closed his eyes, trying to recall the faces of his half-forgotten lovers. He'd had a number of them, some in this very bed, but it hadn't ever been like this. He'd never been a selfish lover, but neither had any of his lovers' pleasure meant more to him than his own.

But Francesca wasn't his lover, she was his *wife*.

That must be why. Of course, it was. What else could it—

"I hope you're not falling asleep." A hot, sinuous tongue wrapped around his earlobe. "I don't know how you could be, with *that*."

"*That*? You mean my cock?" He opened his eyes and glanced down at himself. "Now you've offended him."

"I beg your . . . *his* pardon." She stroked her palm back and forth over his thigh. "Perhaps I can do something to soothe his feelings."

She circled his belly button with her thumb, then let her fingers wander lower. He'd tugged his pantaloons over his hips when he went to fetch the tray, but now she loosened his falls and teased her finger under the waistband.

Giles hissed out a breath between his teeth, his head falling back against the pillow. "Perhaps you can." He lifted his hips, tugged his pantaloons off and threw them over the side of the bed.

She teased her fingertips over his rib cage and down his belly, then paused to trace a pattern low on his hip before circling her thumb around his moist tip.

"God." A ragged moan broke from his chest, and his hips jerked against the bed.

"Is he feeling soothed?" Her tongue circled his earlobe, licking him before her teeth closed down in a gentle nip.

His hips shot forward at the delicious twinge of pain. "Not, ah . . . not yet."

She teased him with another light caress, but when his hips jerked again and a pained groan left his lips, she wrapped her hand around his cock and stroked him, caressing him from base to tip. "Ah, *yes*, sweetheart, please."

He thrust into each of her long, slow strokes, panting as he drove his cock into her tight fist, until he let out a strangled cry and came harder than he ever had before, hot jets of his seed coating her hand and his stomach.

"Oh!" She gasped in surprise, but she stayed with him until his pleasure faded and his body went slack, his head falling back against the pillow.

Once he'd caught his breath, he rose from the bed to fetch a cloth, tending to her first before cleaning himself, then he returned to the bed and stretched out on his side, facing her. "Good morning," he murmured, brushing her hair back from her face.

She smiled at him. "It has been, yes."

He traced her jaw, tipped her face up to his with a finger under her chin, and then his lips were on hers, his tongue gentle, coaxing her until she opened for him with a soft moan. He kissed her deeply, his hands wrapped in her hair, and she sighed—a small sound, soft, the gentlest puff of air against his lips before her mouth went soft and pliant under his.

When he drew back, he gathered a handful of her hair between his fingers and brought it to his mouth, his eyes never leaving hers as he brushed the dark strands across his lips.

She laid her hand against his face, her palm warm on his cheek, and as he gazed down into those sleepy blue eyes, a wave of some emotion rolled over him—something simple and pure that he'd never felt before. He was still pondering what it could be when he drifted to sleep, Francesca's hand still cradling his face.

When he woke again, her hand was gone. He reached out and patted the bed next to him, but Francesca was gone, too, only cold, silk sheets where her warm body had been.

"Francesca?" He opened his eyes, blinking groggily. "There you are."

She was standing next to the side table, the sheet wrapped tightly around her, a folded newspaper in her hand and a half-finished cup of tea sitting on the tray before her. "Come back to bed, sweetheart."

She didn't answer, but when she looked up from the newspaper, her blue eyes, so warm only a short while ago, were now as cold as an arctic lake.

The blood in his veins froze to ice. *No*. God, no—

"The *Morning Post* has a short piece about our marriage." She held up the paper.

"Francesca—"

"It's strange, really. At first, I wondered why they didn't seem at all surprised that a grand duke such as yourself would choose such a humble bride, but then I read a little further, and I understand it now. I'm the only person in London who's surprised at our marriage, aren't I?"

He vaulted from the bed, casting about for his pantaloons. This wasn't an argument he wanted to have without his pantaloons. "Listen to me, Francesca—"

"The blue ball gown. *You* sent it to me."

"I did." He swallowed, but it was past time for her to know the truth. "I was there at Madame Laurent's that day, in a private waiting room next door to your dressing room. I heard Lady Edith mocking you, and I couldn't bear it. I wanted you to have the gown, so I sent it to you. Is that truly so wicked, Francesca, that you can't forgive me for it?"

"It's not about the gown, as you know very well. You shouldn't have sent it to me. If I'd known it was from you, I never would have worn it, and you never would have been forced to offer for me, but—"

"*Forced!* Francesca, no. You can't possibly believe I—"

"What, Giles?" Her voice had gone dangerously soft. "That you used me to salvage your reputation? Of course, I believe it. You've never made a secret of the fact that you'd do anything to protect your family from scandal. It was the reason you intended to marry Susannah, and the reason you married me."

"No! I didn't . . . that's not—"

"It worked out rather well for you, all told. The *ton* is certain to be much happier with you for marrying me than they would have been had you married Susannah. It was, after all, *my* family your father destroyed, not hers. There's a certain justice to it. But of course, you've thought of all that, haven't you, Giles? Otherwise, I wouldn't be here."

Dear God, this was a disaster. He had to find a way to make her understand that he . . . that he—

"A ruination, of all things." She laughed, but it was a hard, cold sound. "To think you were worried about my appearing in Hyde Park without a chaperone! It seems ludicrous now, doesn't it?"

"Not so ludicrous, when you consider the incident at the Marble Arch appeared in the *Morning Post*." Not just that incident, either, but his radish comment, and the details of their encounter at his mother's musical evening. It still troubled him. Until he knew how that gossip had reached the newspapers, things would never be right between them. "Can you explain, Francesca, how the *Post* could have reported our private conversation at the Marble Arch with such accuracy?"

"You don't think . . ." She trailed off, the color draining

from her face. "Are you accusing *me* of telling tales to the scandal sheets?"

He opened his mouth, but closed it again without a word. It hadn't been her. He had only to look at her face to see it.

She tossed the newspaper aside, marched across the bedchamber, and seized the blue ball gown, which was draped over a chair.

"Francesca, what are you—"

"It wasn't me who went to the *Morning Post*. It was Susannah." She tugged a folded paper from some mysterious pocket in the gown, marched back across the bedchamber, and shoved it into his hands.

"Lady Susannah? Why would she . . ." But she'd been there each time, hadn't she? At Lord Hasting's ball and at the Marble Arch, and she'd been sitting right next to Francesca at his mother's musical evening, where she could easily have overheard everything that was said between them.

"She's been in love with Lord Ormsby for months. She wanted to marry *him*, Giles. It was my uncle Edward who insisted on the marriage between the two of you. It seems Susannah becoming a mere marchioness wasn't enough for him. Dear God, when I think of all the people he's hurt, the lives he's ruined."

All at once, the fight seemed to go out of her. Her shoulders sagged, and she buried her face in her hands. Pain seared through him, his chest aching if his heart were being torn from it. He started toward her. "Francesca, please—"

"No!" She held up a hand to stop him. "I don't want . . . please don't touch me."

He froze, his hands falling helplessly to his sides.

"Susannah thought a few unflattering pieces in the *Post* might tarnish your reputation just enough to make her father listen to her pleas to end your betrothal. I might have told her it wouldn't work." She let out a bitter laugh. "He wanted his daughter made a duchess. Her happiness wasn't of any importance to him at all."

He was reading Susannah's letter, hardly able to believe the quiet little mouse he'd once been betrothed to could have concocted such a scheme, but then how well had he really known Lady Susannah?

Not well at all, it seemed. "She mentions the *Morning Post*, but nothing about the *Cock and Bull*, which printed all those lies about your ruination. Did she have a hand in that?"

Francesca collapsed into a chair as if her legs had given out. "No, it must have been someone else. She'd already left London by then and anyway, Susannah would never risk my reputation that way, no matter how desperate she was."

No, she wouldn't. Her affection for Francesca was sincere and undeniable, nor did it make sense for her to confess to the other offenses, and lie about this one. "Who, then?"

She gave a weary shrug. "I don't know. Does it matter? The damage is done."

It mattered a great deal to *him*. "Someone told lies about you, Francesca," he gritted through clenched teeth. "They hurt you, and destroyed your reputation." He was going to find whoever had done it and see to it they were made to pay for their viciousness.

"You married me, Giles," she said dully. "My reputation has been magically restored, along with your own. Convenient, isn't it?"

"If I had told you the truth, would you have agreed to marry me?" But even as the words left his mouth, he wished them back again. He'd coerced her into the marriage precisely *because* he'd withheld the truth.

"No! That's why you should have told me. I'm not some pawn on a chessboard you can move about as it suits you, Giles. I have a right to make my own decisions, but you stole that right from me when you pretended you cared for me to persuade me to marry you."

Had he pretended? God, he no longer knew. None of this made sense anymore.

"Francesca, please listen to me." He crossed the bed-chamber and dropped to his knees, grasping her hands in his. "I made a mistake, and I sincerely beg your pardon for it. Can you forgive me? You're my wife, Francesca, and I *do* care for you."

Her gaze met his, and there was such sadness in those blue depths, such disappointment. "When we were in Ashwell, I believed you were being honest with me, Giles. I believed you were a man who *could* be honest, but I'm no longer certain you're the man I thought you were. You *manipulated* me. How can I ever trust you again?"

"Please, Francesca." He buried his face in her lap. "Please—"

"Perhaps it would be better if I retired to your country estate in Kent."

"No! You're not leaving me." If she left now, they'd never find their way back to each other again. No, he couldn't let her go. Not like this.

She drew in a deep breath, then let it out in a sigh. "Very well, but I'd prefer to remain in my own apartments from now on."

He despised the very thought, but he couldn't deny her that. "Of course, if you wish."

"Thank you." She drew her hands free of his and rose stiffly from the chair. "If you'll excuse me, Your Grace."

Then she was gone, through the door that separated their bedchambers, and for all that she closed it quietly behind her, he could hear it echoing still as he lay awake that night, alone in his bed, wrapped in silk sheets that smelled like her, an ocean of unsaid words between them.

CHAPTER 27

Francesca didn't appear in the breakfast room the following morning. Giles waited for her, his coffee turning cold in his cup, until Trevor took pity on him and ventured to hint that Her Grace had taken her breakfast in her bedchamber already that morning.

There'd been no reason to wait any longer after that, and quite likely no reason to appear for either tea or dinner this evening, either. If her scent didn't still linger on him, he might have believed he didn't have a wife at all.

Nothing for it then, but to go off to White's, and hope for a distraction there.

But once he'd climbed into his curricle, he found himself setting his horses' heads toward his mother's townhouse on Harley Street. He hadn't spoken to her or his sisters since the day the *Cock and Bull* had ruined Francesca, and he half expected to find she'd taken Diana, Amy, and Louisa off to Kent, just as she'd said she would.

The stillness of the house seemed to confirm his suspicions, but Tully, his mother's butler, informed him Her Grace was not at home, but that he might find Lady Diana in the small parlor.

Diana was alone, curled up in a window seat with an open

book in her hands, but she wasn't reading. She was staring out the window, looking as forlorn as he'd ever seen her.

He did have a talent for breaking young ladies' hearts, didn't he?

She turned when he closed the door behind him, and a quick smile rose to her lips. "Giles! My goodness, I've been waiting for you to appear for days now. You took your time about it, didn't you?"

"Forgive me." He crossed the room and pressed a kiss to her cheek before dropping down onto the opposite end of the window seat. "Some business took me out of London for the past few days."

"Oh?" She raised an eyebrow. "What sort of business?"

The business of chasing a young lady to Herefordshire, lying to her so convincingly she made the mistake of marrying him, debauching her, then abandoning her to her bedchamber to nurse her broken heart alone.

It hadn't even taken him a full week. Imagine how much havoc he could wreak in a month? The mind boggled.

"You look strange, Giles." Diana's eyes narrowed on his face. "What have you been up to?"

There was no point in drawing it out. "Chasing, courting, and marrying Lady Francesca Stanhope."

Diana's mouth dropped open. "You . . . did you just say you *married* Lady Francesca Stanhope?"

"I did, yes. She's the Duchess of Basingstoke now, and your new sister."

"My new sister! How delightful! Where is she?" Diana leapt to her feet, and the book in her lap dropped to the floor with a thud.

"At my townhouse, alone in her apartments, hiding from me." An unexpected pang pierced his chest at the thought, startling him.

"Oh." Diana dropped back down onto the window seat. "Oh, no. What happened?"

"I've made a mess of it, Diana, and I don't . . ."

I don't know what to do.

The confession tried to claw its way from his throat to his lips, but he choked it back. His mother and sisters relied upon him. They came to him with their problems, and he solved them as best he could, not the other way—

"Oh, just *say* it, will you?" Diana threw her hands up in the air. "Say you don't know what to do, and ask for help, for pity's sake!"

He blinked at her. "Why are you shouting at me?"

"Because I'm tired of you wearing yourself out trying to make everything right for us, and never asking for a thing for yourself! No one can go on like that forever, Giles. We're all permitted a moment of vulnerability now and then, even you!"

"No." He shook his head. "Vulnerability is a luxury I can't afford, Diana."

Hadn't Francesca said something similar to him, once? Yes, the day he'd met her at the Marble Arch for their promenade, when he'd scolded her for being so careless with her reputation. She'd retorted that she didn't care a whit if she was ruined—that it was a luxury, to care about such things as that.

He'd been furious at the time—had thought it an absurd thing for her to say, but now . . . hadn't she been describing something he'd felt himself, but had never known how to put into words?

He had three innocent younger sisters and a mother who, for all that she fancied herself formidable indeed, was still struggling with the consequences of a disastrous marriage.

Weakness was a luxury, and not one he'd ever permitted himself.

"That's the most ridiculous thing I've ever heard." Diana glared at him with her arms crossed over her chest. "You quite mistake the matter, if you suppose you can choose not to be vulnerable. It will come upon you whether you want it to or not, and if you're too arrogant or foolish to ask for help, it will end in ruin, every time."

"Perhaps that's true for you, but I'm—"

"You're *what*, Giles? The grand Duke of Basingstoke? That makes you more susceptible to hubris, not less so."

"*Hubris?* I don't suffer from—"

"You do indeed, brother of mine, so much so I'm amazed they call you Helios instead of Phaethon."

"Helios!" What the devil was she on about? "No one calls me Helios!"

She stared at him for a moment, her face growing redder by the second, and then she burst out laughing. "Oh, my poor, dear brother, how I love you, as blind and foolish as you are!"

Did people really call him Helios? Good Lord. He could have lived the rest of his life quite happily, without ever knowing that. He rose to his feet. "Well, Diana, as illuminating as this visit has been, it's time I—"

"No, wait. I'm sorry." She grabbed the sleeve of his coat with one hand and wiped her eyes with the other. "Just answer me this. Does it matter to you that Francesca is hiding from you? Would you rather she *didn't* hide from you?"

"She's my wife, Diana. Of course, it matters to me. It matters very much."

Diana reached out and squeezed his hand. "I was hoping you'd say that. Now, then. Why is she hiding from you? What happened between you?"

He winced. "I, er . . . I coaxed her into marrying me without telling her the scandal sheets claimed I'd ruined her."

"Oh, dear. That *is* a problem, isn't it?" Diana tapped her lip, thinking. "So now she thinks you—"

"She thinks I only married her to salvage our family's reputation—that I lied to her, and used her." And no wonder. He'd believe the same, if he were her.

Diana raised a brow. "Well, did you?"

This was where things got a trifle murky. "I thought so at first, but I got a bit muddled once I arrived in Herefordshire. Francesca is . . . well, she's intolerable, really, is what she is. You can't imagine how difficult it was to court her."

"I'm sure that's not—"

"She's argumentative, impertinent, stubborn, and not charmed by me in the least. When I first started courting her, she *laughed* at me. Laughed, Diana! She's a dreadful scold, too, always lecturing me for one thing or another."

"Well, at times you can be rather—"

"But she's kind, and clever, and amusing, and so affectionate with her mother, and she has the most remarkable blue eyes, astonishingly blue eyes—dragonfly blue—and she's beautiful, the most beautiful lady I've ever seen, really, and . . . what? Why are you looking at me like that?"

"You're in love with her, Giles." Diana's eyes were shining. "You're madly in love with her."

"*Love*? For God's sake, Diana, I'm not in love with Francesca. I just—"

"Love her. You just *love her*, Giles. Goodness, men are dense."

"That's absurd. I don't love her, but she *is* my wife now, and I don't fancy having a wife who despises the very sight of me. I'd rather we learned to get on together."

"Very well, Giles, if you insist. What matters is the wife you're definitely *not* madly in love with is furious with you, and hiding in her bedchamber because she despises the very sight of you—"

"You don't think she really despises the very sight of me, do you?" Was it truly as bad as that?

"Those were your words, Giles, not mine. Let's concentrate on coaxing her from her bedchamber, shall we?"

"Yes, yes. What should I do? How do I get her to come out of her bedchamber?"

"I haven't the vaguest idea."

He gaped at her. "What do you mean, you haven't the vaguest idea? I thought you said you were going to help me!"

"Of course, I'll help you, but I can't tell you what to do, Giles. I hardly know Francesca, after all. But the thing is, *you* know her. You already know what you have to do to win her trust back. You just don't *know* you know it, if you know what I mean."

"I *don't* know what you mean!" He leapt to his feet, raking his hands through his hair. "For God's sake, you're no help at all!"

"Calm down, brother. My goodness, love has you all worked up, doesn't it?"

"Diana—"

"Think about it, Giles. Think about *her*. Somewhere along the way, she's told you what matters to her, what she wants, what she dreams about. You need to show her you've been listening to her, all along."

He dropped his head into his hands. "Can't I just give her jewels?"

Diana laughed. "You can do that, too, if you like, but any gentleman can give jewels to a lady. Give her something only *you* can give her."

"*What*, though?"

She shook her head. "Only you know that."

Good Lord, but marriage was a dreadful, dreadful business. "Very well. I'll do my best. In the meantime, don't tell Mother I'm married, alright?"

"Don't tell Mother you're *married*? How in the world can I keep such a thing from—"

"You'll have to keep her away from the newspapers, too, I'm afraid. There was already a bit about my marriage in the *Post* this morning, and there are sure to be others."

"Giles! Don't you dare ask me to keep your marriage—"

"I'm sorry, Diana, but my marriage is rather fragile at the moment, and I don't want Mother in the middle of it. Now,

I must get back to my bride. I don't think it's wise for me to leave her alone any longer, do you?"

She huffed out a breath. "You're incorrigible."

"And you, my dear sister, are a perfect angel." He leaned down to kiss her cheek. "Thank you."

He left Diana fuming, but a good deal less forlorn, and had nearly gained the entryway when footsteps ran up behind him. He turned, and Louisa threw herself into his arms. "Good Lord, Louisa, I thought you were Mother. You scared the wits out of me."

"I missed you, Giles! You haven't been here for ages and ages, and I haven't had a violet ice in all that time! You'll take me, won't you? But we'll have to go quickly, before Miss Peck finds me."

"No violet ices today, sprite. I have some other business to tend to today."

Louisa stared at him, her head cocked to the side, then reached out, grabbed a handful of his cheek, and started tugging on it.

"Ouch! What are you doing, Louisa?"

"Trying to make you smile." She gave his cheek one last tug, then gave up. "You look sad, Giles. Are you sad today?"

Clever child, Louisa. One could never hide anything from her. "I am a bit sad today, yes."

She frowned. "Why?"

"Because I got married, and the lady I married doesn't like me very much."

Louisa considered this. "Do you like her?"

"I do like her, sprite. She's my wife, after all. A gentleman is obligated to like his wife." Though no doubt that would be news to the *ton*.

"Oh. Well, why don't you make her like you back, then?"

"I want to, but I'm not sure how to do that, Louisa."

Louisa's face lit up. "I know how!"

"Do you, indeed? How, then?"

"Take her to Astley's Amphitheater!" Louisa gave him a triumphant smile. "She can't help but like you then."

"I don't think that will work." But thinking hadn't gotten him anywhere so far, had it? Thinking, it seemed, wasn't at all compatible with marriage.

Astley's Amphitheater. *Astley's Amphitheater*. Could it actually work?

He pressed a smacking kiss to Louisa's cheek. "Sprite, I think you might be a genius."

Louisa gave him a solemn nod. "I *know*."

This wasn't a business to be undertaken lightly.

Nothing less than his and Francesca's future happiness was at stake, and he wouldn't risk it all by going off half-cocked.

He needed a plan.

So, when he arrived home, despite being tempted to go in search of his wife, he went straight to his study, closed the door, sat down at his desk, and began to write.

He wrote until his hand ached, the sun sank in the sky, and his stomach was rumbling from hours without eating. When he was finished, he sat back and read over what he'd written.

Once he was satisfied, he rang the bell for Trevor.

As always, his butler appeared at once, as if he'd been waiting right outside the study door. "You rang, Your Grace?"

"Yes, Trevor. Go and fetch Digby, and return to my study with him at once, if you please."

"Of course, Your Grace." Trevor hurried off, and returned after a short time with Digby in tow. "How can we help, Your Grace?"

"Here." Giles handed one of the documents he'd just

finished writing to Trevor, and the other to Digby. "Please sit, and read carefully."

Digby and Trevor glanced at each other, then took seats on the settee and began to read.

For some minutes there was only the sound of the fire crackling and the soft crinkle of pages being turned over. Finally, they both finished and looked up at Giles, who was pacing beside the settee.

"Are those instructions clear, gentlemen?"

"Yes, Your Grace," his servants replied in unison.

"This is a matter of some import to me, as you can imagine."

Trevor nodded. "Of course, Your Grace. If I might just enquire, Your Grace. Is this to be kept a secret from Her Grace?"

"Secrets between a husband and wife are dangerous, Trevor, particularly when one's wife is as perceptive as the new Duchess of Basingstoke." Only a fool would try to keep a secret from Francesca. "Don't you agree?"

"I most certainly do, Your Grace."

"I encourage you to look upon the items on your list, Trevor, as *surprises* for Her Grace, rather than secrets to be kept from her. Should that trouble your conscience, you may rest assured that I will reveal all to Her Grace at the appropriate time."

"Yes, Your Grace. A wise plan, indeed."

"Thank you, Trevor. You may go."

Trevor carefully folded the paper, tucked it into his pocket, then with a bow for Giles and a nod to Digby, he departed.

"Now, Digby. As you can see, I'm expecting a great deal from you." He nodded at the paper in Digby's hand. "I've asked for your assistance because I trust you implicitly, Digby."

Digby sat a little straighter. "Yes, Your Grace. Thank you, Your Grace."

"It will be no simple matter, to complete the task I've

assigned you. I won't be displeased with you if you're not able to do so. I ask only that you do your best, Digby."

"I appreciate that, Your Grace. I will do everything I can to see the job done to your satisfaction. One question, if I may?"

"Please."

"This." Digby held up one of the papers Giles had given him. "Are you certain about *this*, Your Grace?"

"Indeed, Digby, I'm quite resolved."

"Very well, Your Grace."

"Before you go, can you tell me if Her Grace has left her apartments at all today?"

"I'm afraid she has not, Your Grace."

"Thank you, Digby. You may go."

Giles continued pacing after his valet was gone, unsure what approach to take with Francesca. On the one hand, a husband of any sense should assume a wife who so assiduously avoided his company would prefer not to see him, and respect her wishes.

But on the other hand, he couldn't stand for the day to end without his seeing her, especially after how they'd left things. The wiser course by far was to wait for Francesca to come to him, but when was a new husband ever wise?

He took the stairs two at a time, but when he reached his bedchamber, he paused by the door to the shared sitting room before entering, struggling to calm his breath.

She wasn't in the sitting room, which left only her bedchamber.

He eyed the door. Predictably, it was closed. Was it locked, as well? Would Francesca go so far as to lock him out of her bedchamber? It was probably better for his bruised pride if he didn't know the answer to that question, so he knocked softly, rather than trying the doorknob. "Francesca?"

For a long, torturous moment there was no sound at all

from the other side of the door, but just as he was about to turn away, he heard a faint rustle, then the soft shuffle of footsteps.

The door opened, and Francesca appeared on the threshold, her dark hair pulled severely back from her face and secured with a blue ribbon. She was pale but composed, yet she looked weary, and her eyes were red.

Weeping. She'd been *weeping*, alone in her bedchamber.

And there was that odd pang in his chest again. Perhaps he was becoming ill.

"Good evening, Your Grace."

He flinched at the formal title, the coolness in a voice that had cried out for him only hours ago, the tight pinch of lips that had parted so invitingly under his own. "I thought you might like to accompany me for a walk in the gardens. It's a pleasant evening, and likely one of the few we have left before winter descends on us."

"No, thank you, Your Grace."

"Very well." He tried to smile, but his heart was sinking. "Will you come downstairs for dinner?"

"Not tonight, Your Grace. Perhaps tomorrow."

He nodded. "Very well. Good night, then, Francesca."

"Good night, Your Grace." She closed the door.

He made his way back to his own bedchamber and threw himself into a chair in front of the fire. Marriage, as it turned out, felt very much like the time his foot had gotten caught under his horse's hoof.

Like five broken toes, only worse.

Thank God he had a plan.

CHAPTER 28

There were only so many hours a lady could stare at the same four walls without losing her wits, even if those walls were papered in a lovely silk damask, with a pattern of roses and wild jasmine done in petal pink and pearl white, on a ground of the most delicious pale orchid color imaginable.

Yes, even then.

Francesca's wits began to desert her after three days, a rather poor showing given the duchess's apartments at Basingstoke House were larger than the entirety of her former home in Ashwell. She should have sailed through for a month or more, but by early afternoon on the third day even the pretty, petal-pink roses looked as if they were judging her.

One thing was certain, however. Her eagerness to escape her apartments had nothing to do with her husband. It certainly had nothing to do with the shadows in his eyes when he'd appeared on her threshold two days ago, or the dejected twist of his lips when she'd closed the door in his face.

She hadn't even noticed his lips. Not at *all*.

It also hadn't a thing to do with the fact that he hadn't returned since then. He hadn't risked another knock on her door, nor had he extended a second invitation to share a walk with him in the gardens.

No doubt he'd lost patience with her, and was preparing

to . . . well, do whatever it was dukes did with recalcitrant duchesses. Thank goodness the days of severed heads on pikes were over, or else she might find herself with a great deal more to worry about than judgmental roses.

"Ahem."

Was that . . . she paused in the middle of her bedchamber, listening.

"Ahem."

Was that a gentleman clearing his throat? It had *sounded* very much like a gentleman clearing his throat, and as it was coming from the sitting room that separated her bedchamber from her husband's, there could be little doubt whose throat it was.

She tiptoed across her bedchamber toward the door.

Boot heels thudding over thick carpet, the faint ring of a teaspoon against porcelain, the soft rustling sound of a newspaper's pages being turned over . . . yes, it was *him*. He was in their shared sitting room at this very moment, not ten paces away from her, just on the other side of the door! Did he know she was listening to him? Could he hear her breathing?

She backed away from the door, slapping her hand over her mouth to cover any telltale signs of respiration, except . . . well, for pity's sake, surely there was no need for such dramatics. It was his sitting room, too. He had every right to be there, just as she had every right to remain in her bedchamber until he'd gone.

Yet soon enough she was creeping forward again, unable to resist. She pressed her ear against the door, but this time, all was quiet on the other side. Had he gone, then? If only she dared open it! Just the tiniest crack, to see if he was still—

"Good morning, Your Grace!" Sarah, her lady's maid, burst into the bedchamber, a sunny smile on her face.

Francesca sprang away from the door, her cheeks heating,

but Sarah didn't seem to notice her guilty flush. "I've got something very nice for you this morning, Your Grace."

"Is it more of that delightful brioche with the currants?" She peeked at the breakfast tray. There *were* a few things she enjoyed about being a duchess, and brioche stuffed with sweet currants was one of them.

"I have those as well, and your chocolate." Sarah set the tray down on a small, round table beside the fireplace and began busily arranging the linens and dishes. "But I'm referring to this, my lady!" She took up the newspaper on the side of the tray and presented it with a flourish. "There's the most delightful little bit about you in the *Morning Post*!"

"God in heaven, not *this* again!" Franny slapped her hands over her eyes—because it was a morning for melodramatics, it seemed—and pointed at the door. "Take it away at once, Sarah! I never wish to lay eyes on the *Morning Post* again!"

"But Your Grace, it really is the sweetest thing, all about how His Grace is utterly besotted with you!"

"Besotted?" Franny peeked through her fingers. "His Grace? With *me*?"

Sarah gave her a puzzled look. "Yes, of course with you, Your Grace. Why, the *Post* has it that His Grace has quite upended the house, just to please you!"

What nonsense. "As usual, the *Post* has gotten it all wrong."

"But there's been ever so much activity these past few days, Your Grace, with all manner of hammering and things, and furnishings being dragged about."

"That may be, but I'm sure it has nothing to do with me."

Sarah's face fell. "I beg your pardon, Your Grace, for bringing the newspaper to you." She poured out the chocolate, then took up the silver tongs and arranged two pieces of brioche on a plate. "Here you are, Your Grace. I'll just take the newspaper away—"

"No! That is, it's quite all right, Sarah. I suppose it won't do any harm for me to glance at it."

"Very good, Your Grace. Will that be all, then?"

"Just one thing, Sarah. Do, ah . . . do the roses look any different to you this morning?" She waved a hand at the wall. "More judgmental, or mocking, somehow?"

Sarah blinked. "I don't believe so, Your Grace."

Yes, it was definitely time for her to leave her bedchamber. "Nothing else for now, Sarah. Thank you."

She waited until the door had closed behind Sarah before turning her attention to the *Post*, which was sitting on the table beside her tray. So, Giles was besotted with her, was he? It was going to be a dreadful shock for London, then, when he bundled into his winged chariot and sent her straight back to Herefordshire.

She snatched the paper up and rifled through it.

Ah, yes, here it was. "The D—of B—Loses his Heart."

She snorted. "I daresay that's news to him."

It was just a short piece, no more than a few dozen lines. That was reassuring, at least. How many lies could they tell in a few dozen lines?

Quite a few, as it turned out, the more egregious among them the claim that the newly wed Duke of Basingstoke was so besotted with his blue-eyed bride he'd stop at nothing to win her affections in return, starting with transforming his morning room into a private music room for his beloved duchess's exclusive use.

A music room, for a duchess who couldn't even play the pianoforte? How absurd!

Giles wasn't going to be pleased when he saw this. It made him sound a bit like a lovesick fool, a duke at the mercy of his duchess—

"Ahem."

She froze with her cup of chocolate halfway to her lips. He was still in the sitting room, perhaps reading the *Post* at this very minute, but if he was in a temper over all of London believing he'd lost his heart to her, it was rather a quiet one.

Perhaps now was as good a time as any to leave her bedchamber. He was her husband, after all, and unless she intended to live the rest of her life within these four walls with those roses condemning her, she'd have to face him sooner or later. There was no sense hiding in her bedchamber and sulking like a child.

She took another fortifying sip of her chocolate, set the cup aside, then rose to her feet and marched through the connecting door before she could change her mind.

Giles was sitting in a chair by the window, his long legs sprawled out in front of him, and a newspaper in his hand.

Not just any newspaper, either, but the *Morning Post*.

"Francesca!" He leapt to his feet, his face lighting up.

"Good morning, Your Grace."

His smile dimmed at her use of his title, which was . . . well, he made it a great deal more difficult for her to continue thinking ill of him when he appeared to be every bit the lovelorn husband the *Post* portrayed him to be.

Then again, he'd appeared every bit a lovelorn suitor in Ashwell, hadn't he, and that had been nothing more than a charade, just as his adoration of Susannah had been. Perhaps he could fool the *Post* with his performance, but she knew better.

"I'm so pleased to see you this morning, Francesca. May I offer you a cup of tea?" He waved a hand at the tea tray on the table by the window.

"No, thank you. I've just finished my chocolate." She ventured farther into the sitting room, unsure what to say. Surprisingly, he seemed equally at a loss, shuffling his feet and darting anxious glances at her in a not very ducal manner, almost as if he was . . . nervous?

No, surely not.

"Er, will you sit down?"

She perched on the edge of the chair, and he resumed his seat across from her.

And they sat there staring at each other without either of them saying a word. She had no idea what he was thinking—his expression gave nothing away—and she was doing her best not to notice how handsome he looked.

It was no easy task.

Why did the pale November sunlight streaming through the window behind him insist on toying with his hair in such a charming manner, turning the fair locks pale gold? Why must his eyes be so very blue, his lips so temptingly red?

It had been three days since she'd kissed those crimson lips, three days since she'd clutched handfuls of that thick golden hair in desperate fingers, writhing underneath him as he brought her to pleasure with his sinful mouth—

"Ahem."

She jerked her gaze to his face. Dear God, she'd been gaping at him like a besotted schoolgirl! Gazing at him, and thinking about his mouth, and his wicked, delicious tongue, and appendages engorged with blood—oh, *why* had her mother put that thought into her head?

He knew it, too. He could read her thoughts on her face, because his blue eyes were darkening, just as they had when he'd . . . when they'd . . .

"I—I suppose you must have seen that nonsense in the *Post*?" She nodded at the paper in his hand, her cheeks on fire. "Er, about your heart, and your blue-eyed duchess, and upending your house, and . . ."

Oh, dear. Perhaps she should have remained in her bed-chamber.

"Nonsense?" He raised an eyebrow. "Which part of it do you suppose is nonsense, Francesca?"

"Why, all of it! The part about the morning room becoming a private music room for my particular use!"

He said nothing, just raised his teacup to his lips, those

blue eyes watching her over the rim of the cup, and . . . and smoldering! He was *smoldering* at her, the villain.

"It *is* nonsense, isn't it?" All at once, she was no longer certain.

He tossed the newspaper aside, rose from his chair, and held out his hand to her. "Why don't you come and see for yourself?"

She stared up at him. Why should he want to take her to see the morning room?

Unless it was no longer a morning room?

"Francesca. Take my hand." It wasn't a command, precisely. His voice was gentle, and he waited patiently, yet at the same time there was something quite *ducal* about him this morning that made her swallow her refusal.

She took his hand and let him lead her from the sitting room and down the grand staircase to the first floor. He'd shown her the house the first day they'd arrived in London, so she'd seen the morning room before, and had admired it then. It was a spacious chamber, with a row of French doors at one end of the room that let out onto a terrace and a garden beyond.

He paused in front of the closed doors, his warm fingers tightening around hers. "I hope this pleases you, Francesca. I want to please you."

There was no time for her to reply, because he threw open the doors then, and led her inside, and everything— her nervousness, the dozens of questions on the edge of her tongue—all vanished in a single, gasped breath.

"*Oh*. Oh, my goodness."

It was still the morning room, in some respects—the beautiful French doors leading out into the garden were still there, of course, along with the magnificent gilt chandeliers, but otherwise, she would hardly have recognized it as the same room. In a matter of three short days, it had been transformed into a light, airy music room fit for . . . well, fit for a duchess.

The walls, formerly a stately gray, had been painted a lovely cream color. The heavy velvet draperies had been removed, and in their place were swathes of pale green silk, and the polished wood floors were now covered with a carpet in cream, green, and gold. She'd never seen a more beautifully elegant room in her life. She could hardly speak, for gazing at it.

"Well, Francesca?" Giles murmured. "Are you pleased?"

She turned to find him standing closer than she'd anticipated, all of his attention focused on her. "Pleased? I think it's the prettiest room I've ever seen, but I don't understand, Giles. Basingstoke House already has a music room."

"Yes, but it's far too formal and grand. It's meant for social occasions and designed to impress guests. This room is private, intimate, and for you alone."

Had he lingered on the word *intimate*, or had she imagined it? "I never expected . . . I don't even know how to play the pianoforte." Still, she couldn't help running a finger over the keys. It was a gorgeous instrument, done in rosewood and inlaid with mother-of-pearl. It took pride of place in the center of the room, but there was a harpsichord against one wall, as well, and a harp in the corner with an exquisite, classical Greek lyre beside it.

"You needn't worry about that. I've hired you a music master. A talented gentleman named Mr. Friedrich, who specializes in teaching harp and pianoforte. You seemed to especially enjoy the Pleyel harp pieces at my mother's musical evening, as well as your cousin's performance of Mozart's Sonata in F on the pianoforte, so I thought we'd start there. I hope that suits."

"You noticed that?"

He stepped closer, his voice lowering to a husky murmur. "I notice everything about you, Francesca. Even then, before I made you mine, I noticed everything."

His. She swallowed.

"Do you know what else I recall from that night, Francesca?" He drew closer, the sleeve of his coat brushing her arm.

Her throat had gone dry, too dry to speak, so she shook her head.

"I noticed that only one person in the room that night was truly enraptured with the music. Only one person among the dozens there who wasn't just politely listening—one person who was feeling the music with her entire body and soul." He pinned her with his blue eyes. "That person was you, Francesca. Only you."

She couldn't look away from him. Dear God, she *couldn't look away from him*.

"That night on the terrace, when we were alone, you told me you'd once loved to play. That you hoped you'd have the chance to learn again, someday." He smiled down at her. "This is your chance."

He remembered everything. All that she'd done, all that she'd said. Somehow, he'd even heard the things she hadn't dared to say.

"Come." He took her hand and seated her on the bench in front of the pianoforte. "Let's see what you remember from the last time you played."

She gave a shaky laugh. "Very little, I daresay. That was ten years ago."

But her hands were already poised over the keys. At first, she was afraid to touch such a lovely instrument, but after a brief hesitation, her fingers found their positions, and the first few measures of Beethoven's Moonlight Sonata filled the room.

It was a clumsy performance—halting, and rife with slips and misplaced notes. He stood quietly beside her while she fumbled through the piece, but strangely, she wasn't ashamed for him to hear her mistakes.

She played and played, the music coming back to her in

fits and starts, her confidence growing as the keys under her fingers began to feel more familiar, and her old music teacher's voice filled her head.

Relax your fingers, Francesca. Less pedal, if you please, Francesca. Don't rush the tempo! Posture, posture, posture . . .

"You'll wear yourself out, Francesca."

She looked up from the keys, dazed, to find Giles had settled on the bench beside her. The very *narrow* bench—so narrow his thigh was only a breath away from hers, their heads bent together over the keys, and he smelled so good, like fresh air and a faint trace of wintergreen-scented soap. She inhaled deeply, his intoxicating scent filling her head.

Oh, no. Had she just *sniffed* his hair?

She leapt to her feet, panic buzzing in her chest like a swarm of bees. The beautiful music room, the music teacher, and the pianoforte . . . only the coldest of ladies could be insensible of the effort he'd made to please her, but when it came to her husband, she wasn't in danger of coldness or insensibility.

With him, her danger was in being too warm, too susceptible, too softhearted. It would be so easy to simply forgive him, to open her heart the last little crack and make a place for him inside it, but once he was there . . .

What if he chose to break it? What if he persuaded her to trust him, and once she let her guard down, he broke it again?

And again, and again—

"Francesca?" Giles jumped up as well, his brow creasing. "Is something wrong?"

"No, I—I'm merely fatigued. I believe I'll return to my bedchamber." Oh, when had she become such a coward?

"I see. Of course, if you're fatigued, you should rest." He smiled down at her, but the flickering shadows were back in his eyes. "May I take you upstairs?"

"No! I mean, it's quite all right, Your Grace. I can find my way up by myself."

He bowed, but the hurt in his eyes followed her out the door of her lovely new music room, up the stairs, and into her bedchamber where the roses were waiting for her, their pretty pink petals dripping with disdain.

CHAPTER 29

The following week.

"That's the third time you've brought your fork to your mouth, Basingstoke." Grantham set his own fork aside, a frown on his lips. "And the third time you've put it down again without taking a bite."

Giles frowned at his fork, but Grantham was right—there was a rather pathetic bite of beef dangling from the tines. His stomach should have been growling angrily by now, too, given he hadn't eaten any breakfast.

He never used to mind dining alone. If anyone had asked him prior to his marriage, he would have said he preferred it, but sitting alone in the breakfast parlor this morning, staring at the door hoping his wife would materialize while he attempted to choke down eggs and toast was not an experience he cared to repeat.

"Poor showing, indeed, Basingstoke." Montford slid a succulent bit of beef from his own fork into his mouth. "What the devil's wrong with you this afternoon?"

Giles eyed the bit of beef, his stomach roiling. "Not a thing."

"Then why are you all rumpled? You look as if you just rolled out of bed. Thank goodness I didn't succeed in stealing

Digby from you. He . . . what, Basingstoke? Why are you looking at me like that?"

"For God's sake, Montford, keep away from my servants, will you?"

"I don't see what all the fuss is." Montford considered the toe of his boot. "The man knows his way around boot blacking, and he's got a light touch with a cravat. Anyway, he refused. He's disappointingly loyal to you."

Giles sighed. "Never mind Digby. I need your help, gentlemen, and with a rather delicate task."

Grantham huffed out a breath. "What is it this time, Basingstoke? It seems to me you have everything you could want. You're no longer ruined, your family's reputation has been restored. What more could you ask for?"

What more, indeed? Once upon a time, that would have been enough, but now—

"And you have your duchess." Montford finished his meal and patted his lips with a serviette. "And a damn fine one she is, if you don't mind me saying so, Basingstoke."

"I *do* mind it, Montford." Giles dropped his fork onto his plate with a clatter. "I don't need you to tell me how lovely my wife is."

He *knew* how lovely she was, from her cloud of dark hair to her perfect pink toes, and every delectable curve and hollow in between, but it was looking as if he'd have to rely on his memory to ever see that glorious sight again.

But he hadn't come here to grumble about his unsatisfied desires. He'd come to grumble about something else entirely. "That story in the *Cock and Bull*, gentleman. I want to know who's behind it."

"Why should that matter now?" Montford speared a slice of beef from Giles's plate and popped it into his mouth. "The quickest way to put an end to a ruination scandal is to marry the lady, and you've done that. She's the duchess now, and no one would dare breathe a word against the Duchess of Basingstoke."

"Some scoundrel insulted my wife, Montford, and told lies about her to all of London—lies that are certainly still being repeated in every *ton* drawing room even now, despite Francesca's becoming my duchess. You can't think I'm simply going to let it go."

Montford shrugged. "I would, if I were you. You've got better things to do than chase some villain all over London."

"Better than restoring my wife's reputation, Montford? I don't see what."

"I only mean to say, Basingstoke, that I wouldn't be wasting my time with the gossips if I had such a delectable creature awaiting my attentions at home—"

Giles slammed his fist down on the table with enough force to make the utensils jump. "Don't speak of my wife as if she's one of your mistresses!"

Half a dozen gentlemen turned in their direction, and Montford exchanged a wide-eyed look with Grantham. "Beg pardon, Basingstoke. No offence meant."

Damn it. It wouldn't do to shout at poor Montford. It wasn't his fault Giles had made a mess of his marriage. "Forgive me, Montford. I'm not myself."

Grantham frowned at him. "What's the trouble, Basingstoke? Is the duchess demanding you find and punish the offender?"

Francesca, demanding? Hardly. "No. She hasn't asked me for anything."

Not for a single, blessed thing. Not since their wedding night.

"What brought this on, then? Is there some other trouble between you and the duchess? You've scarcely been married for two weeks."

Two weeks, yes, and things between him and Francesca grew more stilted every day.

She was scrupulously polite to him, but she was distant, the impudence seemingly drained from her tongue, the spirit in her blue eyes now a wariness that made his chest tight every time their gazes met. Gone was the temptress from their wedding night, swallowed up by an unfailingly gracious duchess who was as unlike the lady he'd married as midnight was to daybreak.

He *had* caught her gazing at him once or twice, but she hadn't returned to his bed, nor had she indicated in any way that she'd welcome his appearance in hers. So, each night he retired to his bedchamber alone, and lay awake half the night tormented by dreams of the taste of her lips, the drift of her silky hair between his fingers, the delightful pressure of her thighs against his hips as he . . .

Ahem. This was neither the time nor the place for such heated memories.

Back to the matter at hand. "The problem, gentlemen, is that as long as the villain who tarnished Francesca's reputation is permitted to go unpunished, there's nothing to keep them from doing it again. I intend to put a stop to it before they get the opportunity, but I'll need your help."

"I still don't see why you want to stir up this sordid business, Basingstoke. Far better to let it drop. You'll only drag the *ton*'s attention back to it."

"I can't let it drop, Montford."

"Well, why the devil not?"

"Well, if you ask Diana, it's because I'm madly in love with my wife, and can't bear the thought that anyone would hurt her, or some other similar romantic foolishness."

There was a shocked silence, then Montford threw his hands up in the air. "*Love*? For God's sake, Basingstoke, why would you destroy a perfectly good marriage by doing something so reckless as falling in love with your wife?"

"Do you take me for a fool, Montford? I told you, I'm not in love with Francesca." The very idea was preposterous.

"Though Diana would say one doesn't choose whether or not to fall in love. It just happens."

"It just *happens*!" Montford looked horrified. "That's bloody terrifying, Basingstoke. If it could happen to a hard-hearted devil like you, it could happen to any one of us."

"For God's sake, Montford, pull yourself together," Grantham snapped. "I'm certain Basingstoke isn't in love with the duchess. No doubt it's just a particularly virulent case of lust. She is very beautiful."

"Diana insists it's love." It was utter nonsense, of course, though curiously, what he felt for Francesca wasn't simply lust, either. That is, he did want her in his bed—desperately, in fact—but holding her while she slept hadn't been *entirely* repulsive to him.

Indeed, it had been rather pleasant. She smelled good, and she had the most adorable way of burrowing into his chest—

"Lady Diana would know better than *you*, Basingstoke." Montford shook his head. "It's a bloody mess, is what it is. You poor bastard. What's to be done? How do you get free of it?"

"It's not a septic limb, Montford. You can't just lop it off, and hope for the best. From what I understand, the only treatment is to make the object of one's affections fall in love with them in return." It was either that, or spend the remainder of one's days madly in love with a lady who couldn't manage more than a polite smile in return for his affections.

Unrequited love must be a devil of a business. As bad as things were with Francesca, at least he had the comfort of knowing he hadn't fallen hopelessly in love with her.

He'd simply keep moving forward with the plan he'd set out. The music room had eased tensions between them somewhat. Perhaps today's adventure would result in an even more ardent response.

"You mean to say, Basingstoke, that the only cure for love

is *more love*?" Montford snatched up his glass of wine and drained it in one gulp. "Christ, that's diabolical."

"Never mind love, Montford. The matter at hand is the villain who told lies about Francesca to the *Cock and Bull*. I will not sit idly by while some blackguard maligns my duchess."

Grantham set his fork aside with a sigh. "Very well, Basingstoke. What is it you'd have us do?"

"Find out who he—or she—is, nothing more." He had his own suspicions, but no proof, and he needed to be certain. "I'll see to it from there. I'd start with Madame Laurent. I've a notion the trouble began there, the day before Lady Sandham's ball. Perhaps she knows something."

"Very stealthy, indeed. Come along then, Grantham. It's the least we can do for poor Basingstoke." Montford shook his head and rose to his feet with a sigh. "It's a tragic day, indeed, when a perfectly good duke is ruined by love."

Francesca was playing the pianoforte in her music room when Giles returned to Basingstoke House. She'd taken to playing for an hour or two after her lessons with Mr. Friedrich, and was improving by leaps and bounds. Friedrich was delighted with her, and claimed he'd never had a pupil with such an accurate ear for pitch, or better natural musical taste.

Giles lingered outside the music room, listening as she ran through her scales, then eased the door open and, without disturbing her, seated himself on a settee nearby and listened as she progressed into the Moonlight Sonata, which she'd mastered, and then on to the piece she was learning now, Mozart's Sonata Facile.

It had become a habit of his, to creep downstairs to the music room after her lessons had ended, so he might listen to her play. She never objected to his presence, but only smiled politely at him when he entered, then instantly returned her attention to her music, as if he wasn't in the room at all.

She was dressed in pink today, a color he favored on her, her dark hair swept back from her face and secured in a knot at the back of her neck with a simple pink ribbon. She had the loveliest neck, long and slender, her skin so pale and soft, and untouched by anyone but him. How many times had he kissed that secret skin, the one night they'd spent together?

Not enough. Not nearly enough.

What would she do if he came up behind her now and dropped the softest of kisses into that fragrant hollow between her neck and shoulder? Would she send him away, or would she turn on the bench, open her arms to him, and slide them around his neck?

He stared at that tempting curve as the notes of Sonata Facile tripped one over the next, her body swaying with the movement of her hands on the keys, so lost in his fantasy he could almost see it unfolding—see himself rising to his feet, crossing the room and leaning over her, his hands braced on either side of the pianoforte, her breath catching as he drew closer, and closer—

"Good afternoon, Your Grace."

He blinked, the fantasy dissolving into a far less titillating reality. He was seated on the settee still, ten paces or more away from Francesca, who was seated on the bench, though she'd stopped playing and had turned to face him. "Did you have a pleasant outing this afternoon, Your Grace?"

Your Grace, still. He hid a wince. "Pleasant enough, yes. I dined at White's with Montford and Grantham. Both expressed themselves eager to make your acquaintance at the theater next week."

"How kind."

"You enjoyed your lesson today? Mr. Friedrich is forever raving about how quickly you're improving."

"He thinks I might try Sonatina in G next." She smiled again—so excruciatingly polite—but she'd risen from the bench and was edging toward the door, no doubt to escape upstairs. She no longer kept solely to her bedchamber, but Basingstoke House was a grand, sprawling place. She didn't need to remain in her bedchamber to avoid *him*.

But not this time. He rose from the settee and caught her gently by the wrist, stopping her before she could escape through the door. "No, Francesca. Not today."

Her eyebrows shot up. "I—I beg your pardon?"

"I've arranged an outing for us this afternoon."

"What sort of outing?"

She sounded so suspicious he couldn't help but laugh. "Nothing so terrible as what you're clearly imagining. It's a surprise, Francesca. I—I hope you'll enjoy it."

He might have just informed her he was dragging her to a public hanging, for all the enthusiasm she showed, but his exceptionally gracious duchess never, ever argued with him. Unlike Lady Francesca, who could hardly open her mouth without a deluge of impertinence streaming from her pretty pink lips.

One would think he'd be pleased with his quiet, docile duchess, but he wasn't.

Not at all.

"Very well, Your Grace. Shall I go upstairs and change?"

"You'll need a wrap, as it's cold outside, but otherwise you're just fine as you are. You, ah, you look very pretty today, Francesca," he added, awkwardly enough. There'd been a time, hadn't there, when he'd paid ladies compliments easily enough?

"Thank you, Your Grace."

Another *Your Grace*—he'd be happy never to hear those two words from her lips again—but her cheeks colored, and she offered him a smile a degree or two warmer than her polite, frozen one before she turned and ran up the stairs.

It was a start, at least.

She returned to the entryway a short time later, a navy-blue pelisse over her pink gown, and soon enough they were in the carriage and on their way to Lambeth.

CHAPTER 30

The inside of the carriage was smaller than it used to be. Franny shifted against the squabs and tucked her legs more tightly under her skirts, but no matter how much she squirmed, the space separating her from her husband remained dangerously narrow.

Yes, it was certainly tighter, closer, more intimate.

Had the carriage somehow dwindled in size since the last time she'd been in it? Narrowed, perhaps? Or had her husband's long, muscular legs somehow become longer and more muscular since their memorable ride from Ashwell to London on the day of their wedding?

One of his knees was nearly touching hers. If she dared to move an inch, her skirts brushed against his pantaloons. If she angled her knees to the left, her toes would be scandalously close to coming into contact with the tips of his boots, and if she slid them to the right, she was nearly certain to encounter his legs.

Nothing but madness lay in that direction.

Whichever way she turned, the tiny sliver of space on which her sanity now hinged would vanish, and there'd be . . . touching.

Touching, after nearly two weeks of painful, heartrending distance.

But they were only his *knees*, for pity's sake. Not his hands, or his lips, or his broad, powerful chest. Not his thighs, or any other, er, appendages in the general vicinity of his thighs. There was no reason in the world the possibility of his knees against her own should be stealing her breath and setting her all aquiver.

But here she was.

It wasn't as if he was doing anything at all to encourage her, either. He was all politeness, all courteous attentiveness when he'd handed her into the carriage, but he'd hardly spared her a glance since then. He hadn't spoken a word, or ventured so much as a smile in her direction, and he kept his gaze focused on the streets of London passing by his window.

And his knees weren't, after all, touching hers. Not quite.

Had he forgotten she was here? If he had, could she really blame him?

A sigh hovered on her lips, but she swallowed it back and turned her own gaze away, toward the window. How had they come to such a strange impasse as this? As angry as she'd been with him when she'd found out about their ruination scandal, in her worst imaginings she never dreamed they would come to *this*.

They'd hadn't exchanged more than a dozen words each day since the day after their wedding, and those they had managed to squeeze from their lips had been awkward, wary. If they went on thus much longer, they'd no longer remember how to talk to each other at all, and they'd be doomed to remain in this peculiar wasteland forever.

It was up to her to find some sort of compromise between them—she could sense that much, sense him holding back, treading cautiously, watching her and waiting—but she didn't have the first idea where to begin.

Then again, perhaps she was mistaken, and he wasn't waiting for a thing from her. Perhaps he was perfectly content with the way things were. Isn't this what *ton* marriages were, after all? Long periods of silence interspersed with polite small talk? Maybe this was precisely what he expected of his duchess—

"We've arrived, Francesca."

"Arrived?" Oh, yes. He was taking her somewhere, wasn't he? That was the point of this torturous carriage ride.

The coachman had brought them to a stop outside a tall, narrow building with two pairs of windows, the lower pair set into graceful arches directly above a portico with two lit lanterns hanging from the front of it. A dozen or so people were gathered underneath it, chattering and laughing as they sheltered from a chilly autumn wind.

She pressed her nose closer to the glass. That building. There was nothing remarkable about it, yet for all its ordinariness, it was familiar, somehow. The laughing crowds, the porticoed front entrance, and Westminster Bridge in the background . . .

"Oh, my goodness! Are we going to Astley's Amphitheater?" She'd never before been inside, but she'd know that building anywhere. She turned to Giles, a hand over her mouth. "Is that the surprise? We're going to the circus?"

"It's called Davis's Amphitheater now, since John Astley retired, but it's still the circus, so yes." He smiled, his first since they'd climbed into the carriage. "We're going to the circus."

"How wonderful! Whatever made you think of bringing me here?"

"My six-year-old sister, Louisa, of all people. I mentioned you were, er . . ."

He trailed off, and his cheeks . . . was he *blushing*? What in the world had he told his six-year-old sister that could possibly make him blush?

"I mentioned you were a trifle homesick for Herefordshire, and she suggested I bring you to Astley's Amphitheater to cheer you up."

"Did she really? What a delightfully clever child."

"Far cleverer than most of the peers in London, yes, though to be fair, to Louisa's mind, a trip to Astley's Amphitheater followed by a violet ice at Gunter's is the solution to every problem."

"Well, I can't help but agree with her. The violet ices are the best kind."

He grinned, and just like that, they were talking again, the words and smiles flowing easily between them. Louisa was a genius.

"You did tell me once you'd always wanted to go to Astley's Amphitheater, when you were a child. Do you remember? That morning in Ashwell, when we walked to High Street, you said you—"

"That I'd longed to see it, and never got the chance. I remember."

Her father had always meant to take her, but then in the blink of an eye he'd been gone, and soon afterward, she and her mother had been banished to Herefordshire, and her visit to Astley's had become just another lost thing, one in an endless parade of lost things.

She glanced out the window again, sucking in a deep breath to keep her eyes from filling with tears. This was no occasion for weeping, certainly. It had taken more than a decade for her to have her trip to Astley's, but here she was, at last!

"Francesca? You're certain this is a pleasant surprise? Because you look as if you're about to burst into tears. If you don't want to go—"

"No! No, I—I want to go, so much, Giles! Indeed, I couldn't have asked for a nicer surprise." Impulsively, she seized his hand, her fingers tight around his. She mustn't let him think for one instant that she wasn't thrilled. "I just never expected you would . . ." Remember something she'd said in passing, that nearly anyone else would have forgotten at once as merely a childish whim, and utterly insignificant. "I never expected this."

"You're pleased, then?"

"So pleased! But you don't think it's silly?" She faltered. "I'm not six years old any longer. I suppose I'm a bit old for the circus."

"Nonsense. One is never too old for the circus." He handed her down from the carriage, but instead of releasing her, he kept her hand in his as they made their way inside.

Giles took her to a box on the third tier, and it was rather like being perched on top of the world, with the stage and the circus ring far below them. It was the perfect vantage point from which to see the entertainments, while also having a view of the building itself, which was magnificent in its own right. "My goodness, it's enormous! I've never seen such a large stage."

"It's one of the largest in London, I believe. It's cleverly designed, as well, with every seat offering an unobstructed view."

"Is the ceiling meant to look like the sky?" It was painted a pale blue mottled with white at the edges, as if clouds were floating by. A grand chandelier hung from the center of the circle, a wonder of glass and blazing light.

"Louisa thought so, so I suppose it must be."

"I'm dizzy from simply trying to see it all." Where did she even start? Where did she look first? Each way she turned her eyes met one fascinating thing or another, whether it was the fantastical scenery and decorations, or the ring in front of the stage with the seating arranged around it, so close it appeared as if the patrons on the ground level could touch the horses as they paraded around the ring.

"If you're dizzy now, you're sure to swoon when the program begins." He gave her a teasing smile.

"Nonsense. I never swoon, Your Grace." She hung over the edge of the box, taking in everything and nodding while he described his visit with his two youngest sisters some weeks earlier.

"Louisa and Amy had a vigorous debate on the merits of the different exhibits, with Louisa arguing for the trick riders, while Amy insisted the pantomimes were far superior to anything a horse and rider could do. They nearly came to blows."

She laughed at that. "And you, Your Grace? What was your favorite exhibit, and were you prepared to defend your choice with fisticuffs?"

"Me? I don't have a favorite. I only came for the girls' sake."

"Is that so?" She held back another laugh. "Then you have no opinion at all?"

"Well, since you demand it, I suppose I'd have to choose the military pantomimes. They have moving sets, and the horses are trained to maneuver through them. It's quite a spectacle, with troops of horses dashing about and the riders in military costumes, with cymbals crashing, and such. Philip Astley—John Astley's brother—was a cavalryman, you know."

"I didn't know, but now that I do, I will certainly look to the pantomimes with an eye for military accuracy."

He might play at nonchalance all he liked, but the enthusiasm in his eyes gave him away, like a boy playing with toy soldiers. To her, his delight in the pantomimes was far more engaging than his ducal charm, perhaps in part because he appeared totally unaware of it. "Do they engage in actual battles?"

"Oh, yes. Real cavalry and infantry battles. Last time there were as many as five horses galloping around the theater at once, with one rider managing all of them. It's amazingly lifelike, especially when the horses charge."

Just then the chandelier above them dimmed. A swell of music from the orchestra signaled the program was about to begin, and they settled into the box to watch.

And what a program it was! If she had thousands of words and a lifetime in which to do it, she could never hope to describe it all, but it lived up to her every childlike expectation, in a way so few adult things did.

The equestrian antics and pantomimes; the burletta, complete with comedic ballads and singing and dancing; the mechanical wonders; the whimsical scenery and the fireworks; and of course, the spectacular military pantomime—it was at once everything her child's heart had dreamed of, and more than she'd ever dared hope for.

She was still dazed with it all when Giles led her from the theater after the performance, her head swimming as she tried to commit it all to memory during the carriage ride home. The stars were still in her eyes when he escorted her to the door of her bedchamber and raised her hand to his lips.

Nothing less than the lingering kiss he pressed to her fingers could have distracted her from the glittering spectacle still playing behind her eyelids, but the moment he bent over her hand, her every nerve jumped to life, her breath stuttering in her lungs, her lower belly tightening in anticipation.

It was a casual kiss, a mere brush of his lips, but there was nothing casual about the way he looked at her as his mouth lingered over her gloved fingers. "Goodnight, Your Grace," he murmured, his breath warming the silk.

For an instant, she could only gaze into those blue eyes, every word she wanted to say vanishing in the wake of that sweet kiss, but when he turned away from her toward his own bedchamber, her mind jolted with panic. She couldn't let him leave without telling him how much tonight had meant to her.

Say something, anything.

"How did you know?" Dear God, she sounded a perfect fool, but that cryptic question was enough, it seemed. He turned back to face her, and his blue eyes were alight with a hope that made her heart wrench painfully in her chest.

"How did I know what, Francesca?"

His voice lingered over her name, his tongue caressing each syllable, the tenderness underlying the heat stealing her breath. "How did you know how much it mattered? Astley's, I mean. I don't believe I said more than half a dozen words to you about it, that day in Ashwell. How could you have known what it meant to me, from so few words?"

He thought about it for a moment, then shook his head. "I'm not sure. Something about the expression on your face when you mentioned it, or perhaps I knew because it would have mattered to *me*, had I been in your place."

"My place?"

"When you spoke of Astley's, I could see it was tangled up with your memories of your father. I couldn't imagine that didn't mean something to you, Francesca."

She swallowed against the sudden raw ache in her throat.

He'd heard far more than she'd imagined that day. He'd heard her, and then he'd put himself in her place. The morning after her wedding night, she would have said such a thing was impossible, that he wasn't a man who could ever understand so completely how another person might feel, but before that, when they'd been together in Ashwell . . .

She wouldn't have said so, then. She'd accepted his proposals because he'd shown her in a dozen different ways that he *was* that man.

Every time he braved the mud to venture out into the garden with her. When they'd gone to High Street, and he'd quizzed Mr. Westcott about the teas that might best suit her mother, and later, when the box had arrived, and she'd found a cone of sugar and drinking chocolate inside. When her mother had swooned, and he'd caught her and carried her to her bed, and later, when he'd returned to Ashwell with Dr. Baillie.

Even before that, too, when he'd sent her the blue ball gown, because he hadn't liked overhearing her aunt Edith mocking her. Then last week, with the pianoforte, and today, with the circus. All those times, he'd put himself in her place, while she never once tried to put herself in his.

So selfish of her, so unfair.

But perhaps it wasn't too late.

She didn't think. She didn't try to reason with herself, nor did she listen to the doubts that drifted through her mind. She simply lay her hand against his cheek, and rising to her tiptoes, pressed her lips against his.

For an instant he froze, then he drew back, gazing down at her with dark, shimmering blue eyes. "So sweet, Francesca." He reached for her, stroking his thumb down her cheek and teasing it across her lower lip. Once, and then again, until she parted her lips for him.

Time narrowed and contracted until there was just the two of them, her face tipped up to his, their breath mingling. He leaned closer, his mouth grazing her ear, her temple. "Your skin flushes pink wherever I touch you."

But he didn't kiss her. She waited, breath held, but long, quiet moments passed, and still, he didn't kiss her.

Did he know her skin still burned when she thought about his kisses? That at night, alone in her bed, she fell asleep to the memory of his lips taking hers? That her heart had soared the first time he'd kissed her? It had felt like coming home, that kiss—it had felt, at last, like everything she'd ever wanted was within her grasp, and she only had to reach out and take it.

But he hadn't, it seemed, felt the same way, because even when he looked into her eyes, and she reached up to trace the line of his lips, he didn't kiss her.

"Giles, I . . ." She trailed off, unsure what to say.

He stepped back, and her hand fell away from his face.

"Sweet dreams, Francesca." He pressed his lips to her forehead again, and then he was gone, leaving her with a pounding heart, and the warm imprint of his lips against her skin.

CHAPTER 31

"The newspapers have outdone themselves this time, Digby."

"Have they indeed, Your Grace?" Digby was busily tidying up the shaving implements while Giles, freshly shaved and coiffed, was sprawled in a chair before the fire with an open newspaper in his hands.

"Yes. Just listen. 'Nothing could equal the delight with which the Duchess of Basingstoke observed the wondrous spectacle of Mr. Davis's circus pageantry. No one who looked upon her beaming countenance could fail to be charmed by such childlike awe, least of all the duke, who remains as captivated as ever with his lovely bride, and could not take his eyes off her.'"

Childlike? There was nothing childlike about Francesca. One had only to kiss those achingly sweet lips to know that.

"That's very good indeed, Your Grace." Digby tested the razor's blade with a careful swipe of his thumb, then wrapped it in a clean cloth and replaced it in its leather case.

"If there's one thing the newspapers can be relied upon to do, Digby, it's to snap up every little tidbit they're offered like a child does a sugarplum." One merely had to be careful to offer only those sugarplums that suited the purpose. His purpose was to protect Francesca from any ugliness the scandal sheets might be contemplating.

It was far more difficult for the more sordid scandal sheets to claim he'd only married Francesca because he'd "ruined" her, when the *Morning Post* had a new story nearly every day about how besotted the Duke of Basingstoke was with his duchess.

"Indeed, Your Grace. London quite adores their new duchess."

"As they should. Nothing new has appeared in the *Cock and Bull*, or any of the others, has it, Digby?"

"No, Your Grace. Not a word."

"Good."

Fortunately, protecting Francesca required nothing more than telling the truth. He *was* captivated by her. Captivated, charmed, besotted, infatuated, and without the least bloody idea in the world what to do about any of it.

Why hadn't he kissed her last night? God knows he'd wanted to, and she'd been right there in front of him, on her tiptoes, no less, her face raised to his, and he'd kissed her on the forehead.

On the *forehead*, as if she were Louisa, and he was tucking her into bed. He folded the newspaper and tossed it aside, disgusted with himself. "Has the Duchess emerged from her bedchamber yet, Digby?"

"Yes, Your Grace. She took her tray in the sitting room this morning."

"The sitting room?" She hadn't ventured into the sitting room in the morning for more than a week. Could she have been hoping to find him there? Had she forgiven him for his clumsiness last night? Was it too late for them to have breakfast together?

"Yes, Your Grace. I rather thought she was waiting for you."

He scrambled to his feet and leapt toward the connecting

door. Damn it, why hadn't he thought to check the sitting room this morning? But perhaps he wasn't too late. Perhaps she was still there, and they might—

"I beg your pardon, Your Grace, but Her Grace retired to her dressing room an hour ago with Madame Laurent. I believe the modiste has come to fit the duchess for a new theater gown."

"Yes, of course. I forgot." It would be their first formal appearance together as the Duke and Duchess of Basingstoke. "That reminds me, Digby. Have you made any progress on that other matter I gave you?"

"Alas, Your Grace, I haven't had much success as of yet, but I remain hopeful."

Giles blew out a breath. "Every reasonable effort is being made, Digby?"

"Indeed, Your Grace, I assure you it is."

There was nothing else for it but to wait and see, then. "I trust you to do your best, Digby."

"Thank you, Your Grace. I will, indeed."

Giles took up the newspaper he'd tossed aside and wandered into the sitting room, leaving Digby in peace to fuss over his linens. He seated himself in the chair beside the window and resumed reading the newspaper where he'd left off, but there was nothing there to hold his attention.

Perhaps he should go off to White's and see if Montford or Grantham were about. Or he could take a ride in Green Park or make a visit to Rundell, Bridge & Rundell. He wanted to select a piece of jewelry for Francesca to wear to the theater next week, but it would be difficult to do so without knowing anything about her gown.

A visit to Tattersalls, then? Weston's? His mother's?

Good God, was he really contemplating a visit to Harley Street when he was hiding a duchess in his townhouse, right under his mother's nose?

Things had come to a sad pass, indeed.

Nothing, it seemed, was appealing enough to rouse his arse from his chair. It was all just so intolerably *dull*. Rather pathetic, really, for a gentleman who'd never before had any trouble amusing himself.

His attention wandered back to the sitting room door. How long did it take a modiste to measure one small woman for a theater gown, for God's sake?

Not that he was sitting about waiting for Francesca, of course, but he hadn't heard her play the pianoforte yet today. A visit to White's was all very well, but not nearly as diverting as listening to his wife play the Sonatina in G, and he'd quite like to know what color gown she'd chosen to wear to the theater.

Blue, to match her eyes, or pink, to match her lips?

Dear God, her lips. Why in God's name hadn't he kissed her last night? It was the first time she'd ever sought his lips, and instead of kissing her until she was sighing for him, and then taking her to his bed as any sane man would have done, he'd let her slip through his fingers.

What the devil was the matter with him?

He'd wanted nothing more than to take her to his bed last night—to wrap that beautiful hair around his fist and hold her close to him while he pressed his mouth against her neck and pushed his hips into hers, so she could feel how much he wanted her. To touch every inch of her smooth skin, his lips taking over where his fingers left off until he'd kissed her everywhere.

But he hadn't done it.

No, instead, he'd dropped a chaste kiss on her forehead and left her to spend the night alone in her bedchamber. She'd been disappointed, too.

No, it was worse than that. She'd been baffled and hurt.

Why, then? Why had he done it?

Because . . . damn it, the answer was there, lurking in the

back of his mind, but trying to get his hands around it was like groping in the dark.

He hadn't kissed her, because if he had, nothing could have stopped him from gathering her into his arms and taking her to his bed, and he couldn't do that, for all that he'd been half mad with desire for her, because . . .

Because once he had her in his arms, he wouldn't give her up again.

Not for anything.

As much he wanted her, as desperate as he was for her, when she came back to him, it would be because she wanted him, body and soul, and for no lesser reason than that. He wouldn't have his wife tumbling into his bed while her mind was clouded with desire, then regretting it the next day, because . . .

Because it would hurt her, and he couldn't hurt Francesca, ever, because . . .

Because her pain was his, just as her pleasure was. Because when she was sad or struggling, his chest felt hollow, and when she was smiling, his lips curved upwards right along with hers, and—

Dear God.

He rose unsteadily to his feet, the paper slipping from his hands and drifting to the floor.

He was *in love with her*. He *loved* her. He *loved* Francesca.

He wasn't just charmed, or captivated, or even smitten, as those words implied a temporary condition, a malady that would fade with time.

This was *not* that.

This was like bloody quicksand. He'd been up to his neck in it before he ever realized he'd fallen over the edge, and thrashing about did no good at all. It only made him sink deeper.

He *adored* her. He would do anything she asked of him.

He shook his head, dazed. How had this happened? When?

When he hadn't been looking, evidently. But why had there been no warning? Wasn't there meant to be a warning?

Love, of all wretched things. Twenty-eight successful years without dipping a single toe in it, and now he was drowning, all because of a pair of damnable, beautiful blue eyes.

Yet could he say with any truth that he'd go back to the man he'd been before he'd found Francesca, if he had the chance?

No. God, no. Never.

Falling in love with her was the best thing that had ever happened to him. It was just alarming to discover it had been going on for so long without his knowing it.

Montford was right all along. Love *was* diabolical.

His preoccupation with Francesca hadn't started on his mother's terrace on the night of her musical evening. It hadn't started at the Marble Arch, or in Wilmot's ballroom, when she'd refused to dance with him, or even at Lord Hasting's ball.

No, it had started before that, the first time he'd ever laid eyes on her, when he'd stumbled across her in Stanhope's garden, her shabby cloak caught on a spike, with her wide blue eyes and impertinent mouth and her secrets. Even then, he'd wanted to take her apart, to see inside her, touch every part of her with his hands and his mouth until she couldn't remember a time when he hadn't been there.

Everything that had followed . . . their first kiss in her mother's garden in Ashwell, her hands against his chest and his arms around her waist, her silky dark hair coming loose and tumbling all around him, the first moment her shy, sweet tongue touched his—all of that had happened because he was in love with her.

He'd dreamed a dozen dreams of her since then, of her lips chasing his while he weaved his fingers through her hair and tangled his hands in all that long, dark silk. He'd dreamed of bringing her to her climax, only to do it all over again as soon as her breathless cries faded from his ears.

But none of that meant anything, unless she was *his*.

If he had to wait weeks for her to be certain of him, or even months, then he'd wait. Though in truth he'd prefer not to have to wait any more than a few hours. Or minutes. Yes, minutes would be better than—

". . . dramatic shade is perfectly divine with your coloring, Your Grace!"

Was that Madame Laurent? He stilled, listening.

"Honestly, Your Grace, this gown is my favorite creation this season."

Yes, it was certainly Madame Laurent, her voice carrying clearly through the sitting room door. Had it been left ajar?

"Why, the *ton* will be positively green with envy when they see you in this at the theater next week. I don't mind saying, Your Grace, that I can hardly wait to witness it."

"Now that you mention the *ton*, Madame Laurent," Francesca said, her sweet voice floating through the door. "I wonder if you happen to know a young lady by the name of Prudence Thorne?"

Prudence Thorne? He didn't recognize the name.

"Why, yes, Your Grace. I know Miss Thorne. I made a few gowns for her at the start of the season. She's a lovely young lady. A pity, really, that her season was cut short."

"Was it, indeed? Forgive me, Madame Laurent, but I met Miss Thorne early in the season, and I've looked everywhere for her since, but she vanished after Lord Hasting's ball, and I never saw her again."

"It's rather a sad story, Your Grace. Miss Thorne was obliged to give up her season, I'm afraid." Madame Laurent lowered her voice. "Her father, Major Thorne, got into some difficulties with a wager in Lord Hasting's card room, and Miss Thorne thought it prudent to take him back to Surrey."

"Oh, dear. How dreadful. I'm sorry to hear it. She was

the first lady I met when I arrived in London, and I did so enjoy her company. I was looking forward to our becoming friends."

Friends. Yes, Francesca must feel the lack of friends, mustn't she?

She and Lady Susannah—that is, the Marchioness of Ormsby—were engaged in a lively correspondence now, but Lord and Lady Ormsby didn't intend a return to London until next season, after the scandal from their elopement had died down, and it was several weeks yet before Lady Maria would be well enough to leave Bath.

Francesca must feel quite alone here. Didn't ladies need other ladies to speak to on occasion? This was the first he'd heard of Prudence Thorne, but there was no mistaking the longing in Francesca's voice when she'd said the lady's name.

I was looking forward to our becoming friends . . .

Where had Madame Laurent said Miss Thorne lived? Surrey?

Surrey wasn't all that far from London—

". . . back to my shop to see if I can find that lace. It will trim the gown to perfection, I assure you, Your Grace. Shall I return tomorrow with it? It won't take but a moment to add it to the waistline. I've a few other bits and pieces for you, as well, and can bring those with me, if you like."

"If you'd be so kind, Madame Laurent."

"Of course, Your Grace." There was a shuffle of footsteps, then the door that led from Francesca's bedchamber to the corridor opened, and Madame Laurent called out a cheerful good-bye.

Then, nothing but silence.

He waited for some time, but there wasn't as much as a whisper from inside Francesca's bedchamber. No footsteps, not even the faint rustle of silk.

Had Francesca retreated to her dressing closet, then?

He rose and crept toward the sitting room door, and yes, it *was* slightly ajar. One small push was all it would take to widen the gap another half inch, just enough for him to peek inside, but was he really so desperate he'd resort to spying on his own wife?

Surely, he had more self-control than that! Only a manner-less brute of a husband would burst into his wife's private bedchamber without an invitation. No, if Francesca wished to see him, she'd come in search of him.

Well, then, that was settled. He turned away from the door and marched back to his chair, positively brimming with virtuousness, but as it turned out, virtue was a poor, fleeting thing, and most certainly *not* its own reward, because soon enough he abandoned his chair again, and crept to the sitting room door.

It remained open, and the bedchamber was still and silent.

Francesca had no doubt returned to her dressing room. If he did peek inside, he'd likely find only an empty bed-chamber.

Unless . . .

Was it possible she'd left the door open on purpose, for him? Could it be there was an enchanting, possibly half-dressed duchess waiting for him to enter her bedchamber right at this very moment?

No, that was too much to hope for.

But it wouldn't do any harm to check, surely? He could simply pop his head in, make certain all was well, then close the door securely after him.

All perfectly innocent, of course. Noble, even.

Slowly, quietly, he eased the door open wider, but he stopped short, his breath snagging in his chest when he saw what was waiting for him on the other side.

Francesca hadn't returned to her dressing room.

She was standing in front of the full-length looking glass in her bedchamber, but she wasn't studying her reflection.

She was watching the sitting room door behind her, a small smile on her lips. "You took your time, didn't you, Your Grace? I thought you were going to stand out there forever."

Ah, now *that* sounded very much like an invitation, one he wouldn't dream of refusing a second time. He stepped into her bedchamber and closed the door behind him.

"This is my gown for the theater next week." She held out the skirts, her eyes still on his in the glass. "Do you approve, Your Grace?"

The gown was a deep violet color, the silk so fine it shimmered like an amethyst waterfall even in the muted light inside her bedchamber. The bodice was cut low, revealing a generous expanse of her creamy skin. Dainty puffed sleeves of the finest embroidered lace in an even deeper shade of violet emphasized her slender shoulders, and an overdress of the same lace floated out behind her.

He knew next to nothing about ladies' gowns—he knew what he liked, and little more than that—but this gown was unlike any other he'd ever seen before. It wasn't a gown for a young lady from the country who was as yet unsure of her place in London.

No, this was a gown for a duchess.

His duchess, a lady unlike any other lady in all of London.

"You're very quiet, Your Grace. Are you displeased with the gown?"

He prowled closer, a low, ragged sound rumbling in his chest, a sound he'd never heard himself make before.

Two bright spots of color appeared in her cheeks, a shiver rippling over her as he moved closer, until he was directly behind her, the folds of violet lace brushing against his pantaloons. "Giles?"

Her eyes had fallen to half-mast, a spray of goosebumps rising on her skin, and she was trembling for him, every inch of her waiting for the touch she knew was coming. Where would it land? Her waist, or her hip? The few locks of hair that had freed themselves from her ribbon, and were now drifting in a dark cloud over her shoulders?

No. None of those places.

For long, aching moments, he didn't touch her at all. "Do you want me, Francesca?"

Her eyes dropped closed, then opened again and met his in the glass, those dragonfly-blue irises swallowed by her dark pupils. "Yes."

He traced one finger over the lacy sleeve of her gown, but still, he didn't touch her. "If you have me, you will have all of me, and you will give me all of you in return. Nothing less. If you come to my bed, Francesca, I won't ever let you leave it again. You're mine forever then, and I'm yours. Do you understand?"

She swayed against him, the sensuous arch of her spine touching his chest. "Yes."

"Is that what you want? To be mine?" He held his breath, waiting.

"Yes." No hesitation.

Then, only then, did his lips find the back of her neck, the skin there so soft and fragrant, so smooth under the tip of his tongue.

"Oh." She gasped as he dropped another kiss there, his breath stirring the wispy curls at her hairline. "Oh, Giles."

He dragged the tip of his tongue up the back of her neck, then caught her hands in his and brought them up to either side of the looking glass. He closed her fingers tight around the edges and splayed one hand over the gentle curve of her belly to steady her.

"Hold on, sweetheart."

CHAPTER 32

Francesca's shy gaze met his in the mirror. "I thought you weren't going to come in here, just now. After last night, when you didn't . . . I thought you might not want me anymore."

"No. That will never happen, Francesca." Giles lowered his head to her neck and inhaled her scent. Fresh air, a faint hint of rosemary-scented soap, and *her*. "But I needed you to be sure you wanted me, before I touched you again."

She drew in a shaky breath. "Do you still want *me*?"

"I will *never* not want you, sweetheart. I can't stay away from you." He circled one gentle fingertip over the soft skin between her shoulder blades, then dragged it slowly down her spine. "I want you more than I want my next breath."

Her blue eyes were wide, her pulse fluttering in her throat. "I—I missed you, Giles."

A sound tore loose from his chest—a groan, a sigh—he didn't know which. He wanted to sink to his knees for her and stay there forever. He stroked his fingertips over the base of her spine. "I missed you, too, sweetheart. So much."

She was silent for a moment, then she let out a nervous little laugh. "I'm not sure what to do now."

"You don't have to do anything." He pressed a soft kiss under her ear, his cock swelling against his falls as he trailed his tongue over her fragrant skin. "Just let me make you feel good."

She nodded, her eyes so wide and trusting it made his throat ache. There'd never been a chance he wouldn't find his way back to her. Everything that had ever stood between them collapsed like a sandcastle in the tide as soon as he admitted the truth to himself.

In the end, it was simple. He was hers. He was *hers*, and that was all that mattered.

He rested one hand on her hip and let his thumb trace that luscious curve, the silk slippery under his fingertips. "Have I ever told you that I adore your neck?" He brushed her hair aside and touched his open mouth to her nape. "It's been driving me mad ever since that first night in the garden."

She shivered as he dropped damp kisses along the side of her neck. "It has?"

"God, yes." He caught her earlobe between his teeth, his stomach tightening with want at her soft gasp as he nipped at it. "I've dreamed about kissing it again. Biting it." He sucked a tiny fold of her skin into his mouth and teased it with his tongue. "You have the most sensuous neck I've ever seen."

"I've never thought about my neck before."

He managed a hoarse chuckle. "I've thought about it enough for both of us."

"Oh?" She smiled at him in the looking glass. "What else have you thought about?"

He nuzzled his face into the hollow of her shoulder. "All of you. Everything, Francesca." He loosened the buttons at the back of her gown and slipped his hand under the edge of her bodice, her skin so warm and soft under his palm. "Here." He stroked his other hand over the curve of her belly in teasing circles. "And here. I've devoted hours to thinking of you here."

"Oh." Francesca's breath came faster, and her eyelids grew heavy. "That's so . . . oh."

God, he wanted to fist that violet silk, raise her skirts, and sink his fingers inside her, but he held off, holding onto his control by a thread. A gentleman didn't rush a lady in the bedchamber, no matter how desperate he was for her.

"I've thought about wrapping your hair around my hand and holding you with your mouth against my chest." He pulled the pins from her hair, gathered the thick, dark locks in his hand and draped them over one of her shoulders, baring her skin to his lips. "I want to taste every inch of you. Is that alright, sweetheart?"

"Yes. I—I want you to."

He dragged his teeth lightly over her neck again, a low groan escaping him. Her neck might very well prove to be the death of him. His cock was so hard he feared he was one caress away from disgracing himself, and she hadn't even touched him yet. "You taste so good, Francesca."

She met his gaze in the glass, her pink lips curving, her voice a raspy whisper. "What else have you thought about, Giles? What will you do to me next?"

God, he could come just from the sight of that wicked, sly little smile. "I stroke your breasts until your nipples are so hard for me, sweetheart."

She gasped, as if his blunt words excited her, her heavy gaze holding his. "How do you stroke them? With your hands? Or your tongue?"

Good Lord, what a question. His cock twitched, the tip pushing up over the edge of his waistband. His innocent wife was as clever in the bedchamber as she was everywhere else, that pert mouth of hers sweet and wicked at once.

It had been made for him, that mouth.

"My hands first." He slid his fingers a little deeper into her bodice and teased the edge of a fingernail gently over one of her nipples, then stopped and waited. "Tell me what you want, sweetheart."

She jerked against him, her sweet curves pushing against

the front of his falls, a maneuver his cock heartily approved of. He licked her earlobe, then brought his mouth close to her ear. "Ask for what you want, Francesca. You only have to ask, and I'll give you everything."

"Touch me."

Her breathlessness, that pleading note in her voice made him wild, undid him. Quickly, he reached down and unbuttoned his falls, freeing his painfully confined cock. "Here, sweetheart?" He traced the undersides of her breasts, then dragged his palm lightly over one of her nipples. "Is this where you need to be touched?"

"Yes," she breathed. "Yes."

He caught one taut peak between his finger and thumb, pinching lightly, a slow smile curving his lips when she shuddered against him. "Does that feel good, sweetheart?"

She let out a choked whimper.

"Answer me, Francesca." He dragged her sleeve down, baring her shoulder, still working her nipple, mesmerized by their reflection in the looking glass, the eroticism of his fingers toying with the rosy peak. "Tell me how it feels."

Her fingers tightened around the edge of the glass, her knuckles whitening. "It's so good, Giles. It makes me ache."

"Where, sweetheart?" He dropped a kiss onto her shoulder. "Show me where you ache."

She took his hand and pressed his palm against her breast. "Here."

"Yes. Where else?"

He held his breath as she slid his hand down between her breasts, over her rib cage, then lower, lower, his fingers dragging over the swell of her belly, then lower still, into the sweet, warm space between her thighs. "Here. I ache here."

"Do you need me to touch you there, sweetheart?" he whispered, easing her skirts up and tracing her damp folds with gentle fingers.

A sharp cry left her lips. "Yes, like that. Please, Giles."

He went still, his gaze locked on her face. Her lips were parted, her cheeks flushed with desire, her eyelids heavy over dark blue eyes. His breath caught at the sight of her before him in her lovely violet gown, one of his hands inside her bodice, the other under her skirts, her nipples peaked for him, taut against his teasing fingers. "God, Francesca, just look at you. So beautiful, sweetheart. You're so beautiful, I can't breathe."

A soft cry left her lips, and her head fell back against his shoulder.

"No. Look at yourself." He released her breast, took her chin in his hand and gently lifted her head so she might see her own reflection. "Don't hide from me, Francesca, or from yourself."

She drew in a deep breath and met his gaze in the mirror. "I wish I could see myself the way you see me."

He released her chin and stroked his palm down her neck and between her breasts, then stepped away from her just long enough to take his waistcoat off and tear his shirt over his head. He gathered her close again, a groan tearing from his throat when her back touched the bare skin of his chest. He rested both hands on her hips. "I'm going to touch you, Francesca, and I'll tell you what I see. Is that all right?"

She nodded, her gaze never leaving his face. "Yes."

He continued to stroke between her legs with one hand, while the other moved over her lower belly, then up her abdomen. He touched the tip of his tongue to her neck, tasting her there before sliding his mouth up to her ear. "The flutter of your pulse, here." He dipped his fingers into the hollow of her throat. "The way you catch your breath, and the way your skin flushes when I stroke you. It's so lovely, sweetheart. It makes me want to touch you everywhere."

"Where . . ." She swallowed. "Where will you touch me?"

He nipped at her shoulder, his breath tearing from his lungs in ragged pants. "Your breasts." He made quick work of the rest of the buttons at the back of her gown and eased it off her shoulders and down her legs, folds of violet silk puddling on the floor at her feet. "You're so responsive, Francesca." He dragged his fingertips over the dainty pink tips of her nipples. "Does that feel good, sweetheart, when I stroke you like this?"

She caught her lower lip between her teeth. "Yes."

He stroked and tormented the taut peaks with his thumbs until she was trembling in his arms. "I want to lick them, sweetheart. Suck them. I will, later. Do you think I can make you climax that way? Just by sucking your nipples?"

"I . . ." Her eyelashes fluttered. "I don't know. I've never felt anything so . . . I've never . . ."

"Hold onto the glass, sweetheart." He hissed when she leaned forward and her palms hit the glass. "Yes, Francesca. Just like that."

He slipped his fingers between her thighs again, a groan tearing from his throat when he found her dripping for him, drenched in honey. "You're so wet for me, sweetheart. Do you need me right here?" He teased the pad of his finger lightly around her slick nub.

"Ah, Giles. *Please.*"

"Yes, love, yes." He stroked her slowly, his touch whisper soft, giving her just enough to draw out her pleasure, but not enough to send her over the edge.

Not yet.

She writhed against him, her hips working against his taunting fingers, seeking her release, but he kept her balanced on the edge for long, breathless moments, working her with quick flicks of his fingers until she was close, then slowing and gentling his strokes only to bring her back to the peak again and again, her sweet, desperate cries driving him mad.

"Lean back against me, sweetheart. I'm going to give you what you need. Watch yourself in the glass while I make you come."

He gave her one long, lingering stroke, then another, and that was all it took. She cried out, her body undulating against his as he took her over the edge at last, her bottom lip caught in her teeth as she shuddered and panted through her release, and Dear God, he'd never seen anything as beautiful as his wife finding her pleasure.

He couldn't take his eyes off her.

It seemed to go on forever, the shudders wracking her, her lovely pink lips parted and pleading, his cock surging harder against her as she cried out for him, sobbed for him, begged him not to stop, not to stop . . .

And he didn't. He didn't stop until the tension drained from her body, her fingers went slack around the edges of the looking glass, and she fell back into his arms, boneless.

Only then did he scoop her up, holding her tight against his chest as he crossed to the bed. He laid her down, crawled in beside her, then gathered her close against him. Her breathing calmed, then evened out as she fell into a light doze.

It had been a near thing, but he hadn't disgraced himself.

Yes, he was as hard as a poker, the head of his cock a furious red, and there wasn't enough blood left in his other head to do even the simplest mathematics, but the wife he adored was beside him, her cheeks still flushed from the climax he'd given her, and somehow, he'd managed not to ruin her lovely new theater gown.

Not a bad morning's work, really. Not by any measure.

When Franny woke a short time later, she found Giles sprawled on his back, one arm around her shoulders, the other folded behind his head, and a smug smile on his lips.

A triumphant, very *masculine* smile.

She raised her head from his chest and propped herself up on her elbow. "You look pleased with yourself, Your Grace."

He chuckled, then pulled her closer and draped his arm

over her waist. "I was just thinking I'm the only man who ever gets to hold you like this. The only man who ever gets to see how beautiful you are when you climax."

"Giles!" She laughed, her cheeks heating. "What a thing to say!"

"I'm a possessive, selfish man, wife. Knowing you're mine, and mine alone gives me a great deal of satisfaction, indeed."

Selfish?

He'd just given her incredible pleasure, and now he was lying next to her with what appeared to be a painfully swollen appendage—a swelling for which he hadn't demanded any relief—and he thought he was being selfish?

She eyed his appendage. It was striking—long, thick, and hard, the tip flushed a deep red, and throbbing against the roped muscles of his abdomen with every one of his heartbeats.

She'd given his appendage a good deal of thought in the two weeks since they'd last shared a bed.

His, ah . . . his cock, that is.

She couldn't take her eyes off it now. Impossibly, it seemed to grow larger as she stared at it. It arched toward his belly button, waiting for her to . . . to what? Well, she wasn't quite sure. She was a novice when it came to cocks, but even she knew he needed release.

Badly.

She could stroke him. He'd shown her how to do that.

But he'd also put his mouth on her that one time, and it had felt so heavenly, so impossibly, toe curlingly *good* she might have actually swooned a little. If his mouth on her made her feel that good, mightn't her mouth on him have the same result? She wanted to find out, but it was a bit nerve-wracking, taking a fussy organ like that into her mouth. What if she got nervous, and maimed him with an accidental slip of her teeth?

He let out a low moan. "It's driving me mad, the way you're staring at my cock."

It *was*? If he could become that aroused just because she was looking at it, what would he do if she took it into her mouth? There was only one way to know for certain.

She laid a hand on his hip. "Take off your pantaloons, Giles. I want to see you. Touch you."

She hardly had time to blink before he'd torn off his pantaloons and sent them sailing across the bedchamber. Then he fell back against the bed, his chest heaving.

Well. He was eager enough.

She touched her tongue to her bottom lip. She'd never done anything like this before—hadn't even known one *could* do such a thing as this, but the bedchamber was no place for cowardice.

And really, how difficult could it be? Surely, she'd figure it out as she went along. She drew in a deep breath, leaned over him, and kissed her way down his torso. His stomach muscles tensed as she went lower, then lower still—

"Francesca, what are you doing?" He sounded as if he was having trouble catching his breath. "You don't mean to—"

"Hush." She gave the tip of his cock an experimental lick, and a strangled moan left his lips.

Oh, no. Had she hurt him? She drew back quickly, but he didn't appear to be in any pain. His cock appeared as willing as ever, still hard and beautifully flushed, and he was clutching the sheets in his fists, his lips open and his head arched against the pillow, his neck straining.

Well, that was promising. She leaned over him again, drew the plump head into her mouth, and suckled the tip.

His hips shot off the bed. "Ah, God, *Francesca.*"

My goodness, this was going much better than she'd thought it would. She was going on pure instinct, but everything she did seemed to drive him wild.

The next time she took him as deep as she could. She

couldn't hold him in her mouth for long, but she suckled him hard, her lips wrapped tightly around his length, her tongue teasing over him before she released him from her mouth to take a deep breath.

"Francesca, do you know what you're . . . ah!" He let out another desperate groan as she took him into her mouth again, his hips jerking and his fair hair hanging in a damp tangle over his fierce blue eyes. "*Francesca.* Sweetheart, you're going to make me come."

Yes. That was what she wanted, to make him lose control, to make him groan and cry out, to find his release. She closed her mouth over him again, and this time his hand came up to cradle the back of her head, his fingers playing gently in her hair as his hips moved in steady, shallow thrusts.

She took him deeper, then deeper still, then all at once he let out a sharp cry. His fingers tightened in her hair, and he drew her head back with a quick tug. A second later his cock pulsed, his powerful body shaking and his back arching as streams of white liquid spurted over his stomach and chest.

"My goodness." She glanced between the puddle on his belly to his face, then back again. "That was . . . well, that was . . ."

"Not a bad morning's work?" He collapsed against the bed, a sleepy, satisfied grin on his lips.

She stared at him for a moment, then threw her head back in a laugh. "Not a bad morning's work, indeed."

CHAPTER 33

The following week.

Beethoven's Sonatina in G was going to be the death of him. He was going to expire right here on a green silk settee in Francesca's music room.

Giles crossed his legs, let out a deep sigh, uncrossed them, shifted from one arse cheek to the other, then crossed his legs again. "A curse upon Beethoven's head! Aren't sonatinas meant to be brief? This one's been dragging on for hours!"

"It's been a minute and a half, Your Grace." Francesca continued playing, her fingers never faltering on the keys.

She was dressed in white today, with a fetching sash of bright blue ribbon around her trim waist, tied in a sweet little bow that rested right in the middle of her back. One quick tug, and there would be nothing between his fingers and the buttons on her gown.

That bow had been taunting him since she sat down on the piano bench.

Cross. Uncross. Shift. Heavy sigh.

She didn't pay him any attention, but continued with her practice, coaxing a quick burst of light notes from the keys, until at last her hand stilled, and the music faded into silence.

He leapt up from the settee. "Are you finished?"

"Yes, I'm—"

"Thank God. Come upstairs, sweet—"

"I'm finished practicing with my left hand." She switched to her right hand and began to play again without so much as a glance at him.

He collapsed back onto the settee with a groan. "You'll regret your cruelty to me, wife, when you finally rise from that bench and turn around to find nothing but a twisted, desiccated corpse where your husband used to be."

"You're quite noisy for a corpse, Your Grace."

"A desiccated corpse," he repeated stubbornly. "A twisted, desiccated corpse with a hard, aching co—"

"Giles! Hush."

"I beg your pardon, madam, but you put me into this state."

"Me? What did I do? I'm merely playing the pianoforte."

"*Do?* Are you under the mistaken impression, wife, that you need to do anything at all to arouse me? The other morning, I woke to find you drooling on my pillow, and it was all I could do not to pounce on you." Really, how was a man meant to get anything done, with such a fetching wife?

"All you could do? As I recall, you *did* pounce on me, Your Grace."

"So, I did, and so I would again this instant, if Herr Beethoven would only get out of my way. *Now* are you finished?"

"I am, indeed."

"At last! Come up—"

"With the first movement."

Did he detect a slight change in the pitch of her voice? A hint of a laugh, perhaps? He raised his head from the back of the settee, and . . . yes, her shoulders were shaking.

His wife—sly, impertinent, adorable wife that she was—was teasing him.

Well then, all wagers were off the table, weren't they?

That being the case . . . he rose from the settee, prowled toward the pianoforte, caught the end of her blue ribbon, and tugged.

"Giles!" The second movement of Sonatina in G ended with an abrupt crash of discordant notes. "What do you think you're doing, you wicked man?"

"Having my way with your bow, madam."

She started to turn on the bench, but he boxed her in with an arm on either side of the pianoforte. "No, Francesca. You haven't finished practicing."

"I can't practice with you doing *that*."

"What? This?" He nudged his face into the crook of her neck, inhaling deeply. "That *is* a pity, but you're meant to practice for two hours, are you not? I'm sorry for your difficulties, but I don't make the rules."

"You're the duke, aren't you?" She gasped as his lips roamed from her neck to her earlobe, nibbling delicately. "Who makes the rules, if not you?"

"Well, perhaps I might be persuaded to make an except—"

He was interrupted by a brief knock on the door, and an instant later, Trevor appeared. "I beg your pardon, Your Graces. His Grace, the Duke of Grantham, and His Grace, the Duke of Montford, are here."

Grantham and Montford and their damnable timing! "Tell them to begone at once, Trevor—"

"Gracious as ever, Basingstoke." Grantham strode into the music room, caught sight of Francesca, and swept into an elegant bow. "Good morning, Your Grace. It's a great pleasure to meet you at last."

"Especially looking so well." Montford glanced from Francesca's scarlet face to Giles's irritated one, his dark eyes dancing. "Quite glowing, indeed."

Giles reluctantly released Francesca's ribbons and handed her up from the piano bench. "Gentlemen, Her Grace, the

Duchess of Basingstoke. Francesca, Their Graces, Grantham and Montford. They're both reprobates, and best avoided."

Francesca laughed and offered each gentleman a curtsy. "Your Grace, and Your Grace."

"That's quite enough grace for one morning, wouldn't you say?" Montford dropped onto the green settee Giles had just vacated and glanced around him. "Why don't I recall this room?"

"It used to be gray." Grantham took the seat beside him.

"Did it, indeed?" Montford looked around again, his brow creasing, then shrugged.

Giles seated Francesca on a nearby settee, settled down beside her, and turned his attention to his friends. Montford and Grantham weren't in the habit of making early morning calls. They must have come because they'd discovered something about the *Cock and Bull* culprit. "Gentlemen? Have you some information for me?"

Grantham hesitated, glancing at Francesca. "Yes, but perhaps it would be best if—"

"It's all right, Grantham. You may speak freely. I have no secrets from my wife."

"Do you not?" Montford gave him a puzzled look. "How curious. I've never heard of such a thing before."

"Never mind, Montford." Grantham shot him a quelling look, then turned back to Giles. "We've found out who is responsible for that story in the *Cock and Bull*. Indeed, they took surprisingly little trouble to hide their identity. I suppose they thought no one would check."

Giles leaned forward. "Who was it?"

Grantham cleared his throat. "Er, well, it's rather a delicate—"

"It was Lady Edith Stanhope."

Francesca gasped. "My aunt?"

"For God's sake, Montford." Grantham glared at him.

"You might have taken a little more care with the duchess's feelings."

"Oh. Yes, of course. I beg your pardon, Your Grace."

"Lady Edith. You're certain?" But it made perfect sense, didn't it? She'd been at Madame Laurent's that day. She'd gotten a close look at the blue ball gown, and would have recognized it at once as the same gown Francesca was wearing at Lady Sandham's ball that evening.

He'd suspected Lady Edith all along. He'd hoped he was wrong—that even a lady as vicious as Lady Edith would draw the line at ruining her own niece—but it seemed he'd given her too much credit. "You're quite sure it was her?"

"Absolutely sure. Madame Laurent claims Lady Edith saw you leave her shop with a dressmakers' box on the afternoon of Lady Sandham's ball. When she saw Her Grace in the blue gown at the ball that evening, she drew her own conclusions."

"Yes, the *wrong* conclusions." The most vindictive, malicious conclusions she could possibly draw. The Stanhopes had already taken everything they could from Francesca, but Lady Edith still wasn't satisfied until she'd stolen Francesca's reputation, too.

But she wasn't going to get away with it. Not this time.

"One of the printer's assistants at the *Cock and Bull* confirmed it." Grantham glanced at Francesca. "I'm sorry for it, Your Grace."

"Thank you, Your Grace, but you may rest easy on my account. There was a time when my aunt's perfidy might have hurt me, but those days have long since passed. I don't pay any attention to her antics now. There's nothing she can do to hurt me anymore."

"That's wise of you, Your Grace." Montford gave Francesca an approving look, but turned a shrewd eye on Giles. "I doubt we can say the same for Basingstoke here, however. He looks as if he's ready to challenge Lady Edith to a duel."

"There will be no duels." No, he had something else in mind for Lady Edith.

"Well, then, now that we've ruined your morning, we'll be on our way." Montford rose to his feet. "Come along, Grantham."

Grantham rose as well, bowing to Francesca. "Your Grace. I look forward to seeing you at the theater this evening."

Giles pressed a quick kiss to Francesca's hand, then followed Grantham and Montford to the door of the music room. "Thank you both. I'm in your debt."

"What are you going to do to Lady Edith, Basingstoke?" Montford asked, glancing over Giles's shoulder at Francesca. "Something dreadful, I hope."

"You'll find out soon enough." Sooner than they anticipated.

"Good. I never cared much for Lady Edith Stanhope. I do, however, quite like your duchess. But she looks like a high-spirited one. Not particularly biddable, eh, Basingstoke?"

Francesca, biddable? "You have no idea, Montford."

"Beautiful, and impertinent." Montford shook his head. "Dreadful combination. You'll have your hands full with that one, Basingstoke."

With any luck, he'd have his hands full of her in the next few minutes. "Yes, well, until tonight then, gentle—"

Crash! The thud of the front door slamming echoed down the hallway, followed by thundering footsteps. "What the devil?"

"Your Grace!" Trevor came rushing down the corridor, his face a mask of horror. "Your Grace," he panted. "I beg your pardon, Your Grace, but your—"

"Giles Frederick Charles Alexander Drew!"

Montford turned wide eyes on Giles. "Christ, Basingstoke. It's your mother, and it sounds like she's—"

"Giles!" His mother was right on Trevor's heels, skirts

whirling in outrage as she marched down the corridor, his three younger sisters trailing reluctantly in her wake.

"Her Grace, the Dowager Duchess of Basing—"

"For pity's sake, Trevor. I'm standing right here. I daresay His Grace can see me."

Trevor blanched. "Er, yes, Your Grace. I beg your pardon, Your Grace."

"Perhaps just a trifle less volume, Mother. You're giving poor Trevor palpitations," Diana begged, coming up behind their mother and shooting an apologetic glance at Giles. "She got to this morning's newspapers before I could stop her."

"What can you *mean*, Giles, marrying without telling me, and asking your poor sister to keep it a secret, and hiding your duchess from me?" His mother braced her hands on her hips, her blue eyes blazing. "I will have an explanation this *instant*!"

"Go," Giles muttered to Grantham and Montford. "Save yourselves while you still can."

"What, and miss this?" Montford rubbed his hands together. "No, Basingstoke. I think we'll stay a bit longer. Won't we, Grantham?"

"Indeed, we will. How do you do, Lady Diana?" Grantham, ever the courteous gentleman, offered Diana a polite bow.

"I'm a bit out of sorts, Your Grace, if you must know. Would you and Montford be so kind as to help me keep my mother from killing my brother?"

"Don't be absurd, Diana," their mother snapped. "There will be no—"

"Giles!" Louisa darted forward and attached herself to his leg. "Did you take your lady to Astley's, like I said you should? She liked the trick riders best, didn't she? See, Amy? I told you the trick riders were the—"

"Oh, will you hush about the trick riders, Louisa?" Amy stamped her foot. "Giles never said she liked them best. I'm certain she was far more impressed with the pantomimes. Isn't that right, Giles?"

"Well, she liked—"

"This isn't *your* house, Amy, it's Giles's house!" Louisa stuck her tongue out at her sister. "I don't have to hush, do I, Giles?"

"In truth, it might be best if you both—"

"Honestly, Giles, I can't understand why you didn't just tell me you wished to marry!" His mother threw her hands up in the air. "Did you suppose I would object? You must know I only want to see you happy. Well, Giles? I'm waiting for an explanation!"

"Shall I bring tea, Your Grace?"

Giles stood in his once peaceful hallway, gaping at the destruction around him. What had happened? One moment he'd been about to relieve Francesca of her ribbons, and now he was surrounded by angry faces. Well, four angry faces— Montford and Grantham were grinning like a pair of devils.

But Diana was red-faced and pinch-lipped as she attempted to separate Amy and Louisa, who were facing off like two bare-knuckle boxers on the verge of a brawl. His mother looked as if she was about to burst into a storm of tears, and Trevor . . .

His unflappable butler looked like a horse about to bolt.

What an unholy mess. He turned on his heel, but before he could escape into the music room and lock the door behind him, Francesca appeared on the threshold.

She saw at one glance that they were on the brink of devastation, but rather than panicking, she turned her sweetest smile on the butler. "Yes, Trevor, please do bring tea, and some of the lemon cake, if you would."

Trevor fled.

"Your Grace," she said to Grantham. "Would you be so good as to escort Lady Diana into the drawing room? The rest of us will follow directly."

Grantham bowed, took Diana's arm, and led her off in the direction of the drawing room.

"Lady Louisa, and Lady Amy, I presume?" Francesca smiled at his two youngest sisters. "How wonderful to meet you both at last. My name is Francesca, and I adored the trick riders and the pantomimes in equal measure. Shall we discuss it further, while we have our tea and cake?"

Amy and Louisa ceased their squabbling at once and turned wide, worshipful eyes on their pretty new sister. "Yes, please, Your Grace," Amy said, remembering her manners at last. She nudged Louisa, who offered Francesca a curtsy. "Lemon cake is my favorite."

"Is it? How fortunate. Go on to the drawing room, then, and we'll join you there in a moment."

Amy and Louisa darted off, their good humor fully restored, and Francesca turned to Montford, eyebrows raised. "Is lemon cake also your favorite, Your Grace?"

Montford chuckled, and slapped Giles on the back. "High-spirited, like I said. I wish you luck, Basingstoke! Forgive me, Your Grace," he added, with a bow to Francesca. "I've a previous engagement and must take my leave." He ambled off toward the front door, still chuckling.

Francesca turned to his mother then, and took both her hands. "Your Grace. I regret you had to find out about our marriage in the newspapers, and not from our own lips. It's inexcusable, and I'm most sorry for it, indeed."

"I daresay I'll recover." His mother gave a watery little sniff. "But I confess it was quite a shock."

"Yes, er . . . ." Francesca blushed. "It was all a bit rushed, really, and perhaps not as orderly as Giles and I might have wished. I'm terribly sorry we hurt your feelings."

"No, my dear girl, not at all." His mother pressed Francesca's hand between her own. "You must understand that my disappointment has nothing at all to do with my son's choice of duchess. I couldn't be more pleased to welcome you to our family."

"You're very kind, and may I say, Your Grace, that my mother speaks of you often, and with great affection."

Francesca said no more about Lady Maria, but her words were enough for his mother, whose eyes took on an unmistakable sheen. Something passed between the two of them then, some sort of understanding, a silent agreement to put the most painful parts of their shared past to rest.

"I would dearly love to see her again." His mother's voice caught. "I've missed my friend."

"She'll be in London next week, Your Grace, and from what I understand from her letters, in much-improved health. She asked me to let you know she's looking forward to seeing you."

"Well then, I have nothing more to wish for." His mother turned to him then, her face soft, all her earlier anger gone. She patted him affectionately on the cheek and murmured, "Well done, Giles," before making her way down the corridor toward the drawing room.

Giles waited until she'd rounded the corner before catching Francesca in his arms. "That was masterful, Your Grace. I've never seen a passel of unruly visitors silenced and dispatched so effortlessly before."

Her blue eyes were twinkling. "You recall all those little old ladies in Ashwell who accused you of being a wicked, conscienceless rake, don't you?"

"Recall them? I still have nightmares about them."

"Well, someone had to take them in hand."

He laughed, drew her close, and pressed his lips to her forehead. "I've never seen Amy and Louisa fall into line so quickly. I've always thought you'd make an excellent cavalry commander, Francesca."

Footsteps approached, and Trevor emerged from around the corner. "I beg your pardon, Your Grace."

Giles sighed. "Yes, Trevor. What is it now? If it's any more of my family, send them away."

"No, er . . . *Her* Grace, Your Grace. You have a visitor, Your Grace."

"A visitor?" Francesca frowned. "Who can that be?"

"It's a Miss Prudence Thorne, Your Grace."

"Prudence Thorne? Miss Thorne! Giles, did you do this?" The smile that lit her face was lovelier to him than the sunrise itself. "I might have had a hand in it, yes."

"But how could you possibly have known about Miss Thorne?"

"Eavesdropping, of course. I heard you ask Madame Laurent about her." He pressed a second kiss to her forehead, and then, because he couldn't resist, another to her lips. "I do hope Miss Prudence Thorne likes lemon cake."

CHAPTER 34

"If I'd had the least idea you were going to marry Helios, Your Grace, I would have remained in London for the entire season."

"Would you believe me, Miss Thorne, if I confided that I hadn't the least idea of it, either?" Francesca glanced at Giles, who'd turned to speak to Grantham in the back row of the theater box, and her heart hitched at the sight of him, just as it always did.

"Certainly not, based on the way you're gazing at him right now, Your Grace." Miss Thorne's hazel eyes were twinkling. "But I distinctly recall you were far less enamored with His Grace at Lord Hasting's ball. Indeed, I recall you being quite annoyed by the nickname Helios, and declaring it utter nonsense."

"It *is* utter nonsense, I assure you." Lady Diana leaned across Franny and laid a hand on Miss Thorne's arm. "Why, he was the naughtiest little boy imaginable, and very far from being godlike, wasn't he, Mother?"

"He was a perfect demon, yes." The dowager duchess cast a fond look at her son. "But I think he's turned out rather well, despite a naturally frolicsome temperament."

"Frolicsome!" Lady Diana snorted. "If he has turned out well, you may thank Francesca for that. He's quite transformed.

It makes one wonder if love might turn every man from a demon to a god. What do you think, Miss Thorne?"

"I think it's rather a risky proposition, my lady."

"Oh? Why is that?"

"If love truly is transformative, then surely it works both ways? Mightn't a lady fall in love with a god, and find herself wed to a demon?"

A brief silence fell, then all four ladies burst into gales of laughter.

"Best to avoid marriage altogether, then." Lady Diana cast a sly glance at her mother.

"Hush, Diana." The dowager duchess rapped her daughter's knuckles with her fan. "Really, am I to be allowed no peace? No sooner do I settle one incorrigible child than I'm burdened with another."

Lady Diana tossed her head. "Miss Thorne agrees with me, don't you, Miss Thorne?"

"I can't say I've ever yearned to join the married state, my lady. I beg your pardon, Your Grace." Miss Thorne smiled at the dowager duchess.

The duchess sniffed. "We'll see. I think you'll both lose your hearts next season, and I'm quite looking forward to witnessing it, I assure you."

Giles had turned at the sound of their laughter, and now he bent his head toward Francesca's. "You're very merry tonight, Your Grace. Are you enjoying yourself?"

"I am, indeed. How could I not?" She slipped her hand into his, a sigh of contentment on her lips. "Once my mother arrives next week, I shall have nothing more to wish for."

It was all quite grand to be a duchess, of course, and to watch the play from an elegant theater box, but all the splendor—the silk gowns and glittering jewels, and dukes and ladies on every side of her—had never much mattered to her.

It didn't, still.

The things she cared about now were the same things she'd cared about when she'd been on her hands and knees in the garden in Ashwell, coaxing rutabagas from the mud. Friends, love and laughter, and a husband she adored, who's heart was as golden as his hair.

A husband she wouldn't trade for Helios, himself.

Giles brought his lips closer to her ear. "I have told you, have I not, how lovely you look tonight?"

His warm breath stirred the curls at her temples, making her shiver. "You have, indeed. Half a dozen times before we left our bedchamber, I believe."

"Ah, yes. I recall now." He reached for her and caught the pendant nestled in the hollow of her throat on the tip of his finger. It was a tiny dragonfly, its dainty wings inlaid with amethysts, diamonds, and sapphires. "Dragonfly blue," he murmured, his gaze meeting hers.

"Dragonfly blue." She caught his hand and pressed a kiss to his gloved fingers. "I have told you, have I not, how much I love your gift?"

"You have." He rested his forehead against hers, his lips curving in a smile. "Half a dozen times before we left our bedchamber, I believe."

"Ah, yes. I recall now."

"Here's Montford at last," Grantham said from behind them.

"Montford?" Miss Thorne tensed beside Francesca. "His Grace, the Duke of Montford?"

Francesca turned to her in surprise. "Yes. Are you acquainted with . . . my goodness, Miss Thorne, you've gone as pale as a ghost!"

Miss Thorne made no reply, only watched as Montford weaved his way toward their theater box, her eyes narrowed and her lips tight.

"Prudence?" Francesca laid a hand on her friend's arm. "Are you unwell?"

"No, I . . . forgive me, Your Grace. I'm quite well. I didn't realize the Duke of Montford would join us in your box tonight."

"Is something amiss?"

Miss Thorne hesitated, biting her lip. "You know I was obliged to leave London just as the season began."

"I do, yes." Madame Laurent had mentioned that Prudence's father, Major Thorne, had taken a significant loss at the card tables, and Prudence had confirmed it during a private chat over tea this afternoon.

"It is a debt of honor, and thus must be discharged, but I despair of ever having the funds to do so. The amount my father owes to the gentleman in question is too great."

"Yes, I remember you said . . . oh. Oh, *no*." Francesca followed Prudence's glance to Montford, who'd just arrived at their box. "You don't mean—"

"I beg your pardon for my tardiness, Basingstoke. How d'ye do, Grantham? Ladies, you're all uniformly lovely this evening." Montford's dark eyes widened as they landed on Miss Thorne. "Good evening, Madam. I don't believe I have the pleasure of knowing you."

Oh, dear. This was dreadfully awkward. "Er, Miss Prudence Thorne, may I present His Grace, the Duke of Montford."

"Miss Thorne." Montford bowed over her hand. "Thorne, Thorne. That name sounds familiar to me, but I'm certain we haven't been introduced, as I'd surely remember *you*, Miss Thorne."

"I believe you're acquainted with my father, Your Grace. Major Thomas Thorne." Prudence's voice was as cold as an arctic blast.

Montford frowned. "Major Thomas Thorne? No, it doesn't sound fam—"

"The card room at Lord Hasting's ball, Your Grace? He lost a large sum of money to you at piquet."

"Oh." Montford released his hold on Prudence's hand. "*That* Major Thorne."

A prolonged silence followed this exchange, and it might have become quite awkward, indeed, if the low murmur of the crowd hadn't risen sharply in volume, distracting them.

"Oh, dear, the gossips are growing restless." Lady Diana glanced at the boxes nearby, one eyebrow arched. "Who do you suppose is their target tonight?"

The other ladies shrugged.

Giles, however, settled back into his seat with the air of a man very much looking forward to the evening's performance. "I believe Lord and Lady Stanhope have arrived."

By now, the boxes on either side of them were buzzing with whispers, and Francesca could see some people had risen from their seats and were craning their necks to get a glimpse of a box on the left side of the theater.

And all the while, the whispers grew louder, then louder still, an occasional hiss rising over the general cacophony.

"Giles." The dowager duchess frowned at her son. "What have you done?"

"Why, nothing at all, Mother, other than reveal the truth. It's a pity Lady Edith didn't think to have a look at the *Cock and Bull* before she and Lord Edward left for the theater this evening. You'd think she would have, as enamored as she is with that particular publication. I daresay if they'd seen the front page, they would have decided to forgo the theater tonight."

A moment later, Uncle Edward, who was looking as pleased with himself as he ever did, entered his box, her aunt Edith on his arm, and the two of them took their seats.

Franny covered her hand with her mouth. "Oh, my goodness. How can they bear to just sit there while everyone is staring at them?"

"They don't yet realize they're the center of it, but they

will, soon enough," Grantham said. "The *ton* has a way of making their disapproval known."

Franny caught Giles's hand in hers, gripping it hard. "What did you tell the *Cock and Bull*?"

"Nothing but the truth, just as I said. That the tale of your ruination was a vicious falsehood invented by Lady Edith Stanhope. That instead of showing you the familial kindness due to a niece from her aunt, she purposely set out to ruin you."

She glanced back toward her uncle Edward's box. Just as Grantham had predicted, he and Aunt Edith had by this point realized *they* were the target of the *ton*'s scorn. Indeed, they would have to be blind not to see it, as a great many people were now staring openly at them, all of them whispering furiously, and some even taunting.

Uncle Edward looked utterly confounded, but Aunt Edith . . . she knew precisely what had happened. Her face went bright red, and then, as her horrified gaze moved from one box to the next, taking in the jeering faces, dead white.

Until, at last, it inevitably met Franny's.

Franny held it for long, charged moments, then deliberately turned her face away.

If she were a better person, perhaps she'd feel pity for them, but she'd couldn't look upon them without thinking of the years of unhappiness she and her mother had endured at their hands.

It had taken more than a decade, but justice had been served at last.

"I left it to the *ton* to decide their fate, and they have."

She turned to her husband and opened her mouth, words of gratitude and hope and love rushing to her lips, but in the end, there was no need for her to say anything at all.

He already knew, because somehow, this man knew her as well as she knew herself.

"I won't allow anyone to hurt you, Francesca." He raised her hand to his lips. "Not ever again."

"Did you enjoy yourself at the theater this evening, Your Grace?"

Franny let her head fall back as Sarah dragged the brush through her hair in long, smooth strokes. "It was quite riveting, yes."

As for whether she'd *enjoyed* it, well, that was a complicated question, given all that had happened with her aunt and uncle, and that awkwardness between Prudence and Montford.

One thing was certain. She hadn't been bored.

"Was the *ton* all staring at you in your violet silk gown? They were, weren't they, and sick with envy, too!"

They'd positively gaped at her, yes—that is, when they hadn't been gaping at her aunt and uncle, though Uncle Edward and Aunt Edith had fled the theater quickly enough when they'd found themselves the objects of a dramatic set-down at the hands of an infuriated *ton*.

If there was one thing the *ton* didn't tolerate, it was the betrayal of one of their own, and for better or worse, London had claimed the new Duchess of Basingstoke as their own.

Giles had made certain of it.

Her kind, attentive, and devastatingly handsome husband, who was at this very moment, waiting in his bedchamber for her.

Perhaps that was enough brushing for tonight. "Thank you, Sarah. You may go."

Sarah laid the brush aside. "Yes, Your Grace."

Franny waited until Sarah had gathered up the violet silk gown and closed the bedchamber door behind her before she jumped up from the dressing table, flew from her bedchamber into the sitting room, and on to the duke's apartments on the other side.

She stopped short when she reached the bedchamber, a gasp on her lips. "Oh, how pretty!"

The soft glow of candlelight permeated the room, gilding everything it touched, including her golden-haired husband, who was reclining on the bed in only his shirtsleeves, a tempting slice of his bare chest on display.

Her heart leapt against her ribs.

Would it always be like this, every time she looked at him?

His lips curved in an inviting smile. "Come here, sweetheart."

He drew the coverlet back, holding out his hand to her, and she crossed the bedchamber, took his hand, and clambered up onto the bed.

"You were so beautiful tonight in your violet silk, Francesca." He caught a lock of her loose hair in his fingers, his eyes a deep, hypnotic blue in the candlelight. "I loved showing off my beautiful duchess, but you are never lovelier to me than you are right now, with your dark hair flowing down your back and candlelight flickering in your eyes."

His sweet words, and the way he was looking at her right now . . . dear God, he was making her melt. "Take me to bed, Your Grace."

"I intend to." He brushed the hair back from her face. "But first, I have something for you."

Another gift? "But you gave me my dragonfly necklace already. Is a duchess not meant to be content with amethysts, diamonds, and sapphires?"

He smiled. "This is a different kind of gift."

She touched her fingertips to his cheek. "Very well, Your Grace."

He pressed a kiss to her palm, then took up a narrow box she hadn't noticed lying on the bed beside him.

A jeweler's box.

"More jewels? Giles, I don't need . . ." She trailed off as the candlelight flickered over the pale gray velvet box.

That box.

She knew that box. The weight of it, the feel of the soft velvet nap against the pads of her fingers, the faint squeak of the hinge as it gave way.

The last time she'd held that box, she'd been weeping, certain she'd never see it again. "Giles," she whispered, her throat catching on his name.

"Open it, sweetheart."

Her hands shaking, her heart in her throat, she did as he bade her, knowing what she'd find nestled inside.

Tears rushed to her eyes as she brushed the pale gray silk wrappings aside and drew out her mother's cameo. It was strung on a length of blue silk ribbon, just as it had been when she'd last seen it.

When she'd last worn it.

She traced a finger over her father's beloved profile—that handsome nose, that proud chin, then turned it over, and yes, there was the inscription.

For Maria, my dearest love. Ever yours, Charles.

She raised her gaze to her husband's face, a sob choking her throat. "How?"

"Digby. I still don't know how he managed to find it, but it's not the first miracle he's worked."

"But there must be dozens of jewelers in London."

"More than a hundred, Digby tells me."

"You asked Digby to find it for me? When?"

"The day after we arrived here from Ashwell."

That was the day they'd argued so bitterly—the day she'd accused him of using her, of treating her like a pawn on a chessboard. While she'd been hiding in her bedchamber, he'd had his servant searching every jeweler's shop in London for her cameo.

Her breath caught on another sob.

"Francesca." He opened his arms to her and she fell into them, her fingers curling in his fine linen shirt. "Don't cry, sweetheart."

Only then did she realize she was weeping, weeping as if her heart were breaking.

But it wasn't. It was cracking open. The heart she'd kept so tightly closed for so long was opening, expanding, the walls falling away to make room for *him*.

"I love you, Francesca. I have since the first moment I saw you, but I'm a very great fool, and didn't realize it. I should have . . . please don't cry, Francesca . . . I should have known, and told you at once, but . . . please, Francesca, I can't bear it when you cry—"

"Shh. These are happy tears." She pressed her fingertips to his lips and with a great, watery, exceedingly unromantic sniff climbed into his lap. "I love you, Giles, with everything I have, and everything I am." She clasped his face in her hands. "My duke."

"My beautiful, blue-eyed duchess." He rested his forehead against hers.

They remained that way for long, quiet moments, their breath mingling, and then the boyish smile she loved so well curved his lips. "It's strange, isn't it, to think we wouldn't be here right now if you hadn't gotten caught on that spike in the garden."

"If I'd never gotten caught on that spike, you never would have called me a muddy radish, or sent me the blue ball gown, or chased me to Ashwell."

"If I hadn't chased to you Ashwell, I wouldn't have been threatened into marrying you by a pack of old ladies with pitchforks at the ready—"

"Giles!" She smacked him in the chest, laughing. "That isn't how it happened!"

"If we hadn't married . . ." He paused to drop a tender kiss on her lips. "We wouldn't have fallen in love, and I wouldn't be holding my duchess in my arms right now, and I wouldn't be the happiest man in all of England."

"Mmm." She pressed a kiss to his chest. "Fate is a strange thing, isn't it?"

"Yes, Your Grace." He tugged her closer, safe in the warm circle of his arms. "A strange and wonderful thing, indeed."

EPILOGUE

Basingstoke Manor
West Farleigh, Kent
Eight months later

"Giles!" Franny darted through the glass doors leading from the south terrace into Giles's study, her chest heaving from her wild dash across the garden. "You must come at once! Someone's dug an enormous pit on the edge of the south lawn!"

"For God's sake, Francesca." Giles rose from behind his desk and caught her by the shoulders. "Please tell me you didn't run all the way here from the south lawn! Have you forgotten your promise already?"

"No, of course not!" Oh, dear. She *had* forgotten, and she'd only just made the promise last night. Her mind was forever in the clouds these days, it seemed. "Very well, it *may* have slipped my mind for an instant, but only because half of the south lawn is missing, and—"

"No excuses, Francesca." Giles's tone was stern, but the hand he laid on her swollen belly was as tender as the brush of a butterfly's wing. "What are you doing, dashing about the south lawn? Aren't you meant to be resting right now?"

Franny bit her lip. "Well, yes, and I was on my way to my bedchamber to do just that, I swear it, but then I saw—"

"The devil you were. You always bite your lip when you're lying." He gave her lower lip a gentle tug, freeing it from her teeth. "Do I need to take you to our bedchamber myself?"

"Well, I can't deny it makes the prospect of a nap a great deal more appealing, but first, there is the rather pressing matter of the destruction of the south lawn—"

"I already know about the south lawn, sweetheart."

She blinked. "You do?"

"Of course. Do you suppose the gardeners took it upon themselves to dig a massive pit in the estate grounds without my directing them to do so?" He grinned down at her. "I am the duke, after all, and quite important, for all that my wayward wife is forever disobeying me."

Disobeying him, indeed. Franny braced her hands on her hips and thrust her chin into the air. "Well, I'm the duchess, and no one said a word to *me* about tearing a hole the size of Hyde Park into the south lawn."

"No, because I knew as soon as you discovered it, you'd be down there sticking your pert little nose into the business, instead of resting as you promised you would." He tapped the end of the nose in question, his grin widening. "And you see, I was right."

Franny huffed, but there was no arguing *that* point. "I'm with child, Giles, not blind. Did you suppose I wouldn't notice an enormous, muddy crater in the south lawn?"

"I did *not* suppose so, Your Grace, because I know very well you never miss a thing." He dropped a kiss onto the end of her nose. "I intended to tell you all about it this afternoon, but since you've been spying on the gardeners—"

"Spying! I never *spied* on—"

"And since you won't take your rest until you know the whole of it, I suppose I haven't any other choice but to take you there now." He drew her arm through his and led her back through the glass doors and onto the terrace. "Come along, then, but you're to go to your nap directly afterward, and no argument."

"Only if you come with me." She squeezed his arm. He was in his shirtsleeves and waistcoat, having foregone his coat as he tended to do when they were in the country, and she marveled as she always did at the flex of solid muscle underneath the fine linen.

He let out a low, husky laugh. "My dear wife, you know you won't get any rest at all if I join you in our bedchamber."

"Not right away, no," she agreed, a little sigh rising to her lips as she admired the way the sun toyed with the golden strands of his hair. What lady in her right mind would choose to sleep when she had such a man in her bed? "But I daresay you'll wear me out enough that I'll drop off to sleep directly afterwards."

"Hmmm. You tempt me, Your Grace, and perhaps I may yet be persuaded, but first, behold!" Giles swept his arm toward the freshly dug pit, which was at the bottom of a rise of ground.

They were standing on the crest of it, and from here she could see the hole was even bigger than she'd first thought, and it wasn't just their gardeners laboring over it, but a dozen men from the village, besides. "Er, yes, I see it. It's spectacular indeed, only what *is* it?"

"What *is* it?" He gave her an indignant look. "Why, it's a pond, of course, or it will be, once it's finished."

"A pond?" She peered down at it. "It's the size of a lake, Giles!"

"Nonsense. It will spread out across an acre of land, a mere fortieth of the size of the Serpentine. That's a pond, by any measure."

By the measure of a duke with an ancestral estate of hundreds of acres, perhaps. "I see. I daresay it will be grand to have a pond, only . . ." She cast the massive hole below them a doubtful glance. "What are we meant to do with it?"

"Whatever we choose. Perhaps I'll row you around it in a boat."

"A boat?" That did sound rather pleasant, but surely there was more to his sudden desire for a pond than an urge to row a boat across it. "Whatever put the idea into your head?"

He was quiet for a moment, his gaze fixed on the workmen hauling away wheelbarrows of dirt, then he turned to her, stroking a hand over her distended belly. "Every child should have a pond for swimming. I always longed for one as a child. My father forbade it, but I . . . well, I have no desire to be the sort of father my father was."

She said nothing for a moment, but reached out and took his hand in hers. He'd spoken of his father more often since they'd discovered she was carrying their child, and though he didn't often speak about the sort of father he hoped to be, she knew he thought about it a great deal. "You're not a thing like him, Giles," she said at last, squeezing his hand. "You never could be."

He shrugged, but the smile he turned on her was grateful. "It also occurred to me your mother would appreciate a pond."

"My mother? Why?"

"Because she's fond of dragonflies, and dragonflies are attracted to water."

"Are they, indeed?"

"Yes. They breed in water, lay their eggs in or near water, and their young hide among the water plants. Once the pond is in, we'll surround it with water lilies, arrowhead and cattails, and other plants that attract dragonflies. And there, on the slope," he pointed to the ground rising up from the flat place where the pond would sit. "We'll plant yarrow, and black-eyed Susans, and butterfly bush for the butterflies."

She swallowed, her heart swelling in her chest. "You've, ah, you've looked into this rather carefully, haven't you?"

"I did, yes. I thought it would be a nice thing for your mother." He shrugged again, but when he turned to her, there was a hint of hesitation in his eyes. "Do you suppose she'll like it?"

"She'll love it, Giles," Franny choked out around the lump in her throat. How could he ever imagine he was anything like his father? He, who was always thinking of ways to please her, or her mother, or his own mother and sisters? Was it any wonder they all adored him? "It will be a lovely thing for her, and she won't expect it, which makes it all the more special."

"Oh, no. Have I made you cry again?" He took her into his arms and urged her head against his chest. "No one would ever guess you hid such a tender heart under that sharp tongue, Francesca. It's a secret for me alone."

"Because of you, Giles." Perhaps she'd always nurtured a secret soft spot in her heart, but it had taken *him* to set it free. "You, and this one here," she added, resting her hand on her belly.

"Ah. Like father, like daughter."

"Or son." She smiled up at him. "Giles Frederick Charles Alexander Drew, the Ninth Duke of Basingstoke."

Giles threw his head back in a laugh. "Good Lord, what a ridiculous mouthful, but as long as he or she has your blue eyes, I'll be content."

He pressed his lips to her brow, but as always happened whenever they touched, the innocent caress quickly turned passionate, and in the next breath his mouth was hot over hers, his tongue tracing her lips. She opened instinctively, meeting him eagerly, and he plundered the depths of her mouth until her knees were shaking, and her body quivering with the desire she never could have imagined was possible until he'd shown it to her.

"Take me to our bedchamber, Giles," she murmured against his lips. "It's time for my nap."

He drew back, his mouth hovering over hers. His hands came up to cradle her face, his thumbs caressing her cheekbones. "Just a nap, Your Grace?"

"Oh no, I think not. A long, delightful afternoon stretches out before us, and we must occupy ourselves somehow, mustn't we?" She gave him an inviting smile and dropped another kiss on his lips before turning and leading him up the hill, his hand still clasped in hers.